W9-AVK-719

THE LAST TRIAL

ALSO BY SCOTT TUROW

Testimony

Identical

Innocent

Limitations

Ordinary Heroes

Ultimate Punishment

Reversible Errors

Personal Injuries

The Laws of Our Fathers

Pleading Guilty

The Burden of Proof

Presumed Innocent

One L

THE LAST TRIAL

SCOTT TUROW

GRAND CENTRAL PUBLISHING
New York Boston

Grand Central Publishing
Hachette Book Group
1290 Avenue of the Americas, New York, NY 10104
grandcentralpublishing.com
twitter.com/grandcentralpub

First Edition: May 2020

Grand Central Publishing is a division of Hachette Book Group, Inc. The Grand Central Publishing name and logo is a trademark of Hachette Book Group, Inc.

In a few places, lines from *The Burden of Proof* (Farrar, Straus and Giroux, 1990) are quoted or closely paraphrased and are gratefully used with permission of the publisher.

Library of Congress Cataloging-in-Publication Data

Names: Turow, Scott, author.
Title: The last trial / Scott Turow.
Description: First Edition. | New York : Grand Central Publishing, 2020.
Identifiers: LCCN 2019049243 | ISBN 9781538748138 (hardcover) | ISBN 9781538748121 | ISBN 9781538748084 (ebook)
Subjects: GSAFD: Legal stories.
Classification: LCC PS3570.U754 L37 2020 | DDC 813/.54—dc23
LC record available at https://lccn.loc.gov/2019049243

ISBN: 978-1-5387-4813-8 (hardcover), 978-1-5387-4812-1 (large print), 978-1-5387-4810-7 (signed edition), 978-1-5387-0300-7 (special signed edition), 978-1-5387-4808-4 (ebook)

Printed in the United States of America

LSC-C

10 9 8 7 6 5 4 3 2 1

For all my grandchildren—those here, those to come

THE LAST TRIAL

PROLOGUE

A woman screams. Shrill and desolate, the brief sound rips through the solemn hush in the corridors of the old federal courthouse.

Within the huge courtroom of the chief judge, the spectators are on their feet. The case on trial here, the criminal prosecution of a world-renowned physician, has been national news, and the gallery has been shoulder-to-shoulder every day. Now most of the onlookers are straining to see what has just happened beyond the walnut rail that bounds the area reserved for the trial participants.

The defendant's lead counsel, a very old man but still quite celebrated, has sagged from sight at the defense table. His client, the accused doctor, who is almost as aged as his attorney, kneels, holding the fallen man's limp hand by the wrist.

"No pulse," the doctor shouts. "Help, please!"

With that, the young woman beside him, who first cried out, takes flight. She is the paralegal on the case and also the old lawyer's granddaughter, and she bulls down the center aisle of the gallery, headed toward the door. Beside the doctor, the attorney's daughter, his law partner for decades, has been largely paralyzed by distress. All along, she has approached this trial, their last case together, with foreboding. Now she is weeping spontaneously, making no sound despite the tears racing down behind her glasses. The two prosecutors, the United States Attorney and his younger assistant, have sped from their seats across the courtroom. Working together, the pair take hold of the figure heaped on the floor.

In her robe, the chief judge has rushed down from the bench, intent on taking control of the scene, but she stops, suddenly mindful that the jury remains here. Like the other onlookers, the jurors are on their feet in the box in various stricken poses. The judge points to the deputy marshal positioned near them and shouts, "Remove the jury, please," then continues forward.

The court security officer, in his blazer and flesh-colored earpiece, has run across the courtroom to help, and with his aid, the prosecutors slowly hoist the old lawyer's body, placing him on his back on the walnut table, as his daughter shoves aside papers and equipment to make room. The old doctor quickly spreads the attorney's suit jacket and rips open his white shirt to expose his chest. The lawyer and the doctor have been friends for decades, and there is a trace of tenderness as the physician briefly presses his ear over the other man's heart, then sets the heel of his palm on the sternum of the inert figure, pumping with both hands at regular intervals.

"Someone breathe for him!" the doctor urges. The judge, who has known the lawyers on both sides for years, reacts first, pinching open the attorney's pale lips and setting her mouth on his as she exhales deeply. The sight seems to bring the daughter back to herself, and after the first dozen or so breaths, she takes over.

The prosecutors and the security officer have stepped back. Perhaps they mean to give the doctor room, or perhaps, like everyone else here, they find the sight of the old lawyer motionless on the table, like a Spartan on his shield, stark and horrifying. A small man, he has nonetheless always been a dominating presence in the courtroom. Now he lies here sadly exposed. Sparse white hairs curl across his breast, and his flesh has the grayish undertone of skim milk. The left side of his chest appears somewhat sunken where the livid mark of a surgical scar follows from just below his nipple all the way to his back. Incongruously, his red, white, and blue necktie, still knotted in his collar, hangs down his naked side.

The young woman who screamed and then fled has returned. She is an odd person. You can see that, not just because of the inch-long nail driven through her nose as decoration, but also from the slightly angry and indifferent way she deals with people. "Move, move," she shouts, dodging up the aisle. She carries a red plastic case in her right hand, where blood is welling from her knuckles. The latch on the box in the corridor that houses the defibrillator was jammed, and after several desperate tries, the lawyer's granddaughter simply punched in the thin glass.

As she passes the front spectators' row, one of the long line of journalists standing there remarks to a colleague beside him, "Talk about going out with your boots on."

Immediately after delivering the equipment to the doctor, the young woman wheels, pointing her bloody hand at the reporter.

"That's shit, Stew," she says. "No way he's dying."

I. OPENING

NOVEMBER 5, 2019

1. THE END

Ladies and Gentlemen of the jury," says Mr. Alejandro Stern. For nearly sixty years, he has offered this greeting to start his defense of the accused, and with the words today, a vapor of melancholy scuttles across his heart. But he is here. We live in the everlasting present. And he knows this much with iron certainty: He has had his turn.

"This is the end," he says. "For me." Without lowering his eyes from the jury, he blindly probes his midsection to fasten the center button on his suit coat, as he always has done after his first few words. "No doubt, you have been thinking, 'The defense lawyer is so very old.' And you are correct, of course. Standing up to the government when the freedom of a good person, like Dr. Kiril Pafko, hangs in the balance is not a task for someone of my age. This will be my final time."

Behind him on the bench, Chief Judge Sonya Klonsky utters an unformed sound, as if clearing her throat. Yet having known Sonny well for thirty years, he understands as clearly as if she had spoken. Were he to say more about his personal situation, the judge will politely cut him off.

"Yet I could not refuse this case," he adds.

"Mr. Stern," Judge Klonsky says, "perhaps you should turn to the proof."

Looking up to her on the carved walnut bench, Stern lets his head droop in a small bow. It is a gesture retained from his boyhood in Argentina, which also left the whisper of an accent that embarrasses him, even now, whenever he hears recordings of his voice.

"Just so, Your Honor," he answers, then turns again to the jury. "Marta and I are proud to stand beside Dr. Pafko at this crucial moment in what has been a long and honored life. Marta, if you would."

Marta Stern rises slowly at the defense table, greeting the jurors with a pleasant smile. As her father sees her, Marta is that unusual person who looks far better in her middle years than she did as a young woman—fit, well coiffed, and at ease. Stern, by contrast, has been withered by age and disease. But even now, he does not need to say she is his daughter. Both are short and thickly built, both show the same awkward combination of wide features. Nodding, Marta resumes her seat at the defense table beside their paralegal, Pinky, Stern's granddaughter.

Stern lifts his hand next to his client.

"Kiril, please." Dr. Pafko, too, comes to his feet, stiffened by age but still tall and attentive to his appearance. A white silk pocket square bubbles above one line of the golden buttons on his double-breasted blazer. His silver hair, streaked by yellow and almost entirely thinned away on top, is swept back debonairly, while his teeth are uneven and small as he attempts a charming smile. "How old a man are you, Kiril?"

"Seventy-eight," Pafko answers at once. Stern's question to his client at a time when only the lawyers are supposed to speak is clearly improper, but Stern knows from long experience that the government's lead counsel, the United States Attorney, Moses Appleton, will bypass minor objections rather than have the jury think he is eager to hide things. Stern wants Kiril's voice to be among the jurors' first impressions, so they will be less disappointed if, as Stern hopes, Kiril never takes the stand in his own defense.

"Seventy-eight," Stern repeats, and tosses his head in mock amazement. "A young man," he adds, and the fourteen jurors, including the two alternates, all smile. "Let me tell you a bit about what the evidence will show concerning Kiril Pafko. He came to the US from Argentina to complete his medical education roughly half a century ago, accompanied by his wife, Donatella, who is there behind him in the first row." Donatella Pafko, a year or two older than Stern, eighty-six or eighty-seven now, sits with a regal air, utterly composed, her white hair gathered into a smooth bun, her face heavily made up and lifted bravely. "He has two children. His daughter, Dara, is seated beside her mother. You will meet his son, Dr. Leopoldo Pafko, called Lep, later as a witness in the case. Lep and Dara have given Donatella and Kiril five grandchildren. Surprisingly, Kiril's grandchildren, too, will figure in the evidence you are going to hear.

"Of course, most of the proof will concern Kiril's professional life. You will learn that Kiril Pafko is both a medical doctor, an MD, and a PhD in biochemistry. For four decades plus, he has been an esteemed professor at Easton University's medical college, here in Kindle County, where he has directed one the world's foremost cancer research labs. Along the way, he also founded a company, Pafko Therapeutics, which puts his research into practice, producing lifesaving cancer medications.

"I apologize now, because in this case you will hear a good deal about cancer. As we learned during voir dire," Stern says, using the term for the judge's questioning of prospective jurors, "many of us have our own sad experience with cancer, through the suffering of a loved one, or even"—Stern meaningfully touches the lapel on his suit jacket—"ourselves. If the fight against cancer may be likened to a worldwide war, then Kiril Pafko has been one of the human race's leading generals and, as the evidence will show you, one of that war's most decorated heroes."

Using his ivory-knobbed walking stick, Stern steps closer to the jurors.

"Despite a light remark or two from me," Stern says, "I am sure you understand that for Dr. Pafko, this case is not a laughing matter. You have heard an excellent opening statement from my friend, Moses Appleton." Stern gestures to the crowded prosecution table beside him, where Moses, a square man in a store-bought suit, screws up his lips and his narrow, faint moustache in suspicion. He clearly regards Stern's compliment as tactical, as it is—but also sincere. After trying half a dozen cases against Moses over the years, Stern knows that the US Attorney's stolid, plainspoken way strikes all but the most blatantly racist jurors as reliable.

"Mr. Appleton has summarized the evidence, as the government would have you see it. For nearly a decade, he says, Pafko Therapeutics, sometimes called PT, worked on a cancer wonder drug called g-Livia. That much is true. What is untrue is Mr. Appleton's claim that the medication received rapid approval from the Food and Drug Administration, the FDA, only because Dr. Pafko falsified the clinical trial data for g-Livia to conceal a series of unexpected deaths. You will learn that Kiril Pafko did nothing like that. But Mr. Appleton maintains that this imagined 'fraud' caused Dr. Pafko's stock in PT to gain several hundred million dollars in value, even while seven cancer patients named in the indictment had their lives cut short.

"In consequence, the prosecutors have charged this seventy-eight-year-old scientist, revered around the globe, as if he were a Mafia don. In Count 1 of the indictment, the government has alleged a strange crime called 'racketeering' that combines a grab bag of state and federal offenses. Kiril Pafko is now accused of fraud, by several different names, of insider stock trading, and if all that were not enough, of murder. *Murder*," Stern repeats and goes completely still for a second. "Not a laughing matter at all."

Pausing for effect, Stern glances to Marta to gauge how he is doing. If the Sterns had followed their long custom, Marta would be addressing the jury in opening. But she has gallantly given way to her father, saying he is entitled to maximum time at center stage for his final bow. The truth, Stern suspects, is that she does not care much for their client, and regards the case as her father's last folly, a misjudgment of age or vanity or both, and, besides all that, a test Stern may no longer be up to.

Marta would say this case has nearly killed Stern once already. Eight months ago, in March, he was sideswiped at high speed on the interstate, as he was driving back from witness interviews at PT. Stern's Cadillac was slammed into a ditch, while Stern himself was unconscious when the ambulance arrived at the hospital, where a subdural hematoma—blood on the brain—required immediate neurosurgery. He was confused for days, but by now the neurologist says his scans are normal—"for a person of eighty-five." The qualification troubles Marta, but Kiril, who after all has a medical education, continues to insist his old friend represent him. In the courtroom, Stern has always been his best self. Yet he also knows that here, the truth emerges through a fierce struggle between the sides that will push him to his very limits.

But for fifty-nine years, Stern has approached every case almost as if he, as much as his client, were on trial. Each day consumes his entire spirit; he will sleep fitfully, as the witnesses take over his dreams. The worst moment, as always, came this morning, the first day of the actual trial, always like a play's opening night. Anxiety was a rodent gnawing on his heart, and the office was in bedlam. Pinky, his granddaughter, was ranting about misfires with the computer slides for Stern's opening. Marta was dashing to and from the conference room issuing last-minute directions for legal research to four young lawyers on loan to Stern & Stern. Vondra, Stern's assistant, kept invading his office to check his trial bag, while in the hallways it looked as if the entire support staff was building the pyramids, loading a long handcart with the huge transfer cases of documents and office equipment that would be needed in the courtroom. In his few instants alone, Stern focused on his opening, trying to etch it into memory, an effort cut short when Kiril and Donatella arrived for a final briefing, during which Stern was required to project an air of utter calm.

And yet this is the life he has been reluctant to forsake. It is not ego or money, the tabloid version of his motives, that have kept him working. The reasons are more personal and complex, for whatever the frequent frustrations of practicing law, the plain truth is that Mr. Alejandro Stern has adored it: The rushing about, the telephone calls, the small breaks of light in the tangle of egos and rules. His clients, his clients! For him, no siren song could be more enticing than an anguished call from someone in dire straits—in his early years, a hooligan in the precinct lockup, or as happens more typically these days, a businessperson with a federal agent at the door. He has always answered with the majestic calm of a superhero: 'Speak to no one. I shall be there momentarily.' What was it? What was this mad devotion to people who were often scoundrels, hoping to avoid a punishment that even Stern knew they deserved, who balked at paying fees, who lied to him routinely, and who scorned him the moment a case was lost? They needed him. Needed him! These weak, injured, even buffoonish characters required the assistance of Mr. Alejandro Stern to make their way. Their lives teetered on the cliff edge of destruction. They wept in his office and swore to murder their turncoat comrades. When sanity returned, they dried their eyes and waited, pathetically, for Stern to tell them what to do. 'Now,' he would say quietly. The work of six decades reduced to a few words.

If some of the central figures in his life—his first wife, Clara, the mother of his children, who died a suicide in 1989; or Peter, his eldest child; or, in rare moods, Helen, who left Stern a widower again two years ago—if they were present to hear Stern sing lyrics about his clients, his family would ask pointedly, 'And what about us?' To their implicit accusation, Stern, ironically, has no defense. The brute fact is that his energies and attention have often been entirely consumed by the courtroom, leaving less than he would have liked for the people he claims to love. All he can offer in response is candor: This is the life I needed to live. At eighty-five, he is certain that without it, he never would have known himself.

2. THE WITNESSES

Timeline of Critical Events

12/9/14

FDA designates g-Livia as Breakthrough Therapy

4/1/15

Eighteen-month clinical trial of g-Livia begins

9/15/16

Kiril Pafko learns of sudden deaths of clinical trial patients on g-Livia; trial database altered to omit deaths

10/27/16

PT submits altered database to FDA for g-Livia approval

1/16/17

g-Livia approved for sale by FDA

8/7/18

K. Pafko tells reporter he's never heard of sudden deaths of g-Livia patients; sells $20 million worth of PT stock

12/12/18

Kiril Pafko indicted

In his opening, Moses was himself, methodical but brief. His great gift with juries is sticking to essentials, and he did a good job explaining a somewhat complicated case, illuminating his 'Timeline' on a sixty-inch monitor wheeled in front of the witness stand. Moses's account started in 2014, when Pafko Therapeutics presented the FDA with early test results for g-Livia. Patients with non–small-cell lung cancer who'd received the medication even for a few months showed dramatic improvements compared to those on the current standard therapies. The disease spread more slowly, and in many cases tumors had actually receded.

The FDA granted g-Livia Breakthrough Therapy designation, which could speed the testing and approval process. In consultation with agency experts, PT planned an eighteen-month clinical trial of g-Livia. Assuming the product again showed the same clear benefits and extended lives, the medication would proceed to final FDA approval and become available for prescription years earlier than normal.

Days away from the completion of that trial in September 2016, troubling reports reached Kiril, through his son, Lep, PT's medical director. Starting in the thirteenth month of the test, roughly a dozen patients at clinical sites around the world had died suddenly for unaccountable reasons that seemed to have no connection to their cancer. Instead of leaving the matter to a panel of outside experts who, by protocol, were supposed to investigate such reports, Kiril looked into the issue on his own. According to

Lep, Kiril told him he had consulted the company in Taiwan administering the trial, which quickly recognized that there had been no sudden deaths. A simple coding error had mislabeled patients who had withdrawn from the study—as patients always do—as fatalities.

The database was changed—corrected, Kiril might say—and soon after submitted to the FDA. In January 2017, the FDA approved g-Livia for sale to the public. PT's share price skyrocketed, especially after a bidding war erupted between two large pharma companies to buy the concern. But in August 2018, before the acquisition by Tolliver, the winner, was completed, a reporter from the *Wall Street Journal* phoned Kiril, seeking comment on a pending story. The *Journal* was about to publish an investigative piece stating that after more than a year on g-Livia, isolated cancer patients were dying suddenly of a suspected allergic reaction. Kiril told the reporter he knew nothing about any sudden deaths, but moments after he put down the phone, he secretly ordered the sale of roughly $20 million worth of PT stock. Once the *Journal* story appeared, the value of Pafko Therapeutics shares plummeted, crashing almost completely several weeks later, when the FDA publicly questioned the clinical trial data for g-Livia. Kiril Pafko's indictment by a federal grand jury in Kindle County followed soon after.

In presenting this summary, Moses has used only forty of the fifty minutes Judge Klonsky has allotted to each side for opening statements. His brevity is meant to signal to the jurors that despite the foreign world of drug testing, the crime is clear. But the US Attorney's simplifications create some opportunities for the defense. Stern asks Moses to bring the Timeline back up on the monitor, a request the prosecutor may not refuse but which causes obvious consternation at the prosecution table, where nine investigators and lawyers are seated. Aside from Moses, the only other person there who will address the jury is a lean young assistant US Attorney with a glossy mop of black hair named Daniel Feld, presently typing on his laptop with the passion of a concert pianist.

"As always," Stern says now to the jury, after elaborating on Kiril's presumption of innocence and the government's heavy burden of proof, "there are two sides to the story and some vital facts Mr. Appleton chose not to mention to you. At the very heart of the charges that the government must prove beyond a reasonable doubt"—Stern, as ever, speaks the last four words with slow weight—"is their claim that Kiril Pafko is responsible for altering the results for the clinical trial of g-Livia in September 2016, erasing evidence of a dozen sudden, baffling deaths. Despite all the fanfare—testimony from Dr. Pafko's colleagues, forensic analysis of Kiril's office computer, records of his phone calls—after all of that, you will learn that"—Stern pauses before again laying emphasis on the next words—"Dr. Kiril Pafko altered nothing. Not in September 2016 or any other time. Nothing."

With that, Stern nods to Pinky, who is triggering her laptop to display slides on the giant monitor, emphasizing Stern's principal points. The Timeline fades out and the phrase "Kiril altered nothing" appears on-screen. Pinky, who is also at times her grandfather's roommate, is a frequently infuriating employee. Marta would have fired her sister's daughter long ago, but Stern continues to hold out hope. Still, he could not contain a swell of relief that Pinky actually showed up at work this morning, or again now when it appears she's kept the slides in the correct order.

"But didn't Mr. Appleton say the results were altered? Yes. But not by Kiril. The changes were made in Taiwan, by Dr. Wendy Hoh, who works for the company that was conducting these trials for PT. You will see Dr. Hoh as a witness, and you will have an opportunity to listen to her. The evidence will show you that her reasons for altering this database were *not* as the government describes.

"In point of fact, you will see that the motives the government imagines are often just that—imaginary. For example, Mr. Appleton suggested that Dr. Pafko committed this fraud in order to become a megamillionaire. Yes, the value of PT's stock rose steeply once g-Livia was approved by the FDA. g-Livia is a remarkable medication, and it was no surprise that big pharma companies immediately wanted to buy PT. But since g-Livia was first given Breakthrough Therapy designation, from that day until today, Kiril Pafko has not grown a penny richer personally by selling PT stock. Mr. Appleton did not think it was important to tell you that."

Pinky reveals a note on the screen reiterating that Kiril made no money, while Stern, accompanied by the solid thump of his cane, again moves toward the jurors, pleased that he seems to have their attention. They are the face of America, all colors, half from the suburbs, seven from Kindle County, their ages ranging from lively-looking Mrs. Murtaugh, a widow of eighty-two, to Don Something, a hip young guy with a ponytail who wants to teach high school. He is already keeping a close eye on Pinky, whom people her age seem to regard as attractive, despite what her grandfather sees as bizarre affectations like the Day-Glo tattoos frescoed on her arms or the nail through her nose.

"But didn't Mr. Appleton say that Dr. Pafko was charged with securities fraud for insider trading, that he sold PT stock right after he received the first call from that *Wall Street Journal* reporter? Yes. But I am not sure you would understand from Mr. Appleton's summary that the stock that was sold was in trust for Dr. Pafko's *grandchildren*." Stern utters that word triumphantly, even though he is well aware that under the insider trading laws, the fact that Kiril's grandchildren profited, rather than Kiril himself, is inconsequential. The jurors will not learn that for weeks, until Judge Klonsky gives them instructions on the law, and at the moment, Marta and Stern are unsure what else they can offer in defense of these charges.

"Now the point I have just illustrated—that the evidence will show another side to things—is something you must bear in mind throughout. While the government is trying to prove its case, it will decide on the witnesses and ask those persons questions first. Then Marta and I get to ask questions, a process referred to as 'cross-examination.' Please, in all instances, be sure to await our inquiries before attempting to form impressions. It will often turn out that some, even much, of the testimony of a witness called by the government actually favors the defense.

"Second, in every case, just as if these witnesses were salespeople who knocked on your door at home, you must ask yourself if this person has something to gain by what they are saying. For instance, at least two of them, both former colleagues of Dr. Pafko's at PT, have been promised by the government that they will not be prosecuted for their role in the events they are testifying about. You will learn that it is the government, and the government alone—not the judge, not you, not me—that has the power to decide whether a person is charged with a crime. Thus, the proof will show quite plainly that these former colleagues of Dr. Pafko's understand their testimony must satisfy the prosecutors.

"Oddly, even though these two executives from PT refused to testify without the government promising not to charge them, both will tell you that so far as they are concerned, they did nothing wrong. Kiril, of course, agrees. He, too, believes that no crime was committed in this case, no intentional fraud, not by him or anyone else, particularly because, as you will see, one of these two nonprosecution witnesses is Kiril's and Donatella's older child, their son, Lep.

"Lep is an MD and PhD like his father, as well as the medical director at PT. Now, it is a very strange, very difficult situation when a son testifies against his father. The evidence will show you, however, that Lep loves his father and his father loves Lep. Both understand that this is a circumstance the government has forced upon them."

"Objection," says Moses for the first time from his seat.

Sonny reflects a second, then shakes her head. "Overruled." Stern takes a second to offer the jury a smile of calm vindication.

"Now, aside from Lep, the second of these nonprosecution witnesses is another very accomplished person with an MD and PhD, Dr. Innis McVie. Dr. McVie is the former executive vice president and chief operating officer at PT who, along with Lep and Kiril, helped found Pafko Therapeutics. She worked beside Dr. Pafko for thirty-two years, first as a researcher in his lab at Easton, and later as second-in-charge at the company. Once g-Livia was approved for sale in January 2017, she left PT. As happens after decades side by side, disagreements had developed between Dr. Pafko and her, although the details need not concern us." Stern offers a little wave at the superfluous. What the jury will not hear, as a result of a defense motion Judge Klonsky ruled on in private in her chambers before the trial started, is that for most of Innis's thirty-two years with Kiril, she was his lover, his 'wife at work,' as some called her, a fact Stern himself learned only after trial preparations were under way. Innis apparently spent her last twenty months at PT in a state of fury after Pafko began carrying on with a far younger officer, the marketing director, Olga Fernandez.

"At any rate, Drs. McVie and Pafko were no longer on good terms, which will be quite apparent to you, because in August 2018, after Dr. Pafko received this call from the *Wall Street Journal* reporter, Kiril phoned Dr. McVie for advice, and—strangely—she decided to record their conversation. Mr. Appleton has said you will hear that recording. If Mr. Appleton changes his mind, have no fear, the defense will play it for you. One thing you will learn is that it was Dr. McVie, not Dr. Pafko, who first suggested that he sell PT stock. And yet the government decided not to prosecute her." Stern wrinkles his mouth and narrows his eyes to suggest the government's decision is imponderable, disturbing.

"So you understand my point. As you hear the witnesses, ask

yourself, please, what stake this person may have in saying what they do. Another example: You will be hearing from agents and officials of the FDA and FBI. Remember they are quite literally testifying for their boss, the government of the United States, which is also prosecuting Kiril. Each, I suspect, would say they want to keep their jobs.

"Some testimony, like that from investment bankers and stockbrokers, will come from people who might have a financial interest in what they are saying. You also will learn that a number of civil lawsuits have been filed seeking money damages from Kiril and PT for the same events addressed in the indictment. It will turn out that some witnesses, here to testify about the heartbreaking deaths of their loved ones, are seeking, and sometimes have been paid, millions and millions of dollars by PT in these civil cases."

"*Objection!*" Across the courtroom, Moses has rocketed to his feet, thundering the word. A second of stillness follows, since it is evident in Moses's bearing that he is a man seldom provoked to fury. "Your Honor," he says, "we have discussed this subject, and the court's ruling was crystal clear."

Staring down grimly at Stern, Judge Klonsky answers. "Indeed, it was. The objection is sustained. The jury will disregard Mr. Stern's last statement."

For another second, the show of anger from the US Attorney and the judge continues to trouble the atmosphere of the huge courtroom, where every seat is filled.

"In fact," Judge Klonsky says, "remembering the outline of your remarks, Mr. Stern, I think it's a good time for a break. Let's take ten minutes." Sonny then tells the jury that until the end of the case, they should not talk among themselves about what they have heard in the courtroom. With that, she motions to the deputy marshal to escort them through a back door to the jury room, where they will gather every day and eventually deliberate.

As the jurors exit, the lawyers come to their feet, while the judge, still clearly vexed, orders the attorneys to meet with her in chambers.

In the meantime, as Marta stands at Stern's shoulder, his daughter whispers, "What the *hell* was that?"

3. FRIENDS

A judge's chambers are her private offices. Sonny's, the impressive space afforded the chief judge of the United States District Court, consist of several rooms that occupy nearly a quarter of the top floor of the grand old federal courthouse. Beside the reception area, three small offices house the law clerks, who help the judge write her opinions, and the docket clerk, Luis, who manages the 450 or so civil and criminal cases over which the judge presides. The remaining area is reserved for the chief judge herself. A huge old Federalist desk is by the windows. Shelves of law books with golden bindings, little more than decorations in the computer era, ring the perimeter, and there is a long dark conference table surrounded by leather executive chairs where the judge holds her meetings. Prominent on the walls are family photos of Sonny's grandchildren and a few courtroom sketches from her earlier career, including one in which Sonny, then an assistant United States Attorney, is portrayed before the jury box, a finger poised. In the background of the watercolor is her trial partner in that case, Moses Appleton, recognizable, like the judge, in leaner, younger days.

Meetings in chambers can be conducted outside the presence of the jury—and the press. Nonetheless, Minnie Aleio, Sonny's court reporter, has taken a place in the corner with her steno machine that transforms shorthand into a transcript. As Moses edges past Stern to find a place on the other side of the conference table, the United States Attorney, still provoked by what has just gone on in court, whispers, "Man, I didn't think we were gonna try this case that way." Moses has always treated the Sterns as a cut above, a better class of defense counsel who, unlike many, eschew underhandedness as a defendant's right, and Stern registers Moses's rebuke as troubling.

The judge, who has not bothered to remove her robe, as she ordinarily does in chambers, has chosen to stand at the end of the table, while the lawyers sit, reemphasizing her authority.

"I decided it's a good moment to have a word with the group. We all know that my long relationships with the lawyers in this case are somewhat unusual. We are all friends here. And we will be friends when this case is over. But I will not allow any of you to impose on my friendship while this case is on trial." With those words, Sonny levels her dark eyes at Stern. "We had extended discussions last week about how to deal with the delicate matter of the many civil lawsuits that are pending against PT and Dr. Pafko."

Kiril's indictment provided a vulture's meal to the plaintiffs' bar. Two days after the first *Journal* article, the Neucriss law firm here in Kindle County had worked its customary magic and had filed multimillion-dollar suits for wrongful death in behalf of five families from across the US, quickly followed by dozens more civil cases brought by the Neucrisses and other personal injury lawyers from coast to coast. Besides those suits, several plaintiffs' class actions have been filed in behalf of PT's shareholders, alleging securities law violations and damages of hundreds of millions of dollars.

The distinction between civil cases, brought by private citizens to seek financial compensation for their injuries, and criminal cases, initiated by the government with the usual goal of sending the defendant to prison, often confuses laypeople. That could be expected to include jurors, who might not understand that in order to convict someone for a crime, the evidence must leave them far more certain—no reasonable doubts about guilt—than in a civil case. For that reason, Sonny was initially inclined to forbid any mention of the civil suits, but during last week's pretrial rulings, she accepted the Sterns' arguments that fairness requires allowing the jury to know that some witnesses stand to profit by their testimony. Even so, the judge said that she would decide what questions were proper, one witness at a time.

"Giving the benefit of the doubt," Sonny says now as she stands over the table directing a hard look at Stern, "I suppose I can see, Sandy, how you misinterpreted my ruling and thought it was all right to mention the civil cases briefly. But I was clear as day that there was to be no mention of the money any witness was seeking or had been paid. In fact, Sandy," Sonny says, "I have a distinct memory of you saying that the jury might take actual settlements as an admission of guilt on Dr. Pafko's part. Am I wrong about that?"

Stern hesitates briefly, just to give appropriate recognition to the judge's ire.

"You surely are not, Your Honor, but I found in the moment that I had changed my mind." In the courtroom, facing the actual jurors and the prospect of the heartsore testimony of persons whose loved one died after taking g-Livia, it was suddenly clear to Stern that Kiril was better off if the jury realized that they did not have to convict Pafko to ensure the grieving families received some compensation. He can see, however, from what swims across the judge's face that this explanation startles her, and she straightens up.

"Yes, Sandy, but I did not change *mine*." With the words, she sets her knuckles on the table, robe billowing, bringing the level of her dark eyes closer to Stern's. "If you, or any other lawyer, disobey my rulings again, then, old friend or not, I will deal with you appropriately."

The omen is absorbed in silence.

The chief judge's long friendship with each of the lawyers in the case is an awkward fact. Stern and she met three decades ago, when Sonny was an Assistant US Attorney investigating Stern's client, his sister's husband. It was a difficult time for both of them. Stern was only weeks past Clara's suicide and Sonny's marriage was collapsing while she was in the late stage of pregnancy. With both lawyers at sea emotionally, there was a dizzy night when they seemed smitten with each other. The infatuation dissolved in the daylight like a dream, entirely unrealized. Now Stern's body is in decay, and while Sonny's robust beauty remains, she has become completely gray and rounder. Yet in Stern's view, the importance of those kinds of attachments in a life never fully fades.

Marta has a more current bond with the judge. She shared a nanny, Everarda, with Sonny for years. They refer to one another as "besties." Work, by longstanding agreement, is never part of their conversations, which reinforces their intimacy, since they speak routinely of husbands, children, the travails of family, what is closest to their hearts.

Because of both Sterns' affinities with the judge, in Sonny's twenty-five years on the bench in state then federal court, neither Sandy nor Marta has ever tried a case before her. It was Moses's ascension to US Attorney that complicated matters. As the drawing on Sonny's wall reflects, Appleton and she were prosecutors together, favored trial partners who forged the bonds of battle. Sonny and her husband, Michael, are probably the best friends Moses and his wife, Sharon, have away from River of Zion Baptist Church, where Moses frequently preaches. When their daughter, Deborah, finished law school, she served for two years as Sonny's law clerk, overlapping for a year with her co-clerk—Dan Feld.

Furthermore, Sonny cannot simply remove herself from Moses's cases. The US Attorney is the government's sole official representative in federal district court, meaning that almost 70 percent of Sonny's trial docket is consumed by criminal and, sometimes, civil matters brought in Moses's name. His reputation is at stake in every one of those cases, whether or not he is present in court. Recusal would require Sonny to stop doing the bulk of her job. Worse, it would burden her fellow judges, who would inherit those cases, an especially unbecoming development inasmuch as the chief judge must prod the other district judges to stay up to date with their caseloads.

Accordingly, when the case was randomly assigned to Judge Klonsky, she sent a joint e-mail to Moses and Stern and Marta. 'Talk among yourselves and in your offices. If you think, on balance, you want a different judge, just e-mail Luis,' her docket clerk, 'and tell him to put it back on the wheel. No hard feelings, I promise.' Moses was the first to hit Reply All and say, 'No objections here.' Marta was less inclined to agree, but Stern pointed out that Kiril's interests favored staying put. Sonny is an excellent trial judge who is fairer to the defense than many of the former prosecutors on the bench, and she is also a lighter touch at sentencing.

Now they are at the first crossroads. Facing Sonny's baleful look, Stern can only speak the truth.

"Your Honor, I was confused," he says. The words are sincere, but the explanation settles in the room like a bad odor. It is a second before Stern recognizes that what he said might be taken as a reference to his age. The judge jolts slightly, while Stern continues to fumble. "I thought that because Your Honor had ruled in response to our objection, we could proceed otherwise." This explanation does not really make sense even to him, and in the end he can offer only abject apologies and a promise that there will be no reoccurrence.

The deeply humane look, which has always been essential to the Sonya Klonsky Stern knows, wars in her face with deeper doubts, but she decides to say no more. She tells the lawyers she will see them in five minutes in the courtroom.

4. G-LIVIA

Across the corridor outside the courtroom doors, in the small Attorney & Witness Room, Stern briefs Kiril and Donatella with studied nonchalance about what transpired in chambers. Then he returns to the defense table, where he finds himself momentarily alone, trying to calm himself by taking in the majesty of the chief judge's courtroom.

First erected in the early 1900s in beaux arts style, the courthouse was undergoing expansion when the market crashed in 1929. The building's intricate architectural detail, finished during the Depression by craftsmen employed by the WPA, required substantial upkeep, and thus the courthouse was briefly abandoned about forty years ago in favor of a glass-and-steel tower built across Federal Square. But the mechanical systems there were a disaster. Stern still recalls a winter day when you could see your breath inside, and old Judge Carrier took the bench in a topcoat and mittens.

The judges returned here. These days the Old Courthouse is a cherished landmark, often portrayed on postcards showing glamour shots of the central staircase of wrought iron and translucent alabaster panels winding beneath the glass-domed roof. Within

Sonny's two-story courtroom, slanting walnut pilasters frame the wide arched windows and naturalistic murals depicting legendary scenes of justice. Overhead, the ceiling coffers are etched in gold, with bizarrely beautiful chandeliers set on the corners, inverted obelisks of greenish copper. For a second, Stern marvels about Beauty, supposedly eternal but often judged so differently across the generations.

Abruptly, the judge returns, and the onlookers and lawyers scurry to their seats. Once the jurors are again in the box, Sonny turns to address them.

"Ladies and Gentlemen, from time to time as the trial proceeds you will hear the lawyers make objections. It may sound like they are being technical, or even trying to hide things from you, but they are doing their job to ensure that this case is decided according to rules for conducting a fair trial. Those rules have been followed for centuries, with good results, and it is my job to decide whether the objections are correct. When, as just happened with Mr. Stern right before our little break, I sustain an objection, then you must do your level best to put what he said out of your minds. It is something I've decided doesn't fit within those time-honored rules."

At the mention of his name, Marta gives her father a solid kick in the ankle under the table. He is actually pleased that she has recovered her sense of humor, since Marta's expression while they were in chambers was stark and alarmed. And he accepts the admonition delivered at the point of her shoe: It is imperative for any trial lawyer to stay on a judge's good side, at least in the presence of the jury. Jurors always love judges, whom they take as their only reliable guide through the strange land of the law.

"Mr. Stern," the judge says, "please proceed. I believe you are going to speak about twenty minutes more."

He responds with an obedient nod and struggles to his feet.

"Ladies and Gentlemen," he says, "in the remainder of my

opening remarks, I want to address Mr. Appleton's most dramatic charge, that Kiril Pafko, MD and PhD, for his own profit, supposedly put a medication on the market with the intention that some patients would needlessly die. The evidence will show that, were it not so grave, this accusation would be laughable."

With his cane, Stern again limps to a place a few feet in front of the jury rail.

"Now let us concede the obvious. It is true, sadly, that patients who were taking g-Livia died, and that those deaths were often a great blow to their loved ones. We all sympathize with their grief. But you do not take g-Livia like an aspirin. You take g-Livia because you are very sick, because you have serious progressive cancer, and because you know that without it, the odds are you will die relatively soon. Yet the prosecution will not and cannot prove, let alone beyond a reasonable doubt, how long any one of the persons named in the indictment would have survived, if they were *not* taking g-Livia."

"Objection," says Moses. Stern's neck is far too arthritic to allow him to look back without moving his entire body, but he revolves smoothly to face Moses. This, too, is something he will miss. Age has made him slow and even clumsier. One knee is irreparably diseased, while arthritic pain radiates along the length of his spine. His balance is perilous. Yet by whatever magic, in the courtroom he has always moved with grace.

"That is not what the government is obliged to show," the US Attorney says. From Moses's settled tone, Stern is certain that this is an objection Moses is making for tactical reasons. But on the bench, Sonny is shaking her head.

"I heard him describing the evidence, Mr. Appleton. Overruled."

"Thank you, Judge Klonsky," says Stern, nodding politely, hoping the jurors conclude that the judge and he are again on good terms. "Yet the most obvious answer to the murder charges is Kiril Pafko's life. For fifty years he has made immense contributions to curing cancer, perhaps greater contributions than any other human being alive.

"To understand, you must learn just a little bit about Kiril's research, which is remarkably complex. But feel no fear, please: I do not really understand what Kiril does, so from me you will hear no long confusing lectures."

In the jury box, they all smile. Stern feels he is already over the first hurdle. Instinctively, juries often dislike the person who speaks for someone accused of a serious crime.

"Cancer, as you know, occurs when cells in an area of our body stop going through the normal cycle of first growing, then eventually dying and being replaced by younger cells. Instead, cancer cells grow uncontrollably. Most often, they form huge masses in our bodies, called tumors." Stern again touches his chest, over his own lungs, which were afflicted. He is far from the only cancer survivor in the room. One of the jurors, a heavy, dour CPA, revealed during voir dire that she has had two bouts of bladder cancer, and Sonny, as a young woman, lost a breast. Her gratitude for the decades of good health she's enjoyed since is one more reason Stern regarded her as a particularly lucky draw for Kiril.

"Since cancer research began, doctors and scientists have longed for the so-called magic bullet, the drug that would stop cancer in its tracks. In 1982, Kiril Pafko was one of three scientists who first discovered that a large percentage of all cancers, including three of the four leading killers—that is lung cancer, colon cancer, and pancreatic cancer—can be traced to a genetic change in a single family of proteins present in every cell in our bodies, the so-called RAS protein. This is a picture of the RAS molecule." Pinky obliges with an image of RAS, a mass of blue and pink and purple circles that looks very much like a bunch of grapes. Stern knows that speaking about RAS, of which his own understanding is limited, may befuddle the jurors briefly, but it will illustrate Kiril Pafko's genius, which is central to the defense.

"RAS is the on-off switch for cell growth. Kiril's discovery was that in cancer, RAS somehow forgets its initial coding, allowing that wild cellular growth to occur. This was a discovery of immense importance, because it offered the first genuine opportunity to stop or even cure this disease.

"You do not need to take my word about the significance of what Dr. Pafko found." Slowly, Stern has made his way behind his client and now places his free hand on Kiril's shoulder. "Because in 1990, Dr. Kiril Pafko received the greatest honor that can be bestowed on any physician, any physiologist, any medical researcher on earth. Kiril Pafko, this man sitting before you, was called to Sweden and awarded the Nobel Prize in Medicine"—Stern once more adds weight to each of those four words—"a prize that has gone previously to people like the doctors who discovered penicillin, who cured tuberculosis, to Doctors Crick and Watson who first identified DNA. That is the company as a scientist that Kiril Pafko keeps." Moses actually filed a motion to prevent any mention of Kiril's Nobel, claiming it is irrelevant, but Sonny ruled that the defendant in a fraud case is always entitled to prove his reputation for honesty and integrity, which is implicit in the prize. Faced with that, Moses, in his opening, mentioned the Nobel in passing, but with Stern's expansive explanation, it feels as if he has suddenly drawn back a curtain to reveal the sun.

"When Kiril's discovery was made, the scientific world assumed that we would soon learn how to reverse the lethal process taking place when RAS somehow forgets its job. But RAS, for more than thirty-five years, has proved 'undruggable,' meaning despite the ardent efforts of thousands of scientists of unquestioned brilliance—despite that, no pharmaceutical product or process has been discovered to make the RAS molecules in tumors function in the healthy way they should.

"But doggedly, decade after decade, Kiril has studied RAS. In 2010, Kiril and Lep published a discovery almost as important as the first. What goes wrong with RAS in cancer is that it attaches to the cell membrane backwards." On the monitor, the RAS protein swims in space until the back side is attached to a larger blob, from which it's separated by a tiny red line.

"And this is where PT enters the story. Kiril, in partnership with Easton University and a venture capital fund, decided nearly twenty years ago to try to put his amazing theoretical discoveries into practice by formulating actual medications. In 2012 and '13, PT developed something called a monoclonal antibody, a mAb for short, a product that mimics our natural immune system. That mAb, which has a long scientific name, which I will now attempt to pronounce for the one and only one time: Gamalimixizumab"—Stern makes a good show of struggling to get the word out of his mouth—"that mAb, thanks to Olga Fernandez, PT's marketing director, received the brand name of g-Livia. What g-Livia does is basically surround the RAS protein on the wrong side." On the screen, a cloud surrounds one end of the bunch of grapes. "With the wrong side disabled, the mutant RAS proteins attach to the cells correctly and send normal signals. Tumors stop growing, and even, sometimes, begin to die." In the animation, RAS turns, and a brief little twinkle sparks on-screen.

"g-Livia is the magic bullet. Although it was tried first on lung cancer, non–small-cell lung cancer, to be precise—these names," says Stern and once more wags his head in chagrin over the difficult nomenclature—"Kiril and many, many other scientists believe that g-Livia will not only stop tumor growth in a host of lung cancers but also in colon cancer, in pancreatic cancer, in bladder cancer." His eyes flinch just slightly toward the female CPA."Quite literally, as many as forty percent, two out of every five persons on the earth cursed by cancer, could be helped, even cured, by g-Livia."

Moses once more has come to his feet. "Your Honor, haven't we gone far beyond what is proper in opening?"

Sonny has been watching Stern so intently that she seems to draw back at realizing Moses is in the room.

"I think I see where this is going, Mr. Appleton. Mr. Stern, are you outlining the evidence that will go to the issues of motive that Mr. Appleton addressed?"

"Just so, Your Honor." Stern offers the judge his deepest bow yet, before revolving toward the jurors. "Her Honor has understood me precisely. My point is simple. The potential to save millions and millions of lives explains the rush to get g-Livia approved by the FDA and in the hands of doctors and patients. The overwhelming goal, purely and simply, was extending lives, Lord knows not ending them, and not, as Mr. Appleton supposes, making hundreds of millions of dollars. You will learn that Kiril had plenty of money already."

"Objection," says Moses. "Dr. Pafko's wealth is not proper evidence under the cases."

Sonny frowns. She seems to recognize that Moses's objections, now uncharacteristically frequent, are an effort to throw Stern off stride.

"I assume you are moving on, Mr. Stern?"

"Just so," says Stern, then comes inches from the jury rail, so he again has their full attention. "What the evidence will show you beyond question is that Kiril Pafko's entire adult life has been focused singularly on one aim: conquering cancer and sparing lives. Virtually every working moment, in the lab at Easton, in his office at PT, has been dedicated to saving you and me." These last words, an appeal to the jurors' personal interests, is improper, but Stern is still capable of complex and instantaneous calculations in the courtroom, even though he routinely struggles to operate his cell phone. He knows that Moses has cornered himself and cannot pop up again to object without looking like a brat.

"So this, then, Ladies and Gentlemen, is the fundamental task before you. You must decide whether the evidence has convinced you beyond a reasonable doubt that a person who has stood on the very highest peak of scientific achievement, a physician revered around the world, a researcher whose name will be remembered long after he, and many of the rest of us, have ended our time on this planet, a doctor, a teacher, a leader, a remarkable innovator, a *Nobel Prize winner* who has labored for five decades now to end the curse of cancer and to prolong millions and millions of lives, whether it is even possible, let alone proven beyond a reasonable doubt, that that same man has become in his last years a fraud and a murderer."

Stern stares down the jury in a second of utter silence before shaking his head vigorously enough to feel the loose flesh wobbling beneath his chin.

"We say that could not happen.

"We say that *did* not happen.

"We say you will find Kiril Pafko not guilty."

5. INNOCENT

The moments after a trial session ends have always felt to Stern like the aftermath of a play, as the pin drop silence gives way abruptly to hubbub. In Sonny's courtroom, the spectators drift to the doors, while the reporters, eager to file their stories, edge ahead. Members of the judge's office staff climb the stairs to the bench to bring Her Honor messages. In the meantime, a herd of attorneys who were waiting in the corridor sift in for Sonny's next matter.

Stern steers his client across the corridor to the attorney-witness room to brief Kiril on what is ahead tomorrow and to wait for the wide-eared reporters loitering in the hallway to disperse. This is where those who are to testify wait before being called into the courtroom, and where attorneys can offer brief counsel to their clients. The preservationists who lovingly tend the public areas of the courthouse don't pay any attention here. The old desk is splintered on its edges, and the wooden barrel chairs are shaky. A single nondescript travel poster for the Skageon region up north hangs askew on the wall beside a discolored venetian blind.

As soon as they are alone, Kiril grasps Stern's hand between both of his own. Pafko's liver-spotted flesh is bedecked in gold, a ring the size of a doubloon and a heavy Rolex on his wrist.

"I stole several glances at the jury," Pafko says about the opening, "and they could not take their eyes from you." Stern tempers his pleasure in his client's compliments with the knowledge that Kiril has never abandoned the Argentinian way and frequently brings forth a river of fulsome bullshit.

Stern briefs Kiril on what to expect tomorrow when the testimony starts, then opens the door. Donatella is on a bench opposite with Dara, their daughter. Striking and dark, Dara bears a strong resemblance to her mother. As such, Dara unwittingly demonstrates what drove Kiril to pursue Donatella relentlessly decades ago in Buenos Aires, notwithstanding the fact that she was already married. As for Donatella, even in her late age, she retains strong cheekbones and penetrating dark eyes. Despite her white hair, her thick eyebrows have remained completely black, like smears of greasepaint.

Stern directs the three Pafkos to the courthouse's central alabaster staircase. With his cane, Stern must go one step at a time. Outside the courthouse doors, he guides Kiril and Donatella and Dara through the melee of reporters shouting questions, and the camera operators who charge like rhinos to get their close-ups. Kiril smiles and waves gamely, as if they were here to hail him, until Stern has the Pafkos safely in the black SUV that has slid to the curb, stealthy as a shark. One of Kiril's principal indulgences since g-Livia was approved is a maroon Maserati convertible, which he drives everywhere. Stern convinced his client it is not a good idea for a man accused of a crime of greed to be photographed at the wheel of a car that costs more than a house in some local neighborhoods. Sonny has told the jurors to shun media coverage of the case, but the instruction is hard to heed for anyone who gets near any kind of screen. In a couple days, after the news organizations have their file footage and photos for the archive, Kiril will be able to drive himself again.

Stern then clumps along the curb, greeting several reporters but otherwise saying nothing to them, until he reaches his Cadillac. The car is driven by a longtime employee of the law office, Ardent Trainor, a long, slender man in his late sixties, who alights to help Stern into the rear seat. The car still has that new-car aroma, which to Stern, in his unrelenting desire to be a real American, has always been the smell of success.

Stern's near-death experience on the highway back in March had many troubling consequences. His Cadillac, a gray 2017 CTS coupe, was totaled. The good news, as they say, is that insurance provided most of the cost of a replacement. The bad is that his children will not let him drive it. With Peter, Stern's doctor son, as their leader, the three made their father promise to limit his time behind the wheel to a rare spin to the local grocery store or the dry cleaners in the little suburban town where he lives.

In the sudden silence as the car door slams, the events of the day can finally be absorbed. Overall, he would say, so far, so good, except for blurting out about the civil settlements, which remains confounding. Every lawyer now and then loses their way as they are speaking, don't they? The lapse, however, is unusual for him.

Yet Stern's principal concern is for his client, who already seems fatigued and old, but worse, uncharacteristically vague. Like many clients, during the investigation and the months leading up to trial, Pafko tried to avoid talking about the case. He has four different phone numbers—home, office, personal cell, business cell—and Stern often had to leave several messages on each line before hearing back. But now that it is all in his face, Kiril is evincing a kind of simpering optimism. Given Pafko's age, one might even fear early dementia, but Stern knows it is more likely the decimating effect of public accusation. For white-collar defendants like Kiril, people accustomed to the power of wealth or prominence, the months after indictment are a special hell. They confront scorn in the eyes of virtually everyone who hears their name, while they are consumed by relentless anxiety over the future, in which the only certainty is it will bear no resemblance to the past.

Yet Stern feared Kiril was on the road to this sad torment once he saw the *Wall Street Journal* story in August 2018. Kiril called Stern a few weeks later to ask Sandy to represent him, within minutes of Pafko being served with a federal grand jury subpoena. The documents the government was seeking made it obvious that the prosecutors already believed the clinical trial for g-Livia had been tampered with. Stern experienced the inevitable schadenfreude of his profession. He was distressed for Kiril but thrilled for himself. A lawyer called upon to salvage the entire social existence of a person formerly held in the highest esteem is like a sorcerer being asked to turn back time. At eighty-five the opportunities to display that wizardry came, even to Sandy Stern, far more rarely. But a few days later, when Kiril had taken the seat customarily occupied by Stern's clients, a crimson leather chair in front of Stern's desk, better sense had prevailed. He told Kiril his best choice would be a younger lawyer, more certain to be beside him for what lay ahead.

'Do you feel incapable?' Kiril had asked. 'To my eye, Sandy, you seem every bit the man I met forty years ago.'

'Well, then, Kiril, our first task is to find someone to check your vision.'

Kiril enjoyed the joke but nevertheless insisted. Knowing his case was in Stern's hands, he said, would give him his first night's sleep in weeks.

Stern continued to resist, yet he realized that it would violate his own deeply rooted sense of loyalty to say no. The truth can be reduced to a few words: He owes Kiril Pafko his life.

In 2007, Stern was first diagnosed with non–small-cell lung cancer. The left lobe of his lung was removed, and he underwent chemotherapy. By 2009, there was a spot on the other side and he received chemo again. In 2011, there was another recurrence and treatment with yet another drug. By 2013, he had full-blown metastatic disease. Al, his internist, who is on staff at Easton Hospital and was aware of Sandy's friendship with Kiril, urged Stern to speak to Dr. Pafko. So far as Stern knew, he was the first human to receive g-Livia, several months before the FDA approved it for initial experimental use on patients. It was an act of mercy by Kiril for a dying friend, and one that, if disclosed, would subject Pafko to risks with both the university and the government.

For Stern, like thousands of other cancer patients after him, the medication has been a miracle. While his cancer is not totally erased, the lesions have retreated throughout his body. For that reason, Stern feels an intense obligation to Kiril—and also to the large universe of other cancer sufferers. The FDA has declared its approval of g-Livia void. The product is off the market in the US, caught up in a maelstrom of lawsuits and administrative actions, while the FDA refuses to set conditions to make the medication available even to patients with no other hope. The outcome of Kiril's trial will clearly push the agency one way or the other. In the meantime, Stern's supply comes from a factory in India and is shipped across the border in brown paper and a shoebox.

So he said yes to Kiril. Pafko, whose old face has something of the texture of a walnut, was brought close to tears.

'Sandy, Sandy,' he said, and toured around the desk to hug his friend. A good eight inches taller than Stern, Kiril held Sandy by the shoulders and sought his eye. 'Truly, Sandy. Truly. You must believe this. What the prosecutors think, that I altered those test results. Truly, I know nothing about that.'

Like a doctor who must face the fact that every body can be overcome by disease, Stern's practice has taught him that almost all souls are vulnerable to wrongdoing. In Pafko's case, there are plenty of what defense lawyers politely call 'bad facts.' Kiril's declaration that he knew nothing about the rash of sudden deaths on g-Livia is flatly contradicted by a screenshot of the clinical trial database, before it was altered, that was found on Kiril's office computer. In fact he even e-mailed the same image to Olga Fernandez, the PT marketing director with whom, back in 2016, he had recently started sleeping. Then there is what Kiril neglected to mention to his lawyers for months, namely that he had sold $20 million worth of the PT shares in his grandchildren's trust, virtually as soon as he was off the phone with the *Journal* reporter in August of 2018.

As a result, Marta long ago wrote off the case—and Kiril. Her judgment was confirmed when the Sterns undertook the pretrial exercise now familiar for deep-pocketed litigants and presented the case to three different mock juries of hired strangers. Supervised by a team of jury consultants, Stern played himself and Marta took Moses's role, and they gave each side's anticipated opening statements. Every time, Kiril was convicted of fraud, as well as insider trading—even murder on the first run-through.

Given those results, Stern, if not his client, accepts that they face long odds at trial. Should the real jury return the same verdicts as the mock groups, Stern has recognized in cold instants alone that Kiril is likely to die in prison. And yet his mind has returned time and again to that first meeting in his office, when Kiril hugged Stern and, with tears brimming in his murky gray eyes, declared that he did not do as the prosecutors claimed. Whatever the lessons of logic and experience, a rush of hope, like a spring rising through the earth, had saturated Stern's heart. He responded as habit and professional detachment had long taught him not to. Nonetheless, in the instant, he meant each word.

Stern had told Kiril, 'I believe you.'

6. MARTA

Here on the thirty-eighth floor of the Morgan Towers, once the Tri-Cities' tallest building, Marta and Sandy have made their offices throughout the thirty-year duration of Stern & Stern. From the two huge windows in his office, he has often taken a meditative moment, staring down at the silver ribbon of the River Kindle, known to the original French trappers who settled here as 'La Chandelle,' the Candle. The word was corrupted by English speakers to 'Kindle,' giving rise to the name of the county, by which this metropolitan area of three million is generally known.

Last weekend, daylight saving time ended, leaving Stern with lingering jet lag. Now, at four thirty, some stunted sun remains, which means that on the plate glass, Stern can see his reflection, which he usually makes a studied effort to avoid. There he confronts the time-scarred face of the other old men he has seen his entire life. The pumpkin-cheeked look he'd become resigned to in middle age is gone. With the cancer, twelve years ago, he lost dangerous amounts of weight, which, for whatever reason, he's largely not regained. According to the scale, he should be the same nimble shape as the slender young man of sixty years ago. And yet, after decades of failing regularly at dieting, he has been chagrined to find he looks, if anything, worse. There is a dark hollowness to his cheeks that suggests illness. His flesh is loose and pallid, like a dish of pudding, and after chemo, he regained only a few patches of white hair behind his ears.

Mired, as he is often, in memories, Stern forces himself back to his desk to check his voice mail, which has been transformed to text on his computer screen. In the old days, after court, he would receive a fistful of phone messages, which he returned late into the night. Today neither call is even about a case. Both are social invitations, one from a widow he's known for many years. At the age of eighty-five, after two marriages, Stern has decided to leave the playing field as a winner. He feels no inclination for companionship or whatever rubric could be applied to romance at his age.

Just as Stern is lifting the phone, Marta stalks into his office without so much as grazing her knuckles on the door. He doesn't need to ask what she is upset about and she is quick to tell him anyway.

"What the hell was that crap in your opening about the civil cases? I can't tell you how relieved I was when Moses stood up to object, because I was about to do it myself."

He does not really have an answer. He tells her, as he's told himself, that he was caught up in the moment.

"Dad, did you see Sonny grab me as we were leaving chambers? She wanted to know if you're losing it." It feels like a thorn in his heart to think that Sonny, who for years joked that when she grew up she wanted to be like Sandy Stern, now sees him as possibly addled.

"Dear God," he says.

"I reassured her, but Jesus, Dad."

It has always been part of the rhythm between them, going back to Marta's college years, that she will assail her father, sometimes ferociously, which he must accept in a mood of calm. The reverse has never been true, even now when Marta has reached her late fifties.

When it comes to her father's criticisms, Marta remains as delicate as vellum.

Stern would prefer that their last trial together be handled in a mood of celebration, but he knows that expectation is as unrealistically sentimental as a corny greeting card. The truth is that Marta is out of sorts for many reasons about this case. When Kiril first phoned Stern, he could not resist sharing the news about this new engagement in an air of triumph as he strode into Marta's office. Instead, he confronted shock and alarm on his daughter's face.

'Dad, are you completely crazy? A case like that could kill you. It's been years since you had a trial longer than two days. Forget about cancer. Your heart could never stand that.'

'My heart is fine,' he answered sharply.

'Really? Is that why Al has you coming in for an EKG every ninety days?' Al Clemente, Stern's internist, has been Marta's close friend since high school. He is an outstanding doctor, but not good at resisting Marta's badgering to disclose supposedly confidential information. 'And besides, Dad, you're the wrong lawyer for Pafko. You and I have seen this a hundred times. Some white-collar big shot in hot water goes to a close friend, so he doesn't have to deal with an attorney who will make him face up to the fact he's guilty. Kiril wants someone he can lie to.'

Stern felt a crestfallen look droop through his face. The thrill of being professionally revived had blinded him to the risks Marta recognized. Seeing that, Stern's daughter softened. She motioned him to one of the armchairs and sat down beside him. He was sure she was going to repeat the same points in a kinder tone.

'Dad, you need to know something. Solomon and I have reached a decision. We're going to retire. I want to start winding up by the end of the year.'

In the moment, it felt as if she was telling him she was going to die. He was too flabbergasted to answer. Marta leaned toward him, her hands joined pleadingly.

'I've loved working with you, Dad. I'm one of the most blessed people I know. But Sol and I have a lot of life left and we want to do other things.'

'What have I been working for?' he finally stammered. It has been his fixed assumption that Marta would be the beneficiary of the years of intense labor, the lost nights and weekends that always have felt to Stern as if they are somehow reflected in the rich glow in his office's dark paneling. But he knew his words were a mistake as soon as he heard himself.

'Jesus, Dad,' Marta said indignantly. 'Talk about manipulative.'

He lifted his hands, he now the one imploring.

'Marta, I apologize. That is not what I should have said. Nor even what I meant. This news requires some adjustment.'

'Half the defense lawyers in this city would be happy to come into this practice. We both know that. My stepping aside is probably going to be a bonanza for you.' She was referring to the price another lawyer would pay to be known as Sandy Stern's law partner and to inherit the flow of calls that will still come here for years.

'This is not about money, Marta,' he answered. It was something of a touché in their conversation and made up a bit for his gaffe of a moment before. Nonetheless, in the ensuing silence, he could do little more than shake his head. 'I had no inkling,' he said.

'Neither did we,' his daughter said, but their logic, as she explained, made sense. Money had long since stopped being an issue for Solomon and her. Their youngest child, Hernando—called Henry for Marta's grandfather—was about to graduate college. There was now an interval when they could travel freely before Clara, their daughter, would presumably begin a family, which would keep them here more. Marta's small eyes were intent as she detailed their thinking.

'It's not as if I'm rejecting you,' she added.

But she was. Not in a way that was inappropriate. Yet she was rejecting what was most important to him, what defined him. She was an outstanding lawyer, but she was admitting that she did not share her father's consuming faith in the law that for him rivaled what many feel for religion.

That night, he slept little, trying to put together the pieces. He went to her the next morning as soon as he arrived at Morgan Towers. Marta's office is of the same large dimensions as Stern's, something he insisted upon. Nevertheless, her space is far less formal than her father's, which she routinely compares to an upscale steak house, with its low light, pleated crimson leather seating, and stained-glass lamps. Marta's office is never neat. There are stacks of papers and boxes all over the room, and the walls are crowded with family pictures and abstract art. The furnishings, mid-century modern, teak-armed pieces, always look to Stern like they have been rescued from Goodwill.

'Marta, sharing my profession with my child, working with you side by side—this has given me a pleasure as deep and fundamental as breath. But we both know that my energy for this is waning. I am grateful you have stayed here as long as you have. When you retire, so will I.'

She was still for a second.

'You can't blackmail me into staying,' she said coldly.

'"Blackmail"?' He had spent most of the night composing these words. Disbelieving and stunned, he sunk into the chair in front of her desk.

Between them, for years, it sometimes seems that there has been a contest to decide which of them is more awkward, more obtuse, the bigger clod. After a second, Marta appeared to recognize that she was today's winner. She swept around her desk and folded her father in her arms. Always quick to cry, she removed her reading glasses to dab at her tears.

'Dad, I would hate to think I was forcing you to shutter the office.'

'You certainly are not. As you pointed out, I could easily combine with a younger partner. This is my choice, Marta.'

'Dad, what will you do, if you aren't practicing? I never even considered that you'd quit.'

'What do other people do? I shall read. Travel if my health holds out. Perhaps I can mediate or consult. I can go down to the Central Branch Courthouse and step up on cases for free.' He'd had that vision for years: nudging aside an overburdened public defender and standing beside some woebegone boy in handcuffs and an orange jumpsuit. In Stern's fantasy, the shock in the courtroom would be as palpable as if Superman had appeared in his cape, announcing he was here to stand up for Truth, Justice, and the American Way. Of course, the reality these days was that if anyone even recognized Stern's name, it would probably be only the judge or the more elderly court personnel, and certainly not his would-be client.

So together Marta and her father made their announcement. Marta agreed to put off retirement until the conclusion of the Pafko trial. After that, Stern & Stern would close its doors. From his colleagues, Stern encountered considerable skepticism. Wasn't he the one who'd always asked why a healthy person would quit doing the one thing in life at which he'd always most desired to succeed? In the worst moments of chemo a decade ago, when he often felt too weak and sick to get out of his chair, he was in the office nonetheless.

After Helen passed, everyone told him that in the first year or two, the survivor of a happy marriage either dies or resolves to go on. But going on doesn't have to mean going on the same way, does it? A period of redefinition could be invigorating. He makes similar statements frequently. But at night, he often feels like he is leaping into a void as terrifying as death. Still, he has not wavered publicly. For Marta and him, *US v. Pafko* will be the end. Which has raised the stakes in many ways.

"Dad, you need to be careful," Marta tells him now. "If I had to read Sonny's mind, she's probably more inclined to think you're playing her by claiming to be old and confused. She knows you well enough to understand how much you'd love your last verdict to be a not guilty, especially in a case no one thinks you can win." Inclined to protest, Stern mutes himself. Winning is like sex—the spirit inevitably craves the next occasion. "But you don't want her thinking you'd step over the line to get that result. You'll end up damaging a relationship that means a lot to both of us. And it will be bad for Kiril if Sonny stops treating you with mega-respect."

He can only nod. He has practiced for sixty years believing that his duty to the law is even greater than his duty to individual clients. It would be catastrophic to his judgment of himself if his last acts in the profession took him beyond the boundaries he has always faithfully observed.

II. MURDER

7. DAY TWO: THE VICTIMS

The government commences its case against Kiril Pafko on Wednesday morning with the testimony of Mrs. Aquina Colquitt of Greenville, Mississippi. Mrs. Colquitt, slow-speaking and unfalteringly polite, is everybody's granny, just a little plump and gray, with large spots of rouge on her cheeks and a springy hairdo that suggests Mrs. Colquitt, even these days, sleeps in curlers. In grim detail, she describes the death of her husband, Herbert. Mr. Colquitt had begun treatment with ġ-Livia virtually the day the medicine shipped, since his oncologist regarded it as Herbert's best hope. But one night, after fourteen months of twice-monthly injections, he became feverish with a rapid heartbeat and was admitted to the hospital. Mrs. Colquitt was with him the next morning for his violent death, as he suffered rigors, choking, and uncontrolled vomiting. Herbert took on a scarlet glow as he struggled for breath, while the code team failed with every lifesaving measure.

"It was like Satan hisself had a grip on Herb and was takin him down," she says. Appealing as Mrs. Colquitt is, the prosecutors have an added reason to make her their first witness. Utterly mystified by Mr. Colquitt's sudden symptoms, his doctors, after receiving the family's permission, assigned a med student working with them to briefly video what was occurring. The clip is only about twenty seconds, but it is devastating.

AUSA Dan Feld, in his first speaking role before the jury, conducts the direct examination. As the monitor finally darkens, Feld gazes at Mrs. Colquitt with an agonized look and whispers "Thank you" before taking his seat. The courtroom remains in reverent silence as Marta approaches the podium.

She introduces herself to Mrs. Colquitt as one of Kiril's lawyers, and then gestures to the defense table. "Mrs. Colquitt, we want to offer our deepest condolences." The Sterns have agreed to play to type, concluding that the jurors are more likely to accept the required display of empathy from a woman.

"Thank you, ma'am," Mrs. Colquitt answers.

"Now, Mrs. Colquitt, let me ask you about your husband's treatment with g-Livia before these final events. Did it seem g-Livia was making him better?"

"Objection," says Feld.

Sonny angles her face warily. "Grounds?"

"Whether g-Livia worked or didn't work for a period of time is irrelevant. The question is solely whether it killed him."

"Ms. Stern?" asks the judge.

"Among other things, Your Honor, the positive effects of g-Livia are relevant to the defendant's intent, which the state must prove beyond a reasonable doubt."

Sonny thinks about that. "Overruled."

"Your Honor, may we be heard?" asks Feld.

"After the witness, Mr. Feld. Ms. Stern may proceed now."

Marta has the court reporter read back the question to Mrs. Colquitt.

"The doctors and the nurses and them, they said he was better."

"Did scans show that his tumors were decreasing in size."

"Yes, ma'am. That's the very thing they said."

"And did he seem better to you?"

"For that first time, yes, ma'am. Much better. He was just sufferin so from the chemo and what all. He was a lot better."

"As far as you were concerned, as his wife, Mrs. Colquitt, would you say that g-Livia had caused Herbert's quality of life to improve?"

"Oh yes, ma'am," she answers. "Until it kill't him. To my mind, that's not what I'd call improvement, you know." There is isolated laughter in the courtroom and Mrs. Colquitt looks about somewhat abashed. "Not tryin to be smart or nothin. But Herbie, he was happier, I'll say that. He had started in lookin at the brighter side, I'd say. Cause he wanted to live, you know." She's avoided tears until now. Equipped with an embroidered hanky wrapped over her hand, she now brings it to her eyes.

On redirect, Feld asks the right question, whether Mrs. Colquitt, having it to do over again, would want her husband treated with g-Livia.

"No, sir, not at all. He just didn't get the time the doctors said they was expectin."

With that, Mrs. Colquitt is excused. Stern notes that every one of the jurors turns to watch her leave the courtroom in the company of her son and daughter-in-law. As a result of their decision to include murder charges against Kiril, the prosecution has scored big to start.

It was Marta, who enjoys a less formal relationship with Moses than Stern, who brought back the astonishing news several months ago that the US Attorney was going to include murder charges against Kiril. It seemed a classic example of what is referred to as 'overcharging' a case, calling a bunion a tumor, with the resulting damage to a prosecutor's credibility.

But as the Sterns continued to prepare Kiril and themselves for his indictment, they began to comprehend Moses's logic. For one thing, the law is far more favorable to the government than Stern had anticipated, given the fact that it has never been applied in a similar context. First degree murder in this state means killing someone unlawfully and knowing, in the words of the statute, that "the acts which cause the death... create a strong probability of death or great bodily harm to the individual or another." The prosecutors say that, in continuing to market g-Livia after finding out that the drug could engender a lethal reaction, Pafko knew there was a strong probability some patients would die.

In dealing with Moses, you can never leave aside the influence of his Old Testament morality. He thinks Kiril is a bad man who has done a bad thing, not only lying for profit, but also subjecting thousands of people to a danger that ended many lives. It's simple justice, in Moses's view, that Pafko stand trial for that.

Yet, as Marta and Stern war-gamed the moves and countermoves that would go on at trial, they recognized that Moses also gained important tactical advantages by alleging murder. A case limited to fraud and securities charges would be tedious, with a lot of bureaucratic testimony. Worse for the government, Kiril's alleged fraud involved fooling the FDA into approving the medication by hiding circumstances—the alleged fatalities—that required further investigation. But in the narrow view of the law, whether anyone actually died because of g-Livia would be irrelevant, and the jury would be instructed not to speculate about that.

With murder charges, on the other hand, the government can prove the fatal effects of g-Livia on specific patients and commence its case with the dramatic testimony of the family members who watched their loved ones perish. The treating physicians will testify next that they could not save their patients, because they were not warned that a severe allergic reaction—which is now the consensus view about what was going wrong—was possible. In the duel of courtroom impressions that is every trial, Kiril must endure a merciless beating at the start.

Yet the murder charges also have enhanced Stern's modest hopes for an acquittal. To the jury, those allegations, not fraud, will become the heart of the prosecution, and there are many obstacles, legal and factual, to proving murder beyond a reasonable doubt. If the Sterns debunk murder, there is a chance the jury will turn its back on Moses's entire case.

Once Mrs. Colquitt is gone, Sonny calls a recess to allow argument on Feld's objection that the defense should be barred from asking the so-called victims whether g-Livia in fact had helped the patients before they died.

"This 'victim' testimony," says Feld, employing the word he can't say often enough, "is being offered only to show that g-Livia actually killed these persons, as the murder statute requires. Whether the drug worked for a period of time is irrelevant." At the end of the day, this is the greatest single weakness of the murder case: g-Livia works. Yes, the murder statute reaches to a gangbanger who kills someone else when shooting at a rival in a drive-by, but could the gang member be convicted of murder if, in firing, he also magically made others invulnerable to bullets? The analogies are imperfect. But the questions are obvious.

Seemingly realizing that the positive effects of g-Livia might mitigate the crime, the government carefully chose the victims named in the indictment. All had stage 2 non–small-cell lung cancer, meaning the disease had progressed no further than the lymph nodes on the same side as the tumor. Thus, with the treatment regimens standard before g-Livia, these patients were all expected to survive longer than the thirteen to eighteen months each had gotten. Even so, the jury will inevitably hear something about g-Livia's benefits, since that is part and parcel of the clinical trials that are central to the government's case. What Feld is arguing now is a legal point, that the good g-Livia did some patients does not constitute a defense to murder.

Rather than raise the issue before trial, the prosecutors seem to have decided that they will fare better on the off chance that they catch the Sterns—and the judge—flat-footed. They have not, however. Marta is armed with several arguments and supporting cases, and it is her last line of attack that seems to gain the most traction with the judge.

"Your Honor," Marta says, "the government needs to show in the words of the state murder statute a 'strong probability' that Dr. Pafko's acts would lead to deaths and he knew that. There is no question, therefore, that the defendant is entitled to show the helpful effects of the medication, since, from his perspective, it affected the probabilities."

"That's a red herring, Your Honor," Feld answers. "The strong probabilities—the overwhelming probability—remained that someone was going to die from this drug, even if it helped some people, even most people."

"Judge," says Marta. "Dr. Pafko's assessment and the probable effects of g-Livia are issues for the jury to decide, not Mr. Feld. And to do that, the jurors must know the full gamut of the results, not just the bad examples the government wants to cherry-pick."

The cases decided by the state courts throw little light on the question of what constitutes 'a strong probability,' mostly because the murder statute has never been applied in a circumstance like this. Sonny leaves the bench for ten minutes, to do her own quick study. Returning, she says simply, "The government's objections are overruled. The defendant may show the positive results of treatment with g-Livia, certainly in the cases of the persons alleged to have been killed. We'll have to hash out the finer questions of law at the end of the case when we get to jury instructions."

This is the Sterns' first concrete victory on Kiril's behalf.

The testimony resumes with the son of a woman who died shortly after a year of receiving g-Livia. For the Sterns, the only strategy that makes sense is to get the so-called victim evidence over as quickly as possible. In the wake of Sonny's ruling, Feld alters his examination of the son to include a question about whether g-Livia improved his mother's condition for a while. Accordingly, when the man's direct is over, Marta stands and says, "You have our deepest condolences. The defense has no questions."

The next witness is Mr. Horace Pratt of Maine. Feld is clearly hamming up this part of the case, and Mr. Pratt gets on the stand looking like the farmer with the pitchfork from the painting *American Gothic*. He is dressed in khakis and a flannel shirt buttoned to his throat.

Before the jury was brought in this morning, Marta raised the issue that got her father in trouble with the judge. The estates of all seven victims named in the indictment filed civil complaints against PT for wrongful death. Despite the prosecutors' objections, the judge ruled that in the five civil cases still pending, brief cross-examination was proper to establish that the relative stood to get some of the money that PT was being asked to pay. It is clearly relevant to a witness's credibility if they might profit elsewhere from what they are saying. On the other hand, the judge barred any inquiry with the two families—including the son who just got off the stand—that have already reached multimillion-dollar settlements with PT, since those witnesses will not get any further financial benefit as a result of their testimony. Before trial, Sonny had said she wanted to make this kind of case-by-case appraisal with each witness, which was why she was so angry when Stern charged ahead without her permission, making matters worse by mentioning the settlements.

On this issue, too, Feld has, in the courtroom saying, chosen to 'take out the sting' by asking about the civil suits on his direct examination. Mrs. Colquitt had answered, 'I don't know so much about that cause my son's been talkin to Lawyer Neucriss.' Mr. Pratt answers similarly that the matter is in the hands of the lawyer for his wife's estate.

"Now, Mr. Pratt," Marta says, when it's her turn, "you are the heir to your wife's estate?"

"True," says Pratt, spare with words.

"And you know, don't you, that your wife's estate has brought a wrongful death action against Pafko Therapeutics?"

Feld stands to object. "He said the estate's lawyer is handling the matter."

The judge squints toward Feld through one eye. Like the Sterns, she clearly suspects Feld of shaping the testimony in pretrial meetings, so the witnesses can sidestep the issue of what they might gain from being here.

"Ms. Stern was asking about what Mr. Pratt knows. Overruled."

"Yep," says Pratt. "Know that."

"And you are being represented in this matter by the Neucriss Law Offices."

"Anthony Neucriss. The son."

"And do you know also that the Neucrisses have asked for damages from PT of $5 million?" The number produces a little ripple in the courtroom.

"I do."

"And do you know also that the Neucriss firm has turned down on your behalf an offer from PT of $2 million."

Feld objects indignantly. This question is on the borderline and Sonny hesitates. In the interval, Pratt answers.

"Not two million to me," he says. "Neucriss gets forty percent, so for me it's hardly over a million."

Stern catches Mrs. Murtaugh, the elderly widow on the jury, allowing her mouth to sour. There is a different face now on Mr. Pratt's grief.

Sonny says, "I'll limit further cross to the *ad damnum*," using a term the jury is not meant to understand. With the other victim witnesses, Marta can only ask about the amount of damages the families are seeking.

Even with that limitation, Marta is able to point out that three of the remaining five 'victim' witnesses stand to benefit from the pending litigation. Two of the families are also clients of the Neucriss office, whose first cases were filed less than forty-eight hours after the *Wall Street Journal* story appeared. How the Neucrisses managed to track down these patients and sign them up before other attorneys is a mystery that the Sterns and the large firms that represent PT in these civil cases have had no success in solving. But Pete, the father, now almost ninety, is still known among Kindle County lawyers as the Prince of Darkness, and has been finding underhanded ways to worm into juicy personal injury matters since the days of his first marriage, when his father-in-law, a lieutenant in the Traffic Division, instructed all the cops in his command to hand out Neucriss's card at accident scenes. Indeed, Stern recalls the wire service photos of the elder Neucriss stalking through the streets of Bhopal, India, after the infamous chemical spill there, his briefcase stuffed with retainer agreements and an Army gas mask over his face.

After the 'victims,' the government next calls several of the attending physicians, who testify to their utter mystification about what was happening to their patients. There are points for cross-examination, but they can all be made with the pathologist whom the government will call next. Stern and Marta know from prior experience they have an opportunity to gain some ground with Dr. Rogers, and their hope is that the government is forced to call her before Sonny recesses the trial for today. But the judge adjourns after the last doctor climbs down. The first day of evidence in *United States v. Pafko* concludes with the prosecutors far ahead.

8. PAINT

Facing his first long trial in years, Stern had known his energy could not possibly match what it once was, but he is shocked by how drained he is after court. He's done little more than watch today, but even so, the high-tension focus the courtroom requires, combined with the drama of yesterday, has sapped him. His synapses, neurons—wherever it is that thought forms—are too fatigued to function. He even feels a few feathery traces of the tachycardia that besets him now and then and concerns Al, his internist. Stern has promised Marta and himself he will not be heroic when he wears down. After a word to Kiril, then his daughter, Stern summons Ardent and is soon in the Cadillac on the way home to the West Bank. He is well prepared for tomorrow's crosses and he can review any materials he needs by remote connection from home. It is better to rest in advance.

After Helen and Stern were married in 1990, both sold the houses, less than a mile apart, where they'd raised their children with their first spouses. Together they bought this place, a one-floor brick cottage with a shake roof. It has a nice master suite, an updated kitchen, a guest wing to encourage visits from out-of-town children, and the large garden Helen loved to tend. Pregnant, if unspoken, was the realization that they were both likely to die here. Now that mission is half accomplished.

Having been widowed once before, there is a disconcerting familiarity to the vacancy Stern experiences whenever he enters the empty house. He knows how to turn on several TVs so there is a burble of background noise, how to swim through the occasional disconnected sensations of already being a ghost, just lurking here on earth. Helen's departure, like Clara's, had come with no warning. He woke one day as a married person and by noon was alone. Helen died of a cerebral aneurysm on the elliptical at the community health club. Is it somewhat easier because he has been through this before? Perhaps, on some level, he accepted the impermanence that's implicit in any second marriage. After Clara's suicide, he had been shipwrecked. But that was suicide. Now his grief feels more prolonged. With Stern's cancer there had been a period of mourning, of leave-taking, between Helen and him, but then g-Livia had worked its miracle. Now he can only hope Helen felt his intense gratitude to her for the brilliant light, the real joy, she had shone into his life.

Once through the door, Stern barely has the strength to stagger to the living room. Helen came into the marriage with an ill-trained little dog, a Jack Russell terrier named Gomer, and when the pooch died he was quickly replaced by Gomer II and now Gomer III. Unlike his predecessors, Gomer III did not bare his teeth at Stern when he approached Helen, but the dog was largely as proprietary of his mistress as the others. The only recognition Stern ever made of the unlikely event of Helen passing first was insisting, before Gomer III came from the rescue shelter, that his wife recruit someone else to take the dog if Stern survived her. But Gomer is too high-strung to be trusted around Helen's grandchildren. To his unending chagrin, Stern has been left with the animal, who gives every indication of blaming him for Helen's disappearance. He feeds Gomer III every morning and each night, and with Pinky's help continues to arrange for the walkers and groomers. In return, he receives next to no gratitude. Gomer wags his little whip of a tail now, but only because he expects his evening victuals.

Stern drops his briefcase and pours a finger of scotch, then falls into the black Herman Miller chair that looks out on Helen's garden, a wreck again this year without her tender hand. He does not know how long he has been asleep when he is awakened by Pinky rattling through the kitchen.

"Dinner, Pops? Did you eat?"

In the fog of waking, he actually needs a moment to recall.

"Soup?" Pinky's culinary skills are limited, but he seldom has an appetite at night. Chef Boyardee is good enough as a prop for his efforts at conversation with Pinky.

Stern is still unsure if it is accurate to say Pinky lives here. Within the family, Pinky tended to have two principal defenders, Stern and Helen. Stern's love for his granddaughter exceeds his understanding. It is simply there in his heart, and Helen, a partner who always understood what was essential to him, took up Pinky's cause as her own. For several years, Helen had encouraged Pinky to use the guest wing here as a landing spot when, as always seemed to happen, she reached the end of a live-in relationship of roughly six months' duration with a boyfriend or girlfriend. Stern was always secretly elated by her unannounced return. With no warning, she would drift into the kitchen around eight thirty a.m., grab something from the refrigerator, and let him know that she would like a ride to work. Given that pattern, Stern was shocked a few months back when he heard Pinky say offhandedly in the office, 'I'm sort of taking care of my grandfather these days.'

Stern's children had undoubtedly encouraged her. Pinky might not be long on practical skills, but she could go to the grocery store, do the laundry, and dial 911 when, as will someday happen, she finds her grandfather collapsed on the kitchen floor. Being Pinky, however, she still disappears for days without warning.

They eat their soup together at the breakfast bar in the kitchen as Pinky flips through messages on her phone. Gomer, who clearly has more affection for her than for Stern, plops down at her feet.

"And what did you make of today's court proceedings?" Stern asks when she appears to be resting her thumbs. Pinky does not always hear what is said to her, but this time she shakes her head dolefully.

"I thought you stomped it yesterday, Pops, but today—" She stops. A fine athlete like her father, a former Division I football player, Pinky had been a competitive snowboarder until a fractured vertebra put an abrupt end to her hopes for a college scholarship. She still reverts often to boarders' lingo. "Today, I thought they marched all over Pafko's ass. Is it gonna be like that every day?"

"I expect not, Pinky. I believe we have quite a bit to say for Kiril."

"That's good," she says. "But he's guilty, right?"

Stern actually finds himself offended for his client's sake. Has she been listening to her Aunt Marta?

"Pinky, why would you say that?" It would be unlike Pinky to have made a rigorous evaluation of the evidence.

"No, I mean, the defendant's always guilty. I mean, *I* was always guilty."

While Pinky was in high school, Stern appeared in court in behalf of his granddaughter so often after drug arrests, which increased in frequency after she broke her back, that he would grimly joke about having to jettison the rest of his practice. Finally, he found himself sharing with her a hard-learned lesson: In life there are those who get away with things and others who don't. Pinky's natural defiance puts her in the second group.

For a while, Pinky's interactions with the cops seemed to have had a beneficial effect. Like many young people who have their scuffles with the justice system, she later decided she wanted to enter law enforcement. It took her nearly six years to get her college degree in police science; then she shocked everyone, except Helen, by acing the entrance exam for the KCUPF, the Kindle County Unified Police Force. But days before she was to start, Pinky lost her place in the academy. It was not her prior arrest record, as Stern at first suspected, since juvenile offenses weren't considered. Instead she had tested positive for Ecstacy and cannabis. To her grandfather, she expressed amazement that the surefire steps she'd read about on the Internet to thwart drug testing had failed. Abstinence, apparently, had never been a serious option.

"Which reminds me," she says. "I brought a letter home from the office for you." She goes to her pocketbook on the kitchen counter and returns with a business-size envelope, folded in quarters. "Read it," she says. "It's kind of interesting."

The letterhead and logo at the top of the page belong to an outfit called Elstner Labs, a respected firm in the realm of forensic chemistry and engineering. Elstner has performed a chemical analysis on something called 'the reference specimen.' Two dense paragraphs follow, full of words that are beyond him: 'X-ray powder diffractometry'; 'Fourier transform infrared spectrometry and pyrolysis.' Eventually, he understands that Elstner analyzed a paint sample. One testing track confirmed the major crystalline components of the paint, the other characterized its organic makeup. In the letter's second to last paragraph, Elstner concludes that there is a high degree of likelihood that the source of the paint was a 2017 Chevy Malibu of a color called Vanilla White.

Although Stern would prefer not to admit it to Marta, there are moments when he is entirely befuddled, when his brain seems to be grinding without establishing a connection to the world beyond. Usually, the phenomenon is over in a few seconds, but not this time. Stern has placed the letter on the quartz countertop and stares at it with his fingertips laid against his forehead, as if his hand were an antenna that will finally receive a signal. But it is futile.

"Pinky, I am sorry, but I do not understand what this has to do with Kiril's case."

"Kiril? It's about your accident."

"In March?"

"Right. I got that paint from your car."

He stares. "Pinky, my car was gray." Or is that his new car? For an instant, he feels a stark fear about what he has again revealed. But no. No. Both are gray, the new Cadillac and the old Cadillac, just different shades.

"Pops, it's from the car that hit you."

"Ah," he says with relief, now that he understands. The driver who'd smashed into Stern's front end at ninety miles an hour never stopped. Only one witness remained on the scene to speak to the Sheriff's Police, and she, bless her, was far more concerned about Stern's life than recalling the offending vehicle. Her account confirmed that the collision was not Stern's fault, but she was not someone who could tell you make and model, even if that car was sitting right in front of her. Light-colored, she'd told the police.

That was no surprise to Stern. He had one memory of the wreck, which he dwelled on in the hospital. He recalled seeing a white sedan with the cream-colored parking decal of PT in the lower right corner of the rear window. He'd demanded that the police investigate and, with his brain healing, perseverated, requesting at least once every hour that he be allowed to communicate this information to a detective. Finally, when he was more collected, a Greenwood County Sheriff's Police investigator stopped by in the company of a neurosurgical resident. Both were women in their thirties, and together they patiently explained the fallacies of his recollection.

His last clear memories were of exiting the parking lot at PT's low-slung white suburban facility in Greenwood County. As he'd left there, the resident said, he'd undoubtedly seen a car in front of him with the oval PT sticker.

'When a brain has absorbed this kind of insult,' Dr. Seau explained, 'memories get stuck together in peculiar ways. It's a bit like dreams. I know it's what you recall—'

'Quite vividly,' Stern answered.

'Yes,' said the cop, now intervening, 'but that's not possible. The front end of that car hit you right near your driver's side door. You never could have seen the rear window. You were already skidding at a forty-five-degree angle toward the culvert.' Largely as a courtesy to Stern, the cops had gone to the parking lot at PT a few days after the accident, but, as they would have predicted, there was no vehicle there that showed front-end damage.

Stern had recovered his reason by the time the detective and resident visited him together. He understood. But he felt like Galileo after being told that he had to accept that the sun circled the earth. He knew what he knew. And there was white paint left on his car.

'That's what I saw,' he told Pinky, who in that period visited him every day.

'And the cops won't investigate?'

Stern explained. Pinky nodded in her millennial way several times before saying, 'Okay, so I'll follow up.'

Brain-injured or not, Stern knew this was implausible. Whatever Pinky's education, she had neither the resources nor the attention span to duplicate a police investigation. But that she took her grandfather seriously, when everyone else dismissed what he was saying, touched him.

To the best of his memory, Pinky's announcement that she would look into things was the end of that effort. With Pinky, follow-through was a term best expressed with an acre of white space between the words. But she had apparently gone to the salvage yard where the Cadillac was waiting for the insurance adjuster to declare it a total loss. There she scraped off the remnants of the long streaks of white paint, which had been deposited by the offending vehicle on the crushed front end of Stern's Cadillac, and sent them to Elstner Labs.

He again looks at the correspondence.

"This letter is dated in July, Pinky."

"Yeah, right." The expression familiar to everyone who knows Pinky well enters her soft face, the 'I messed up' look, as her nice green eyes dart to the floor. "But you know, like, I never get mail in the office."

"I see," says Stern. "The letter was on your desk?"

"That's what Vondra says. She found it the other day, because we got a past-due notice about Elstner's bill."

"I see. Those are expensive tests, Pinky."

"You told me in the hospital I could spend a thousand."

No chance he'd remember that. Things were a scramble.

"A thousand would be a very good price for such tests, Pinky."

"Yeah," she says, "it was more."

No point in asking how much more. It is already done, and Stern's native frugality has always ended with his grandchildren. Marta, who rarely allows Pinky's missteps to pass, will show him the bill eventually, in any case.

"And have you given any thought to the next move, now that you have this information?" Stern asks her.

"I'm going to go back to the Greenwood cop and see if she can look through the DMV records and scope out how many white 2017 Chevy Malibus are registered around there."

Stern nods. He would bet there are hundreds, if not thousands, of white 2017 Malibus in the vicinity, which would make further investigation impractical. But failure is such a frequent outcome for Pinky that he keeps his thoughts to himself.

"Well, I shall look forward to hearing what they say," he answers.

Pinky smiles, clearly happy to have escaped any upbraiding for spending too much money on the paint analysis. He briefly grasps her hand, washes out his soup bowl, and goes off to his bedroom with his laptop to study for tomorrow before he is reclaimed by sleep.

9. DAY THREE: EXPERTS

Dr. Bonita Rogers is called next by the government. Feld asks the questions necessary to qualify her as an expert on pathology, and she then testifies that she has examined the postmortem reports of all seven victims named in the indictment and their extensive medical histories. Based on that, Dr. Rogers has reached the opinion that all expired due to a severe allergic reaction to g-Livia.

Stern has done battle with Dr. Rogers before. She is in her early forties, shapely and with hair as orange as an orangutan's, as well as large green eyes that stand out in a starkly pale complexion. Good-looking witnesses—like good-looking lawyers—often have an advantage because they hold the jurors' attention. Yet over the years, Stern has found that pathologists, whose practice often concentrates on the dead, occasionally prove to be socially inept, and in Dr. Rogers's case the good impression she makes does not last long.

"Dr. Rogers," Stern says, rising cumbrously for cross. As an accommodation to Stern's age, the judge has offered to allow him to question witnesses from his seat. Notwithstanding the round of laughter he got, Stern meant it when he told the judge that he did not think his brain would work as well with his backside pressed into a chair.

"Mr. Stern." Rogers smiles, but the fact that she knows his name without an introduction is a good sign to the jury that this is another episode in a long-running contest.

"Now, Dr. Rogers, is there no medical treatment for an acute allergic reaction?"

"There are treatment options. But the physician needs to recognize what is occurring. Without proper warnings about the possibility of an allergic response to g-Livia, that was far more difficult." That was the prosecutors' point in calling the treating doctors yesterday, so they each could say they'd been utterly baffled.

With Dr. Rogers's testimony, both sides are walking a very narrow bridge over dangerous seas. The prosecutors have charged only seven deaths in their indictment, even though by the time g-Livia was withdrawn from the market, there were more than one hundred fatalities for which anaphylaxis—meaning allergic shock—was the suspected cause. In the indictment, Moses named only the most unambiguous cases, where the deaths were precipitous, the patients had the clearest expectation of living longer, and the attending doctors and the family members would make the deepest impression on the jurors. (Kiril is not charged with homicide for the twelve sudden deaths during the clinical trial, because he had no warning at that point of potentially fatal problems.) Any testimony from Rogers referring directly to the other postapproval deaths will lead to a mistrial motion from the Sterns, claiming Kiril is being tried for uncharged crimes. The defense, therefore, must do nothing on cross-examination that would make it fair for the prosecutors to refer to the many other fatalities.

"Now, you are not trained as an allergist, Dr. Rogers, are you?"

"No."

"Well, if any of the next questions are beyond your competence, Dr. Rogers, please say so."

The word 'competence' provokes a glower.

"Did you, as an expert, conduct a search for other allergies these patients might have had in common?"

"I read their medical histories."

"But to render your opinion, you did no investigation beyond that?"

"Right."

"Do certain foods trigger serious allergic responses that are known to come on suddenly later in life?"

"I guess that happens."

"Are shellfish allergies, for instance, known to develop that way?"

"I've heard that, but as you say, Mr. Stern, I'm not an allergist." She offers a little smart-ass grin.

"Do you know whether any of these seven people who you say died from g-Livia—do you know, for example, whether they had eaten shellfish within twenty-four hours of their deaths?"

Rogers smirks. "I doubt it."

"You doubt whether you know or whether they ate shellfish?"

"Shellfish."

"Based on what evidence?"

"It's not in their medical histories."

"Yet the entire basis for your testimony is that the treating physicians didn't recognize that they were dealing with an allergic response. So they would have had no basis to ask about what the patient ate, correct?"

"I guess," she says. "But it would be quite a coincidence if all seven of these people had eaten shellfish."

"But there are many other agents known to cause sudden and fatal allergic responses, are there not? Tree nuts? Pesticides? It is a long list, is it not? And you do not know for certain whether these seven people might have developed late-life allergies to something other than g-Livia, correct?"

Rogers reluctantly agrees.

“Now, you told us that there were no proper warnings about the possibility of an allergic response to g-Livia. Do you recall saying that a moment ago?”

“I do.”

“What is the product insert, Dr. Rogers? Are you familiar with that term?”

“Of course,” she answers. A snide wince shrinks one side of her face. “A product insert, a PI, is all those pages of small print you receive in the prescription box.”

“May I show you the PI for g-Livia? Marked as Defense Exhibit-1?” After a few more preliminaries, Stern asks Dr. Rogers to read aloud a sentence that is highlighted from the PI on-screen.

“g-Livia is a monoclonal antibody. mAbs have been known to cause serious allergic reactions in some patients.”

It was Pinky, shockingly, who’d found this note. She can’t put papers back in the correct file, yet, a bit of a savant, she can digest pages of small print with remarkable speed.

“So there was in fact a proper warning about potential allergic reactions that accompanied g-Livia?”

“I’m not sure I’d say that.”

“Really? Is there something improper about that warning?”

“It’s standard, Mr. Stern. It’s like the side-effects warnings you hear on TV commercials that no one pays attention to.”

“Certainly, if you had a patient experiencing a reaction you could not understand, the PI would be a good place to look for a possible explanation?”

“If a patient is in crisis, I’m not sure that’s the time to try to read eight pages of mice type.”

“Yes or no, Dr. Rogers, would a good doctor look at the PI if the doctor had any thought that a medication might be causing the patient’s crisis?”

“A good doctor might do that. In my view, it doesn’t make you a bad doctor if you don’t.”

"Now, you told me before that there are treatment options, if a doctor recognizes a severe allergic reaction. Please describe them."

She mentions massive doses of antihistamines and epinephrine.

"And if those treatments had been administered, could they have saved any of the seven patients named in the indictment?"

"There is no way to know, Mr. Stern."

"I did not say 'would,' Dr. Rogers. I asked 'could.'" The more uncooperative Dr. Rogers is—and she is inevitably combative—the better for the defense. "Are there cases in the medical literature where patients with these symptoms have been treated with antihistamines or epinephrine or stimulants and survived?" Stern is careful to ask about the literature and not other g-Livia cases. Alert doctors saved hundreds of g-Livia patients, but mentioning that would open the door to talking about other deaths as well.

Rogers answers that there are such cases.

"And in the event of those treatments, is it true that the probability of death by allergic response is reduced?"

"'Probability.'" She clearly doesn't know it is a loaded word. In order to convict Kiril of murder, the jury will need to find that he recognized a 'strong probability' of fatalities. "The probabilities are reduced, yes."

Stern stops and angles his face to the side, so the jurors know this is an important answer, then takes his seat.

The prosecution has made a better choice with their next witness, Dr. Bruno Kapech. Kapech is an oncologist and epidemiologist called to testify about cancer survival rates and the prospects that each of the seven patients named in the indictment would have lived longer had they not been treated with g-Livia. In an unfortunate coincidence for the defense, Kapech is, like Kiril, a chaired professor at Easton Medical College. His testimony comes with the implication that those who know Kiril best have turned against him. Pafko has told the Sterns that, as you would expect, there is no love lost between Kapech and him, although the grudge has nothing to do with medical judgments, but rather a factional dispute about the choice of the current dean of the med school.

Nevertheless, Kapech smiles briefly at Kiril as he assumes the stand. Kapech is in his midfifties, gray and overweight with a black goatee. In his thick Israeli accent, that turns short vowels into long ones and all r's into a faint growl, Kapech explains his extensive educational background and his board certification in three different areas. Next, Feld elicits a concise description of how cancer survival rates are calculated. Among stage 2 patients with non–small-cell lung cancer, the rates vary depending on age, race, and gender, the size of the tumor first discovered, where it is within the lung, the number of lymph nodes affected, and even the date of diagnosis, since survival rates, blessedly, are on the rise. Following that, Feld has Kapech explain the accepted treatment before g-Livia: surgery then chemo with one of several agents, the regimen Stern first underwent himself.

That done, Kapech moves on to the prospects for survival of the seven 'victims' named in the indictment. The most recent data from the National Institutes of Health indicates that 52 percent of stage 2 patients would live twenty months or longer, he says; 36 percent would make it to the five-year mark. Going through the variables he's already listed, Kapech predicts that the median survival time for each of these patients would be even longer than indicated by the general data.

Marta is usually better with technical witnesses, but the Sterns agreed that Sandy may have an edge with Kapech, whom Stern has met at a number of Easton events. Always a supporter of the university whose education changed his life, Stern, since receiving g-Livia, has made several large donations to the medical college. He has chatted with Kapech, a vice dean, at a few fund-raisers, conversations that inevitably turned to Stern's own condition. When Stern rises for cross, Kapech offers a warm smile.

"Sandy," he says. "They tell me I should call you 'Mr. Stern' today."

"And I shall call you Dr. Kapech."

Kapech nods, even offers a brief, jovial laugh.

"So let me ask you about the first of these deaths we heard about. Mr. Herbert Colquitt, this gentleman from Mississippi. How long exactly would Mr. Colquitt have lived, if he had not been treated with g-Livia, but rather one of the standard therapies you have described?"

Kapech, who does not mind hearing himself speak, repeats his answers about his calculation of Mr. Colquitt's median survival time—thirty-seven months.

"Meaning," says Stern, "that according to the studies, and taking account of all the variables you identified, if we had, say, a thousand people just like Mr. Colquitt, half would live longer than thirty-seven months and half less."

"Yes."

"But let us talk, please, about Mr. Colquitt. How long would *he* have lived?"

Kapech responds with a patient smile. "I can't tell you how long I will live,"—'leef' Kapech pronounces the word—"or you, Mr. Stern. I can only tell you what the studies show."

"Are you saying you don't know how long Mr. Colquitt would have lived?"

"I gave you my answer."

"Which is that you don't know, Doctor, correct?"

Feld objects that Stern's question was asked and answered. In order to keep trials from going on forever, a lawyer may ask the same question just once.

The judge intervenes: "Do you know exactly how long Mr. Colquitt would have lived, if he hadn't been treated with g-Livia?"

"Of course not," says Dr. Kapech. He then turns back to Stern.

"Now, Dr. Kapech, how many stage two patients who get one of the other standard therapies—how many live *less* than the fourteen months that Mr. Colquitt survived?"

"I don't really know. I can look, if you like."

"Please do."

Even Kiril grants Bruno's expertise, but Kapech does not commonly testify as an expert and he is unfamiliar with the stagecraft of trials. Rather than consult the armload of books and papers he brought with him into the courtroom, he reaches into the inner pocket of his suit coat for his phone and pokes at it for quite some time. In the interval, Stern sees a couple of the jurors, who seem to have bonded, exchange a look. The two, a middle-aged African-American man and the younger guy with the ponytail, share smirks, apparently amused that a supposed expert goes no deeper than what shows up on his phone.

As Kapech continues swiping and scrolling, it suddenly strikes Stern how truly odd it is to be talking about stage 2 non–small-cell lung cancer as something that happens to other people. He, in fact, is one of these statistics. When the word 'cancer' came out of Al Clemente's mouth, it was as if a comic book monster had exhaled a dark poisonous fog. His heart pinched in his chest, and Stern's breath left him. Truly, here was what the wordsmiths had in mind when they referred to 'a dread disease.' Cancer, Stern learned, was anxiety as much as physical symptoms. What seemed worst, as the diagnosis settled into him over the next days, was not merely that he was dying, but that he would not die well. Treatment for malignancies had become only a little better than the tortures of a CIA black site. Chemotherapy, unbearable nausea, surgery, disfigurement. His heart went out to Helen, who, being brave and loyal, would have to put up with all of this. He wanted to encourage her to treat him like a Spartan elder and drop him on a mountainside. Yet perhaps the worst part of all was facing the fact that he was not courageous enough to do that willingly. Like most humans, he would struggle to go on, beg for his life as it were.

"The National Cancer Institute says that for all lung and bronchus cancers, forty-seven percent of patients live one year."

"Fifty-three percent do not?"

"Yes, but survival rates are higher for non–small-cell than small-cell cancer. And eight of nine lung cancers are NSC. Then about thirty percent are diagnosed at stage two. Based on the available data, I'd say ballpark that fewer than thirty percent of stage two patients expire before fourteen months."

"So going back to Mr. Colquitt, the gentleman from Mississippi, there's a thirty percent chance that he wouldn't have survived the fourteen months that he did on g-Livia. In that range?"

"In that range. But let's be fair to everyone and say twenty-five to thirty percent."

Kapech means to be evenhanded, but his willingness to bargain with the truth is one more thing that might inspire the jurors to doubt him.

Across the courtroom, Stern stops to scrutinize Kapech. He clearly enjoys being known as the great authority, but whatever his gripes with Kiril, Bruno certainly doesn't appear to be slanting the data. Stern's sense is that if he solicits opinions from Kapech, rather than challenging the ones he's offered, Kapech will remain friendly. Lawyers are always taught not to ask a question on cross-examination to which they don't know the answer, but Stern's instinct is that there is an opportunity for the defense here.

"So you would say as an epidemiologist, Dr. Kapech, that there is a strong probability that Mr. Colquitt or anyone else diagnosed with stage two non–small-cell lung cancer would live longer than fourteen months?"

Kapech pulls a mouth. "I can't say a 'strong probability.' A good chance, yes. A strong probability, no. It's all semantics, of course, but to me a strong probability is closer to eighty-five to ninety percent."

The jury doesn't get it yet, because they have not been instructed on the law. Right now, this back and forth between Stern and Kapech probably sounds like nitpicking. But if there was not a strong probability that the victims named in the indictment would have lived longer than they did, Kiril could not have committed murder. You can't kill a ghost. Bottom line, the government's main epidemiological expert has just testified in effect that Kiril is not guilty. When Stern turns briefly, he sees that Marta has lifted a hand to her mouth to conceal a smile.

Having scored like this, Stern knows that he should sit down. But he has that feeling of momentum he has often experienced during a successful cross-examination.

"Now, to be clear, Dr. Kapech, patients diagnosed with stage two non–small-cell lung cancer have a very serious disease, which unfortunately is likely to end their lives eventually, no matter what the treatment."

"I can't disagree," says Bruno Kapech.

"And in your testimony, you are simply contrasting what happened to these particular patients against what might have been predicted, had they followed treatments standard before g-Livia became available."

"Correct."

"But would you agree that the one-year survival rates on g-Livia show that it *is* a better choice for the first year, even given these isolated reactions?"

Feld objects on relevance, but Sonny overrules him. Her face has darkened as she looks at the prosecution table.

"Yes, Mr. Stern, the one-year data is far better. But as you know, we make these judgments based on five-year rates. Because g-Livia has been removed from the market, we don't have any longer-range data, even anecdotal reports. So we don't know how many patients would develop a fatal allergic response over the longer period."

Stern stops. Something is wrong about what Kapech just said.

"By 'anecdotal reports,' you mean reports about what happened to particular patients, rather than a disciplined study?"

"Exactly."

"But you are familiar with some anecdotal reports about extended use of g-Livia, are you not?"

"Not that I am aware of," says Kapech.

Stern knows that isn't true. Kapech and he have talked not only about Stern's case but about six other patients who started getting g-Livia after him in late 2013 and early 2014. Stern included, five of them are still alive.

"Well, Doctor, you are quite familiar with at least one report, are you not, about non–small-cell patients who have survived on g-Livia longer than five years?"

"No." Kapech shakes his head firmly.

"You are not familiar with *my* medical history, Dr. Kapech?"

Across the courtroom, Feld shrieks, "Objection!" and behind him Moses booms the word again, in the same tone of outrage he used when Stern mentioned the civil cases during opening.

Stern looks back. There is an iron rule against a lawyer becoming a witness before the jury. He takes the point and waves at Kapech.

"Withdrawn," he says. "Nothing further."

"Mr. Stern!" says Sonny. He sees only now when he looks up to the bench that he has badly misunderstood the gravity of the situation. The judge stares down darkly.

"Remove the jury," she says with a gesture at Ginny Taylor, the deputy marshal in her blue uniform. The jurors are gone quickly. Stern realizes that he lost track of things. Because of his memories of the trauma of his diagnosis, and his acquaintance with Kapech outside the courtroom, he got entirely caught up in their byplay.

"I apologize, Your Honor." He starts to explain but the judge is shaking her gray head quite deliberately.

"No, Mr. Stern. I have warned you already that I was not going to tolerate any more infractions. You know your medical condition has no place in this case. If you can't follow the rules, I am telling you right now that I will order that Ms. Stern conduct the defense alone."

It is part of the job for defense lawyers to quarrel with judges, but the sharpness of the rebuke, particularly coming from Sonny, whom he counts as a dear friend, makes Stern feel as if he has been run through by a lance. Losing Kiril's case is an accepted risk. Being removed as out of control, however, is a humiliation that will follow him to the grave. He suddenly feels weak with confusion and grief and falls into a chair at the defense table, leaving it to Marta to approach the bench, while Feld and Moses follow. Feld speaks while the US Attorney, deeply aggravated, turns back to glower at Stern, who suddenly recognizes that he may have permanently damaged this relationship as well.

Although Marta counts Moses as a friend, Stern and Moses's connection is principally professional. Yet there has always seemed to be deep respect on both sides. As prosecutors are inevitably, Moses is intensely judgmental, but he also strives to be fair and has always been willing to listen to Stern's arguments in behalf of his clients. In press interviews, Stern sung Moses's praises following his appointment as US Attorney two years ago, after nearly a decade as first assistant. Stern was one of the few in the legal community unsurprised that Moses has always been a registered Republican.

Moses grew up in the Grace Street projects, coming of age in sadly familiar circumstances, raised by his mother and grandmother while his father, whom Moses never really knew, was doing thirty years at Rudyard penitentiary. Among Moses's more harrowing stories of his childhood is how his mother would occasionally lay his sister and him in the bathtub to protect them from gunfire in the hallway. Mrs. Appleton worked double shifts on an assembly line to pay for Catholic school for both her children, although their weekends were spent at her side at River of Zion. Moses was one of only twelve boys in his class to finish high school, following which he enlisted in the Marine Corps. Afterward, he went to college on the GI Bill, then enrolled in law school, which he attended at night while driving a UPS truck all day. Along the way, Moses developed fixed views about what is fairest for people like him who start with nothing: Stability. Rules followed by everyone. An even-handed system of rewards. Notwithstanding the demands of being US Attorney, he still tutors once a week at St. Gregory's, where he attended grade school.

The same personal code also makes him an exceptional gentleman. When Judge Klonsky told Stern he could question witnesses while seated, Moses said that if Sandy took that option, the prosecutors would follow suit. Moses's apparent conclusion that Stern in late age has grown dishonorable makes Stern feel like he did as a scolded schoolchild, scoured by shame.

In the meantime, Marta, knowing how painful this moment has become for her father, is defending him vehemently.

"Your Honor," she says. "I urge you to question Dr. Kapech outside the jury's presence. I have no doubt that you will find that Dr. Kapech *knew* his answers were untruthful."

Feld, unexpectedly, raises a hand to intervene.

"While I was preparing Bruno to testify, he told me that he knew Mr. Stern and that he was familiar with Sandy's medical condition, and I told him that none of that should be mentioned in the courtroom. I didn't see how it could possibly be relevant. He obviously misunderstood. But I intended to ask Dr. Kapech to correct his testimony on redirect."

Sonny closes her eyes to take all of this in, then with a quick hand motion rises and leaves the bench, tossing over her shoulder, "I need five."

Marta comes straight back to the defense table, where she whispers for a second to Kiril. Then guiding her father by the elbow, she takes him outside, past two empty courtrooms, until they are alone on one of the walnut pews at the end of the white marble corridor.

By now, Stern's mood has followed a predictable course, going from guilt to indignation, especially in light of what Feld has explained. Stern's dressing down from the judge, he feels, is a response first and foremost to his age. Were he forty years younger, the judge would have known there was more to the story.

"Hear my vow, Marta. If Sonny tries to remove me, I shall go to the appellate court."

"That won't happen, Dad. She was pissed off about what was going on in the courtroom. I think she hates the murder charges. When Kapech gave that answer about strong probabilities, she looked over at Moses like she was going to murder *him*. I nearly laughed out loud."

It dawns on him that that was the moment when he saw Marta concealing her smile. But for now, Stern remains more concerned about his own fate than his client's.

"I am not demented," he says, "and resent that assumption."

"Dad, you're not demented. I would have barricaded the doors to the courtroom if I thought you were. Your judgment, your reasoning, your overall smarts—they're still amazing. But your self-control in a situation like that, when Kapech is suddenly pissing you off, it's not the same. You cried ten times more often in public after Helen died than you did after Mom. I was glad you weren't as closed off anymore, but it's different, and you need to promise me, really promise me, when you feel some kind of unexpected inspiration, you're going to stop and check in with me. Just give me a look."

He nods. He can accept that. Amid all the other shocks, none is deeper than the fact that his feeling for the rules, which has always been like a thin veneer encasing him, failed as his incredulity with Kapech grew.

When they return to the courtroom, Ginny, the deputy in her uniform, has her hand on the back door, meaning the judge is ready to return to the bench.

"Well," Sonny says, once she's settled there, "I had the court reporter come back and read the transcript to me, and I have to say that I see blame on all sides. Mr. Feld, I accept that you would have tried to remedy the situation on redirect, but once you knew that Dr. Kapech's answers under oath were not truthful, especially because he misunderstood instructions from *you*, you needed to come at once to the sidebar or simply stand up and correct him. Mr. Stern, I understand that you were in a difficult situation, but you, too, certainly should have requested a sidebar before asking a question that's ordinarily so far out of bounds."

"I agree," says Stern quickly. He adds a little miniature bow. "There will be no reoccurrence."

"I realize that. And frankly, looking back at the transcript, I am not even certain about the relevance of this part of Dr. Kapech's testimony, but let's leave the matter where it is for now and go on to redirect."

Once a witness is on the stand, he may not discuss his testimony with the lawyers for either side. Thus, Feld's efforts to recover depend on Kapech's ability to take clues from the questions. Kapech does well, considering his lack of courtroom experience.

"When you answered Mr. Stern about 'strong probabilities'—is that a defined epidemiological term?"

"No. Not at all. I was just answering about my own impressions."

"And you certainly weren't using that term in the legal sense."

"No, no. Not at all. I'm a doctor after all. Not a lawyer."

When Kapech steps down, the judge reminds the jurors not to discuss the case with anyone and recesses for the week. Monday was jury selection, an elaborate process given the amount of publicity Kiril's case has had. Sonny does not try cases on Fridays, which are reserved for motions in the hundreds of other cases on her calendar.

When the session ends, Stern catches Kiril by the sleeve and asks to see him back at the office. "Alone," Stern adds quietly. Pafko nods quickly, as if he knows the subject and says he will arrange transportation home for Donatella, then drive to Stern's office.

Downstairs, Stern meets Ardent at the curb. He is completely wrung out again from the emotional toll of what transpired with Sonny. In the end, he thinks she held Feld more to task than him. But that doesn't matter, because he knows that the Sandy Stern of old, the lawyer with the majestic reputation, would have figured out a more skilled response to Kapech's false answers than violating the century-old rule against becoming a witness in the case. In the sealed privacy of the car, he can face the uncomfortable truth that has been gathering like a sad fog around his heart: He is no longer up to this. Marta was right. He should never have agreed to represent Kiril.

But he is already seated on the speeding train. For Kiril's sake, and his own, he needs to summon everything—reinforce his mental discipline, redouble his will. There must be no more foolish mistakes, no more incompetence, no further dancing along the cliff edge of catastrophe. He will never be who he was, but he owes everyone—Sonny, Marta, Moses, himself, and most of all, Pafko—his very best imitation.

10. KIRIL

How had he met Kiril Pafko? As the publicity about *US v. Pafko* has mounted, people have asked Stern now and then, but he has no precise memory. It was more than forty years ago. They were both émigrés from Argentina, both with young families, both gaining traction in their professional communities; there was also the fact, beyond polite mention, that each had been adroit enough to marry a woman of wealth. More than one person had suggested they get to know one another, but all Stern retains of the initial meeting is the sight of Kiril, tall, polished, and handsome, advancing across a large room with a self-assured smile and his hand extended, uttering the standard slang greeting of Buenos Aires: "*Che, pibe*." Hey, kid.

At that point, Kiril had arrived in the Tri-Cities as a young med school professor, fresh from Harvard and already surrounded by an air of renown. Stern was also becoming better established. His years of hustling cases in the corridors of the Kindle County Superior Court, to which he'd resorted after leaving the cushy practice in his father-in-law's office, were behind him, but not the constant immigrant anxiety about whether he would succeed. Because his in-laws were always suspicious of his motives for marrying Clara,

Stern begged his wife not to accept a penny from her parents, but that made the challenge to prove himself more extreme. Words in English still eluded him at the most critical moments in court, and he knew the accent he could not shake bred distrust from judges, cops, and worst, potential clients. Whenever he felt he was failing, he became acutely aware of the three children at home, clamorous with need. As other humans required food, water, shelter, Stern longed to feel secure.

Kiril, on the other hand, was already larger than life. Stern at first saw little common ground. Because of everything he still held against his father, Stern avoided the company of physicians. Pafko was also a fine athlete. Year after year, Kiril reigned as the tennis singles champion at the country club where Stern's in-laws were also members, while Stern barely knew how to hold a racket. Most grating perhaps was Kiril's confidence that everyone liked him, as he overwhelmed them with well-lubricated foreign charm.

Even the fact that Alejandro and Kiril were both Argentinian did not really unite them, since they hailed from far different social strata. The disorder in Europe that began in the 1880s and led to the World Wars brought hundreds of thousands of Europeans to the Land of Silver, which was viewed then as a place of opportunities to rival the US. The Pafkos, wine growers whose vineyards were not far from Bratislava, had left Slovakia for Argentina in 1919, almost a decade ahead of when the Sterns had fled Germany in the face of the rising tide of anti-Semitism. The Pafkos flourished as vintners in Mendoza. The Sterns floundered. Stern's father, a fragile ne'er-do-well doctor, moved his family from place to place, leaving them impoverished when he died at an early age.

It was the two wives, Clara and Donatella, who formed the initial bond. They were kindred souls, both born to wealth, both well-educated, both with deep minds and unyielding discretion. Each was a trained musician. They looked forward to the afternoons once a month when they had lunch and attended the symphony.

The families often ended up together in the summer months, when the Sterns were frequent guests at the country club. Whatever his initial reluctance, Stern began enjoying Kiril's quick mind, his humor, and his skills as a raconteur.

And then, out of nowhere, both men were struck by lightning, united by what passed locally for fame. Their friendship was reinforced because there were few companions who understood what it was like to ride a rocket into the stratosphere of sudden renown. In 1986, Stern defended the chief deputy in the Kindle County Prosecuting Attorney's Office, a married man accused of the murder of a fellow prosecutor, alleged to be his former lover. Tangled with a local election campaign for prosecuting attorney, the case, with its torrid aspects, generated attention coast-to-coast, and Stern found photos of himself, burdened with brown document cases as he lumbered toward court, appearing in publications like *Time* and *People*. He soon learned the workings of the American media, in which attention begets attention. Important clients came with it—corporate executives, then Kindle County's Catholic archbishop, whom Stern kept out of prison despite the many frauds involved in hiding the child born of His Eminence's affair with a fourteen-year-old girl. It became routine for Stern to be introduced to strangers as 'a famous lawyer.' Occasionally, if the new acquaintance seemed to have a sense of humor, and Clara, or later Helen, were present, he would add, 'Please do not be impressed. There are no groupies.'

Kiril's moment came in 1990 when he was awarded the Nobel Prize. Stern was thrilled for Kiril, for Easton, and for Kindle County, always struggling with its designation as 'a second-tier city.' Kiril accepted fame with none of the ambivalence Stern felt about the spotlight. If attention is a narcotic, then Kiril mainlined it. He recounted for months the story of walking into the Matchbook, a tony restaurant in Center City, and having every patron rise to give him a standing ovation the day after the announcement in

Stockholm. g-Livia had inspired another round of national acclaim for Kiril—until the *Wall Street Journal* painted him as a fraud.

Stern has not been in the office long after his moment of resolve in the Cadillac when Kiril arrives. Pafko, as ever, is gallant.

"Sandy, if you are feeling some need to explain about the judge, please do not. I know she is your friend, but it is clear to both Donatella and me that she is quite short-tempered."

Knowing how wrong he was, Stern has not considered how Sonny's agitation with him might have struck the jurors. Kiril could be right that she appeared quick to anger. But it is not the judge whom Stern wants to discuss.

"Kiril, I asked to see you without Donatella to talk for a second about Innis." He is referring to Dr. Innis McVie, Kiril's longtime lover, who left PT in January 2017, after g-Livia was approved and Kiril had taken up with PT's forty-year-old marketing director, Olga Fernandez.

"I see," says Pafko, a bit wary. "What about her?"

"She has finally agreed to meet with me. I am going to Florida to see her tomorrow. I wanted you to know. Pinky is supposed to go out to PT to collect Innis's personnel file, to help me prepare."

"Ah," says Pafko with a wry smile. "Make sure you bring earplugs. You will hear terrible things about me. And truth will not be an obstacle. You know what Shakespeare said, Sandy. 'Hell hath no fury.'"

"Better to know what is coming, Kiril."

"Agreed," says Kiril succinctly. The day last year when Kiril begged Sandy to take his case, Stern could have warned Kiril—and himself—that being someone's criminal defense lawyer is rarely a way to improve your opinion of them. Over the years, there have been exceptions, of course, clients who exhibited impressive bravery, or honesty about themselves. But usually what you discover is disappointing. Stern was entirely unaware that Kiril has apparently long had a woman on the side. That is not unusual for men in power, of course. Nevertheless, as a husband who was rigorously faithful to two wives, Stern takes a dim view of Kiril's behavior. And he is also much too fond of Donatella to accept Pafko's actions as entirely harmless, although Sandy has no clue what she knows.

But if the long relationship with Innis meant much to Kiril, he gives no sign of it today. He clearly prefers not to discuss her, and Stern soon lets Kiril go on his way. After seeing Kiril out, Stern returns to his office, taking up his outpost at the window and reflecting, not for the first time, about how enigmatic he finds his client, and even their relationship.

That first day, when Kiril had hugged him and tearfully declared his innocence, Pafko had stopped on the way to the door to embrace Stern again.

'Thank you, Sandy,' he said, 'thank you. Truly, I regard you as the closest friend I have.'

The declaration was startling, because Stern would never say anything similar. For Kiril and Donatella, Stern holds real affection. The Pafkos, as Stern has viewed them over the decades, are people of depth and values. But Kiril's polished manner is also a barrier; Stern knows little about Kiril at the core.

Nor does that limitation much concern Stern. He would be hard-pressed to name a male—at least one alive—with whom he has profound bonds. Yes, there have been men with whom he feels deep professional affinities developed in the course of hard cases, and always there have been guys to play cards with, to sit beside at the Trappers games. Yet the truth, which he has come to accept in late age, is that his most intimate connections have always been to women—to his mother and his sister, to Helen and Marta, even to Clara during their marriage's early years.

Nevertheless, in the last decade, Kiril has become an important figure in Stern's life and someone to whom Stern feels an instinctive attachment. Having reexperienced in the courtroom today the sense of doom that came with his diagnosis, and the darkness it cast over several years, Stern has a sudden moment of clarity about his deep gratitude to Kiril. Pafko was not simply a doctor who had arranged for Stern to receive a lifesaving medication. What Kiril had dispensed along with g-Livia might have been even more consequential.

While Kiril was assessing Stern's case in 2013, Sandy had met with him in a small examining room at Easton med school. Pafko was in his long white coat and thoroughly in his element. These days he saw few patients, but he was strikingly adept at the one-on-one. By then, Stern had met his share of oncologists. Some felt obliged to be cheerleaders, while others employed the Joe Friday method and limited themselves to blank recitation of the dismal facts. But in the role of treating physician, Kiril had an undeniable magic which exploited his natural charisma. As Stern sat on the edge of the examining table, Kiril had placed his hands on Stern's shoulders and bent forward so they could see one another eye to eye.

'Sandy, I believe in this medication. But I also believe in you. You know, we describe treatment response as a bell curve. At the far end, there are always patients who exceed expectations. Why? Will alone cannot subdue disease, Sandy. But wanting to live and having a reason to do so—every oncologist will tell you that it matters, even though no one can tell you why. You, Sandy, you are the kind of patient who lives, who wins the battle far, far longer than most.'

Kiril peered at him, holding on to Stern almost as if he were Sandy's parent, his grip notable in its strength and comfort. Months later, even before Stern began to see the results of the treatment, he looked back to that moment as the point in time when a fundamental transformation in his attitude had begun. He stopped preparing himself for death and resumed looking forward—to the pleasure of being home with a wife who loved him unreservedly, to watching his grandchildren unfold like blossoms, to absorbing the legacy of a life that, on balance, he felt had been well-lived. And he is deeply in Kiril's debt for that, not just for the time that g-Livia has given Stern, but for the pleasure in living that Kiril somehow renewed.

Now Pafko has asked Stern to return the favor somehow, to prevent Kiril's few remaining good years from being seized from him. The truth, given the facts, is that probably no one on earth can manage the feat. Certainly, as Stern accepted today, the time seems to have passed when Sandy could deliver. But standing at his window in the wake of Kiril's visit, Stern feels more completely than he has in all the months since, his motives for taking the case, and the emotional weight that comes with it.

11. INNIS

From the narrow perspective of a criminal defense lawyer, *US v. Pafko* is an ideal case. The charges require a nuanced defense. The national media attention attracted by the combination of Kiril's Nobel Prize and the extensive publicity and advertising Olga Fernandez organized for g-Livia have raised the excitement level by several powers. Last—and far from incidental—the case promises to be an excellent payday. Rather than the usual arm wrestling to get clients to pay for his services—even the well-heeled don't have much use for their bills after being sentenced to prison—PT's by-laws make Kiril's legal fees the company's responsibility for now.

Furthermore, the wasp's nest of civil actions against the company and Kiril have lessened some burdens on the Sterns. They have entered into joint defense agreements with the huge law firms handling the civil cases, allowing Marta and him to draw on those resources for legal research, e-discovery, consulting experts, even courtroom graphics like the animation of RAS Stern used in his opening. From PT's point of view, it is all money well spent, since Kiril's conviction will all but decide liability in most of the civil matters. In the courtroom, the Sterns prefer the humble appearance of only Marta and Pinky and an old man with a cane facing off against the vast governmental bureaucratic machine represented by the nine people seated at the prosecution table. But back at the Sterns' office, four associates and two paralegals delegated by the Kindle County branch of a national firm can be called on for assistance at any hour—a godsend since, with the doors closing soon at Stern & Stern, many staff members have already moved on to new jobs.

In one area, however, Stern has always preferred to do the work himself. Even in the days when Marta and he had two private investigators on retainer, he liked to see the witnesses face-to-face before confronting them in the courtroom. The decision to leave Stern in charge of interviewing potential witnesses had been arrived at when Marta's children were young, in order to minimize her travel out of town and after-hours meetings.

Even so, Marta initially opposed Stern's trip to Florida to interview Dr. McVie, thinking air travel on top of the rigors of trial was too much. Stern calmed her by promising that after seeing Innis McVie, a limo would drive him two hours across the state so that Stern could rest up Friday night and Saturday at the palatial beachfront house of Stern's sister, Silvia, in West Palm Beach. Marta trusts her aunt as a reliable steward of her father's well-being.

Stern lands in Fort Myers a little after one p.m. on Friday. Dr. McVie, still an avid tennis player, can't see him until three thirty because she is in a tournament. The limo driver, a recent Cuban émigré named Cesar, drives Stern to a nearby crab shack, where Stern invites Cesar to share lunch. The sunshine is a relief after the emotional buffeting of the week, especially now that fall has closed off the skies of Kindle County, where for months it will be like living under a pot lid. After a conversation in halting Spanish about the huge vista of opportunities Cesar sees in this country, they speed down I-75 toward Naples, where Dr. McVie has transplanted herself after her sour departure from PT.

In the last two decades, Stern and Helen had their share of

friends relocate to Florida to escape state income and inheritance taxes up north. As far as Stern is concerned, no amount of money is worth the change. With swamps and alligators inland, and the gated communities and shopping malls in the traffic-clotted towns along the coasts, the state seems to Stern like a giant penal colony for America's elderly, where the residents—like characters in a famous play—have been blinded by the sun and do not realize they are actually in hell.

He and Cesar are almost in Naples when both a text and e-mail arrive from Pinky. Stern looks first at the e-mail, for which he's been waiting. A scan of Innis's personnel file is attached. There are few surprises there, except that Kiril, whose generosity Stern has often heard praised, wisely sent Innis off with a bountiful severance package that added nicely to the thousands of stock options she'd earned.

Pinky's text, by contrast, provides Stern with a little jolt when he opens it. "Look what I saw at PT when I went to get Innis's file!" Attached is a series of photographs Pinky snapped, first from an upstairs window, then on ground level, of a car in the parking lot at Pafko Therapeutics. It is a late-model white Chevrolet, a Malibu according to the stainless-steel nameplate on the vehicle's trunk. Pinky even got a picture of the oval PT parking decal in the rear window. For Stern, the images spark an unearthly sensation, something like déjà vu.

Is this a coincidence or something ominous? Stern wants more time to think this through. He texts Pinky, "Brava! But do no more until we talk." Among other things, he needs to ponder how to address the subject of the white Malibu with Kiril.

Innis McVie's house is in a Naples neighborhood called Port Royal, a haven of the ultrarich. The baronial structures Cesar drives Stern past resemble European castles, fronted by a hundred yards of lawn, with the rear of the residences along the Gulf of Mexico and wide white beaches with sand like sugar. Dr. McVie's orange stucco house, accented with white decorative details, including a balustrade over an interior courtyard, sits at the end of a cul-de-sac and is not as grand as the big mansions. Yet since the residence is positioned right on the water, Stern's guess is that it is still worth more than $10 million, a purchase Innis McVie could easily afford when she cashed out at PT right after g-Livia came to market.

Unlike Kiril's son, Lep, with whom the Sterns have had two tense meetings in the company of his officious Chicago lawyers, Innis McVie largely cast aside her attorney, Rex Halsey, shortly after he'd negotiated her nonprosecution agreement with the government. She has returned Stern's calls herself, saying she has nothing to hide and adding that as the daughter of frugal Scots, she regards legal fees generally as a waste of money. Nonetheless, until recently she has been elusive when Stern has asked to meet. Under the guidance of Rex, with whom she still consults on occasion, Innis at last agreed to see him, but only on the condition that Stern come unaccompanied, so there is no 'prover' to testify if there are disputes about what Innis said. Since witnesses with nonprosecution agreements are usually careful to do nothing to displease the government, including meet with defense lawyers, Stern accepted those terms without reluctance.

Stern has called from the car to announce he is nearby, and Dr. McVie is on her step to greet him, smiling as she stands before a huge arched doorway of mahogany. The front wall of the house sports broad white decorative pilasters and stainless-steel shades half drawn over the huge windows. She calls him Sandy and takes his hand with the imposing grip he'd expect of someone still playing tennis at a competitive level.

Once inside, Stern can see that the rear of the house has a wall of glass, windows that fold back like a fan so they entirely disappear. Outside there is a large pool and a covered patio, enclosed beneath something Floridians refer to as a 'lanai,' roofed and sided with screening that admits sunshine but no bugs or falling vegetation. Moving through, Stern lavishes compliments on the house, which Helen would have described privately as 'overdecorated,' a mix of bold prints and eighteenth-century French antiques. Clearly, there are no grandchildren who visit. In the living room every precious piece has its place. The dreadful pastels of most Florida decorating, including his sister's house, do not dominate. There is a lot of red.

As for Dr. McVie, on first impression she strikes Stern as lively, quick to laugh, and certainly not the embittered shrew Kiril portrayed. A few days short of seventy, she remains striking, with the tidy, small-featured Northern European looks that for at least a century have been accepted as the American ideal of beauty. It appears she took a dip in the ocean when she got home from her tennis match, since her hair is wet, and she wears a modest swim top, a flowered beach skirt, and cork shoes. Stern can see that she retains an athletic form. Her hair, gray and naturally curly, is cut short so she can do without regular styling. Against her tan, her blue eyes are distinct as a beacon.

She points him to a table in the shade, where Stern thanks her for seeing him.

"I don't have a side in this mess, Sandy. And I was curious to meet you, frankly. You're a famous guy."

"I doubt that," he answers, "and whatever I was is largely in the past." He was never attached to the great notoriety that once surrounded him—it was his clients who were famous really, not him. It is unsurprising, though, that Dr. McVie finds fame of interest. Kiril had already shaken the foundations of cancer research when she met him thirty-two years ago. He imagines that Kiril's standing and reputation were part of his attraction.

"When I was young, I thought tennis was going to make me famous," she says. "Then I played Chris Evert. She was thirteen and I was nineteen, and I won three points. That's when I switched to premed." Stern laughs loudly, which pleases Innis.

"Kiril talked about you a lot," she says. "You're a widower?"

"For the second time," he says.

"Yes, Kiril was very fond of your second wife. He says she had a wonderful sense of humor."

"Clara was harder to know, but she had a close relationship with Donatella." Stern wonders if mentioning Donatella might be an error, but Dr. McVie seems to take it in stride, just like her casual references to Kiril. Stern had felt some instinctive need to stick up for Clara. Even with both women gone, he does not compare his two wives. Friends often tell him how much lighter his mood was with Helen, which was inevitable given how deeply depressed Clara often was. But each woman defined a long period of his life that he looks back on with far more satisfaction than doubt; each had given him something that had felt essential at the time.

Dr. McVie's maid sets down a pitcher of lemonade and pours for both of them.

"And you started getting g-Livia right after the dogs and rats, right?"

When she asks how he is doing, Stern tells her that his metastatic disease remains at bay.

"I have reached that blessed state when my doctor now predicts I will die of something else," he says. "On the other hand, at this age, that might come at any moment."

"Oh, you look damn good," says Innis. "I'll bet you see ninety, Sandy. What is that? Another decade or so? You're younger than Kiril, aren't you?"

"Far older," he answers.

It is preposterous to feel flattered to be mistaken for a mere octogenarian. Furthermore, having looked in the mirror, he knows these compliments approach comedy.

"Proves my point," offers Dr. McVie.

Is she flirting? He heard just the faintest trill of that before, when she asked if he was a widower. Despite his many vows, Innis's compliments provoke a little spark of interest. One of the discoveries of late age is that this aspect of being human is indelible. The instincts dim but never disappear. Sex matters. Ever and always. In the years of surgery and chemo, physical passion became rarer for Helen and him, and yet it was still there at the core of what bound them. Stern has never seen sex as the only motivating force in life. Greed, glory, the love of children or God matter as much or more to some. But it is the most secret of our deep desires, revealed only in utter privacy. There is good reason that the Bible refers to the sexual act as 'knowing' someone.

Yet Innis probably means little by it. In Stern's experience, there are attractive men and women who are, if not blind to their sexual power, indifferent to it. But the opposite is more common. Innis has probably been a harmless flirt since she was twelve. Nonetheless, he decides it is best to get down to business. He asks if Moses knows about their meeting.

"I told him," she says. "Mr. Appleton clearly preferred I not do it. He said the only result of this will be to give you a greater opportunity to embarrass me on the witness stand and attack my credibility. Is that true?"

Stern lifts a hand to temporize.

"My first loyalty must be to Kiril. The prosecutors are right about that. But a defense rarely succeeds by trying to make a liar out of every witness. In my mind, the purpose of an interview like this is to find out what you have to say that might benefit Kiril. Those are questions I would be reluctant to ask without knowing the answers, which is why the prosecutors would rather we not speak."

"Oh, I'm sure I have a lot to say about Kiril that's beneficial to him. And I'll say it, even though I am still angrier than hell with him. Enraged, frankly. I'm sure you know why." She glances sidewise over her glass.

"I do," says Stern. Stern has anticipated that Innis's long relationship with Kiril would be a tender area. Along with Lep, she became Kiril's original partner in founding PT. Over the years, when they traveled to scientific meetings, they did not bother with the pretense of two hotel rooms. Indeed, several of the scientists Stern has interviewed in the last year have admitted being shocked when they learned that Kiril was married to someone else.

"But we're not getting into any of this in the courtroom, correct?"

"We made a motion to the judge, which she granted. The parties may say only that you left PT after a disagreement with Kiril."

"I heard that from Rex. Frankly, that's why I decided to sit down with you. Apparently, the prosecutors wanted to trot out all the humiliating details."

That is not completely accurate. Moses is a grown-up and accepts the persistence of what he sees as sin, but sex generally makes him squirm. Although the prosecutors opposed the Sterns' motion, Moses ultimately seemed more interested in getting assurances that Sandy would not paint Innis on cross-examination as the rage-filled reject. With Donatella sitting in the front row in court each day, Kiril's extramarital activities are likely to damage him badly in the eyes of the jury, and Sandy was happy to agree.

"If I knew what I know now," says Innis, "I'm not sure I would have sat down with the prosecutors in the first place. I never imagined they'd try to send Kiril to prison for the rest of his life as a murderer. That strikes me as outrageous."

"I agree, of course, but I would like to hear your view."

"Sandy, there is not a medication without harmful side effects. People die of Tylenol overdoses. g-Livia is an extraordinary medicine. You are living proof. And the FDA is under intense pressure to agree that it can be marketed again, at least for some uses. They've dithered apparently because there was no consensus at first about what was causing these isolated deaths. But there is a broad view now that it is an allergic response, which is a problem that can be dealt with in a clinical setting. The FDA should have concurred by now about administering g-Livia in the most serious cases."

"Oh, I assume Moses and the Justice Department may have some role in that. It is much harder to make a fraud case if Kiril lied to win approval of a product that's back on the market. It suggests that the supposed fraud was immaterial."

"That's nice," says Innis sarcastically. "Patients die so the government can get Kiril?"

"I am sure they have their excuses. But there is a reason, Dr. McVie, that criminal litigation is described as a blood sport."

"Apparently. From what I've read, the whole case against Kiril is grossly exaggerated."

"How so?"

"Frankly, these doctors who testified that they didn't recognize their patients were in allergic shock? They were idiots. You'd treat for that, even if you weren't sure."

"Would you say that on the stand?"

"Of course not," says Innis. She smiles a bit. "Look, Rex has told me from the start to stay in the middle. I've answered the prosecutors' questions, simply and directly, and let the chips fall where they may. But I haven't gone out of my way to stick it to Kiril, and I won't."

Stern watches her in silence for a second, assessing.

"Do I mark myself as an ungrateful guest if I challenge you a bit?"

"Of course not."

"I would say, Dr. McVie—"

"Innis."

"Innis, then. I find it hard to reconcile you saying that you mean Kiril no special harm with recording your phone conversation when he called you after speaking with Ms. Hartung." Hartung is the *Wall Street Journal* reporter who contacted Kiril in August 2018.

It is that recording that makes Innis such a valuable witness to the government, because it virtually convicts Kiril on the insider trading counts. She will also offer testimony pertaining to the fraud charges, but only a paler version of what Lep is going to say anyway. Having spent decades now listening to these taped conversations, it always amazes Stern how frequently people talk past and over each other. Conversation, it turns out, often might as well be occurring between people in two foxholes in the midst of battle.

"Yes, but that was all about Kiril harming *me*."

"How so?"

"Take a look at Kiril's cell phone records."

Stern has done that and is puzzled. "As far as I recall, he hadn't spoken to you in quite some time."

"Yes, but why? Look back eighteen months to when I left. He would not leave me alone. Every time he had two drinks, he was on the phone beseeching me to come back to the company, to come back to him. He kept saying, 'I don't understand why anything needs to be different.' It was insulting, Sandy. And to be honest, very painful." Kiril's gall apparently was unbounded, especially when he was drunk. His hope seemed to be to get Innis to accept demotion from The Other Woman to Another Woman, with Olga now getting second billing behind Donatella. "Finally, I told him that if he kept calling, I would get a protective order."

"A protective order is a far cry from an audio recording."

"No." She shakes her head. "I didn't want him claiming that these calls were just business. And I thought telling him that I was using a recorder was the simplest way to get him off the phone immediately. I know you've listened to it. I told him at the start that we were being taped."

That was true. At the outset, she said, 'Kiril, I am recording this. I have asked you to stop calling.'

'Then turn it off,' he answered. 'I have something I must discuss with you.' Kiril claims he heard a distinct sound, the chirp of a button pushed, and assumed the recording had ceased. And the beep is there. But Innis says Kiril mistook the sound of her putting the phone on speaker, since Kiril had caught her with wet hands at the sink. Kiril's misimpression has no legal significance anyway.

On the recording, Kiril said next he had just learned there are reports that persons treated with g-Livia were experiencing a sudden death syndrome, perhaps an allergic response, after a year on the medication. There followed a beat or two of silence, whose meaning was going to be the subject of fierce dispute at trial. Kiril did not say, 'How is that possible?' or 'Do you know anything about that?' or 'I'm shocked to learn this,' none of a dozen statements a defense lawyer would have scripted for him. But even a skeptic like Marta acknowledges that Kiril seemed surprised and befuddled as he related that information.

On the recording, Innis responded, 'I'm sorry to hear that. But why are you calling me?'

Kiril stammered once or twice. 'Well, what should I do?' he finally asked her.

'Sell your stock?' There was a hiccup of laughter after Innis said this, while Kiril answered with the words destined to fry him, 'Well, I can't do that, can I?'

'I don't know, Kiril. Call a lawyer. None of this concerns me.' She hung up.

Stern asks Innis now, beside her pool, "Would you agree that he sounded surprised when he told you about what the *Journal* was going to print?"

Dr. McVie sways her head to and fro to ponder.

"He certainly sounded to me like he was in a state of shock. You can hear what's there."

"But did he sound surprised by what Hartung, the reporter, was saying about the medication?"

"*I* was surprised," says Innis. "But my principal reaction, Sandy, was that this had nothing to do with me any longer." She hunches forward on her chair again. Her agitated movements have caused her beach wrap to creep up her thighs, revealing her trim legs, unmarked by age. She passes a hand at the skirt but makes no serious effort to readjust it. "Look, you don't need me to reinterpret what's on that recording. You can listen to it for yourself." This again is probably Rex's advice: Don't offer conjecture that will undermine the prosecutors and aggravate them. "I'm simply telling you that I didn't make that recording to get even with Kiril."

"Although you were entitled?"

"Hell yes, I was entitled. For thirty-some years, I spent more time with Kiril than anyone alive. I slept with him, I worked beside him, I listened to him and corrected him when I could. I provided him with ideas and let him take the credit for them. I did all the stupid things that women of my era did for the men they loved. Or thought they loved. Or who they thought loved them." With the last remark, she studies the round wicker table between them and falls briefly into some kind of reverie from which she is slow to extract herself. "Where was I?" she asks finally.

" 'Love,' I believe," says Stern simply.

That earns a bitter smile.

"Right," she says. "Love. But really, what's the point of those words? I was attached to Kiril. Was he the man in my life? Yes. But don't mislead yourself. It was a very complicated relationship. For years, he hired young women in the lab whose looks were their first qualification. He slept with quite a few of them, I'm sure. And I contained my reaction because there were other men in my life, too. How could I do otherwise when he was going home each night to Donatella? Some of those men truly interested me, or excited me. Others I went with largely out of spite." She puts her glass down and waggles her head, like a boxer shaking off a punch. "Let's talk about something else, Sandy. What more can I tell you?"

Stern moves on to his questions that concern the heart of the government's case, Kiril's alleged fraud near the end of the eighteen-month clinical trial that was supposed to pave the way for accelerated approval of g-Livia. PT, like most pharmaceutical manufacturers, had hired an outside concern, Global International, to conduct its testing. During the final months of the trial, a statistician at Global, Dr. Wendy Hoh, noticed there had recently been a spike in sudden fatalities and alerted the associate medical director at PT, who quickly brought the matter to Dr. Lep Pafko.

As Lep told the story, he immediately informed his father. Lep and Kiril agreed that when Lep returned on Monday from a weekend conference in Seattle, these reports would be submitted to a panel of outside experts who served as safety monitors for the trial, and who could properly unmask the data to see if the deaths related to g-Livia. Instead, on Monday, Kiril told Lep he had used a set of codes PT had for emergencies and 'unblinded' the dataset himself, a clear violation of the rules set up when the trial began. But after calling Wendy Hoh, Kiril said they had determined that the supposed sudden deaths were merely a computer glitch, misrepresenting patients who had in fact withdrawn from the study. Dr. Hoh had corrected the database accordingly.

Innis's testimony was more innocuous than Lep's, but she still corroborated Lep on important details. She told Stern that at one point, in September of 2016, Kiril mentioned to her that he was concerned about the dataset from the clinical trial of g-Livia. A few weeks later, when she asked him about it again, Kiril told her the problem had been solved. She never thought about those exchanges again, she says, until the prosecutors began questioning her.

"Did he tell you that he had found that there had been a computer error?" Stern asks.

"It was a few words, Sandy. Frankly, we were barely speaking at that point." Because of Olga, undoubtedly. "It was a conversation in passing, and I asked, as I remember, only because we'd been left alone for a second and I was looking for something to talk about. It was like asking about the weather."

"But nothing he said was inconsistent with having found out that the whole problem was simply a coding error?"

"I suppose. But I don't know what he was referring to when he said the problem was solved."

"Well, Innis, let me ask this. In the years you worked beside Kiril, did you ever see him falsify data?"

"No, I can't say that. But you know, by the time I met Kiril, he was already a very big deal—and he enjoyed that role. A cast of thousands worked for him in the lab. He presided over meetings. But the real scientific work, the observing and recording, was generally being done by others."

"But you regard him as a great scientist, do you not?"

"I regard Kiril as a great something," she says. "As a scientist, he had vision. And God knows, he's an operator. As a grant-getter, he's without rival. But a *great* scientist? I'm not sure what that means. The man or woman who can theorize like Kiril is unusual, but nowhere near as unusual as a scientist who can both theorize *and* imagine how to prove his theory. That person knows how to think both big and small. Kiril is exceptional at the first part, but not the second. The proof, experimental design, tends to bore him. The best scientist I worked with in all those years was Lep."

"Lep?"

"Lep is a great scientist. Not that Kiril will ever let him have the credit he deserves. g-Livia is really much more his work than Kiril's."

In Stern's limited understanding, Lep had short-circuited the usual process of drug development, which is more or less a well-informed version of trial and error. Instead, he used high-level computer modeling to identify the molecule that became g-Livia.

"What Lep did," says Innis, "is going to change pharmaceutical research forever."

"I've heard more than one person say that, Innis, but Lep refuses to accept the credit."

"One could say that Lep is a loyal son. Or that he's learned his place. He's always been very careful not to get between the sun and Kiril."

"You like Lep?"

"Always. Very much. He's very quiet. Wry. Not that the liking was mutual for years. We were proper with each other, but he loves his mother, and I knew that he resented me, which I understood. Over time he got used to me. The irony, of course, is that once Olga came on the scene we became friendlier."

"You speak now?"

"Very rarely. Not in months. But we had a few heart-to-hearts right before I left the company. We came to terms, I would say. You know the saying: 'My enemy's enemy.'" She lifts a hand to signify the rest.

"And Kiril was your common enemy with Lep?"

"Our shared challenge."

She turns to look behind her, where the sun is already getting low.

"May we suspend our conversation for the sunset? It's a local form of worship. Really quite spectacular. You shouldn't miss it. Can you climb stairs?"

"Slowly."

There is a balcony here, offering an unobstructed view down to the shore one hundred yards away, where there is not a soul. The sand itself is extraordinary, soft, and the color of heavy cream.

"How private," says Stern.

She explains that it's high tide, which limits public access. As they look toward the sea, relatively flat today, the housekeeper brings Innis a glass of white wine. Stern asks for more lemonade. For him, this kind of natural glory occasionally produces a few wisps of sadness. The sun has risen and set for eons and soon would be doing so without him to appreciate it. Still, he savors the simple beauty of it, watching the great ball growing rosier and more brilliant as it declines through a few streaks of clouds, soon coloring to that hot fuchsia shade seen nowhere else in life. As Innis promised, the sight is remarkable—there is something pure about the sky. At the end, just as the sun is about to disappear, Stern suddenly sees a strobing flash of green, impossibly brief. He thinks it might be like seeing spots after staring too long into the sun, but Innis cries out, "Did you see it?"

"The green flash?"

"Yes, yes. Amazing." They both gaze silently for a second at the place where the sun had been. "I don't know what the science is—why that part of the spectrum seems to pop that way; I'm guessing it has to do with how the refracted light reflects off the water—but it's very special, isn't it? You're lucky, Sandy. I've owned this place two years and only seen the flash a couple of other times." They turn back to the house. "Are you one of those fellows who walks with luck?"

He did not count his early years or Clara's death as fortunate events. But overall, he'd been quite lucky.

"I would say being alive right now—getting early treatment with g-Livia—that's a piece of luck. I have had more than my share of good fortune. You?"

"I suppose. I'm still trying to figure out if meeting Kiril was a blessing to me or my doom. Here I am, living in splendor. So, just like you, Kiril brought me good things. But on the other hand—" She pauses, just as they reenter the house through an oversize screen door. "I never totally minded being the Other Woman. I still had my independence, fewer responsibilities, but it never dawned on me that, after I had settled for far less than what most people want, he'd take even that away." She looks from Stern quickly, caught up in more visible emotion than she has permitted herself up to now.

Stern decides it is a good time to bring their conversation to an end. He's gotten enough, and he is looking forward to a late dinner with his sister. Eager to find another subject, as they move inside, he says, “I never asked about your tennis match. Did you triumph?”

“Close but no cigar,” she says. “I ran into a great 6. Next month, I move up a division and I’ll be collecting trophies for years.” She smiles, but with evident competitive mettle. On the court, Stern can see, you would not be wise to look for mercy from Innis.

He tells Innis he will go, and together they move toward her front door.

“May I call you again, if I think of other things?” he asks.

“Yes, of course.”

He studies her then and the biggest question emerges unexpectedly, asked as much for his sake as his client’s.

“I suppose I have one more. But it is no small matter. You knew this man on the closest terms for decades. Do you believe he did this?”

“He denies all, I assume.”

Stern never discloses his conversations with his clients. Confidentiality is their inviolable right. When the subject is the insider trading charges, Kiril never quite answers, claiming his mind was a muddle after the reporter called. But as to what had allegedly taken place three years earlier, in late September 2016—unblinding the dataset, calling Wendy Hoh to change the numbers—he continues to deny it all, notwithstanding phone records and computer forensics that corroborate what the government claims, not to mention the screenshot he sent Olga of the dataset before it had been changed.

“Proceed on that assumption,” Stern says.

“And are you going to ask me the same question on the witness stand?”

“Would you rather I not?”

“Yes.”

“Then I promise I shall not.” This, he knows, is not much of a concession. Sonny would never allow the inquiry, not in that raw form.

"Do I believe Kiril did all this?" she asks herself, and studies the beams above them in the entry's high ceiling. "Honestly, I have a great deal of difficulty with the fraud charges. Selling the stock? There's no question he did that."

"You told him to," says Stern. He smiles faintly, to see how combative she will be about sharing the blame. She rolls her bright blue eyes.

"I was clearly being sarcastic."

"And yet he never sold any of his own shares."

This remark brings her up short for a second. Perhaps Stern has told her something she didn't know? She draws back, her head tilted, before returning to the main subject.

"I would never accuse Kiril of being motivated by money. I mean, he was thrilled he was joining the superrich. We weren't really talking, and he still mentioned that to me several times. But I'm sure he took it as another form of acclaim, which is what he's really lived for. And control. He has to be in charge."

"But the fraud you doubt?" says Stern. "Unblinding the dataset? And then bamboozling Wendy Hoh into altering it?"

Innis laughs a little. "'Bamboozling'? He could compete if there were an Olympic event in bullshitting. But unblinding the dataset is a different matter. I really don't think he had the technical acumen. Of course, he's smart enough to figure it out, if he worked at it. But Kiril is like any other seventy-eight-year-old. He doesn't have a native feel for technology. I suspect, if he did it, he had help."

"From?"

"Again, this is between us?" Once he nods, she says, "Olga is a very canny girl. She reported to me directly for a long time. You will meet very few people in this life, Sandy, more nakedly ambitious than that one. Her stock options were worth a fraction of the rest of ours, but if she saw an obstacle to g-Livia's approval, there is no way she'd allow several million dollars to slip from her grasp. At least she didn't sell herself cheap," Innis adds. "You'll never hear me criticize any woman for making the most of her situation. I give her credit for that."

It is difficult to tell if Innis means so much as a syllable of what she's just said.

"Do you have any idea why Kiril would have e-mailed Olga a copy of the unaltered dataset, the one from September 2016 that still showed the deaths?"

Innis's mouth parts slightly. Apparently, she's never heard this detail either.

"Of course not. What does she say?"

To avoid any action a prosecutor might call tampering, Stern rigorously avoids passing information between potential witnesses. Unintentionally, he may already have said more than he should, so he shakes his head a bit.

"How would you react if I told you that Olga doesn't know how to read a clinical trial dataset?"

Innis hoots and slaps her thigh.

"Is *that* what she claims? Of course she knows how to read a dataset. She's been in this industry for twenty years. In all seriousness, Sandy, don't believe a word that woman says. Not one. She's a brazen liar. I know it sounds catty, but take a hard look at her résumé. Do some arithmetic. Consider her job history, see when she graduated college at night in New York. Not to mention giving birth to three kids. See if you can figure out how that woman can claim to be under forty."

Stern knows better than to tell Innis that he's a bit surprised to think Olga is even that old. Innis is pointing at him, her nail polished in crimson.

"If you ever get to the bottom of this, Sandy, I promise you one thing: Olga Fernandez will be standing there."

She walks him out the door. Cesar, invisible in the growing darkness behind the limo's smoked glass, turns over the engine and the headlights illuminate the glittering crushed stone in Innis's drive.

"I had my trepidation about this, Sandy, but all in all, it's been very pleasant to get to know you." She extends her hand at full arm's length, her elbow straight, as professional women sometimes do, to avoid any risks in greater proximity.

"Entirely my pleasure," Stern answers, again feeling her strong grip. He uses the cane to go down the single step, then turns back to wave.

The halogen ground lights surrounding the doorway render her diaphanous wrap all but transparent. Does she know? Probably. She looks very good.

Returning his wave, she starts through the door then turns back.

"Come again when all of this is over, Sandy," she says before ducking inside.

III. FRAUD

WEEK TWO

12. VENTURE CAPITAL

Having gotten in several hard blows by calling Kiril a murderer, on Monday morning Moses and Feld resume a more familiar effort for federal prosecutors: painting Pafko as a greedy crook. White-collar offenses almost always involve someone breaking the law to make a lot of money. After decades of this, Stern tends to view greed as a somewhat ham-handed label for more complex motives, a lust for power or fame, which in turn masks significant self-doubts. But most jurors live with financial anxieties, and prosecutors find it easy to sell them on the notion that the rich are not like them and, in fact, are rich simply because they will do just about anything for money.

To establish that about Kiril Pafko, the government calls into the courtroom Dr. Yan Weill, president of MedInvest, a venture fund owned by a consortium of the nation's three largest investment banks. Dr. Weill is lean and nice-looking, midforties, in a flawless blue suit and a shirt so white it seems illuminated. He is buoyed by an almost insulting level of self-confidence, so glib and quick in his responses that there is a good chance one or two of the men in the jury box hold a secret yearning to climb over the rail and give Yan Weill a couple good smacks.

Stern spent an hour with Weill in his Wall Street office back in September and left more or less liking the man, who is clearly one of those people who believe life should involve an effort to enjoy everything. His laughter—a wall-rocking, high-pitched cackle—erupted frequently as he paused in his answers to Stern to show off items in his office he regarded as hilarious: a piece of amber that somehow fell into Weill's boot when he was in the Amazon; various photos he has captured as a hot-air balloonist; a recent SEC filing for a MedInvest deal in which the general counsel for the company MedInvest was buying was described as "having extensive experience practicing foreign corruption."

As a witness, he displays none of the sobriety, nervousness, or restraint of most people called into federal court. Instead, he has hiked himself forward to the front edge of his seat and provides an instant answer to every question, smiling hugely the whole time.

MedInvest provided much of the early financing for PT, in exchange for a stake in the company that increased as time went on. Once g-Livia headed to clinical testing, PT's stock was offered for sale to the public in order to underwrite the costs. Kiril remained the largest shareholder, followed by MedInvest and Easton University. The big payoff everyone hoped for would come if g-Livia was approved. Once that occurred, the revenues generated by g-Livia sales would drive up the stock price and, in all likelihood, lead to a buyout by a major pharmaceutical manufacturer with the capital and know-how to market a vital drug around the world. The whole plan was unfolding perfectly, including the projected sale to Tolliver, until the *Journal* article appeared in August 2018.

Weill is examined by Dan Feld, who apparently will present the testimony of most of the witnesses for the government. Trying a case is an extraordinary burden for the United States Attorney. When Moses returns after court every evening there are probably ten critical matters—questions in an investigation, disputes that have arisen in other trials—on which he needs to make decisions.

His time on *US v. Pafko* must be husbanded, meaning Feld has to do a larger share of the day-to-day work.

Feld is frequently described as the brainiest of Moses's assistants (although there is often joking that the description originates with Feld). When he left his clerkship with Sonny, he became the so-called liberal clerk whom US Supreme Court Justice Antonin Scalia—always famously open to debate—frequently employed. By reputation, Dan can solve legal problems, digest evidence, or write briefs at twice the speed of most of his colleagues. He is a nice enough young man outside the courtroom, but at trial he is tight as a piano string. His aggressiveness has led to several mistakes already. Stern can see Moses watching Feld far more anxiously than at the start of the proceedings. Of course, Stern knows, the same can probably be said now of the way Marta is watching him.

Both Stern and Marta have agreed that the prosecutors are making an error by characterizing the case as a crime of greed. Yes, the value of Kiril's stock in PT rocketed upward after the approval of g-Livia. And yes, pointing out that his net worth at the high point exceeded $600 million will stir the pot of jury resentments. But the prosecutors' theory has a clear vulnerability, and when he rises for cross, Stern goes straight there.

"Now, as a member of the PT board and a key investor, Mr. Weill, do you keep track of stock sold by so-called corporate insiders—meaning officers, other board members, those kinds of people?"

"I have to," says Weill.

"And can you explain briefly what a 10b5-1 plan is?"

"It's a plan that those corporate insiders agree to in advance, in which each of them specifies exactly when and how much company stock they will sell in the future. The plans are made when there is no material nonpublic information about the company, and the plan covers a pre-agreed period. If you stick to the plan strictly at all times, generally speaking you can avoid liability for insider trading, even if your stock later sells when you know something significant is going on inside the company."

"Was there a 10b5-1 plan adopted at Pafko Therapeutics after the stock went public and clinical testing began?"

"Yes."

"And under that plan, how much of its stock did MedInvest sell?"

"About ten percent. We thought it would be a good time to start recovering some of our investment."

"And under that plan, how many shares of PT did Kiril Pafko sell during that period?"

"None," says Weill.

"None," Stern repeats, and nods slowly, as if he were trying to absorb this information for the first time. "And when I speak of Kiril's shares, were you aware that Dr. Pafko had given away some of his PT stock to trusts for his grandchildren."

"I knew that."

"And were those shares, the grandchildren's shares, included in the 10b5-1 plan?"

"No, because Kiril personally no longer received the benefits from those shares."

"Thank you," says Stern. "And was the 10b5-1 plan amended when PT announced that it had received preliminary indications from the FDA that g-Livia was going to be approved?"

"Yes."

"Now, under that new plan, how much of its stock in PT did MedInvest agree to sell over the next two years?"

"Half."

"At a substantial profit?"

"Very substantial."

"What about the number two person at PT, Dr. Innis McVie? What percentage of her stock did she plan to sell?"

"Basically all of it as soon as various SEC restrictions were lifted."

Stern goes through several other executives and board members, including Lep and his first lieutenant, Hiro Tanakawa, all of whom carried out plans to sell a goodly portion of their holdings in PT shortly after approval. Olga Fernandez had the smallest stake, and she made close to $5 million. It was a bonanza for everyone.

"And what about Kiril Pafko? How many shares did he sell under the 10b5-1 plan that applied to the period surrounding FDA approval of g-Livia?"

"None."

"None?" For the benefit of the jury, Stern squints at Weill, as if he cannot possibly understand. "Zero? Dr. Pafko harvested none of the hundreds of millions of dollars in appreciated value of his stock Mr. Feld asked you about?"

Feld objects that the question has been asked and answered, but Sonny allows it, because Stern has asked now about value, not shares.

"And after FDA approval, did the stock price increase again as word spread about the possibility of a buyout of PT by a much bigger pharmaceutical manufacturer?"

"Yes."

"Did MedInvest make plans to sell the rest of its shares?"

"A tender offer—a public offer to buy all of PT's shares—would terminate the 10b5-1 plan and eliminate any restrictions on exercise of the stock options that officers and board members of the company had. Because of market anticipation, it's almost always better to sell when the tender offer is agreed to rather than waiting for the deal to close, since there can be complications. So yes, MedInvest sold its stake after the board accepted Tolliver's offer."

"And what about Kiril?"

"Nope. He still didn't sell. He was going to hold on to his stock until the last moment."

"And did you ever talk with Kiril about why he had not planned to sell any of his shares?"

"I did. A few times."

"Foundation," objects Feld, meaning Weill must say where and when the conversation took place and who was present.

"Well, the time I remember best was when Kiril picked me up at the airport. It was fall 2017. Beautiful day and the top was down on his convertible and we were driving out to PT headquarters in Greenwood County."

"And what did you and he say at the time?"

"Objection, hearsay," says Feld. The rule against hearsay evidence is simple enough on its face. A fact—that the sky is blue—may not be proven by offering as evidence how someone described the sky when they were outside court. To establish the color, the witness must be here to say they saw that shade and then be subject to cross-examination. But the supposed rule has about thirty recognized exceptions that make its application an opaque mess. Stern would estimate that at least a third of the judges before whom he's tried cases don't understand the hearsay rule thoroughly. The exception Stern invokes is, as he says, "state of mind," meaning that Kiril's statement is not being offered to prove the sky is blue, only that Kiril thought it was. And the judge allows it on that basis.

"Well, the substance of what he said—" says Weill.

"Objection again," says Feld. With the relentless objections, Feld might as well light up a neon sign that says, What's coming is bad for the government.

"Dr. Weill," says Sonny. "Do you remember exactly what Dr. Pafko said?"

Weill, always happy, cackles again, a sound that is almost a shriek.

"I do, but it's not for prime time."

"We're all grown-ups," answers Sonny.

"Well, the stock was way up. Tolliver's bid for the company had been announced, and Kiril was free to sell. His stake was probably worth half a billion at that moment. I said that most people would take some money off the table, but he just waved his hand at me.

We were joking a lot, and Kiril said, 'Yan, I don't give two loose turds about money. I haven't for years. I married rich.'"

Stern, who's never heard the verbatim quote, finds his jaw hanging open, while the courtroom dissolves in laughter. There will be no topping that and he heads back to his seat. Kiril, whom Stern and Marta have cautioned repeatedly about not reacting to the evidence, has nonetheless dropped his face into his hands in embarrassment, while behind him, Donatella, always the master of proper social response, has joined the laughter. She places a hand briefly over her eyes beneath those black brows and continues turning her white head in a way that suggests that this is another in a long line of Kiril's faux pas.

13. HER PLAN

The rest of Monday involves a slow immersion in the FDA's complicated multiyear approval process for new medications. The government's witness is Dr. Maithripala Jayasundara, who says cheerfully that he is known as Dr. Mat. Agreeable as he is, Dr. Mat is also ponderous and quickly loses the attention of most of the jurors as he goes through the many phases of testing and documentation required by the FDA. The process begins with trials on animals, then tests on a small number of humans, aimed at figuring out an effective dose of the medication. Then clinical trials begin, culminating in the double-blind trials regarded as the gold standard. Each step is guided by an intricate regulatory framework, which Dr. Mat explains in far too much detail, especially since many of those rules do not apply to the small number of medications like g-Livia that are designated as Breakthrough Therapies and reach the market early through a process known as 'accelerated approval.'

After Dr. Mat finally leaves the stand, Kiril's personal assistant at PT, Janelle Morris, is called next by the prosecution. Janelle has worked for Pafko since PT was founded and continues to this day, even though Kiril now appears in the office infrequently after being suspended by the company without pay as the indictment neared.

Janelle has also been the point person for all document requests and subpoenas to the company, and in the opinion of both Sterns she is a wonder of efficiency.

Now Feld asks her to identify Kiril's signature on the Investigational New Drug Application that PT submitted to the FDA late in 2013 to start the testing process. Although it's on the monitor, Feld has Janelle read out the undertaking both Lep, as chief medical officer, and Kiril, as CEO, subscribed to: "'I agree to conduct the investigation in accordance with all . . . applicable regulatory requirements.'"

When Janelle—a tall, stately woman—is excused, she makes sure to pass by the defense table and to place a hand on Kiril's shoulder that he grabs and squeezes fondly. Kiril is described by the staff as a good boss who always asks about their families and remembers the details. Viewing him cynically, Marta might say that Pafko always loves to have someone to charm, but his employees regard his warmth and Donatella's as genuine.

Sonny recesses. After seeing out the Pafkos, Stern returns to the office briefly to confer with Marta. Tomorrow's pivotal cross-examination of the principal witness from the FDA will be her responsibility, and she has been doing research for months.

"Dad, you look like the weekend in Florida with Aunt Silvia did you good. How was Dr. McVie?"

"Innis is an interesting person," he says.

"Oh, 'Innis,'" says Marta, and smiles as she turns her face askance.

"Please," her father answers, although the truth is that she has recurred in Stern's thoughts more frequently than he might have guessed. "At any rate, she does not seem especially eager to put a knife into Kiril."

He goes downstairs to the Cadillac with Ardent. Marta is right that he enjoyed the weekend with his sister. Stern's love for Silvia is unlike his feelings, no matter how deep, for anyone else in his life—there is something purer and less burdened in it. She had been seventeen when their mother died, and Stern, five years the elder, had assumed that his role toward her would become somewhat parental, but their needs proved less predictable. They have looked after one another. Stern and his sister, by the habit of a lifetime, speak each day. Occasionally they are on the phone for an hour, but most often their conversations last barely a minute. 'So, busy?' 'Yes, of course. You?' Silvia, too, has been widowed now for the second time.

Never having had children of her own, Silvia is very close with each of Stern's kids and their offspring. That means Stern often learns details from Silvia, which have not been confided to him, especially about his son. Peter is living with his husband and an infant daughter in San Francisco and is still often snarky or combative with his father.

At home, Pinky informs Stern that she is going out for the night, which is obvious from her attire. Very often she dresses in outlandish colors, fuchsia and neon greens to match her tattoos, but tonight it's a darker look: Huge slashes of mascara like the Nike swoosh darken the area under her eyes, and she wears a nose ring on each side dangling from the nail. She has on a leather skirt, black tights, a heavy belt decorated with a silver watch chain, a skimpy bustier, and a black leather vest studded with what appear to be the heads of armor-piercing bullets. Around her neck is a black leather dog collar.

She gives her grandfather a full inventory of the frozen dinners and puts one he likes into the oven. She is clearly eager to leave, but suddenly snaps her fingers, recalling something.

"The Malibu! How about that? What'd you think?"

"I am not sure what to think, Pinky. Did you contact the Greenwood Sheriff's Police to find out how many white 2017 Malibus are registered in the county?" If there are thousands, the significance of her sighting diminishes, but as Stern might have predicted, Pinky hasn't gotten around to that yet.

"But I haven't finished telling you the whole story," she says. "You know, I saw that white Malibu out the window. As soon as I had Dr. McVie's file, I ran out to the parking lot to grab a couple photos and text them to you. And just as I finished, this security guy comes along in his golf cart and asks if I need something."

"I hope you did not explain," says Stern. He would not want Kiril hearing about this from the PT staff rather than from his lawyer.

"I just told him I forgot where I parked my car." She smiles. "I'm good at fooling people, Pops."

That is probably the case, Stern thinks, but largely because Pinky is so off-center that most people would have a hard time guessing what she has in mind.

"So he's, like, driving me back to visitor parking, and, whoa, there's another white Malibu. I asked him—his name is Oscar, and I'm, like, 'Oscar, like really, everybody here got a '17 Malibu for a ride?' and he laughs and says they're pool cars."

"Pool cars?"

"PT owns them. They're trying to be all green and crunchy, so they pay for people to take the light rail out there, but, like, if a salesperson has to go see a client, or the researchers have got a meeting at Easton, they sign a car out. Oscar says PT owns six white Malibus. Hybrids."

Pinky is sure she's onto something. But she's also ahead of herself.

"Pinky, are you remembering what our friend Detective Swanson told us? She walked through the PT lot while I was in the hospital and saw no car there with serious body damage."

"Yeah, but Pops, that's always seemed pretty lame to me. Somebody nearly wipes you out and runs for it, they're not gonna bring some wrecked car back to the PT lot, are they? Oscar is bound to ask questions. I say whoever hit you took the Malibu to a body shop straight off. What kind of detective is Swanson not to figure that out?"

A detective who was trying to humor an old man, Stern could answer.

"Well, certainly, Pinky, someone must keep track of these vehicles. They would notice if one of them was missing for several days, no?"

"Maybe. Maybe they sign cars out for a week at a time. I mean, we should investigate a little, right?"

He wonders if experience with Pinky is causing him to give less credence than he should to her suspicions. He believed he'd seen the PT parking decal in the back window of the car that hit him. And it was paint from a white Malibu on his Cadillac.

"I mean, Pops, I was wondering if I could ask Janelle to see if they have sign-out records for that week when you got hit. For the pool cars?"

"Pinky, I am obliged to mention this first to Kiril. We must tell him before we try to prove that someone from PT committed a felony."

"Okay, but you'll ask him, right? To see the records?"

"I shall."

Pinky, as usual, is happy to be indulged. She reminds Stern about his dinner in the oven and with that departs, leaving him with the customary knot of feelings his granddaughter engenders. He could ask where she is going—especially so early on a Monday night—but she is not likely to answer. On the occasions she has, Stern would have been happier not to know. S&M tonight? Possibly, from her getup, but he'd rather not imagine. And there is no point in asking who she's meeting, since he is unlikely to recognize the names. Pinky does not really have old friends. Most of the kids from high school, for example, with whom she often got into trouble, have straightened out, paired off, even started families. Many probably regard Pinky as a relic of a troubled time to which they don't want to return. When Pinky goes out she generally seems headed to some kind of group mash at a club. Pinky is on the curvier side—

no swimsuit model but a pretty girl with even features and lovely eyes, and when she goes out clubbing she seems to have no trouble finding someone to sleep with. No matter how upside down it seems to Stern, sex appears to be her principal means of connecting to other people.

Pinky had been christened—literally, to please her father's Lutheran family—Clarice in memory of Clara, but Stern's daughter Kate could not bear to utter something so much like her mother's name when she was still in deep mourning. Instead, while Kate waited to hit on something better, her husband's dotty ninety-six-year-old grandmother, who could never remember the baby's actual name, had started calling her 'Pinky' because of her coloring.

Pinky was indeed a beautiful rosy baby, but trouble from the start—colicky, sleepless, always bawling as an infant, then later a problem in school, where she tended to isolate herself. Within the family, there is constant conversation about what is wrong with her. 'Wrong' is never said aloud, but everyone over the years has freely conceded to being infuriated by the young woman. Kate, who coexisted for decades in grudging silence with John, that useless lunkhead of a husband she'd finally kicked to the curb a decade ago, regularly points out that her eldest child is the only human on earth with whom Kate has ever gotten into screaming battles. After years of visits to a counselor, Kate has taken to calling Pinky 'oppositional.' Peter, Stern's son, who can be severe, once called Pinky a 'dimwit.' Marta refers to Pinky as 'somewhere on the spectrum.' Even Stern sometimes cannot find the words for her judgment. No more than a year ago, he became aware of an uproar Pinky was causing in the office by posting photos of her sexual encounters on Snapchat. Pinky, it should be said, has her own way of explaining her frequent social mishaps. 'After a while,' she once told her grandfather, 'I just find everyone annoying.'

He is worried that Pinky, now about to turn thirty, is on the verge of becoming a permanently lost soul. But this concern, like so many others, is tamed by the knowledge that he will not be here to see how the story plays out.

He had never been so divorced from reality as to fail to anticipate getting old. He foresaw many parts of this—the fingers that seem like stone, the way he has become the old man who holds up everyone behind him. But he did not guess at how natural it would feel to be retreating from the world. Caring goes on, but you accept more and more that you have limited time and, thus, effect. Your connections in the present dwindle, as peers die, as you lose your spouse. You are at a distance and it requires more effort to understand what everyone else is saying—not least of all because he can barely hear, even with an aid in each ear. (Last week, he stared at Marta in his office doorway and asked, 'Why are you talking about frying tuna?' She was exasperated immediately. 'I said, "We should try this opportunity."')

While studying the scientific aspects of Kiril's trial, he had a startling and sudden recognition of Nature's plan: We mix and mate as part of her goal to combine and recast DNA. She is eternally looking for a better set of chromosomes. From her perspective, humans are essentially a race of shape-shifters, present temporarily before leaving our genetic material behind. We are all Nature's fools, tricked by instinct into believing in the importance of The Self.

14. FDA

Dr. Alexandra Robb's title virtually breathes the word 'bureaucrat'—director of the FDA's Office of Hematology and Oncology Products in the Center for Drug Evaluation and Research. On the stand, however, she is the image of professional competence. In her late forties, she is well kept, wearing a pinstripe suit and shoulder-length dark hair with a natural wave. Seeing her across the courtroom, Stern thinks she may have some African ancestry, or a grandparent from somewhere on the Indian subcontinent. Her look, these days, is blessedly best identified merely as 'American.'

As a sign of her importance to the prosecution case, Dr. Robb is questioned by Moses. He goes first through her background. Her education, like that of every other health professional who has testified, seems to have taken forever. She has both an MD and a master's in public health and is board certified in oncology. She spent years as a professor before joining the FDA. After a few more questions, Moses asks the court to qualify Dr. Robb as an expert, meaning she will be allowed to offer opinions about the clinical trial process for cancer drugs.

"Dr. Robb," he says, "does the Food and Drug Administration do any pharmaceutical testing on its own?"

"No. That is very expensive. Makers of medications are principally responsible for testing their products."

"What is the FDA's role in pharma testing?"

"We establish standards aimed at ensuring that those tests are objective and complete. We then analyze the results to determine if a particular medication has been shown to be safe and effective."

"In the United States, may a pharmaceutical product be sold without the approval of the FDA?"

"No drug or biologic product may be transported across state lines without the FDA's approval. Effectively that means they cannot be marketed to the American public without our say-so." A biologic, Stern has learned, is a medication derived from naturally occurring living material rather than something synthesized in a test tube. g-Livia is a biologic, since the medicine originates from a mouse antibody, which has been bioengineered to be identical to the proteins humans deploy against foreign cells.

"Are you familiar with a medication trade-named g-Livia?"

"I certainly am."

"What was your first professional contact with the product?"

"I attended a meeting in August 2014."

"Who was there?" She names three doctors from PT, including Kiril and Lep, and a small crowd from the FDA, including the project manager; the medical officer who evaluates trial data; a statistician; a pharmacologist; a pharmacokineticist, who traces how a medication is absorbed; a chemist; and a microbiologist. Even then a buzz about g-Livia was starting among cancer specialists and on Wall Street, thanks again to Olga Fernandez.

"And when you refer to Kiril Pafko, do you see that gentleman in the courtroom today?"

"Stipulated," says Marta immediately without looking up from her notes. She will cross Dr. Robb for the defense. Most judges insist that only the lawyer who will examine the witness may address issues raised by the testimony. In this case, Marta is trying to avoid an uncomfortable moment for their client. Custom would call for Kiril to rise and to be pointed out by Dr. Robb, just to be certain that he is the same person she is talking about. Both Sterns find that finger-pointing demeaning to the defendant. To avoid that, Marta has agreed—stipulated—that Kiril is who Dr. Robb means.

Sonny does not allow Moses to answer and says, "Record will reflect stipulated identification of Defendant Pafko." For his part, Moses appears slightly perturbed, but he goes on to the substance of the meeting in 2014 in DC.

"Well," says Dr. Robb, "the project manager wrote out a memo, which I know both sides have, but the sum and substance was that we had approved the Investigational New Drug Application for the product at the end of 2013. The PT people wanted to tell us—"

"Excuse me," says Marta, standing quickly. "May we know who spoke?"

"I'm sorry," says Dr. Robb. "The principal speaker for PT was the medical director, Dr. Lep Pafko, although Dr. Kiril Pafko said a few words to start. He told us that even in the early phases of clinical testing on animals, and some very limited dosage studies on humans, they had seen what they regarded as remarkable results." It was his cancer, Stern knew, along with a couple of other cases, that Kiril and Lep had spoken about in DC. "A prominent lawyer" is how he's described in the documents. Again, for a second, he is drawn back to that time in his life when a bad death seemed so close.

"And did the team from Pafko Therapeutics have any requests?"

"Yes. They were going to file an additional application, asking to have g-Livia designated as a Breakthrough Therapy."

"And what is Breakthrough Therapy designation?"

"It means the FDA has agreed to an established process to expedite the development and review of a medication."

"And what is required for a medicine to be designated a Breakthrough Therapy?"

"The drug or biologic must be for a serious condition, and preliminary clinical evidence must indicate that it may constitute a substantial improvement over available treatments."

"And how is the approval process for Breakthrough Therapy sped up—or expedited, as you put it?"

"FDA staff will work more closely with the manufacturer, to design clinical trials, for example, that meet our criteria. In addition, the drug or biologic is eligible for expedited review, including a process called accelerated approval."

With Moses prompting, she then goes on to explain accelerated approval, which means the FDA will allow a medication into the marketplace with less than the three to four years of clinical testing usually required. Instead, the drug is approved based on a so-called surrogate endpoint, a shorter period when, for similar medicines, the benefits are normally clearly established.

Dr. Robb is probably the most polished and effective witness the government has called yet, treating a mass of technical material with clarity, and the jury appears to be following her closely. That is not good for Kiril but, in Stern's view, just as well. The saying is that a stupid jury is a prosecution jury. Jurors who can't understand the evidence can only fall back on their native prejudices, which usually include a belief that defendants are ipso facto guilty. On the other hand, Stern has seen instances when a jury's confusion led to reasonable doubts. But theory is beside the point. In the last six decades, Stern has learned that you can only be who you are. A jury that prefers style over substance is not likely to be wowed by Sandy Stern. For him, an appeal to jurors' innate intelligence has always been the best approach. At this stage, after a week and a half, he can usually get a good sense of what is going on in the jury box, even though he does his best not to study them for prolonged periods, which Stern knows makes some jurors feel like animals in the zoo. This bunch seems extremely alert, and several smile whenever he gets to his feet. Either they like him—or find him ridiculous.

"And after granting Breakthrough Therapy designation, did the FDA and PT arrive at a plan for a clinical trial that would support accelerated approval?"

"We did."

"Can you explain what a double-blind clinical trial is?"

"Yes. The most objective way to test a medication is to compare it against another treatment whose effectiveness has already been well documented. That kind of comparative trial means some patients will receive the new medication that is being evaluated, while others receive the therapy that is within the current standard of care. A trial is double blind when neither the patients nor the physicians and their site staff know which medication the patient is receiving. In order to ensure that that veil of ignorance is maintained, usually the manufacturer and others directly involved in the testing don't know either."

Dr. Robb then details a series of meetings between her and her staff on one side and Lep and his chief deputies on the other. Kiril was not at any of these conferences, a point Marta emphasizes by popping up and asking each time for Dr. Robb to name who was present. As a result of these discussions, PT and the FDA agreed on a double-blind clinical trial designed to last eighteen months and involving two hundred patients receiving g-Livia and another two hundred receiving an established form of chemo. The test protocol, the size of a dictionary, is marked as an exhibit by Moses and entered into evidence.

"And with regard to that clinical trial, did PT intend to conduct this test itself?"

"No, they hired an outside concern, Global International, which is a clinical research organization, a company that specializes in conducting clinical trials."

"Is it typical for a pharmaceutical manufacturer to hire a clinical research organization, called a CRO for short?"

"At the FDA we do not deal directly with CROs, but most clinical trials we review these days have been conducted by those kinds of organizations. May I explain?"

"Please," answers Moses, as if they have not rehearsed Dr. Robb's testimony several times.

"A clinical trial must be conducted in strict compliance with that testing plan, the protocol, which the FDA has approved. The medication is then administered by expert physicians, called investigators, and for the sake of objectivity at dozens of different sites, very often located all over the world. Very few pharma manufacturers have the resources to do all that themselves."

"And how are the patients monitored?"

"Typically, the investigators and their staffs examine the patients regularly and also perform various tests and imaging."

"And what happens with that information?"

"The investigative staff regularly keys coded reports for each patient into a database maintained by the CRO."

"And is that database of results public?"

"Not during the test. As I've said, in order to maintain the double blind, the results of a clinical trial are ordinarily kept secret until the end, except for safety monitoring that is done in such a way as to isolate it from the trial sponsor and all participants."

"What does 'unblinding data' mean?"

"That means looking at all the data, including the part that is most sensitive, the codes that show which medication the trial participants are receiving."

"Should unblinding be reported to the FDA?"

"As I said, there is some confidential safety monitoring. Other than that, under our regulations, any unblinding that occurs outside the test protocol must be reported to us."

"And were you informed in September 2016 or any time thereafter that Dr. Kiril Pafko had unblinded the g-Livia dataset?"

"Objection," says Marta. "That assumes a fact not in evidence."

Sonny says, "Restate the question, Mr. Appleton."

"Was the FDA ever informed that the g-Livia dataset had been unblinded before the conclusion of the clinical trial?"

"No. Never. I searched my records and the agency records and we received no reports of any unblindings during the trial, even by the safety monitors, who apparently found no reason to do so."

"Now, what is an 'adverse event'?"

"That's an event during the course of a clinical trial that adversely affects the health of a patient who is a study subject. Adverse events are always supposed to be documented in the trial database."

"And what is a 'serious adverse event'?"

"A serious adverse event is one that potentially compromises the life of a trial participant."

"Is dying a serious adverse event?" asks the US Attorney. Moses's courtroom demeanor is so stolid than he can ask a question like that without seeming like a wise-guy. Dr. Robb, however, can't contain a faint smile.

"Definitely."

"Are serious adverse events in a clinical trial supposed to be reported to the FDA by regulation?"

"Absolutely."

Moses pauses then to show Dr. Robb an exhibit labeled 'Pafko Computer-A,' which he asks to display to the jury. The Sterns could object, because the exhibit can't be formally admitted until the FBI forensic experts have explained how they obtained the screenshot of the Global International database from Kiril's office computer. Yet there is little to be gained by that tactic, since Dr. Robb, as an expert, can testify about the exhibit anyway. In the courtroom, sometimes the best the defense can do is feign nonchalance.

"Now, calling your attention, Dr. Robb, to Pafko Computer-A. What does that appear to be?"

"It appears to be a tabular summary, a table of results, from the g-Livia clinical trial database. The data has been unblinded and sorted for all serious adverse events in the prior six months, that would be from March 15, 2016, through September 15, 2016, the day the database was created."

"And by 'unblinded,' you mean the data is sorted to show which patients are receiving g-Livia?"

"Yes."

"And among the g-Livia patients are there any fatalities listed?"

"Yes. You can see those in the far-right corner on the page. There are fourteen of them, and twelve are coded to show the cause of death as 'not disease related.' Of those twelve, ten occurred in the prior quarter."

"And what else can you tell us by looking at Pafko Computer-A about those deaths?"

"The investigators have keyed in data about each of those twelve episodes that are strikingly similar: high fevers, rigors, elevated blood pressure. Each is described as sudden onset, with death occurring within thirty-six hours of hospitalization, usually far sooner than that."

"And what conclusions do you draw as an expert looking at that database?"

"To me it is very clear that twelve patients who had been treated with g-Livia for more than a year had died in the last six months for reasons that had no visible relationship to their underlying cancer. The frequency of those mortalities seems to be rising recently."

"Are those serious adverse events that should have been reported to the FDA?"

"Without question."

"And if you had seen Pafko Computer-A, or received a report containing similar information, what would you have done?"

"I would have suspended the approval process for g-Livia immediately in order to investigate further."

"Next I want to show you an exhibit called Global-A. What does that appear to be?"

"That is a similar tabular summary reflecting the database for the g-Livia patients in the trial for the prior six months, but this one is dated September 16, 2016."

"Is it similar to Pafko Computer-A?"

"It is very very similar to Pafko Computer-A, but not the same."

"And how does it differ?"

"The twelve sudden deaths are entirely omitted in Global-A."

"And if you had been presented with this data, as opposed to Pafko Computer-A, the screenshot from a day before, what would your response have been?"

"I wouldn't have had a response. All appears well."

Moses then shows her PT's formal request to market g-Livia, something called a Biologics License Application, which was filed in October 2016. The document is marked as Government Exhibit-1.

"And how does the data in Global-A compare to the data that was presented in support of PT's marketing application, Government Exhibit-1?"

"It is the same. There is more data, a great deal more, attached to Government Exhibit-1, which incorporated something called a clinical study report. But all the data in Global-A is part of GX-1."

"And with regard to Government Exhibit-1, PT's markeing application, did you attend a meeting at the FDA with representatives of Pafko Therapeutics on October 27, 2016?"

"I did."

"And who was present from PT?"

There was Kiril and Lep and Tanakawa, she says, as well as the same mob from the FDA.

"And was the data contained in the clinical study report that is part of Government Exhibit-1 discussed?"

"Yes. The numbers seemed to show that g-Livia was a great advance over existing therapies."

"And did you have any conversation with the defendant, Kiril Pafko?"

"I did. As the meeting was ending, I shook his hand and said, 'Congratulations, you seem to have done it again.' "

"And what did you mean by that?"

"I meant that g-Livia appeared to be an advance in cancer treatment as great as the discovery of RAS, for which Dr. Pafko had received the Nobel."

"Now, when you talk about approval of a medication, who makes that decision at the FDA?"

"If we are talking about cancer treatments, the marketing applications, like Government Exhibit-1, ends up on my desk with the recommendation of my colleagues and a panel of outside experts called a drug advisory committee. Ordinarily, I make a recommendation to the commissioner and my other superiors, based on the opinions within the agency and my own review of the evidence."

"And how many cancer treatments have been approved by the FDA without your recommendation in the last six years?"

"None."

"And had you been aware, Dr. Robb, of the data shown in Pafko Computer-A, would you have supported accelerated approval for g-Livia in January 2017?"

"Absolutely not."

Moses goes back to check with Feld that he's made all his points. Feld in fact has something else and Moses nods and returns to his customary place at the podium.

"Have you examined the PI, the product insert for g-Livia?"

"I have."

"There is a warning there about possible adverse effects of mAbs—monoclonal antibodies. Is that warning adequate in your view?"

"Completely inadequate. It is little more than boilerplate. When there is an identifiable risk of a lethal complication or side effect from a medication, we require a black box warning."

"And what is that?"

"Exactly what it sounds like, a box in the PI with a thick black border around language describing the possible problem. The point of the black box," says Dr. Robb, "is so that the doctor and the patient can't miss it."

As an illustrative exhibit, Moses introduces a page from the PI for another product with a black box warning and then displays it on the monitor. It absorbs most of the page and is as dramatic-looking as it sounds.

With that, Moses turns to Marta and says, "Your witness." Humble as he is, Moses still shows just the faintest cat-and-canary smile. Dr. Robb has cleaned Kiril's clock.

Marta comes to her feet. In her father's opinion, Marta is an excellent trial lawyer, poised in court and never without her wits. She is more adept than Stern, both with legal argument and the technical mastery needed to confront an expert witness. She is also especially good cross-examining certain men—including many older police officers—who tend to be riled by strong women. But over the years, both Sterns have accepted, with little actually said, that Marta does not have the same courtroom flair as her father. On cross, Stern prepares feverishly, scribbling notes, selecting exhibits, plotting an anticipated order to his questions, but then flies by instinct once he is on his feet. Marta prefers to stick to a script. By tacit agreement, the spotlight moments usually go to Stern, but they both see Robb as a better witness for Marta for a couple of reasons. Marta by now is far better versed in the complex FDA regulations. What's more, a woman confronting another woman may play better with the jury, since Dr. Robb is in for a hard time, as is evident as soon as Marta has introduced herself.

"Dr. Robb, I want to read you a quote from the *New England Journal of Medicine* from an article published sixteen years ago. 'If Massachusetts announced tomorrow that it was going to license persons to operate something as potentially dangerous as a motor vehicle on the basis of a test drivers had given themselves, the response would almost certainly be national outrage. And yet, with billions of dollars at stake, and, more important, hundreds of millions of lives, we allow America's pharmaceutical industry to test the safety and efficacy of their products for the public marketplace on their own, with limited government oversight. We can hardly profess surprise when that process produces unreliable, even fatal results.'"

Moses has risen, shaking his head.

"Objection, Your Honor, the pharmaceutical testing process is not on trial."

Marta intervenes. "Before you rule, Your Honor, may I finish the question?"

Sonny lifts a hand half-heartedly.

"Do you know who wrote those words, Dr. Robb?"

Robb has been smiling ruefully since Marta started reading.

"I do. It was Dr. Jason Cardenal."

"And who is Dr. Cardenal?"

"He is currently the commissioner of the Food and Drug Administration."

"The head of the agency?"

"Yes."

"Same objection," says Moses. "That is irrelevant."

Sonny looks at Marta with one eye closed, and Marta responds.

"First, Your Honor, Mr. Appleton asked why the FDA doesn't

perform pharmaceutical testing. Dr. Robb said it is too expensive, as if that is all there is to the subject. Second, Dr. Robb is the government's main witness to establish that the FDA was supposedly defrauded. It is relevant if the head of the agency has publicly warned that the nature of the system renders the information the FDA receives inherently suspect."

Sonny smiles fleetingly.

"I don't know about your second reason, Ms. Stern, but I accept the first. The objection is overruled."

Dr. Robb interjects, "Dr. Cardenal has said often in public that he's changed his views."

"Move to strike," says Marta.

"Granted." Sonny turns to Robb. "Dr. Robb, please don't volunteer remarks. Wait for the lawyers to ask you questions."

Robb nods, somewhat chastened. Cardenal's article proposed a system of government testing of new drugs and biologics, paid for by a small charge on every pharmaceutical product sold in the US. The pharma industry objected vehemently, as did many in Congress who thought this would create a monstrous new federal bureaucracy. Others feared that the proposed system would be even more vulnerable to the influence of lobbyists. Cardenal's idea, despite widespread support from the medical community, went nowhere.

Marta, in the meantime, starts down the main road of her cross, as she's previewed it for her father.

"Is it a fair summary of your direct testimony, Dr. Robb, that as you sit here today, you would not recommend approval of g-Livia, if you had seen the database for the g-Livia clinical trial, Government Exhibit Pafko Computer-A, as it existed on September 15, 2016?"

"Correct."

The point of emphasis for Marta is that Robb today holds the same opinion about g-Livia. His daughter has explained to Stern that Robb can't say anything else, since it is essential to the FDA's efforts to void its approval of g-Livia.

"And the standard for whether the FDA approves a medication, meaning okays it to be sold in the US—the standard is whether the medication has been shown to be safe and effective, true?"

"True."

"So in deciding whether or not to approve a medication, you are not making a moral judgment, correct?"

"I don't understand."

"Hypothetically, if you concluded a medication is safe and effective under FDA standards, you would recommend approval, even if there were serious errors or omissions or even outright lies in the application, right?"

"I'm not sure how the hypothetical is possible—how I could feel sure that a medication is safe and effective if the drug sponsor had lied to us. I need to think about that. But yes, we're not making moral judgments."

"But fraud is beside the point in terms of the opinion you expressed about approval?"

"I don't think it's beside the point for everyone in the agency. As you know, the FDA declared—"

"Excuse me," Marta quickly interjects, with a hand raised. Dr. Robb was about to refer to the administrative action the FDA has commenced to declare its approval of g-Livia void because it was based on fraud. That is one more piece of civil litigation Sonny has ruled that the jury is not supposed to hear about.

Marta says, "I'm only asking questions of you, Dr. Robb, not anyone else in your agency. You're the person here to testify."

"I understand."

"And you're saying, as you sit here today, that the only reason you wouldn't support approval of g-Livia is because those twelve deaths shown on Pafko Computer-A raise questions in your mind about whether the medication is safe and effective?"

Robb pouts a lip and takes an instant to ponder.

"That's what I'm saying."

"And for purposes of making that judgment, it also doesn't matter whether those deaths should have been reported as serious adverse events, does it?"

"Well, I'm not sure I can say it doesn't matter."

"Can you name an instance, Dr. Robb, when the FDA refused to approve a medication solely because there had been regulatory violation?"

Robb hesitates, then says, "I need to think about that."

Marta returns to the defense table and picks up a paperback volume of the same dimensions as the Kindle County phone book.

"Is this a copy of the Code of Federal Regulations containing most of the rules your agency has formally established for clinical trials?" It is actually a large-print version that looks considerably more imposing than the standard publication, but Robb, apparently in mind of Sonny's directive about not volunteering, simply says yes.

"And how often does it happen, Dr. Robb, that a sponsoring organization like a pharmaceutical manufacturer fails to comply with each and every one of these regulations during a clinical trial?"

"I would guess it happens every day. But not all these regulations are of equal importance."

Marta moves to strike the second sentence and Sonny allows the motion. The judge turns to Dr. Robb.

"Dr. Robb," she says, "again, please don't volunteer. Listen to the question and answer the question. Don't force me to make you go stand in the corner."

Robb actually laughs and so does much of the courtroom.

Sonny continues. "Mr. Appleton over there is a very fine lawyer, and if he thinks there are other facts the jury should know, he'll ask you about them after Ms. Stern is through."

"Gotcha," says Robb.

Marta is a few feet in front of Robb, still holding the copy of the regs.

"In fact, Dr. Robb, going back to the question I asked just a moment ago, most medications would not be approved by your agency, if regulatory violations by themselves prevented that."

Robb's brow is knotted as she assesses the question.

"Touché," she says at last.

"I'm not fencing with you, Doctor."

"I understand. I guess what you're saying is more or less right."

"By the way, Dr. Robb, do you know how many of the CEOs of companies who failed to report adverse events accurately were prosecuted?"

"Objection," says Moses, and Sonny sustains him quickly. The fact someone else got away with bad behavior has no bearing on the guilt of the defendant.

"But the point, Dr. Robb, in terms of your testimony today, is that your opinion that you would not support approval of g-Livia—that opinion is not based on any reporting failure?"

"Asked and answered," says Moses.

"The question is a little different, but I think we all have gotten the point, Ms. Stern. All that matters for approval is whether g-Livia is safe and effective. Please move ahead."

As is typical in many white-collar cases, the Sterns are trying to conduct a defense reminiscent of the old joke about the man who gets sued after his dog bites a neighbor. At trial, the man offers three defenses: (1) I always keep my dog on a chain. He couldn't have bitten my neighbor. (2) My dog is very old and has no teeth. He couldn't have bitten my neighbor. (3) I don't have a dog.

Stern hopes that at the end of the case the evidence will allow them to argue that Kiril never asked Wendy Hoh to alter the trial data. But if the jury concludes otherwise, the Sterns want to be able to say the alteration didn't matter anyway, that it wasn't 'material' in the word of the law. And Marta is moving methodically toward this goal by getting Robb to agree that neither lying in itself nor failing to follow the letter of regulations are determinative in deciding whether g-Livia meets the FDA standard.

"And with regard to safe and effective, how does the FDA define 'safe'?" Marta asks.

"Well, we approve a drug based on a determination that its benefits outweigh the known and potential risks to the intended patient population."

"So even if a medication in fact kills a certain number of patients, it can still be safe enough for FDA approval?"

"In theory."

"In fact, isn't it? Your center and your companion centers on biologics and devices approve items for the market, knowing that there is a strong probability that someone will die, do they not?" Not incidentally, Marta is repeating the 'strong probability' language of the murder statute.

"And many more lives will be saved. But yes."

"Now, in the course of preparing for your testimony, Dr. Robb, were you allowed to review a transcript of the testimony that Dr. Bruno Kapech gave in this case?"

Moses objects to 'allowed.' The normal rule that witnesses should be isolated from what others have said in court does not apply to experts. Sonny instead directs Marta to rephrase, and Robb says she is not aware of what Kapech told the jury.

"Are you familiar with Dr. Kapech's reputation as an oncological epidemiologist?"

"Very much so."

"A renowned figure in this area?"

"No question."

"Now, in order to discuss your opinions, I'm going to show you part of the transcript of Dr. Kapech's testimony. Do you see that?" After a few more preliminaries, two typed transcript pages go up on the monitor.

"Dr. Kapech told all of us that somewhere between twenty-five and thirty percent of patients with stage two non–small-cell lung cancer will die of their cancer in less than fourteen months."

"Okay," says Robb.

"Now I want to go back to Pafko Computer-A, which is the g-Livia trial database as it existed on September 15, 2016." Pinky puts it back on the screen. "That's seventeen months after the study began, right?"

Robb nods and the judge tells her to answer out loud. She says yes.

"We haven't talked much about the other arm of that trial, involving the chemo that was the standard of care, which g-Livia was being compared to. Do you recall what the fatality rate was in the other arm?"

Moses objects that the results of the other side of the g-Livia clinical trial are irrelevant, but Sonny overrules him. The rules of evidence always allow the remainder of a document to be received if a portion has been shown to the jury.

"I knew once. My memory is that the g-Livia numbers were significantly better. My guess is that on the other arm, the mortality rate exceeded twenty percent."

"Well, let's not guess," says Marta. She then introduces the other portion of the database, which shows that forty-nine of the patients who began the study had died at that point in time. Given the fact that eight subjects had withdrawn from that arm—a routine occurrence, Robb agrees—a tad more than 25 percent of the patients receiving the standard treatment had passed away at that point in time.

"Now, by contrast, Pafko Computer-A shows that six percent of the patients in the study died of this sudden onset phenomenon, correct?"

"Yes."

"But only another five percent of the patients had died of reasons seemingly related to their cancer."

Robb hesitates, which allows Marta to take her through the database line by line. After a good five minutes of that, Robb agrees that five percent—ten patients—appear to have died of cancer-related causes.

"So at that time, roughly seventeen months into the study, eleven percent of the patients on g-Livia had died versus more than twenty-five percent receiving the standard treatment. Correct?"

"That's what the numbers show."

"Which would mean g-Livia was 'safe,' as you explained the safe-and-effective standard?"

Robb is smiling, as if Marta is a naughty child. The doctor looks up to Sonny.

"May I explain?"

"Answer the question, please, Dr. Robb."

"Yes, if the world stopped turning at seventeen months, g-Livia was safer than the standard therapy."

"Even including these sudden deaths?"

"Yes, but those deaths began after about thirteen months of treatment with g-Livia. What no one knows from these numbers is whether, if you continue to administer g-Livia, eighty percent of patients will expire from this sudden death phenomenon within the next year. That is the question that's raised by those mortalities. And because of that, I couldn't and can't say g-Livia is safe."

"g-Livia couldn't be deemed safe because you didn't know what would happen over time?"

"And because I didn't know what the cause of death was. These patients were dying mysteriously. Most of the investigators had listed MI, myocardial infarction—"

"Heart attack?"

"Heart attack as the cause of death, because they saw these cases in isolation. But once you realize it's a wider-spread problem, there are many other possibilites that must be investigated. Cancer patients all take a lot of drugs, so it might have been a fatal interaction between medications. There might be a manufacturing issue with g-Livia. If you gave me time, I could list several more possibilities."

"But as we sit here today, Doctor—*today*—a medical consensus has developed that what was causing these deaths is an allergic reaction, right?"

"Generally, yes. The pathologists who have looked at the symptoms are fairly uniform in that conclusion. It is very very unusual for a medication to cause an allergic response only after a year. You'd expect to see manifestations of that in some patients far sooner. So even now, I have questions. There might be something added to the drug—say, an excipient—that's causing the response. And it could even be, frankly, that g-Livia on its own over time causes a fundamental change in body chemistry that leads to that allergic reaction."

"But from a safety perspective, Dr. Robb, what you assess is not *why* there is an allergic response, but whether it can be contained, correct?"

"Well, one usually goes with the other, but in general I'd say that is true."

"Dr. Robb, has the FDA approved medications that are known to cause allergic reactions in patients?"

"Of course."

"Many?"

"Many."

"Some that can cause reactions that are very severe, even fatal?"

"Okay."

"And in approving the medications, the FDA requires that black box warning you mentioned?"

"Yes."

"And sometimes you also require something called a REMS, a Risk Evaluation and Mitigation Strategy, that might require that g-Livia could only be administered in certain circumstances? You might say injections can only take place in a hospital setting, and that a patient must remain there for seventy-two hours after the injection?"

"I suppose."

"Has the FDA done that in the past in the case of medications that might cause an anaphylactic response?"

Robb smiles with faint bitterness.

"I'm sure you have examples at hand, Ms. Stern."

Marta smiles, too. She has Robb under control.

"But the point, Dr. Robb, is that there are established means to deal with even severe allergic reactions, steps that greatly reduce the possibility of a patient dying?"

"I would say in general that's true, but we don't know how effective those measures might be with the reaction g-Livia provokes."

"But given medical learning, can you say as you sit here that they would be *likely* to reduce the number of fatal reactions?"

"'Likely'? Yes. But I'd want to see the results in a trial to be sure."

"Okay. And the other concern you expressed is not knowing how widespread allergic reactions would become the longer patients took g-Livia. Right?"

"Right."

"Now what is a confirmatory study?"

"That's a study a drug sponsor or manufacturer undertakes after we've granted accelerated approval. In other words, because accelerated approval takes place after shorter trials, we ask the manufacturer to track a patient population that's receiving the medication over a longer period."

"And are you aware that Pafko Therapeutics complied with the FDA's requirements and carried out a confirmatory study of g-Livia among a thousand patients, including more than a hundred who had been part of the original double-blind trial?"

Moses is already on his feet. He objects to any reference to the confirmatory study. After trying to hash out the matter at sidebar,

Sonny has the jury removed. The prosecutors have clearly known that the later study would come up, and they have many arguments about why the judge should preclude any reference to it. It was planned for three years but lasted only twenty-three months until g-Livia was removed from the market. Because of that, the data collected has not been 'scrubbed,' as the scientists would put it, to account for statistical anomalies. More important, Moses says, is that the fraud charged in the indictment was complete when Pafko doctored the data and allowed it to be submitted to the FDA, so later developments shouldn't matter.

In most instances, Moses's argument would prevail. But Dr. Robb has been allowed to testify as an expert. Her testimony is less circumscribed than a lay witness's, and therefore her cross-examiner should get more latitude to explore the basis of her expert opinions.

"Dr. Robb," says Marta, "has repeatedly stated that her judgment that g-Livia is not safe and effective continues to apply today. Accordingly, Dr. Pafko is entitled to challenge that opinion—and her expertise—with any data developed up until this moment."

After a bit more argument, Sonny agrees with Marta. Moses can raise his questions about the value of the raw data from the confirmatory study on redirect, the judge says.

Dr. Robb is brought back to the courtroom and the summary page for the confirmatory study is illuminated on the screen.

"Dr. Robb, let me remind you that Dr. Kapech told us that twenty-five to thirty percent of patients with stage two non–small-cell lung cancer die by fourteen months. Now, just looking at the raw numbers for the confirmatory study, what percentage of patients on g-Livia, including those who'd died of what we now know are allergic deaths—what percentage had died after twenty-three months?"

"It still appears to be about thirteen percent." Oddly, the rate of allergic deaths held steady in the confirmatory study. The oncological community is small enough that word of these sudden deaths had spread and some specialists, on their own, had apparently started treating for an allergic response, even without the black-box warning.

"And assuming that statistical scrubbing verified those numbers, is that an important difference?"

"As we look at things in the world of oncology, it's very significant. Assuming those are accurate numbers, it would be a very important increase in survival rates."

"And so, Dr. Robb, assuming a successful risk mitigation strategy were in place for allergic reactions, and assuming the data from the confirmatory study was verified by statisticians—assuming all of that, would you still conclude today that g-Livia is not safe and effective?"

Robb takes an unhappy instant to stew.

"I can't speak for the entire FDA."

"As we have said before, Dr. Robb, you, not your other colleagues, are on the witness stand. Is it still your expert opinion today that g-Livia is not safe and effective, given the assumptions I've stated?"

"That's a lot to assume. I can assume people stop getting cancer, too."

Sonny interrupts. "Enough temporizing, Dr. Robb. Ms. Stern is entitled to an answer to her question." Although Stern wouldn't have anticipated this, given the Sonny he knows in private, Kiril was right when he observed that she is a little short-tempered in court. After more than twenty years on the bench, her patience for the standard courtroom hijinks, from both lawyers and witnesses, has worn thin, a common condition among long-serving judges. But the scolding from the bench seems again to intimidate Robb. She straightens up, although her face remains dark and troubled.

"Those are large assumptions. But if they were valid, then I guess I would probably hesitate to express the same opinion today. But you know, sitting here, answering hypotheticals, it's kind of a thought experiment. And what we do, what I do, it's not imaginary. It's people's lives. In practice, if I were answering the question for real, I would need to take a lot more time and look at a number of factors much more carefully than I can just sitting right here."

Marta stares at Robb across the courtroom, and Stern has to stifle himself from reaching out to hold his daughter back. Robb has done her best to qualify her answer, but within the cascade of words is the critical phrase—'I would hesitate to express the same opinion today.' If Marta goes back at Robb again, the doctor is likely to retract some or all of that.

Standing silent, Marta reaches the same conclusion on her own. Having taken a second, she has absorbed the charged air in the courtroom, which suggests that everyone here understands that Robb has made a critical concession. Legally, Moses is right that the jury is still entitled to conclude that Kiril committed a fraud in 2016. But what Robb has acknowledged leaves the people in the jury box to decide whether they are really going to convict a seventy-eight-year-old Nobel Prize winner for fudging the numbers regarding a medication that demonstrably saves lives and which we know today should probably be approved anyway.

Marta returns to the defense table to drop off the pages of the confirmatory study she has been holding. She appears ready to sit down, which might be a good idea, but she raises her hand to make clear she's not done.

"One more point, Dr. Robb. Now, you say you met with representatives of PT in Washington on several occasions to discuss g-Livia. Between the first meeting in 2014, when PT was first seeking Breakthrough Therapy designation, and the last in October 2016, how many meetings did you take part in, in total?"

"Four, I believe."

"And was Dr. Kiril Pafko present at any of those four meetings?"

"The first and the last."

"Who was the principal representative of PT each time?"

"Dr. Lep Pafko."

"And in October 2016, when the results of the clinical trial were presented to the FDA, who spoke for the company?"

"For the most part? Kiril said a few words, but Dr. Lep Pafko did most of the talking."

Marta then has Pinky show on the screen the cover page of PT's marketing application for g-Livia, Government Exhibit-1.

"And this part of the document, the form FDA 356h, has fields thirty to thirty-five, where someone called the Responsible Official certifies that PT has complied with all applicable laws and regulations. Was that certification true?"

"No, not in my view."

"And the person who made these certifications, that person was Dr. Kiril Pafko, the defendant on trial here, was it not?"

Robb smiles. The signature is right there on the screen.

"No."

"Who was it, then?"

"Dr. Lep Pafko, the medical director and senior vice president."

"Dr. Lep?"

Marta pauses to give Dr. Robb a querulous, uncomprehending look, then announces she has nothing further.

Sonny calls for the lunch recess. As soon as the jury is gone, Stern rises to grasp Marta by both shoulders.

"Brilliant," he tells her. "You have never been better."

Marta beams, relishing her father's praise. Pinky and several of the lawyers from the big firms involved in the civil cases, who have been observing from the gallery, gather around to quietly compliment Marta. Stern turns away to leave Marta to her admirers and notices only then that behind Kiril, Donatella has slid forward on the first pew. Her hand is on the back of her husband's chair, and the look she is giving Stern beneath those thick black eyebrows is forbidding enough to chill his heart. She rises then and leans toward Stern.

"Sandy," she whispers, in a gentle tone entirely at odds with what Stern just saw from her, "please allow Kiril and me to take you to lunch."

15. HIS MOTHER'S SON

By now, with many fewer photographers assigned to cover the daily trial sessions, Kiril has started driving himself and Donatella to court, parking at the Hotel Gresham a couple of blocks away. As Stern and the Pafkos are moving slowly down the courthouse's central staircase, beside the alabaster panels, Kiril phones the valet there. The young man has the Pafkos' car at the curb when the three elderly people arrive. It is not Kiril's Maserati, but his old Cadillac. Over the years, Pafko bought several cars from the same dealer as Stern, a former client to whom Sandy referred Kiril. The gray CTS is Donatella's now.

"Where is the Italian masterpiece?" Stern asks about the Maserati, and Donatella responds.

"Kiril now has two cars," she says. "His is in the shop so often that he takes mine three days a week." This is a relatively lighthearted jab. At her age, Donatella probably doesn't drive much more often than Stern these days, and Kiril concedes that the Maserati is gorgeous but so delicate, it sometimes feels the car is allergic to pavement.

They are at the University Club in minutes. The look inside is medieval, furnishings fit for King Arthur, ponderous pieces of carved oak and red leather that complement the oak wainscoting. The gothic dining room towers nearly three stories above, with flying buttresses and stained-glass panels between them.

Once they are seated, Donatella chats amiably, describing a cello recital Kiril and she attended last night starring fourteen-year-old Steffi, Lep's oldest child. Greta, Lep's wife, is a German chemist whom he met when they were in grad school, but she is also an accomplished musician. As Donatella speaks, Stern is struck again by her impressive combination of will and grace. She is always dressed magnificently, today in a soft skirt with the rough texture and color of lamb's wool and a black embroidered jacket, and her self-confidence is radiant. Her diamonds are large and worn unapologetically, like merit badges. In the meetings with Stern she has attended now and then, Donatella has customarily been silent, but today when the subject turns to the trial, motive grips her like a fever.

"Sandy, this business about Lep must stop at once," she says. "Kiril will not save his neck by putting his son's in the noose."

Pafko says nothing but nods emphatically. His old-fashioned gallantry in his wife's company has always made Kiril acquiescent to her, at least in the presence of others. Stern has long accepted that no relationship is more complex than marriage, nor more unknowable to outsiders. And where children stand in those intricate arrangements is often nuanced and unique. This is another of Nature's great tricks. Two people develop such intense passion for one another that they create other individuals to get between them. But Lep's place in his mother's emotional hierarchy is obvious.

"Donatella, my dear," says Stern, "a criminal case is won by raising doubts—reasonable doubts. I can assure you that neither Marta nor I have any intention of arguing at the end of this case that Lep is guilty of these crimes. That notion, candidly, does not stand up to extended analysis. But any reason the jurors might find on their own to allow Kiril to go free is acceptable, is it not? I know Lep is deeply concerned about his father. Very often, we plant a thought and let it go. And that is surely our intention here. Let me remind you, Donatella, that Lep has immunity. There is no harm in nodding in another direction, is there?"

Donatella does not seem to accept the explanation. She shakes her head, the flesh of her face moving in a loose way that suddenly makes her look truly old.

"But Lep still has decades left in his career," she says. "If that is in tatters after this trial, that is no victory for any of us."

She looks across the table to her husband, who again nods obediently.

Lep, come what may, is going to be left with at least $100 million. And he will control the company soon enough anyway, whether Kiril goes to the penitentiary or retires. More to the point, suspicions will rub off on Lep if the jury finds he spent years working at the elbow of a crook.

Stern has already scheduled a meeting at the office with Kiril alone after court today. They are to begin deciding what to present by way of defense, and Stern makes a mental note to add Donatella's admonition to the agenda. Kiril has told Stern more than once that he knows nothing to implicate Lep, although he has never been as absolute as what Stern has just heard from Donatella.

"I will certainly abide by your wishes," Stern says. "In truth, I doubt we have much more to say in court on this subject."

The end of Marta's cross-examination is probably the only part Stern might have recast. She had told him last night that she was going to 'ring the Lep bell,' but subtlety has never been Marta's strength.

Lunch is soon over. Donatella and Kiril need to make a quick stop at a shop nearby to select a birthday gift for one of their grandsons, and Stern taxis back to the courthouse by himself, still processing their conversation.

'Lep did it!' has long been the most tempting defense in this case. It was Lep, for instance, who as medical director held the codes to unblind the database, in the event they were ever needed, and Lep who handled most of the communications with the FDA. Lep also could have identified himself as 'Dr. Pafko' on the phone with Wendy Hoh. Whenever Stern indulges his sentimental hopes about Kiril's innocence, his mind drifts in this direction.

The problem is that when Marta and he have considered blaming Lep, they collide head-on with the facts. Lep never would have attempted something so ham-handed as trying to flim-flam Wendy Hoh. Experts agree that a man with a doctorate in computer science could have come up with far more elegant—and surreptitious—means of altering the database and the underlying information. More to the point, Lep also has a locked alibi. Kiril was still on his computer, e-mailing the image of the unaltered database to Olga, when airline records show unequivocally that Lep had already boarded his plane to Seattle, and obviously was headed there from home while the call records from Kiril's office show he was on the phone with Wendy Hoh.

On the other hand, the fact that Lep is not the principal culprit does not mean he was as clueless as he will piously maintain on the witness stand. Marta, in particular, has long insisted—with no convincing counterargument from Stern—that if they suddenly came into possession of a time machine, they would find Kiril deciding to call Wendy Hoh out of panic, then telling Lep all about his success with her upon his son's return. That had been the order of the two men's lives for decades, with Kiril inalterably in charge and Lep unfalteringly obedient, having lived for close to fifty years with nothing more essential to him than his father's approval. As Marta has pointed out tartly, a man like Kiril, who has paraded his infidelities in front of his son for decades, is not likely to suddenly develop a sense of shame or discretion about other misbehavior.

Lep is represented by lawyers from Chicago, who bargained hard for the immunity he ultimately received. Stern was not allowed to speak with Lep until he had completed his testimony before the grand jury. Once Lep had done so, the attorneys had agreed to two interviews, perhaps at Lep's insistence. But they were tense meetings in which Lep related the tale of his father's culpability that he had already told the prosecutors, a story in which Lep's own responsibility was entirely minimized.

As a disincentive to the Sterns, the lawyers had insisted that they—and Lep—come to their offices in a Chicago skyscraper with commanding views of the lake. Seated across from Lep, along with Marta, in a grand conference room that was all windows, Stern found it difficult to establish much rapport, although he has known Lep since he was a boy. Even as a youngster Lep had fine manners, as you would expect of Donatella's child. He always greeted Mr. Stern by name, shook hands as he looked Sandy in the eye, and responded to questions politely, if briefly. Stern can remember Lep at the end of the country club dinner table one night, occupying himself, even in the summer, with a math workbook. He must have been about nine, and when Stern looked over at what the boy was doing, he remarked aloud, something like 'Good grief!' because he could not comprehend a single line of the calculations on the page. In response, Lep offered a sealed smile worthy of Mona Lisa. It was not really childish pride he was exhibiting. He was instead seemingly acknowledging that Stern had discovered his secret, that the complexity of the mathematics allowed him to move through a world of largely impenetrable privacy. It was as if he was keeping a diary that he knew his parents would never be able to read.

Roughly forty years later, in his lawyers' conference room, Lep remained a person rigorously self-contained. Although he shows flashes of wry humor, for the most part Lep is as taciturn as Kiril is garrulous. Except for his commitment to his father's profession, Lep is unlike Kiril in almost every way. He dresses in scuffed corduroy and denim, while his father is one of the few men Stern has ever known who actually looks comfortable in an ascot. Lep takes his height from Donatella's family and is close to six foot five, with dirty blond hair beginning to gray and scalloped on each side by male pattern baldness. He has an elegant sharp-featured Slavic handsomeness, but his quick, uncertain eyes lend his looks a somewhat fragile undercurrent, like some agonized poet. Kiril has frequently related, a bit enviously, that Lep has never seemed to notice the women who threw themselves at him, particularly when he was younger.

No one Stern has spoken to about Lep is anything other than deeply impressed by him as a scientist, especially by his capacities in the burgeoning field of computer-aided medical research, in which digital models of disease are constructed and then cured. Unfathomably to Stern, Lep had conceived of the g-Livia compound by programming supercomputers at Easton to behave like the new quantum computers that don't even exist yet.

For all the wonder Lep's colleagues express about what he accomplished, the man himself is self-effacing.

'I didn't do anything except pour the information into a bigger mechanical brain,' Lep said during his first interview with the Sterns. 'It was my father who recognized that the problems in RAS signaling were related to the positioning of the molecule.' A couple of the scientists at PT have quietly insisted that it was actually Lep who first theorized about how a mAb would have the potential to turn RAS around, but by habit Lep seems unwilling to diminish his father's contributions.

Lep's testimony in this case, by contrast, is less original: Blame Kiril for everything whenever possible. Lep is going to testify to conversations with his father that Kiril swears never occurred.

'Is Lep lying?' Stern asked Kiril when he met with Pafko the week after interviewing Lep in Chicago.

'I would never say that about Lep,' Kiril answered mildly. 'For some reason, it's what he remembers.'

'Kiril,' Stern said. 'If he is not lying, I do not understand how we can explain this.'

'Nor I, Sandy. It's why I am in this predicament.'

Stern and Marta have taken it for granted that Kiril will say nothing to implicate Lep. That is understandable, both as a father and because Kiril knows where the principal blame lies anyway. What Stern did not recognize before lunch was what had stiffened Kiril's resolve to take the fall alone. But the inspiration is clear now.

Donatella.

16. OLGA

Back in court, Moses's redirect has largely been foretold by his objections. Robb agrees that the confirmatory study done after g-Livia was approved has not been statistically verified, and she explains the importance of that at some length. She also says that the success of a Risk Evaluation and Mitigation Strategy for g-Livia remains unproven. Nevertheless, because Moses was prohibited from talking to her outside court until her testimony is complete, he does not take the chance of asking her again whether she continues to believe today that g-Livia has not yet been proven safe and effective. That's probably better strategy for the prosecution anyway. Their case is about what happened in 2016. In line with that, the US Attorney's last question on redirect is whether anything Marta asked Dr. Robb or showed her changed her opinion that she would not have recommended approval of g-Livia had she seen the correct data at that time.

"Absolutely not," Robb answers.

The next witness, Mal Jenkins, is an FBI forensic computer examiner from DC. He explains that Kiril's office computer was seized pursuant to a search warrant in the fall of 2018 and taken to the FBI computer lab. After detailing the process of how an expert examines a hard drive, Jenkins gets to the core of the matter: the screenshot Robb testified about, the unblinded summary table, revealing the twelve sudden deaths of g-Livia patients for reasons coded as 'unexplained,' meaning no apparent relationship to cancer. The screenshot, Government Exhibit Pafko Computer-A, was found on the drive of the computer in Kiril's office at PT, Jenkins says, created at about eight p.m. on September 15, 2016. This is the single most damning piece of documentary evidence in the cases against Kiril, since it confirms that he knew all about the twelve deaths.

Stern cross-examines.

"Now, Special Agent Jenkins, I am certain that in your experience, you have dealt with efforts to remove incriminating evidence from computers."

"Definitely."

"And is it fair to say there are innumerable means of attempting to do that?"

"Countless," says Jenkins.

"You can simply delete the data, right?"

"Not effective, but yes, you can do that."

"There is a process called wiping to remove data, is there not?"

"There is."

"You can restore your computer to the factory defaults, can you not, essentially removing all work done on the computer?"

"You could try that."

"There are even programs one can purchase for the sole purpose of removing data and leaving no trace of it?"

"They work better than anything else you've mentioned, but they're not faultless."

"And with regard to this screenshot, Pafko Computer-A, did you find any evidence of an effort to delete it, remove it, conceal it in any way in 2016?"

"No."

"But certainly, after this article appeared in the *Wall Street*

Journal in August of 2018, suggesting problems with g-Livia, certainly after that, there was some sign that Dr. Pafko tried to hide this evidence, was there not?"

"No."

"No deletion, no wiping, no cleaning program?"

"No, sir."

"And what about after the FDA announced in the fall of 2018 that it had identified problems in the database for the g-Livia clinical trial? Surely there was some evidence of an effort to delete this image then?"

"If there was, I found no sign of it."

"So this screenshot, Pafko Computer-A, was sitting there for close to three years, as it were, waiting for you to find it?"

Feld objects that the question is argumentative, as it is, and Stern withdraws it before Sonny can rule.

"Now, Special Agent Jenkins, aside from the evidence that this screenshot was created on September 15, 2016, was there any other use of that image?"

"It was also e-mailed once."

"When?"

"That night. September 15, 2016. A little after eight p.m."

"And who did that e-mail go to?"

"A Ms. Fernandez."

"That would be Ms. Olga Fernandez, the director of marketing and public communications at Pafko Therapeutics?"

"Yes, sir."

"And were you present two years later, in the fall of 2018, when Ms. Fernandez was interviewed about this e-mail by investigators from the FBI?"

"Yes, sir. I was one of the two agents who visited with her."

"What did she tell you?"

"Objection. Hearsay," says Feld.

Stern has been careful to ask this question while he is facing the jury and does his best to look shocked. He then executes a slow stage turn to peer over his shoulder at Feld. In the meantime, Marta's pen has hit the floor, the warning that he has wandered onto dangerous ground. When Stern glances to the bench, Sonny is glaring at him, which Stern instantly regards as entirely unfair. There is nothing unethical in asking a question that invites hearsay. It's competent evidence, unless it's excluded after objection. Dr. Robb's testimony was a virtual fountain of hearsay, with all her accounts of what Lep and others had said at the FDA, far from this courtroom and outside Kiril's presence. But Stern knows he is on Old Lawyer Probation and apparently must live by different rules. He shrugs, as much for Sonny's and Marta's sakes as the jury's, and returns to his seat, doing his best not to look perturbed.

To Jenkins—and Stern, who has interviewed Olga—she said the same thing basically, that she noticed the e-mail with the screenshot of the unaltered dataset attached in her inbox the next morning, September 16. She happened to see Kiril a few minutes later.

'I asked him what it was he'd sent me?' Olga told Stern. 'He had no clue what I was talking about. *Nada.* I asked him three times. He said he didn't remember sending me any e-mail with attachments. So I just deleted it.'

This piece of testimony is so favorable to Kiril that a wise defense lawyer would treat it with great caution. The FBI, in fact, seems to have heard it with complete disbelief. At Jenkins's request, Olga surrendered her office computer to him. Jenkins took it back to DC, where he concluded that what she had said was absolutely true. The e-mail from Kiril was received but never opened, and promptly deleted early on September 16, 2016.

Even with the forensic corroboration, however, there is, as Marta would say, the strong smell of bullshit in the air. Marta finds it incredible that Olga hesitated to open an e-mail from the CEO, not to mention a man she was sleeping with. 'Dad, you know damn well what happened. Olga was already fooling around with Kiril, so she knew the clinical trial was messed up. And when she saw that e-mail, she went running to Kiril and said, "Why are you involving me in this crap? I just work here."'

Then there is Innis's theory, which Stern has more trouble working out, that Olga is actually the Big Bad Guy. In this version, the e-mail is part and parcel of Olga convincing Kiril to call Wendy Hoh at Global to trick her into changing the database.

Whatever the truth, the decision about calling Olga as a witness must be made carefully, and only after asking Kiril some questions in private that Stern has avoided up until now.

Kiril sends Donatella home by Uber, while the valet again delivers the gray Cadillac to the curb where Pafko and Stern await it. This time, before going through the cumbersome process of sitting down, Stern spends a moment staring at the car.

"What?" asks Kiril from behind the wheel.

"I am thinking about my Cadillac that was smashed up," he answers, but says no more. On the drive to the office, Kiril spends most of the time on the phone, but he does not appear much affected by the fact that the government has introduced its most damaging piece of written evidence against him. It is a blessing in many ways to Kiril that he is in such a deep state of denial. For Stern, it has always been easy to imagine how terrifying it would be to have the massive forces of government pinioning you, inspecting, judging, prospecting for your secrets with a ruthlessness that must feel as if they are tearing through your flesh. Routinely, white-collar clients claim they would receive better treatment in a totalitarian state. This, of course, is in sharp contrast to the poor persons Stern has represented, who are all long accustomed to the random power of law enforcement to ransack their lives.

Yet whether his clients have been rich or poor, their rationalizations for their crimes have almost always been unfathomable to Stern. Yes, of course, a hungry man steals bread. But why would

Kiril Pafko do something as shortsighted as cheat to win approval of a product he knew was bound to have lethal side effects? Could he really have hoped g-Livia would be less fatal just because the FDA had put its seal of approval on it? And yet Stern has learned over the decades that this kind of magical thinking is typical of criminal defendants, at least the ones who have found themselves seated in the pleated leather armchair in front of Stern's desk that Kiril occupies now. In the end, all guilty clients have one thing in common: At the moment of completing the crime, each was convinced against all reason they would not get caught.

"Kiril," Stern says once they are settled, "let me try to go through my small agenda quickly."

The first subject, of course, is what went on at lunch today with Donatella. Being diplomatic, Stern says, "It is always better to be able to present a jury with an alternate hypothesis."

But Pafko placidly shakes his head.

"I have sworn to Donatella there will be no more of that. Please be certain Marta understands."

This instruction will make Lep's cross-examination, which might come as early as next week, a good deal more difficult. But Stern doesn't quarrel. The wisdom is enduring that if a man had a talent for making good decisions, he wouldn't be on trial in federal court for serious felonies.

"Also, we need to begin considering the evidence to offer for the defense."

"Certainly," says Kiril, "I will testify."

Stern's client has stuck to this position every time the subject has come up. Marta finds it unsurprising that the first instinct of a man who has charmed his way through life is to attempt more of the same. But Kiril has no explanation for much of the evidence against him, except to shrug. Unblinding the dataset, which Agent Jenkins demonstrated this afternoon was accomplished on Kiril's computer? He didn't do it. The screenshot? He had no idea it was there. Lep's testimony? No memory of anything like that. Kiril's plan is to smile and shake his head in mystification.

The only potential corroboration on any of these critical points might come through Olga. The problem, of course, is the first question on cross-examination: 'Ms. Fernandez, you and Dr. Pafko had an intimate relationship for some time, didn't you?' (That assumes the questioner is Moses. Feld would feign to be struggling to find a better word than 'fucking.')

When Stern has made somewhat delicate efforts to delve into the relationship with Olga, Kiril has brushed it aside. 'All in the past,' he has said.

'The past, Kiril? Last year? Last night?'

Kiril laughed and fluttered his manicured hand. 'Not to worry.'

If that really were true, there is a chance that Sonny might bar the prosecutors' questions about the affair. Kiril is not on trial for being a philanderer, and a past romance might be regarded as having no present bearing on Olga's testimony. Sonny has already reached that conclusion about Innis, although the rules are much different in Olga's case, since the defense will put her credibility at issue by calling her to the stand.

"I have tried not to pry, Kiril. But this is critical. Is your relationship with Olga—the intimate part of that—is it truly over?"

He smiles. "Well, certainly that is what I have told Donatella." Seeing Stern's face fall, Kiril adds, "Sorry to jest, Sandy. Yes. I think she is a remarkable young woman, but we have had nothing to do with each other in that way for a couple of years now. She called a halt to it, if you must know."

"I do not need those details," says Stern, who wants to know as little as possible that will embarrass him around Donatella. "But with your wife in the courtroom, the jury will not take well at all to evidence of your unfaithfulness." Stern explains that it must be completely accurate if he tells the judge that Olga and Kiril are no longer lovers. "I am in quite a bit of hot water with the judge already. If I tell her something like this that turns out to be untrue, she could even remove me as your lawyer."

"Not to worry, Sandy," says Kiril again, which still falls short of the absolute reassurance Stern would like.

But even disregarding Kiril's coyness, there is the more fundamental problem, which Marta raises often: Olga is not the kind of witness who is likely to make a good impression on the jurors, particularly the women. Force and ambition radiate from Olga with solar intensity. She would be frightening if you were in her way. She speaks English at the speed of her native Puerto Rican Spanish and is full of tense kinetic strength, even on the rare occasions she is sitting still.

There is, on the other hand, much to be said in Olga's behalf. For one thing, if IQ were measured in street smarts, she would be Einstein, which makes her very good at her job. She was born into utter poverty in a remote village in Puerto Rico and has fought like a lynx every day since to gain ground. She is thrice divorced, with three daughters whom she has raised with the assistance of her mother.

Stern, in fact, feels some kinship with Olga. He was a young man struggling to find a foothold in this huge, complex country, fumbling with English. His feeling memory of those years is a cyclone of anxiety and striving. He knows what Olga must have experienced, moving to the mainland with an accent and ambition so powerful that it kept her up at night. He understands, too, how hunger for security can drive acquisitive passion.

But Olga received none of the tempering Stern did through his upper-class education at Easton College. Her degree was earned at night in New York—indeed, after Innis's points about Olga's résumé, Stern suspects the BA listed may never have been awarded. Somehow, though, she was hired in Kindle County to become a pharmaceutical salesperson and moved here. And in that world—famous back then for the underhanded tactics reps used to win doctors' loyalty—she learned, as the saying went, to use what she had. Is Olga beautiful? Not really. She is, in the Yiddish Stern was raised speaking, a little zaftig—hefty. She is short, not even Stern's height in her heels, brownish and freckled in a land that always favored the fair, and round-faced with a broad nose and small intense eyes. Incongruously, her hair has been straightened, puffed out, and dyed blond.

But Stern has never heard anyone call Olga unattractive. She is one of those people who broadcasts almost the same sexual allure and willingness that would be created if she walked into the room naked. Her clothes, in fact, are always a tight squeeze; she probably reinforces buttons and zippers to get the desired effect. Even in the office, her blouses are opened far enough to display some décolletage. Stern judges not. Would he have walked around with his fly open, if it helped him get cases instead of earning him laughter? Probably. Yet it is hard to imagine jurors like Mrs. Murtaugh or the CPA responding well to her. With Kiril's reassurance that his intimate times with Olga are over, Marta and Stern will have to decide whether it is worth the considerable risks of calling Olga to the stand, assuming the judge can be persuaded to restrict cross to omit the details of their personal relationship.

"One last thing," Stern says. "Kiril, you recall that I had a traffic accident when I was returning last March from PT. You remember."

"Of course. I was afraid, Sandy, you would never recover."

"And did I tell you that my clearest memory of the car that struck me was the PT medallion in the rear window?"

Kiril laughs. "Tell me? Me and every other person who came to visit, Sandy. For several days, it seemed to be the only thought in your head. But you said that the neurologist and the police eventually convinced you that memory was an illusion."

Stern describes Pinky's investigation, ignoring Kiril's grin when his granddaughter's name first comes up. As Sandy continues,

Pafko's worn face loses its customary look of good cheer. His thick eyebrows are drawn downward in obvious concern, when Stern concludes, "She wants the sign-out records from the motor pool."

"I apologize, Sandy, but what is the bearing on my defense?"

"I am indulging Pinky, Kiril. You understand."

He shakes his head. "Not really."

Pafko is one of those clients who has given his lawyers carte blanche with every avenue of defense, although it is easy to display largesse when the corporation is paying all expenses.

"Well, I suppose, Kiril, taking this to the logical extreme, if someone from PT were trying to get rid of your lawyer, that could be quite relevant."

Pafko draws back. "Is that truly what you think happened, Sandy?"

"No, in candor, Kiril, I think that is entirely far-fetched."

"Then I see no point in pursuing it."

The two men eye each other. Stern, as happens rarely, can think of nothing to say. Wise or not, the client has the right to his secrets. And Kiril has a point anyway, that his defense team doesn't need to go off on a frolic and detour while he is basically on trial for his life.

Kiril stands, once more looking cheerful, and goes to the closed door of the office. With his hand on the knob, he turns back.

"It is an amusing thought, though, Sandy."

"What is?"

"Someone out there doesn't want you to know I am innocent."

17. THE NIGHT

Wednesday is one of the sessions full of perfunctory testimony that every trial inevitably includes. Dr. Hera Peraklites, who was the chair of the Data Monitoring Committee for the g-Livia trial, the outside safety experts, testifies that if she had seen Pafko Computer-A, the unaltered database, she would have insisted PT inform the FDA. Dr. Peraklites is an owlish presence on the stand—stout, bespectacled, middle-aged, and a bit full of herself. She basically retracts her direct during Marta's cross, admitting she would feel no obligation to inform the FDA if she were convinced there had been no sudden deaths but simply a computer error.

The rest of Wednesday bogs down with protracted argument about the exhibit already shown to Dr. Robb, Global-A. It is a forensic reconstruction of how the image found on Kiril's computer would have looked on September 16, 2016, after Wendy Hoh had corrected the g-Livia trial database, purportedly at Kiril's request. Marta has been exercised about this exhibit since before trial, because Global International has no records of what its database showed on that date, as opposed to September 30, 2016, when the study concluded. No one—not Wendy Hoh, not Kiril, nor any employees of PT or Global—ever saw this table on September 16. As such, Marta regards the exhibit as a fictitious corroboration of Wendy Hoh.

Marta is correct, as far as her father is concerned, but she's also being stubbornly legalistic, as his daughter is sometimes apt to be. The clinical trial study that went to the FDA in October makes no mention of the sudden deaths, and that is Kiril's real problem and the heart of the crime for which he's been indicted. As far as Stern is concerned, Global-A is a favor to the defense, since it gives them something to attack and question in argument. He is not unhappy when Sonny ultimately overrules Marta's objection, although it seems as if Sonny finally understands Marta's point, too late. As happens to judges, she cornered herself with her earlier ruling allowing the jury to see the exhibit when Robb was testifying. If she were to reverse herself now, the judge would be admitting an error that the defense would hammer on appeal.

Around three thirty, the prosecutors announce that their next witness, Dr. Wendy Hoh, had trouble with her connection in Chicago. Just the mention of Dr. Hoh's name is the most dramatic thing to happen all day, and Stern can feel attention rise throughout the courtroom. But everyone will have to wait until tomorrow morning to hear from her. Sonny recesses early.

Back in the office, Pinky, who saw Kiril in the office yesterday, comes to Stern to find out when they will get the records for the sign-outs from late March for PT's Malibu fleet.

"That will not happen, Pinky. Kiril does not approve."

She responds with a dramatic "Wha-a-a-t?"

"I was a bit surprised, Pinky, but in thinking about it, I understand. He doesn't want his legal team distracted in the middle of a trial that will determine the course of the rest of his life."

"Bullshit," she says. "What's he hiding?"

"Really, Pinky. Do you think Kiril had anything to do with running me off the road? What sense does that make? There are simpler ways to get rid of your lawyer—such as firing him."

Even Pinky can't argue that point. Instead, she comes at him from another angle.

"But I mean, can he really tell us not to get the records? He's not even CEO anymore."

"He is our client, Pinky. His wishes are quite literally our command."

While she broods unhappily, Stern offers a related thought. "In fact, Pinky, I was struck by something else yesterday. Kiril still drives his old Cadillac from time to time."

"Does it look like yours?"

"Not identical, but close enough to be mistaken." Kiril's car is a year older and a slightly different shade. When Stern bought his car, he was amused to find that GM produced the CTS in three tones of gray, not to mention silver. Stern's color was called 'Moonstone.' Kiril and Donatella's car is just a bit lighter.

Marta wanders in at that moment to discuss Wendy Hoh's cross-examination. Because of his daughter's impatience with Pinky, Stern has told Marta nothing about the Malibus, and she reacts with typical annoyance when they fill her in.

"Good God. You're wasting time with this in the middle of trial?"

Pinky appears on the verge of one of her frequent dustups with her aunt, but she sees the look in her grandfather's eyes and reluctantly retreats. Over the years, Stern has made many friends at the bar, and done many favors as a result, but he is not sure that after the doors close here anyone is enough indebted to Stern to become Pinky's employer—at least not for long. He has spoken about it with Rick, Helen's son, to whom they have already started referring some of their cases. Payback, and a somewhat tenuous family connection, will probably give Pinky a landing spot, but it is questionable whether she can keep the job in the long run. At his desk, he withstands the ember of hurt and worry ignited by Pinky, which so often blisters his heart.

Instead, he decides to take advantage of the shortened trial day and go home. He is again weary, and feels himself deep into a moment of retreat, when the stress and anxiety of trial seem to have briefly exhausted his ability to care about anything.

He has his soup and by six thirty is in his pajamas. He has a hard time reading for pleasure while he is in the midst of trial, since his mind always seems to wander back to the courtroom. Instead, he turns on the TV. It is a dead season in sports, before any interesting basketball and hockey, and there is no football worth watching on a Wednesday night, although the violence of the game is slowly erasing its appeal to Stern. And he has given up on the news. Everything about Trump, from what the man does to the strident, saturation coverage he inspires on the various channels, upsets Stern.

Instead, he decides to sleep, more out of preference than exhaustion. The longer Stern lives, the more mysterious the night becomes to him, and yet the more he looks forward to it. When he removes his hearing aids, the ensuing silence has a softness, and the world he withdraws to is only his. He has a tactile memory of the long embrace of his slumber beside Helen, the touching and parting and coming back together—his hand on her hip as he descended and rose against the borders of consciousness. Vitality drains away so slowly that there is really no noticing, and yet he feels certain he has experienced no dimming of the fundamental sensation of being alive. He wonders often, Was I really experiencing more as a child, as a young man? Or was it merely that my legs and arms worked better?

In his dreams, he still runs like a deer.

18. WENDY HOH

Thursday gets off to another slow start because Sonny has an emergency grand jury matter, which keeps her in chambers with several lawyers, including Moses, for nearly an hour. But by 10:00 a.m., the prosecutors have called their climactic witness on the fraud counts, Dr. Wendy Hoh. Dr. Hoh is not an MD. She is instead a statistician who serves as chief integrity officer at Global International Testing Corp. She lives in Taiwan, an operational hub for Global International, and has agreed to come to the US for the Pafko trial—although she didn't have much choice if she wanted to keep her job. For Global—and Dr. Hoh—it's imperative that they pin all blame for the altered database on Kiril, in hopes of avoiding lasting damage to their reputation for scientific integrity.

More so than any other witness thus far, Dr. Hoh is visibly and shriekingly tense. She grips the wooden rail of the witness stand with both hands, almost as if she fears getting thrown overboard by rough seas. She also struggles with spoken English, or perhaps American accents. She wears large round glasses and tips her head to the same side each time a question is put to her. As soon as she thinks she understands, she jumps in with a response. Her examination by Feld sounds a little like a quiz show, as if Dr. Hoh were pounding her buzzer and shouting out her guesses about what Feld wants to know. He treats her patiently, however, and eventually convinces her to listen to the entire question.

Although Stern generally avoids confessing the fact, he has long accepted privately that in many ways he has enjoyed spending his adult life among criminals. He has developed an aesthete's appreciation for the knavishness, the guile, the selfish cleverness of so many of his clients, appreciating human misbehavior for its miserable creativity. In almost every criminal case, there is a moment that combines inspired imagination with sheer audacity in a way that leaves Stern gasping, and full of perverse admiration for conduct he knows he would never have the courage to attempt. Kiril's phone call with Wendy Hoh is that instant in *US v. Pafko*.

As Dr. Hoh tells the story, part of her job was to audit the g-Livia clinical database from time to time to make sure results appeared to be recorded correctly. Performing that check in the summer of 2016, she had noticed that there had been a spike in sudden fatalities in recent months. Because the trial was double blind, Dr. Hoh did not know if the deaths were occurring among patients receiving g-Livia or the comparison drug, but she eventually decided she was required to alert her contact at PT, Dr. Tanakawa, Lep's number two. She called him more than three years ago on September 14, 2016. Later that week, at a little after 9:30 a.m. on September 16 in Taiwan—7:30 p.m. the night before in Kindle County—she was in her office when her inside line rang. The caller identified himself as Dr. Kiril Pafko. He told her that PT's safety monitors had responded to her call to Dr. Tanakawa by unblinding the data and site codes for the incidents that concerned her, and had quickly determined that what had been recorded as sudden deaths were in fact a programming error. After speaking to the investigators,

Pafko said, it was clear that the patients listed as having passed away had merely withdrawn from the study at earlier dates. As a number of witnesses have conceded, patient withdrawals from clinical studies are commonplace. Some subjects can't tolerate the medication because of side effects like nausea. Others are 'non-compliant,' which means they don't show up for appointments or respond to follow-up calls from the site staff.

"And what did Dr. Pafko ask you to do?" Feld asks.

"Change data," says Dr. Hoh.

"And did you?"

"Why not?" answers Dr. Hoh. "He say they investigate. Must be so. Dr. Pafko, he win Nobel Prize."

As Stern jots notes on his yellow legal pad, he smiles with bitter chagrin. After objecting initially, Moses and Feld have had a good time hanging the Nobel Prize around Kiril's neck. Dr. Robb had implied on Tuesday that the FDA was far more willing to believe PT for the same reason.

Unmentioned by Dr. Hoh is the fact that major clinical trials are a huge revenue item for Global International. Therefore keeping the customer—that is, the pharmaceutical manufacturer—happy is important. Whatever the reason, Wendy Hoh altered the dataset while she and Kiril were on the phone, following up with a memo to her quality control team about the computer glitch. As Dr. Hoh explains, a programming error made much more sense to her as a statistician than thinking that 6 percent of the patients taking g-Livia had suddenly dropped dead over a few months after generally prospering on the medication for a year.

There is no question that Wendy Hoh's testimony is the worst evidence against Kiril in the case, and the hardest for Stern to square with Pafko's proclamations of innocence. Here again, Marta has been persuasive in her reconstruction of what probably occurred: Kiril made this phone call as a hasty last-ditch effort to see if he could prevent going back to square one with g-Livia testing.

Once he succeeded, no matter how unlikely the gambit had seemed when he'd tried it, his goose was cooked.

Stern begins his cross-examination from his seat, hoping to seem less confrontational to Dr. Hoh.

"Now, Dr. Hoh, you say you spoke to Dr. Pafko?"

"Yes, we speak."

"And how many times before had you spoken to Dr. Kiril Pafko?"

"Oh, never. Never never. Very excited. Dr. Pafko a big name."

"So you were not able to recognize his voice based on prior experience?"

"Oh, no. But very exciting. Nobel Prize winner calling."

"And to the best of your recollection, Dr. Hoh, what did he say when he called?"

"Say, 'This Dr. Pafko. Hello, need to talk.' You know."

"And your principal contact at PT usually is Dr. Tanakawa?"

"Yes, yes."

"Have you talked to other people at PT?"

"Most time is e-mail. Call is upside down. Three p.m. Taiwan, one a.m. PT. Not call much at all. Also better for me. Write English much better than speak."

Dr. Hoh's answer about what was said to start the call would provide some support to suggest it was Lep on the phone. But there are two problems. For one, Stern is mindful of Donatella and Kiril's admonitions. More pertinent, he knows that the next piece of evidence the government is going to introduce is the phone records from Kiril's office extension, showing a twenty-minute call to Taiwan.

"But you have no way to know, Dr. Hoh, do you, whether the person you spoke to was telling you what he honestly believed? Namely, that the deaths were recorded as a programming error."

"Objection."

Sonny shakes her head and overrules. Hoh, who, as she has

acknowledged, is not good with the nuances of spoken English, keeps answering that she believed what she was being told until, after Stern's third effort at the question, she finally comprehends and sits back.

"How I know that?" she asks, a bit astonished.

Dr. Hoh's nervousness requires no explanation. She had messed up by so eagerly taking the correction over the phone without investigating further. Her alacrity in pleasing the customer, no matter how widely encouraged in practice by the sales team, is something the company must now scowl at.

"Dr. Hoh, when was the first time you discussed this phone call you say you had with someone who called himself Dr. Pafko—when did you first discuss that conversation, after it had taken place?"

She shakes her head.

"You do not recall?"

"No, no."

"Did anyone at your company ever talk to you about an article in the *Wall Street Journal* concerning g-Livia?"

"Oh." She smiles and nods with the exaggerated vigor of a puppet. "Yeah yeah yeah. Talk FDA investigator."

"That was Mr. Khan, who is sitting over here at the prosecution table?"

She nods and smiles at Khan, an immaculately kept man with a strikingly wide part in his glistening black hair.

"And do you remember learning some time later that the FDA was questioning some of the data in the trial of g-Livia? Were you aware of those news stories?"

She nods again, six or seven times in rapid succession, and Sonny tells Dr. Hoh she must respond out loud, so it can be recorded by Minnie, the court reporter sitting below the witness stand. Dr. Hoh listens to the judge, then nods the same way. Sonny smiles and says that the record will reflect the witness indicated yes.

"Dr. Hoh, I see a note in the memo Agent Khan made about your meeting that you 'now recall' speaking with a Dr. Pafko. Did you say that to Agent Khan, that you *now* recalled speaking to this Dr. Pafko?"

"Yeah, I say that."

"So that leads me to ask this: When the news was published, suggesting that data might have been altered, did anyone at Global International ask you whether you knew anything about the dataset being changed?"

"Oh oh oh," says Wendy Hoh, to indicate she now understands where Stern's questioning is going.

"Does that mean that you were asked by someone at Global?"

Wendy Hoh looks straight down at her lap. Stern has got her.

"Maybe not."

"Maybe you did speak to people at Global or maybe you did not?"

"Say I maybe no remember. No idea how data change."

"But that was untrue?"

On the stand, Dr. Hoh has slumped and appears on the verge of tears. She was undone, Stern suspected, by the memo she had sent to Quality Control, which her superiors found after she first claimed not to remember anything about how the data was altered.

"Very scare," says Wendy Hoh. "Very important, Dr. Pafko, do what he say and now in *Wall Street*."

It is always helpful to the defense when a principal government witness admits that she's lied. But there is only so far Stern can go in this instance. Marta and he had no idea what to expect from Dr. Hoh, who would not agree to speak to them before trial. It was Pinky who focused on the phrase, 'now recalls,' and with that, they had hopes of painting Hoh as a wanton liar. In the moment, however, it's clear that the jury is not likely to regard her as a schemer. She appears to be a numbers nerd with limited social skills, and fairly straightforward, given how scared she clearly is. The jury is not likely to take well to any effort to humiliate or punish her.

The other issue Stern must steer around during his cross is the memo to Quality Control that Dr. Hoh wrote in September 2016 right after talking to Kiril. Before trial, the Sterns had a significant victory when the judge granted their motion to exclude the memo from evidence as hearsay. It's not a business record because it's not a regular practice at Global to alter data. But if Stern now implies that Wendy Hoh is making up her testimony to save her job, the memo will be received in evidence under a different hearsay exception to show she's saying the same thing today she said before being accused of lying.

Instead, in another of those sudden intuitions Marta would tell him he is too old to trust, he abruptly decides to move in another direction.

"You were very excited, you say, to talk to a Nobel Prize winner?"

"So exciting!" she says.

"And was it exciting to be involved in the test of a drug as potentially important as g-Livia?"

"Big drug," she says. "Very 'portant."

Finally, he asks her about the substantial prospective earnings for Global if the trial continued. She nods with enthusiasm with each answer, clearly eager to please now, as if that will make up for the clumsy lie she told at work.

"But you were aware when you spoke to this person who said he was Dr. Pafko that several million dollars were at stake for your company in further trials?"

"Sure sure," says Wendy Hoh. "Big business, Livia. Big."

On redirect, Feld seems to think that Stern was suggesting Global decided to alter the results on its own to make money. Dr. Hoh is bewildered by the questions Feld is asking to refute this notion, but she ultimately denies that her bosses gave her instructions to change the dataset.

Instead of recrossing, Stern stands, smiles warmly, and says merely, “Thank you, Dr. Hoh, for coming so far.”

When her father sits, Marta is clearly perturbed.

“I don’t know what you think you’re doing,” she murmurs with her teeth clenched.

“Just a dotty old man,” he whispers.

19. TAKING THE PRIZE

Stern and Marta both regard the idea of Kiril testifying in his own defense as a prelude to disaster. Kiril's denials will sound idiotic. He does not, for example, want to offer a subtly different version of the conversation with Wendy Hoh. Instead, notwithstanding the call records from his office phone, Kiril claims he never spoke to the woman at all.

Yet it is a criminal defendant's absolute right to testify. In fact, the federal practice is that if Kiril decides not to 'get up,' as they say, he needs to tell the judge on the record that he is voluntarily waiving the opportunity the constitution gives him to tell the jury his story. In his current state of mind, he will never get through the required discussion with Sonny without saying his lawyers twisted his arm.

Thus, Stern and Marta have agreed that the best way to keep Kiril off the stand is to appeal to his ego. In a fraud case, a defendant always may offer evidence to show he has a sterling reputation for honesty and integrity. If several eminent scientists come to court and say essentially that the Kiril Pafko they know would never do anything like what's alleged in the indictment, it might be easier to persuade Kiril that his own denials are superfluous.

For these purposes, no witnesses are likely to be more impressive to the jury than the two medical researchers who shared the Nobel with Kiril almost thirty years ago. They were colleagues and competitors, researchers of enormous stature who are independent authorities, unlike the people who have worked in Kiril's lab and might be seen as indebted to him. It turns out that one of Kiril's fellow Nobelists, Elena Marchetti, passed away a decade ago. But Basem Kateb has recently returned to Harvard as an emeritus professor, after serving for a decade as chancellor of the Rockefeller University, a preeminent research institution in New York. Stern wrote to Kateb, then logged several calls to his office before the doctor's assistant said Kateb had allocated twenty minutes to Stern late on Friday afternoon, the day after Wendy Hoh's testimony, when Sonny, as usual, will not hold court.

Stern takes a morning flight and reaches Boston in time for his appointment at the main campus of Dana-Farber Cancer Institute on Brookline Avenue, situated amid Harvard's vast med school and hospital complex in Kenmore, not that far from Fenway Park. Stern read about Kateb on the plane. He is Algerian, from an upper-class Muslim family who fled to France at the height of the Algerian War. Although Kateb's first languages were Arabic and French, he found his place in the universe of medical research, a land whose denizens conversed in the idiom of science worldwide.

Stern presumes that, as with his own relationship with Kiril, Kateb had found common ground with Pafko in their émigré experiences. They had been rough contemporaries at Harvard, and Kiril had brightly asked Stern to give 'Bah' his best. They were friendly, Kiril said, never close, but peers who'd shared their field's highest honor.

The office Stern is escorted into is a way station for Kateb near his lab, and probably a fraction of the size of his faculty office at the medical school. This room, no more than eight by ten, reflects a very busy mind. Kateb has been back at Harvard only a few months, after returning to the Boston area where his kids and grandchildren live. A pillar of Bankers boxes, taller than Stern, rises in one corner. Two huge computer monitors occupy the doctor's desk, and the bookshelves reaching to the high ceiling show the uneven projecting edges of ramparts of papers.

In his long white lab coat, Kateb sweeps in a minute after Stern has been seated in a stiff office chair of molded plastic and stainless steel. He shakes Stern's hand perfunctorily and immediately slides behind his desk to stare at the computer screen. It becomes clear soon enough that he is trying to recall who he's meeting.

"Stern or Stein?"

"Stern."

"Someone said 'Stein' at one point. And this is about Pafko, is it?"

Kateb, only a few years younger than Stern, remains wiry and energetic. He wears heavy black glasses, above which his gray-shot eyebrows are almost as bushy as a squirrel's tail. He is dark complected, his nose prominent. The light of intelligence in his black eyes is intense.

Stern explains why he is here. He leaves the hard part, getting Dr. Kateb to come to Kindle County to testify, for later in the conversation.

"So, you're the defense lawyer?" Kateb asks.

"Just so," says Stern.

"My assistant told me you were the prosecutor."

"I am sorry. I hope I said nothing to mislead her."

"No matter," he says. "You're here. I'd have spoken to you, too, if I had the time. And what is it you want to know, Stern?"

Stern's initial impression is that Kateb is a person he would like, and who might enjoy Stern as well, if they had the time for a real acquaintance. That is one of the tragedies of aging, appreciating how many good and interesting people have passed by unknown. Busy as he is, Kateb impresses Stern by the speed with which comprehension passes into his face. He listens very well. Stern explains how Kiril's reputation for integrity is impugned by the charges.

"Well." Kateb stops and screws up his mouth for one second, as if trying out the taste of his words. "Stein?"

"Stern."

"Stern, yes. Forgive me. Well, Stern, I don't think I have anything for you."

"I see. I was hoping, given how long you have been in the same field, how much your careers have been linked, that you might be able to say something in Kiril's behalf. He is in a difficult spot. He seems to think you are fond of him."

"Fond? I've always enjoyed him. Complete rogue. Very funny. He and I once had a horrible delay at O'Hare. Nine hours. We were on our way to Delhi. He bought an entire bottle of Johnnie Walker Blue from one of the bars and he kept me laughing. Wonderful raconteur. Or I was drunk enough to think so. So yes, I enjoy his company. Always have. He's just a shit scientist."

Stern, never prone to verbal eruptions, cannot contain himself now.

"With a Nobel Prize?"

"Even a Nobel. There are always undeserving winners in this life, Mr. Stern, in every arena. Right? He's not the only one. How many successful attorneys do you know who are, on the whole, idiots?"

"You regard Kiril's Nobel as undeserving?"

"Very much so. At least if you ask me."

Stern finds himself somewhat indignant but tries not to show it and put Kateb off.

"My understanding was that your findings—yours and Dr. Marchetti's and Kiril's—were published virtually simultaneously in 1982."

"That much is true. But how did he get there? He was definitely on the track of the human oncogene, the genetic causes of cancer—many of us were. But check the literature. See what Kiril was publishing before the experiments that identified the mutant RAS proteins in lung cancer tumors. You won't see much that anticipates the discovery. In the field, we had thought for a while that human cancers were the product of retroviruses. They are not. So we began searching elsewhere. By the late 1970s, we successfully induced oncogenic changes in RAS in mice. Finding similar changes occurring naturally in human cancer cells was the big breakthrough, because we could then identify RAS as the culprit—codon 12, to be precise, a piece of DNA in the molecule. That's what my work and Elena's established. And Pafko's, of course, if you want to call it his work."

"I do not understand. Did Kiril not perform the experiments?"

"No, they definitely undertook the experiments and research at Easton. But I believe he lifted the experiment's protocol."

"How? From where?"

"From me. Here. Pafko visited his old colleagues at Harvard often in those days. The documents were on my desk, then they were gone. I can't say I thought much of it at the time. I misplace things, always have. One reason I sat around drinking with Pafko years later at O'Hare was in the hope that if he were three sheets to the wind, he might admit what he'd done. But he's canny. When I asked how he could have possibly conceived of those experiments, given his prior work, he laughed and said something like 'Great minds, great minds.' It was bullshit, if you pardon me."

"And you've chosen to say nothing all these years?"

"A few confreres here know my suspicions. But a lawyer, Mr. Stern, is the last person who ought to be expressing surprise. If I disputed Kiril's right to claim credit for the discovery, it would have led to years of litigation, in the law courts and in the scientific journals. My life's work would become fighting Pafko instead of doing research. And what real proof did I have? I'll always believe I'm right. Kiril was broiling in jealousy of me. I stayed here with tenure, while he ended up in the boondocks."

Kateb means Kindle County. Stern grimaces but says nothing. He is familiar with chauvinism from those on the East Coast, who speak of Stern's adopted hometown as the third or fourth circle of hell.

"And to my way of thinking, I made the right judgment," Kateb adds. "Do you think it made any difference if there were two co-winners of the Nobel or three, except for having to split the prize money? I have been very fortunate. As for Pafko, the years have basically delivered their verdict on him."

"Meaning his current troubles?"

"That is certainly one thing. From what I read, he's virtually certain to die in the penitentiary. I would say what goes around comes around. You may not agree."

"I am rather hopeful, actually, about the outcome of the trial." That's a great overstatement, but as Kiril's lawyer he is obliged to evince confidence.

"No matter, really. His career overall has made my point."

"Might you explain?"

"It's rather simple. You know the routine in big science, Mr. Stern. Most famous scientists make a pathbreaking discovery in their youth, they see around some scientific corner and then spend the rest of their careers teasing out the implications. For some reason, that far-sightedness disappears in the great majority of us. For Kiril, it happened earlier than most. He was ablaze with potential when he got here, but by the time they turned him out the door, he had flamed out. Instead, he's been a kind of walking hoax. I can't count the number of his papers in the last three decades that have been debunked—experiments where no one can duplicate his results, conclusions that go far beyond the actual evidence. I don't mean to be immodest, but compare his CV to mine. How many major institutions has he been invited to head? Count his honorary degrees, or the scientific societies that have given him awards. More's the pity, too. He and Lep published their paper concerning their new RAS discoveries in 2010, where they identified the receptor errors in oncogenic RAS. Take a look. Virtually no one followed up on it. The unspoken assumption in the ten or twelve places that matter was that it was more Pafko bullshit. No one was more shocked than I was when it turned out g-Livia was a successful therapy. I still don't understand how he accomplished the initial research either. Looking back, I assumed he'd stolen it from someone else, a real scientist, but no one has come forward to say that. I actually checked the literature before you got here. But no—even a broken clock is right twice a day. Yet you can count on Kiril to fuck it up. His misbehavior has forced g-Livia off the market. It will be a while before the FDA allows it to be prescribed again, and thousands of patients will have died in the interval."

Still ringing in shock and dismay, Stern is a bit slow to process what Kateb is saying. But it seems likely that if Basem Kateb were the US Attorney, he also would have brought murder charges against Kiril—not for giving patients g-Livia, but rather, for creating a situation in which cancer sufferers were denied it.

"And you have no date to speak to the prosecutors?" Stern asks.

"Not as yet. Should they ever call, yes, I will see them. I take it you won't be handing them my number."

"As they say, Doctor, that is not my job."

"I would think not. Nor will I be picking up the phone on my own. As I told you, I decided decades ago not to waste my time trying to discipline Kiril. I'm not about to start now. And I can assure you, Mr. Stern, it will take the jaws of life to get me on the witness stand." Dr. Kateb has no idea of the power of a federal district court judge, even one in a backwater like Kindle County, who could bring him there in handcuffs if he chose to defy a subpoena. Nonetheless, Kateb's commitment to keep his own counsel is the only marginally hopeful news Stern can bring home from an otherwise devastating meeting.

In the taxi back to Logan, Stern finds himself completely at sea, more and more confused by what Kateb had to say. It contradicts everything Stern has taken for granted about Kiril for decades. But his knowledge base is narrow. Kiril's colleagues at home, both at the universities and in the company, are eager to accept his eminence, because rubbing elbows with a Nobelist enhances their own reputations and that of the institutions they are part of. Almost all would be the losers if they cried out that the emperor had no clothes.

But was that the truth? Kateb was offering only his opinion. Nevertheless, he was very convincing. And it explains Kiril's decision to move into pharmaceutical manufacturing, which has always seemed somewhat unorthodox to Stern. The dozen or so researchers in his field who matter wanted nothing to do with Kiril, so he was forced to go in a new direction.

Stern meets Marta Saturday morning at the office. Crunch time in the trial is upon them. Moses called on Friday to announce that the prosecutors will be calling Lep Pafko next. He will be Marta's witness, but the hill will only get steeper from there for both Sterns, when the government goes on to the largely bulletproof part of their case against Kiril, the insider trading charges.

Naturally, Marta is far less surprised than her father by what Kateb said.

"So much for calling reputation witnesses," she says. Even if they could still find a person willing to say the right things, it would never be worth the risk that the government would counter with someone like Kateb. That would turn that avenue of defense into a stroll off a cliff. In fact, this is the one thousandth reason Kiril must not testify. Once he does, the government will be free to attack Pafko's character for truthfulness and integrity with the testimony of the scientists Kateb alluded to who regard Kiril and his work as tantamount to a hoax. Moses and Feld are probably already lying in wait, hoping the Sterns take that misstep.

Marta, who has long assumed the worst about Kiril, is cavalier, but Stern remains crestfallen. It is not so much that Kiril fooled him. A part of Stern had listened to Marta shouting warnings. And life, too, has taught him caution. When Clara died, a woman he'd lived with for more than thirty years, he found that there were parts of her character that were unknown continents. He had resided with a large piece of her, but not the entire woman. With mere friends or social acquaintances or clients, one's knowledge of their interior reaches is no better than what tourists absorb about a place through a couple of visits. But even the little bit about the man Stern thought he could take for granted after forty years has been debunked.

Instead, he sits in his office straining to get any fix on the kind of person Kiril really is. Stern can't imagine what went on inside the man, as he was standing before the King of Sweden to receive his medal, only a few feet away from the person from whom he had literally stolen the right to acclaim. Did he bother to rationalize? Or did he simply pretend even to himself that the theft had never occurred? The latter was Stern's guess. But that, in truth, was the only thing we could do when it came to the inner life of others—guess. Donne had declared that no person is an island. He had it exactly wrong.

We all are.

20. HIS FATHER'S SON

On Monday morning, as Stern is visiting the men's room before the start of court, Lep Pafko emerges from one of the stalls and ends up beside Stern at the next sink. They are the only two people here. Lep looks as bad as you might expect, gray and strained. Perhaps it is Stern's imagination, but he thinks he sees a brief tremor in Lep's lip. Whatever his professional obligations, Stern cannot help but commiserate with a man he has known since Lep was a child.

As the water runs, Stern says, "I am sure this is very difficult for you, Lep."

Lep's fair eyes drift toward Stern and he manages a wry smile.

"You have no idea," he says.

"Your father understands that you have children at home and that you are in a difficult position."

Instead of accepting what is meant to be comforting, Lep turns sharply toward Stern, the same smile now only on one side of his mouth.

"You're a good lawyer, Sandy. But has my father actually said that to you? That he understands the position I'm in?"

Of course Kiril has not. Kiril does his best to avoid talking about Lep. Whenever he does speak of his son, his answers about Lep's prospective testimony are little more than non sequiturs. When Stern does not reply to Lep's question, he emits a bitter little snort.

"You don't need to work me before I get up there, Sandy. I couldn't feel worse. Or guiltier. I mean, he's my father. How else am I going to feel? But please don't tell me what he understands about me. This whole situation has given me some clarity." Lep, like the doctor he is, stands with his long, pale hands, still wet, raised in the air. "I've spent my life at PT turning a blind eye to all the stupid and upsetting things Kiril has done. And he made sure this time I couldn't accept it. But I doubt he's spent a second thinking about the position he put me in. That's not his nature."

Startled by the depth of Lep's anger, Stern, too, is motionless with his wet hands beside the sink.

"And I love PT. I love working there, and I'm proud as hell of this medication. You've been out to the facility a million times. Right over the front door, there's that huge sign that says 'Pafko Therapeutics.' And when I walk beneath it every morning, I love the fact that what's up there is my name, too. But tell me the truth. Do you think that's ever dawned on Kiril? That it's not just his name on the door?"

Lep shakes his head and walks to the dispenser for a paper towel, and is gone in a second. This is the frankest encounter Stern has had with Lep, perhaps ever, and Stern can't help being struck by what emerged. The boy with the math book whom Stern sat next to at the dinner table decades ago relished being able to escape into a world beyond his parents' control. He could be obedient while remaining true to himself. But as an adult, he knows that what he took as a child for freedom was, when it came to his father, simply being ignored.

Despite the inconvenient timing with court about to commence, this confrontation inevitably brings to mind Stern's own angry doctor-son. The deep sadness creeps over him that regularly accompanies Stern's reflections about Peter, a gloom as immobilizing as if Stern had tumbled into a vat of glue. Sixty years along in the ordeal of being Peter's father, Stern still cannot name anything that might explain why they are so deeply and reflexively at odds. In the complex aftermath of Clara's death, during which Peter behaved badly, they had stepped back from each other. Stern had decided to stop apologizing for himself. Peter chose physical distance and, within a year, took a job as a hospitalist at Kaiser in San Francisco.

It was Helen who, not long after Stern and she had become serious, stated out loud the suspicions Stern had long kept to himself. 'Peter is gay.' He was relieved to hear her say that, mostly because it offered the hope that Peter's hostility was rooted in assumptions about his father that could be disproved. When Peter finally came out to Stern a decade later, it was the moment Stern had awaited so the healing in their relationship could begin.

'I know you're too old-fashioned to accept this,' Peter said.

Stern answered, 'Peter, I am too old-fashioned to reject my children, particularly over something that is none of my business, does no imaginable harm to any other human being, and which frankly holds the prospect of perhaps making you happier at last.'

Stern opened his arms to his son, who was a full head taller, and Peter slowly accepted the embrace. But there was no transformation between them. Three years ago, Peter married Tran, a young doctor who had been a resident in training on Peter's service. The two had adopted a beautiful little Mexican girl, Rosa, but Stern, the child's sole living grandfather, had seen and held her only once, when Peter came to town last year virtually unannounced for the med school graduation party for Marta's daughter. Despite broad hints, Stern has never been invited to visit the Bay Area.

Standing in his stinky surroundings, Stern feels almost crushed by the brute force of irony. God only knows what infractions Peter accuses his father of. He made Peter's mother unhappy? He had been self-concerned and worked too hard instead of being the kind of involved father Peter wanted? Stern will never accept the complete accuracy of either charge, but fine, say there is some fragment of truth. Contrast his behavior with Kiril's, who all his life has exerted a selfish dominion over Lep, has stood in the sun and left his son in shadow, carried on affairs in Lep's face, and may even have embroiled his son in actual criminality. And yet, notwithstanding his anger, Lep remains guilty and reluctant about what he must do, while Peter would be running to the witness stand for the moment he's always seemingly yearned for—to be able to publicly declare that his father is a shit.

So again, Sandy Stern confronts a fundamental truth of his existence: The law is humanity's sanctuary, where we retreat from unreason. And humans need the law, because they need to believe there is some justice to their interactions, a justice that God or Fate or the Universe, call it what you like, will never provide on their own.

A few minutes later, somewhat recovered, Stern takes his seat beside Marta, as court is about to begin.

"I had an encounter with Lep in the men's room," he whispers to his daughter. "This may go very badly for Kiril."

Marta turns to him sharply, but the judge is coming on the bench and they must stand.

Moses is already at the podium and as soon as Sonny nods, he says, "Leopoldo Pafko." Erect and slow, Lep enters the silent courtroom and comes forward. In the years before the death penalty was blessedly declared unconstitutional here by the State Supreme

Court, Stern had two clients who were executed. Regarding it as the essence of his duty as a defense lawyer to stand beside his client no matter what, Stern attended, seated next to the family members of the victims in a row of hard chairs on the other side of a window looking into the death chamber and the gurney to which the man to die was strapped. For a week after, he suffered intense migraines for the only times in his life. On both occasions, he could not comprehend why his client chose to walk into the room, still in manacles and leg irons. Were it he, Stern thought, he'd make them drag him. He is reminded of those two men, Ray Sarkis and Tyrone Wallace, as he watches Lep walk before Sonny and raise his hand to take the oath.

Bad as he appeared in the men's room, Lep's usual anxious look is even more extreme as he assumes the stand. His brow is compressed and his face appears frozen. His tongue runs over his lips frequently, and he squints at Moses single-mindedly.

Unlike Innis, Lep received a formal grant of immunity and, in response to Moses's crisp questioning, Lep explains his understanding of the terms and the need to tell the truth. Then Moses goes to the obvious.

"Would you rather not be here, Dr. Pafko?"

"With all my heart," he answers.

Watching, Stern sees a few jurors smile tightly, including the female CPA, the cancer survivor who, Stern has decided, does not regard the defense with much warmth.

Accompanying Lep as he entered a few minutes ago was his wife, Greta, the tallish German immigrant Lep met while he was finishing his MD-PhD at Harvard and MIT. Greta herself was completing a doctorate in chemistry, and once they returned to Kindle County, she worked at PT until the second of their three daughters was born. She is a concert-quality violist who taught all three girls different instruments, so the four females in Lep's house often entertain visitors with string quartets.

Crude theory would declare that sons gravitate toward women like their mothers, and to Stern's observation, Greta is similar to Donatella in some ways—long, pretty, and always composed—and in others not like her at all. If Greta ever wore makeup or fashionable clothes, she has given that up amidst the toil of motherhood. She also lacks almost all of her mother-in-law's social grace and warmth. On the other hand, at least according to Kiril, she exerts the same gravitational control over Lep's household. As Lep's testimony begins, his eyes dart frequently toward Greta, appearing to seek approval, which she delivers with a subtle nod. Donatella is planted on the pew, right next to her daughter-in-law. They are on the prosecutor's side of the courtroom, nearer the jury, but that perhaps is merely because they have better sight lines to the witness stand.

And so, with precision, Lep relates the tale he has promised the prosecutors he would tell. He elaborates his impressive education, two postgraduate fellowships, various awards, and then his appointment in both the medical college and the Computer Science Department at Easton, leading to his work in his father's lab and at PT. He then gets to the meat of the matter, describing his duties as director of medical research at Pafko Therapeutics and his role in the development of g-Livia.

On September 15, 2016, a little more than two weeks before the clinical trial was to conclude, Dr. Tanakawa told Lep about a concerned call he had received from Dr. Wendy Hoh the prior day, suggesting that in recent months there had been a surge of sudden fatalities in the study.

"And what did you do after speaking to Dr. Tanakawa?"

"I went immediately into my father's office, which is next door to mine."

"Did you have a conversation?"

"Yes, of course."

"What was said by each of you?"

"I can't tell you exact words. But we were both somewhat concerned. Every indication we had was that g-Livia was performing remarkably. My dad said to me, 'Well, let's take a look.'"

"What did you understand that to mean?"

"That we should unblind the database ourselves to see if the patients who were dying suddenly were on g-Livia."

"And what did you do in response to your father's remark?"

"I went to my office for the unblinding codes we'd gotten from Global at the start of the trial. Under the protocol, they were to be utilized in the event of an emergency situation regarding patient safety. I brought them back with me, but by then I had second thoughts. Overall, I felt the unblinding should be done by the outside safety monitors, perhaps in conversation with the agency."

"What 'agency'?"

"The FDA."

"What did your father say?"

"He didn't agree at first. We were both upset at the prospect of a problem for the medication, so close to the end of the trial. But I was tight for time. I had a late plane to Seattle, where I gave a presentation at a conference the following morning. Greta, my wife"—he stops for a somewhat obligatory smile as he nods in her direction—"was flying out the next day, and we were going to hike for two days on the Olympic Peninsula. I still had work to do on my slides for the speech, and I also needed to pack, and so I told my dad, Kiril, we should put a pin in this until Monday. I told him we'd be better off with time to think."

"What did he say?"

"He was unhappy but agreed to wait."

"And where did you leave the unblinding codes?"

"I am not positive, but I think I left them there in his office." 'I am not positive' is a new addition. Stern's heart perks up at the prospect that notwithstanding the bitterness Lep displayed in the men's room, he is going to do his best to take it easy on his father. Moses pauses, breaking his set meter, apparently fearing the same thing.

"Now, you say you and your father were upset. Was there any conversation between the two of you about his concerns?"

"He didn't need to explain. He'd said often enough that he felt we were under time pressure with g-Livia."

"Foundation," says Marta, meaning she wants to know exactly where and when that comment was made and Kiril's exact words.

"We had the same conversation countless times. His office, my office. At least once a month, he'd say something on the subject."

"And what was that?" asks Moses.

Marta objects to Lep summarizing a number of conversations and Sonny waves her off.

"Subject to further objection," says Sonny to Lep, "you may continue." Usually, during the testimony, Sonny takes notes on a legal pad and, when things are predictable, looks over other papers—motions, rulings. But she has turned about completely to face Lep and is sitting back in her tall leather chair to assess him. Like everyone else here, she is captivated by the family drama, as old as Oedipus holding a sword over his father's head.

"Please tell us what Kiril said to you about time pressure," says Moses.

"He was concerned that if the approval process dragged on the way these things often do, he wouldn't live to see the end of it. I'd try to reassure him that he was in great shape and would outlast even the FDA." Having heard from the FDA officials about the complicated rigmarole of pharmaceutical testing, several of the jurors and reporters laugh spontaneously.

"And did you do as your father and you had agreed and see him first thing Monday morning?"

"I saw him, but actually he came into my office as soon as I got there."

"Did you have a conversation?"

"We did."

"What was said?"

"Well, this I remember word for word. He said, 'I have great news.'"

"And did you ask what the great news was?"

"Yes, naturally. He told me that after I left the prior Thursday, September 15, he had been too upset to wait. He had called Wendy Hoh at Global. He had a lot of questions, he said, trying to be sure what we'd heard about were genuine results, and by the end of the day Friday, Dr. Hoh had called back."

"Did your father tell you what he claimed Dr. Hoh said?"

"Objection to 'claimed,'" says Marta.

"Sustained." Looking down at Lep, Sonny says, "Just tell us, Dr. Pafko, what the elder Dr. Pafko said."

Nodding as he absorbs the judge's instruction, Lep takes a second to adjust himself on the stand.

"He said that she, Wendy, had told him that she'd spoken to many of the investigators who'd reported these deaths and realized they had been recorded in error. It was a computer programming problem. The dozen patients had all withdrawn from the trial earlier, but had been listed as non-cancer-related fatalities in the prior two quarters."

"Was that the end of the conversation?"

"No. He told me that Wendy, Dr. Hoh, had corrected the dataset, and that there was really nothing further to worry about."

"Did you agree?"

"I went and talked it over with Tanakawa. We were both a little uneasy—"

"Object to 'we.'"

"Just speak for yourself, Dr. Pafko," Sonny tells him.

"Right," says Lep. "I was uneasy. But frankly, I didn't want to get into any unblinding, or more conversations with the investigators, since even the little that Wendy had done, according to my father, put the integrity of the trial at risk, if we needed to continue it."

"So you took no other steps?"

"No, Tanakawa and I went online, entered the database, and did a run for serious adverse events for the prior 180 days. There were many, but no sudden deaths. So it was clear that what my dad said was true and that Wendy had investigated and corrected the database. We were both satisfied."

"Now, did your father tell you at any point that *he* had unblinded the dataset that Thursday night?"

"No, he's never said that to me."

"And did you know at that time that these supposed computer errors had occurred only in the g-Livia arm of the study?"

"No. I thought it was a generalized problem."

"Now let me show you a document in evidence as Pafko Computer-A." The screenshot from Kiril's office computer. "Have you ever seen that dataset before?"

"In your office."

"Never before we showed it to you?"

"No."

"And did Dr. Kiril Pafko ever relate any of the data contained there, showing twelve sudden deaths among g-Livia patients?"

"Never."

"And as an expert medical researcher, if you had seen that dataset, what would you have done?"

"There was no choice. I would have immediately informed the safety monitors and the FDA."

"But given what your father had told you, did you believe you needed to report suspected serious adverse events under the FDA regulations?"

"No. Accepting what my father told me, as confirmed by the Global database, there had been no measurable increase in serious adverse events."

Not incidentally, Lep's supposed gullibility is greatly to his advantage in the civil suits, since it reduces his personal liability.

Moses goes through the FDA meetings that Kiril attended between 2014 and 2016 and later, but there's little new information there. Lep's testimony ends with him saying that before he signed the marketing application, Government Exhibit-1, which verifies the truth of everything contained in the hundreds of pages attached, he had informed Kiril and asked him if it was okay to proceed. Kiril said yes.

Appleton turns to Marta and says, "Your witness."

She is up quickly and tells Lep to hold on to the first few pages of Government Exhibit-1, which Moses was asking Lep about at the end of his direct. She has Lep again identify his signature.

"The application, Government Exhibit-1—as Mr. Appleton just pointed out to you—it contains a representation that all FDA regulations have been complied with, does it not?"

"Yes."

"At the time the document was prepared and signed, did you believe that to be true?"

Marta is standing, but she has not departed from the defense table, so that she is beside Kiril, ensuring that Lep has no choice about looking at his father, which he did not do once while Moses was questioning him. Even so, Lep appears to be trying hard to hold Marta's eye.

"I did."

"And based on your own knowledge, what you've observed personally, and leaving aside gossip or anything you've seen or read, is that still the case?"

It is a dangerous question, but Marta has vetted it with Lep's lawyers. Despite that, after what Stern saw in the men's room, he would have skipped the inquiry, but Lep answers, "Based on what I know personally, it is still the case."

Lep has just taken most of the sting out of his direct. As far as the son is concerned, nobody has shown him that his father deliberately lied about anything. That might be blind loyalty or like believing in unicorns, but notwithstanding the great anger he feels with his father, Lep will do whatever he can to help Kiril, as long as he doesn't violate his deal with the government. With thoughts of Peter still not far away, Stern feels like standing up and cheering for Lep.

Marta goes to the witness stand, takes the signature page of the application from him, then crosses the courtroom and drops the document on the prosecutors' table from waist height, as if now it's nothing but rubbish. Stern meant what he told Marta last week—she is leaving the profession on a high note. She has always been effective in court, but not with the same freewheeling confidence she's exhibited the last several days. A bit awkward-looking, always socially ill at ease, Marta, like her father, found a second self in the courtroom, becoming the person she needed to be for the sake of her client—adept, appealing, and smart, not as a show-off but rather someone who is there to explain on behalf of a person who deserves to be understood. For Marta, like Stern, it has been the same fundamental experience, born into this lumpy body and discovering a forum where you sometimes had the grace of a dancer. For Peter, working with his father would have been like the torture of Prometheus, who according to Greek myths was chained to a post while his guts were eaten each morning by a vulture. But for Marta, it has been liberating. Stern gives himself no credit. It was her decision alone. But beginning with *US v. Cavarelli*, her first criminal trial, which they won against Moses decades ago, her unhappy youth ended. She soon married Solomon, then was a mother managing a high-powered career, a person with an impossibly full life who still bounded out of bed every morning to face a wide realm of responsibilities, all of which, on balance, she loved. Stern understands that by now she's had enough—a widespread reaction of lawyers in their late fifties. But he is proud of how well this life has suited her, how good she looks in her closing moments in their shared calling.

"Now, you said when you departed from PT on September 15, 2016, to go home to pack, you may have left the unblinding codes with your father."

"I may have," says Lep. "I may not have."

"And you worked side by side with your father for close to twenty years?"

"Yes."

"You yourself have a doctorate in computer science?"

"Yes."

"In your opinion, how would you characterize your father's computer skills?"

Moses objects that this is not proper opinion testimony, but Sonny overrules him.

"I would describe his skills as pretty basic. If he needed something with a computer, generally he asked me or somebody else."

"And in your opinion, given his computer skills, could Kiril Pafko have unblinded the dataset?"

Moses objects again, and Marta and he move to the sidebar. While they are gone, Stern feels the weight of someone's eyes and glances back to find Donatella's thick dark brows pinched in a reproachful look. It requires a second for Stern to understand that it is Marta's question that has upset her. If Kiril didn't do the unblinding, then, as Donatella sees it, it might have been Lep. But Marta implied no such thing. She is merely questioning the government's entire reconstruction of events. In response, Stern scowls back at Donatella. She would throw Kiril off the cliff rather than see her son within a mile of the edge.

When Marta returns from the sidebar, the judge sustains Moses's objection, but she allows the next question, which is whether applying the unblinding codes requires more than what Lep would classify as basic computer skills.

"I would say so," Lep answers.

She then asks a question contained in a note Stern handed her, a thought he had while she was conferring with Moses and the judge, an idea for his closing.

"And by the way, given your father's basic computer skills, did you happen to learn his computer password?"

Lep smiles for the first time. "He drove the IT people crazy, because he insisted on something he wouldn't forget. It was eight '1's. Because of all the arguments with IT, everyone in the C-suite knew it."

Given the constraints Kiril and Donatella have imposed, Marta has little more ground to cover.

"Now, you have worked beside your father since you finished your fellowship after your PhD, correct?"

"Yes."

"And by the way, I don't think we've gone through the formality of having you identify for the record the person you have been referring to as your father. That would be the gentleman beside me, the defendant in this case, Dr. Kiril Pafko?" With that, Marta, using a gesture like a conductor at the end of a symphony, beckons Kiril to rise, so that he is staring straight at his son. Lep takes some time before answering yes, and Marta holds Kiril's elbow so he does not sit again, but continues to face Lep.

"And as a distinguished scientist yourself, do you have an opinion about your father's honesty and integrity as a scientist?" The question is carefully framed. Marta didn't ask 'as a husband' or 'as a person.' And Lep's lawyers have promised he will deliver. Nonetheless, it is a high-wire moment for the defense, even assuming Lep remains friendly, because the question could open the door for the prosecutors to call witnesses like Kateb. On balance, Stern and Marta have agreed that Sonny will take this as proper cross-examination, designed to limit the effect of the testimony the prosecutors elicited, rather than establishing a separate beachhead in the defense to which the government would be entitled to respond.

"Yes," says Lep.

"What is that opinion?"

"The highest."

"Even today?"

"Even today."

"Nothing further."

"Brava," Stern whispers when Marta sits down.

The redirect of Lep is brief. Moses is clearly stung by Lep's testimony that even today he would sign the marketing application. The US Attorney asks a few questions aimed at getting Lep to agree that if the uncorrected dataset, Pafko Computer-A, were accurate then the regs required reporting those deaths. That, in turn, would make the application false. But Lep says—correctly—that regulations about reporting serious adverse events are complex and leave a great deal to the judgment of the trial sponsor. Moses absorbs the answer, glowering briefly at Lep. Yet Moses's wisdom in the courtroom is hard won. He could quarrel more with Lep in front of the jury, even attack him, but that would only deepen the impression that the government has been damaged. Besides, Moses knows he can blunt Lep's cross in argument: 'Of course, a son wants to believe his father isn't a liar, but how does that stand up to the facts?'

Accordingly, after a few more questions, Moses stops. Marta declines to recross and Sonny tells Lep he may step down and declares a recess for lunch.

While the jury is still on its way out, Lep comes straight from the witness stand to his father, who stands to receive his son in his arms. Lep gives one anguished outcry and shakes with sobs.

Several of the jurors have stopped to watch. Stern feels some instinct to intervene, fearing that this display on balance is not helpful to Kiril. But if nothing else, the sight of the two men locked in each other's arms demonstrates how torturous the entire circumstance has been to both of them. When Lep has recovered, with a wad of Kleenex pressed to the middle of his face, he finds his wife and starts out of the courtroom with her, arm in arm. Donatella is a step behind.

21. INNIS RETURNS

Over the weekend, the prosecutors made another change to their witness list, deciding to call an FDA lawyer to testify about the many regulations underpinning some of the fraud counts. She comes to the stand Monday afternoon, following the morning session with Lep. Her testimony is clearly a response to Dr. Robb's cross and Robb's concession that current information seems to show that g-Livia is 'safe' for the market.

The lawyer, Emilia Dash, has been pressed into service with less preparation than might be ideal, and Marta has a field day with her on cross-examination. Ms. Dash is unaware of a 2012 FDA white paper that concluded that adverse events are routinely underreported in the course of clinical trials. Then it turns out that one of the 'regulations' Ms. Dash claims PT—and Kiril—violated is actually an FDA guideline, which is, in legal terms, no better than a suggestion. Because the pharmaceutical industry tends to battle any effort by the FDA to promulgate new rules, the agency often is limited to publishing guidance. The drug makers who want their products approved tend to follow these advisories when it suits them, but in the courtroom the difference between what is done in practice and what is done because the law requires it is critical, and Ms. Dash ends up deeply embarrassed.

When Sonny adjourns in the afternoon, it has been a far better day for the defense than Stern anticipated this morning. He returns to the office in the company of Cecil Jonas, a senior partner at a DC firm representing PT in its new battles with the FDA over the agency's effort to retract its approval of g-Livia. Cecil has come to town to observe the proceedings. The success of Marta's cross-examinations of the FDA witnesses is due in no small measure to the hours Cecil has spent tutoring her.

But no matter how thorough Cecil's expertise on pharmaceutical law, that does not make him a maven about everything that happens in the courtroom, which he is not inclined to recognize. Perhaps the steepest cost of the aid the Sterns have received from the many big firms involved in the countless civil matters brought against PT and Kiril is having to endure hours of advice from various senior partners about how Stern should proceed with the defense. Almost none of these lawyers has ever tried a criminal case. They are successful 'litigators,' meaning they are skilled in taking depositions and negotiating settlements, but with very limited experience with juries. That makes them a little like adolescent boys in a locker room in Stern's day, pretending to know a lot about sex. After watching the proceedings, Jonas seems to think that Kiril is on the verge of acquittal, an idea Stern gently dispels.

"Cecil," Stern tells him, "I cannot count the number of prosecutions where Marta and I felt we had decimated every witness for the government, and the jury returned with a guilty verdict even before we had time to leave the courthouse for lunch." This, regrettably, is not false modesty. Unlike civil cases, where the venire come to court knowing nothing about either side, juries usually start criminal cases with faith in the prosecutors whom they tend to regard as public servants working for them. Stern shares with Cecil the watchword Marta and he have learned to live by: 'The zombies keep coming.' The phrase is borrowed from Henry, Marta's younger son, who, when he was twelve, offered that quick summary of a video game he was playing. No matter how many zombies the good guys kill off, there are always more, and one inevitably will get you. Sooner or later a jury throws up its hands at the notion that person after person has shown up on the witness stand to lie, or that time and again the government has gotten things wrong.

Eventually, once Stern sees Cecil off, he gets to his voice mail, where he is surprised to find a message from Innis McVie. He had written to her after their meeting in Naples, telling her he hoped to arrange to speak to her again briefly about one point. In her message, Innis says she returned to Kindle County over the weekend and asks Stern to call, which he does. She seems delighted to hear his voice.

"Sandy!"

She explains she has come in to meet with the prosecutors before she testifies, probably later this week. Her niece also held off the christening of a new baby until Innis could attend yesterday.

"You said you wanted to talk again," says Innis. "Is it business?"

"More or less."

"Disappointing," she answers, with a charming little trill. When Stern was single thirty years ago, after Clara's death, he was shocked to find that the same women who would have found him invisible in high school or college, and would have taken his interest in them as downright insulting—those same women now sometimes seemed to find him attractive. He thought of Helen that way, truth told. And logically speaking, at this stage Stern should be at an even greater advantage now that the Grim Reaper is reducing the field of his competitors every day. Nonetheless, Stern still regards Innis's flirting as dubious. He knows he has little to offer her. She could pass for fifteen years younger, while anyone looking hard at Stern would be inclined to call a coffin maker. Freud's theories about females are often called into question these days with some reason, but in Stern's mind the Viennese doctor had gotten to something eternal about the gulf between the genders when he asked with desperation, What do women want?

Innis and he agree to meet the following morning for breakfast at the University Club, where Stern often uses Marta's membership. The club is close to the courthouse and to the PT condo Innis says she is still entitled to stay in for a couple more months under her severance agreement with the company.

As Stern is packing up to leave the office, he finds Pinky in his doorway. He can guess the subject from the way she looks around first to see if her aunt is within earshot.

"So, like, Detective Swanson finally called me back," says Pinky.

"Yes?" he says impatiently.

"Swanson said about 165 white 2017 Malibus are registered in Greenwood County, according to the DMV."

"And six of them are at PT?" Overall, Stern would have guessed there might be more of the cars in the area, but the numbers are neither here nor there. Granted, he was hit only a couple of miles from PT, yet there is still a good chance all this is no more than a coincidence. "What did Detective Swanson say about your research?"

"Totally bored. She said what you said: There weren't any cars with front-end damage in the PT lot. But when I told her that maybe somebody went straight to the body shop with the Malibu, she said, Well then, get your client's records for those cars."

"Yes, Pinky, but our client does not want us to do that. Nor are we going to stage an end run by encouraging the police to ask instead."

From the way her face falls, Stern can tell that is exactly what she had in mind.

"Pinky, I cannot imagine a starker conflict of interest than initiating a police investigation of our client, or the people he is allied with, when he has ordered us to leave the matter alone."

It is all Pinky can do to keep herself from writhing with disappointment like a seven-year-old, but she heads back to the conference room, where she and the borrowed associates and paralegals are going over all of Kiril's brokerage records in preparation for the next phase of the case.

Stern enters the hoity-toity preserve of the University Club Tuesday morning in a mood of dismay. What troubles him is realizing how comfortable he has grown moving through a world of wealth. He is rich by any measure, and his kids—given Solomon's excellent investment advice about their inheritances from their mother—are even richer than their father. Stern's age peers in the legal world have become, almost to a person, well-minted members of the upper class, and you would classify his neighbors in the West Bank the same way. His childhood in poverty still clings to him like the scent of smoke after a fire, and among the many reasons he has always insisted on continuing his free representation of poor clients is to see again firsthand how different this nation looks to its less blessed citizens. If he didn't practice that kind of mindfulness, he could pass through his present life feeling utterly untouched by the harsh realities they often face.

Marta joined the University Club because it offers excellent athletic facilities, but Stern, especially in his present emotional state, finds it a palace of amusing pretense. The stained glass and flying buttresses and yellowed oak are meant to imitate the East Coast and its world of white wealth from which, in fact, most of the settlers of Kindle County had been deliberately excluded. Chief among them was the first European to arrive here, a trapper and trader named Jean-Baptiste Point DuSable, for whom the central municipality in the Tri-Cities is named, and who, even today, many locals do not realize was black.

Stern finds Innis waiting in the lobby, her back to him as she studies a wall of photos of former club presidents. She turns when he calls, and her beauty evokes an appropriately conflicted response in Stern. Professionally, he is committed to ignoring her attractiveness. Then again, it is hard not to be struck by her appearance, a well-preserved version of the perfect *goyishe* sweethearts like Doris Day who were the dainty goddesses of Stern's youth. Dr. McVie is dressed for business in a tailored black suit and high heels, which make her a few inches taller than he. She is carefully made up, unlike the afternoon they met in Naples when she was fresh from the sea. Caught off guard at first, Stern realizes only now what Innis has been staring at: Donatella's photo on the wall. When women were finally welcomed into the club's upper ranks about twenty years ago, Donatella had served on the board of directors here, and then did a brief term as president.

"Always watching," Innis jokes, with a sideward nod to the photograph.

They move to the elevator. In Dr. McVie's company, he finds his balance better and tucks his cane beneath his arm. As soon as the waiter has served coffee, Stern, still in mind of the photo in the lobby, says, "Is it too personal to ask how Donatella and you dealt with one another?"

"It was smoother than you might think. She is a formidable person. Very very bright. She was civil to me. In public, I always had the sense that we were engaged in a contest to see who could appear more unruffled by the other. I'm sure she'd be quite polite to me now, even warm. After all, she's won. I'm out. She remains. In whatever position that is."

Stern offers a rumble of sound in agreement. "I have to admit, the Pafkos' arrangement puzzles me. I have known Kiril and Donatella for decades, and Clara and I, Helen and I—we thought of the two as especially well settled. Now I find that was far from the complete picture. I could probably say as much about anyone's marriage, but I am still having trouble fitting the pieces together. Not only did Kiril have another part of his life that I am sure was quite important to him"—Stern nods to Innis—"but I have come to assume Donatella recognized and accepted that."

"It always seemed that way, although believe it or not, nobody ever said it out loud. I'm probably the last person who can explain why Donatella acquiesced." Innis manages a laugh. "I would never tell you that they were not deeply attached to each other. But I never had any deep insights into their bond. Kiril always presented their relationship as very dour, even bitter. I understood things were being slanted for my consumption. But as I got the story, Donatella was the darkness and I was the light. Still, I took it for granted that he could never make do with just one of us."

Stern asks if Innis was content with that, and she struggles with the question, twisting her shoulders a bit.

"Well, this is getting quite personal, isn't it?"

"It goes without saying that you may simply tell me to mind my own business." He wonders for a second, if Dr. McVie and he had met on another footing—say the one she's seemed at moments to toy with—if this were, God save him, a date, how Innis might have explained her years with Kiril to him? He was a widower. She was what? A discarded mistress of three decades? His guess is that she would simply slam the door on it and describe herself as someone not to wallow in the past.

"Well, it's personal, but it's nothing I'm afraid to say. It's just rather difficult to explain to somebody else. There is something of the poet in Kiril. He pretends so beautifully. He had his own little walled garden where I joined him. When we were together, Donatella did not exist. I was not sharing. I had him to myself. We both fully believed that in those moments." She nods, struck by the accuracy of her own explanation, while Stern absorbs what she's said: 'Kiril pretends so beautifully.' That accounts for a great deal, including what Basem Kateb told him last week, which Stern, naturally, remains determined to keep to himself.

"I don't want to sound like a blushing teenager," Innis adds. "I knew I was accepting less than most people want. But I came to recognize that suited me very well." She stops then and smirks suddenly as she looks at Stern. "You're very good at getting me talking, aren't you, Sandy?"

"I am very interested."

"Well, that's the right thing to say. I'll protect myself and won't ask why." She laughs again, then spends a moment in silence, the bright blue eyes downcast, clearly deciding if she is willing to continue. At last, she tosses up her hands, as if to say, What the hell. "You know, I came to terms, Sandy, with who I am. When I was about five years into this with Kiril, I met a man. A lawyer, by the way."

"From Kindle County?"

"Around here. He might even be someone you know. I'll be discreet, however, since the fellow's long since married someone else. But he asked me first. To marry him? And so it was all before me—a so-called normal life. The window was closing, but I was fairly sure I could have carried a pregnancy. He seemed willing, although I wasn't sure what kind of father he was to the kids he had already. But I had to ask myself, Is that what you want? And the answer, Sandy, ultimately was no. That picture of coming home to a place I shared every day with somebody else, where every decision was a negotiation of some kind—I could not imagine that. I would have felt confined. The truth, Sandy, is that I am not a nester. I don't want it. Oh, I love romance. I admit that. The initial phases, that delicious madness, screwing until you're raw? I relish all of that. When I first met Kiril, we would lay in bed and cut out paper hearts for one another. I'm seventy, and I still don't think I'm done with that." She looks across the table with a fleet, risqué smile.

At eighty-five, Stern, too, is unwilling to accept that he could no longer fully experience that moment. But even if he weren't Kiril's lawyer, Innis's last remarks sharpen the realization that they are not a good match. What she just confessed about her limited interest in intimacy is unappealing to him. It is hard enough to get close to someone who is eager to share her life. With Innis, by her own word, you would soon run headlong into walls. That had been the failing of his first marriage. He would never do that again voluntarily, certainly not when his time left might be measured in days.

"I am very touched by your candor, Innis. Truly. But you are at the nub of what puzzled me after our initial conversation. In Florida and again now you have said that both you and Kiril pursued other interests from time to time."

"That was so for years," she says.

"Then I have to ask this: What was it about Olga that caused you to turn your back on Kiril and leave PT? It sounds, frankly, like she was merely more of the same."

Innis issues a brief derisive sound, a harrumph, rearing back to view him with more distance.

"You know, Sandy, an hour from now when I think back about this conversation, I'm going to ask myself, Why didn't I tell him to ask his client all these damn questions?"

Her protest is sincere, but Stern also senses that there is another piece of Innis that enjoys reliving her time with Kiril. He feels no need to retreat.

"You would be well within your rights in saying that to me. But as I suspect you know, Kiril has a unique ability to evade questions he does not care to answer, given my closeness with Donatella."

She hoots. "I'll say."

"When I signed on, I had no idea that Kiril's personal life was going to matter in understanding the circumstances at the time"—he nearly said 'of the crime' but that would be bad form—"everything happened."

"Believe me, Sandy, you won't be learning all of that from me." He sits back slightly, somewhat puzzled by the remark. Was there yet another woman with whom Kiril was spending time as the g-Livia trial neared its end? On balance, he decides he is just as happy not to know. "The answer to the question you asked is simple. Why was Olga different? Because he told all of us—Olga, me, Lep, even ultimately Donatella—that he was going to leave his wife for her. At the age of seventy-five, he wanted a divorce to marry Olga. That was the last straw, Sandy. I had been the other woman for thirty-two years. And I had accepted the inevitability of that, that I could not supplant the woman he had already married, the mother of his children. And I know, I just told you I had no interest in marrying anyone. But I'll be damned if I was going to settle for not being asked. To stick around and play second fiddle to Olga? That was beyond insulting."

"But he didn't leave Donatella."

"Of course not. He's terrified of her."

"Is she temperamental?"

"Not especially. But powerful. Surely you see that. I imagine at some level she convinced him she was the key to everything he had accomplished, that without her he would be some flimsy imitation of himself, like one of those life-size cutouts of athletes or politicians that people prop up in windows as a joke."

"And do you know what transpired between Kiril and Donatella?"

"I know what Lep told me. We had a long conversation about six months after I left PT. Whether what Lep said is true, I can't say. You have a better source of information than me."

"Granted, but do you mind repeating what Lep said?"

Again, she pulls her mouth around to determine how much that idea displeases her.

"Here are the basics. Kiril put Olga off for many months, claiming there was too much tumult in his life dealing with the final approval of g-Livia. He promised he would tell Donatella as soon as the product was on the market."

"That is when you left, correct?"

"January 18, 2017. We had this very lavish bash at headquarters—Champagne fountains and chilled lobsters. A celebrity chef. It was otherworldly for me. I had worked twelve hours a day for years to get the company on its feet and this amazing medication onto the market. Now I was done. Kiril, naturally, gave me more stock options and a gorgeous severance package—salary, moving expenses, business cell, use of the condo here when I need it—for two years, way more time than I needed, even with the various restrictions, to liquidate almost all of my stock. I was completely set, rich as an heiress. But when I walked out the door, I was leaving most of my life behind, and only because I felt I'd been forced to do that." With that, Innis flushes. "Hmm," she says, clearly surprised by the rush of emotion. She shakes her head of tight curls and touches the linen napkin to her eyes daintily, still careful of her makeup.

"Better to stop?" asks Stern.

"There's not much left. Where were we?"

"Kiril was going to tell Donatella after that party."

"He did apparently. I never would have believed it. But Lep says he did."

"Any idea from Lep how Donatella responded?" Stern could imagine. Mrs. Pafko was near eighty-five then and had put up with more than her share for decades.

"According to Lep, Donatella stared at Kiril for a minute when he said he was leaving and then said, 'No you're not.' And walked out of the room. And, at least at that point, the subject was never discussed again."

"And how did Olga receive that?"

"Exactly as you would think. She cut it off with Kiril immediately." Sitting here, Stern finds the first thing in this entire conversation he is glad to hear: Kiril actually told him the truth when he maintained that Olga is part of his past. Innis, too, is smiling about the same fact. She says, "I'm sure Olga is bitter and pissed off. Even after all the litigation—this trial and the civil cases—Kiril will be a very rich man, meaning Olga would have been a very rich widow, sooner or later. It probably killed her to find out that her ship had sailed. I can't believe she stayed at the company. She probably still thinks Kiril will change his mind if she keeps shaking her ta-tas in his face."

Innis enjoys her own humor and Stern's smiles. He's half inclined to say a word on Olga's behalf. When you have been very very poor, it is often difficult to think of money as anything but the first element of life. People who tell you there are more essential ingredients to happiness might as well be telling you there are more important activities than breathing. He knows that for all his internal laments when he walked in here this morning, it is not merely accidental that he migrated into this world of wealth. Yet Stern knows that Innis would get up and leave, if he started speaking up for Olga.

As it is, for Innis the tale is at an end. Given her emotional reaction a minute before, Stern is happy to let the subject go. They chat for the next half an hour about Naples. Innis says that after a lapse of roughly fifty years, she has started going to Presbyterian services again every Sunday and has been shocked by the comfort she takes from it, perhaps because it connects her again to her parents. The church and the people she's met there are the better part of her social circle, since she has never managed the knack of becoming truly friendly with the women she plays tennis against.

They stand up as the time for court nears. In the lobby, Innis takes his hand, moves toward him, stops, and then on second thought, finishes her motion by kissing him swiftly on the cheek.

"So I will see you next in court?" she says. She is back to being herself: The tennis player, the competitor, brilliant Innis McVie smiles at the thought. She might as well have put up a sign that reads, YOU DON'T SCARE ME.

IV. INSIDER TRADING

22. THE REPORTER

As Stern and Marta assess the case, the murder charges are preposterous and the fraud counts are vulnerable, in large part because g-Livia has proved to be such a valuable medication. But the insider trading charges are another matter. Less than an hour after Kiril heard from the *Wall Street Journal*'s Gila Hartung that she was going to report that g-Livia users were dying of suspected allergic reactions, and while those facts were unknown to the public, Kiril's broker received orders to sell over $20 million worth of PT stock that Pafko had previously gifted to trusts he'd set up for his grandchildren. Publication of Hartung's story sent the price of PT shares crashing. By selling early, Kiril had saved his grandchildren over $19 million, measured by the stock's low point.

Tuesday morning is absorbed with testimony from lawyers, first an attorney from the SEC who testifies as an expert on the insider trading laws, and then Mort Minsky from a big Kindle County firm that acts as PT's principal outside counsel. He details the elaborate restrictions on the PT executives about selling company stock, except under the 10b5-1 plan, and the many steps Minsky and his firm took to impress those limitations on PT's officers and employees. Stern has never cared that much for Mort, whom he has known for years, and so he enjoys cross-examining him. Mort grows increasingly frustrated in trying to explain the questionable distinctions in this area between insiders and tippees, those who owe duties to shareholders and those who don't. By the end, Stern is able to propose a series of hypotheticals to which Mort must repeatedly answer, "I don't know, the law is unclear." His answers are correct, but given the pompous certainty he exhibited on direct, Mort ends up looking just a little bit silly.

After lunch, the prosecutors are ready for perhaps their most damaging witness on these counts, Gila Hartung, from the *Wall Street Journal*. Ms. Hartung's name is announced by Moses, and the journalist walks briskly through the heavy upholstered doors of the courtroom, with three lawyers from the Wall Street firm that represents the *Journal* following her like spaniels. All three—an older man, a middle-aged man, and a young woman—clutch their briefcases in their right hands and proceed single file behind their client, before taking their seats in the narrow area reserved for them in the first row. The space on the front courtroom pews set aside for the press has been full since the trial began, but is so overcrowded today that many of the reporters have room only to put their butts on the edge of the seats where they've wedged themselves in. The testimony of another journalist is always of great interest to people in the news business, not to mention the fact that Gila Hartung is a celebrity in her own right.

Like so many of the government's witnesses, Ms. Hartung does not arrive on the stand without some baggage, although the Sterns expect to take advantage of only one set of problems. Stern has read about Gila Hartung for at least twenty-five years, since her personal life began making news. At the time, Hartung was a well-established investigative journalist with the *Boston Globe* and a part-time teacher at Boston University. One of Hartung's students paid an unannounced visit to her teacher's Swampscott home and was stunned to find Hartung answering the door in a shapeless housedress, a brown wig, and pearls. In those days, Hartung's first name was Gilbert, and in public she lived the role she'd been doomed to by her birth anatomy.

The moment between teacher and student—her name was Joanna Riles—is taught these days in virtually every journalism class in America, because Gilbert Hartung refused to stand in the way of the student's scoop. Riles's fond account of her reactions to discovering her teacher's secret, and her testimonial to the enduring value of Hartung's mentorship, appeared in the *Globe*, Hartung's own paper. The freelance piece ended up propelling Riles's career—she is now a well-known sports reporter who appears often on talk shows. For her part, Hartung took being outed as an occasion for self-scrutiny. Gilbert began gender reassignment treatment and wrote a celebrated book about her transformation. She continued her journalistic career, marked by two different Pulitzer Prizes for investigative work.

On the witness stand, Hartung's appearance is unorthodox, since she stands nearly six foot three without high heels, and still favors her old men's suits, albeit restructured for her new shape. Her hair is long and gray and untamed by a stylist's hand, and she applies little makeup. In her early sixties, she is jowly and somewhat stout. But she seems accustomed to and unfazed by the first reactions to her looks. It is an unseemly aspect of the trial lawyer's job occasionally to exploit the benighted opinions of some jurors, but the Sterns have studied enough videos of Gila Hartung to know that would be a losing ploy. Once she starts speaking, the eccentricities of her appearance vaporize. Something wise and deeply humane emanates from Gila Hartung. Most of the jurors would simply regard her as strange-looking, as people sometimes are—consider Pinky—but also quite appealing.

The other issue that bedevils Hartung's testimony is likely to be more problematic for her, although it is the same one that always preoccupies journalists whenever they are called to the witness stand. Members of the press, fierce champions of the free flow of information, who regularly go tearing off to the appellate courts to battle a judge's orders sealing transcripts or trial documents, promptly forget all about the public's right to know when they are required to testify. Now they try to conceal anything that might betray the sources for their stories.

There have already been several skirmishes with the *Journal*'s lawyers, who have proven equally hostile to the government and the defense. What they want from both sides is to go away and leave Ms. Hartung alone. They have argued long and hard with Moses that Hartung's testimony is unnecessary in light of what Kiril said in his recorded phone call with Innis McVie. But the prosecutors could not accede, because Kiril made at least one critical statement to Hartung that he hadn't repeated later to Innis.

In their dealings with Moses, Miller Sullivan, the lead counsel, and his colleagues ultimately conceded only that Ms. Hartung would testify to what had been published in the paper. Beyond that, the attorneys were as fearsome and unbending as New York lawyers often are as a matter of style, and they wouldn't even produce Ms. Hartung's notes of her conversation with Kiril until the Circuit Court of Appeals affirmed Sonny's order to do so a few days before trial. After all that, briefs and counter-briefs and oral arguments in two courts, Stern and Marta were chagrined to find that the notes fully corroborated Hartung's story.

At the start of Ms. Hartung's testimony, Moses introduces himself to her and asks whether they have spoken before. They have not. All preparations, including the questions Moses will ask, have been relayed through the lawyers. Reduced to the basics, her direct examination lasts no more than a couple of minutes.

After getting Hartung's name and occupation, Moses asks, "On August 7, 2018, did you call the office of Dr. Kiril Pafko at Pafko Therapeutics?"

Hartung is precise in her response. "I dialed 322-466-1010."

"Did you believe that to be Dr. Kiril Pafko's office?"

"I did."

"Did you reach him?"

"Not at first. I left a message and my cell phone number with a person who said she was Dr. Pafko's assistant. I received a return call approximately half an hour later." Calls from business journalists were routine for Kiril in those days, almost all of them fawning over the extraordinary success of PT.

"And how did the person on the other end identify himself?"

"He said he was Kiril Pafko."

"Were you familiar with Dr. Pafko's voice?"

"I had seen several YouTubes of Dr. Pafko in the course of researching my article."

"Did the voice of the person you spoke to match that of the person you'd seen on the Internet?"

"That was my strong impression."

"And what did you say to Dr. Pafko?"

"I introduced myself and explained that I was an investigative reporter with the *Journal*. I said that I had now spoken to several physicians who all told me that they had patients who had been taking g Livia for a little over a year when they had experienced a sudden and violent death, which the doctors now felt was consistent with an allergic reaction. I asked Dr. Pafko for his comment and whether, specifically, he was aware of any reports of sudden deaths, perhaps an allergic reaction, related to the product."

"And what did he say?" asks Moses.

"At first, nothing. He was silent for some seconds. Then he said, 'I know nothing about that. I've never heard anything about sudden deaths or allergic reactions with g-Livia.'" It is that statement, in particular, that required Moses to call Gila Hartung to the witness stand, since the screenshot from Kiril's computer proves he was lying.

"Did he say anything else?"

"He asked if he could have a couple of hours to investigate further. He promised to call me back before my deadline at four p.m. Eastern."

"Did he?"

"No."

"Did you hear from anyone else on behalf of PT?"

"A lawyer named Ringel from New York called me. He told me they represented Pafko Therapeutics and were investigating what I had said to Dr. Pafko. Mr. Ringel asked me to withhold publication until they had sorted things out."

"And what did you say?"

"I said I would speak to my editors and that I did not expect them to agree. He then warned me about the legal consequences of publishing false and damaging information. That was the end of our call."

The *Journal* went to press. The headline read CANCER SUPERDRUG QUESTIONED and appeared on the first business page, with the lead paragraph carried in a squib on the front left of the paper, where the day's big stories were summarized. "Physicians have begun to report unanticipated fatal side effects from the cancer superdrug g-Livia, which has made the manufacturer, Pafko Therapeutics, the hottest biotech stock of the last eighteen months. According to doctors contacted by the *Journal*, patients in their second year of treatment with the drug, a monoclonal antibody, have experienced sudden deaths that medical experts believe may be an unexpected allergic reaction to g-Livia. Dr. Kiril Pafko, a former Nobel Prize winner in Medicine who is the CEO of PT, said, 'I've never heard anything about sudden deaths or allergic reactions with g-Livia.'"

PT stock lost 50 percent of its value the next day, and its price was reduced to pennies several weeks later when the follow-up story broke that the FDA was now questioning the clinical trial of g-Livia.

Job well done, Moses faces Stern with a tight smile and says, "Your witness."

The old adage about trying cases says, 'If you have the facts, argue the facts. But if you have only the law, argue the law.' Because the Sixth Amendment to the Constitution guarantees defendants a right to confront their accusers, a witness has to be subject to full cross-examination. If the witness—Ms. Hartung—refuses to answer questions Judge Klonsky deems relevant, there will be two consequences. First, Ms. Hartung will be held in contempt and sent to the federal jail across the street. Without any cruel intent, that would be very good news for Kiril, because of the second result: the judge would probably also be forced to strike Hartung's testimony and order the jury to disregard it. In fact, the Sterns might even succeed with a motion for a mistrial, meaning the prosecution would have to start the case again from scratch.

To exploit that possibility and to discourage Gila Hartung from testifying, Sandy and Marta subpoenaed Ms. Hartung's phone records—cell phone, office, and home—her computer, and all her e-mails and notes from the period when she was working on her stories about PT. The New York lawyers chartered a private jet to fly in and file their emergency motions to quash the Sterns' subpoenas. Rather than rule on the subpoenas in general, Sonny ordered the lawyers to bring the documents with them and said she will evaluate the need for the records one question at a time, as Hartung testifies.

Ironically, the reporter's testimony has already changed the predictable geometries in the courtroom. Hartung's lawyers would be happy if she weren't cross-examined at all, but Moses will not support any restriction that would cause the judge to strike Hartung's testimony or that would jeopardize a conviction on appeal. Then there is Sonny herself. Although the press seldom chooses to report the fact, the Supreme Court of the United States decided long ago that a reporter has no privilege to refuse to testify in a federal criminal case. Despite that, Stern has no expectation that Sonny's usual latitude with the defense will prevail here. Personal affinities always matter, and Sonny Klonsky has been happily married for over twenty years to a journalist, Seth Weissman, a syndicated national columnist who has had no end of legal confrontations throughout his career, including being called as a witness in criminal cases twice before. The Sterns know all about this, because Marta had been Seth's lawyer on both occasions.

"Ms. Hartung. My name is Alejandro Stern. We have not met?"

"We have not. I've only read about you."

He nods, smiling just a trifle, to acknowledge the compliment.

"And these three handsome people in the first row here, they are your lawyers?"

"They are the paper's lawyers."

"Do you know whether they have been willing to discuss your testimony with me, as opposed to with Mr. Appleton?"

Moses objects on relevance. Sonny lifts her chin to reflect then says, "Sustained."

"Very well," answers Stern. His tone is meant to say, as Pinky would put it, 'It's on.'

"You said you told Dr. Pafko that you had spoken to several doctors."

"Yes."

"May I have the names of those doctors, please?"

All three lawyers for the paper stand up in the first row, and Moses, just behind them, also comes to his feet.

"Beyond the scope," Moses says, meaning that the question goes further than what is fairly invited by the questions and answers on direct. Sonny overrules him.

Hartung offers two guesses. "I can't recall precisely," she acknowledges.

"Do you have notes that would refresh your recollection?" asks

Stern naturally, as if he does not know he is about to set off World War III.

"I would expect."

"And where are those notes?"

"I believe the lawyers have them."

The problem is that once Ms. Hartung reviews the notes, Stern—and Moses—will have the right to see them, too, since a lawyer is entitled to review any materials a witness uses to prepare for testimony, in order to determine if the notes, rather than the witness's memory, influenced what the witness is saying. The idea of the lawyers for either side scouring a reporter's notebooks for helpful information is a nightmare for journalists, who depend on the confidentiality of their sources.

Miller Sullivan—lean, tall, and bald—steps forward and says, "Your Honor, may I be heard?"

Sonny grimaces and sighs but finally orders the jury excused.

"Mr. Sullivan," she says, as soon as the jurors are out of the courtroom, "I am going to let you be heard once. So you better say whatever you think I need to know right now."

What is an advantage for Sullivan—Sonny's sympathy for journalists—is also a detriment, since she has a personal interest in the law in this area, meaning Sullivan can't get away with any exaggerations about what the courts have said. Given that, Sullivan, like most litigators, takes more time than he should. He waxes on nobly about the First Amendment, but Sonny knows that the Supreme Court has tended to look at this issue in a narrow way. Producing a reporter's notes does not prevent the reporter or the newspaper that employs her from publishing her stories, meaning producing the notes does not violate the First Amendment. As far as Stern—and Marta—are concerned personally, this thinking is asinine—if one reporter is forced to produce her notes, the next reporter will be more wary about what they print, which is just the kind of restriction on publication that the First Amendment was seemingly designed to prevent. But it's the law and good for their client. Because Marta has handled the motions leading up to this point, Sonny allows her to argue, and Marta prevails. Sullivan's efforts to keep Ms. Hartung from reviewing her notes is overruled by the judge.

"Mr. Stern's question is clearly within the scope of the direct," Sonny says. "Ms. Hartung says she spoke to several doctors. Mr. Stern is entitled to test the accuracy of her recollection and whether she told Dr. Pafko the truth."

Once the jury is back in the box, Sullivan produces two spiral stenographer's notebooks from his briefcase. With Sonny's permission, he stands beside Ms. Hartung, and Stern and Moses are allowed to look over Sullivan's shoulder. He uses his hands to shield everything on the four pages he shows Ms. Hartung, except the doctors' names. She reads them off one by one, five in total.

With that done, Sullivan resumes his seat in the first row. He is barely down when Stern asks, "And tell us, please, what motivated you to call these doctors? Had someone told you they were likely to have information that would interest you?"

Sullivan jumps up again and says, "Your Honor."

Moses is up, too, and says, "This is irrelevant."

Stern answers, "This is highly relevant, and we would urge the court to allow us to explain why."

In exasperation, Sonny squeezes her eyes shut, sighs audibly, and again orders the jury excused. When they're gone again, Sonny lights into Sullivan first.

"Mr. Sullivan, I've allowed you to interrupt this trial to assert the important interests you represent. I understand your point of view. I will assume that you object to any inquiry by Mr. Stern that goes beyond the four corners of the article your client published. But the question Mr. Stern just asked states the obvious. We all know that Ms. Hartung did not contact those doctors because she has telepathy."

"But Your Honor," says Sullivan, "that invites the next question, which is who Ms. Hartung spoke to."

Understanding where Sonny's sympathies will lie, Marta races in to explain the relevance of the identity of the persons who first pointed Hartung at the doctors. Over the next few minutes, she lays out three arguments. First, whoever gave Ms. Hartung this information was not someone sympathetic to PT or Kiril Pafko. That bias is relevant, if the source is someone who has or will testify for the government. Second, if the information came out of any of the government agencies involved in the case, that would break various rules of confidentiality and might even bring into question the entire legal basis for the prosecution. The Sterns, and the teams of civil lawyers working on the cases against PT, have long suspected a leak from the FDA, where someone noticed the response pattern with g-Livia and felt a newspaper report would be more effective in getting g-Livia off the market than going through an internal process in the agency that PT would fight every step of the way.

Sonny does not appear completely sold by either point, but Marta saves for last her most telling argument.

"And finally, Your Honor, in order to be guilty of these insider trading charges, Dr. Pafko must have traded on the basis of material, nonpublic information. If Ms. Hartung's story was based on publicly available information, her phone call to Dr. Pafko cannot support the indictment."

Feld addresses the last point, saying that 'nonpublic' under the securities laws means the information wasn't available to persons buying or selling stock. Sullivan wants to add something, but Sonny is losing patience with the whole discussion, probably because her heart and her head are taking her in different directions. She points at the New York lawyer and says, "Mr. Sullivan, sit down please. You are a stranger to these proceedings and will not be heard further.

"Anything else, Ms. Stern?"

Sandy steps back in.

"Your Honor knows that one question on cross-examination often begets another. The defense has its arms tied behind its back because of the failure of Ms. Hartung and her lawyers to comply with our subpoenas."

"Duly noted, Mr. Stern. You will be allowed to question Ms. Hartung, but only within the bounds you yourself have noted with your various theories of relevance: bias of witnesses, breach of governmental rules of confidentiality, and whether Ms. Hartung's story sprung from public information. Bring in the jury."

Stern watches the fourteen return. By now, they have assigned themselves seats in the jury box and file in in that order. Establishing these customs on their own, with no instruction from the judge, generally indicates a group that will deliberate cooperatively and reach a verdict, notwithstanding their differences of opinion. At the moment, none of them appears lighthearted. Extended discussions outside the jury's presence, especially when they are excluded question after question, predictably irritate them—if they're supposed to decide a human being's fate, why can't they know everything?

Pinky has located a copy of the witness list the government produced in the week before trial. In order to mask their actual intentions, as well as to avoid defense claims of surprise, these lists are always wildly overinclusive. Feld had written down 125 names. Stern shows the three pages to Hartung.

"Now, prior to either of the two articles you published about Dr. Pafko or g-Livia, did you have any communication with any of those persons?"

Hartung takes her time. After studying the list, she sets it down, and says, "No."

Stern is not surprised but still feels somewhat deflated.

"And in connection with preparation of the article you published on August 8, 2018, did you communicate with anyone at the Food and Drug Administration?"

"Yes," answers Hartung. Her face is blank, but Stern's heart skips. Goal!

"Was your communication oral or in writing?"

"Both."

"And with whom did you communicate?"

"I phoned and e-mailed the office of the commissioner—"

"The head?"

"Yes. I was seeking comment before I ran my story. A public affairs officer, whose name I don't recall, wrote me back saying the FDA had no comment. My requests for an interview were refused."

Hartung's mouth moves sideways, suppressing a smile. She knows she beat Stern on this one.

"No other communication with FDA officials?"

"No."

"Securities Exchange Commission. SEC?"

"Exactly the same. No comment."

"Federal Bureau of Investigation."

"Spoke to no one there."

Marta hands her father a note. He does not understand why Marta wants him to ask the question, but he trusts her, of course.

"Did you have any communication with someone not on the government witness list named Anahit Turchynov?" Turchynov was Kiril's young stockbroker, who is not going to testify in this case, because, as the jury is likely to learn in the next day or two, she is at serious risk of being prosecuted herself.

Moses objects.

Sonny asks, "Have I seen that name in some defense motions?" The Sterns filed a motion demanding that the government give Ms. Turchynov immunity, claiming that her testimony is essential to defense of the insider trading counts. If Ms. Turchynov actually gets on the stand, it is liable to be a catastrophe for Kiril, but the motion was a guaranteed loser. The power to grant a witness immunity is solely the prosecutor's, not the judge's, and Moses has no interest in giving Ms. Turchynov a pass.

After Stern says yes, Sonny requires Hartung to answer.

From the stand, Ms. Hartung's gray eyes seek out her lawyers, and Stern quickly moves into her line of sight.

"Ms. Hartung, are you looking at your attorneys?"

Rebuked, she pulls herself erect, while Stern admonishes her.

"I am going to ask the judge to instruct you not to attempt to communicate with your lawyers in any way while you are testifying. The jury needs your testimony. Not theirs."

Sonny does as Stern requests and Gila Hartung answers, "I'm very sorry, Judge."

Stern presses ahead, asking again if she spoke to Anahit Turchynov.

"It's an unusual name. I would think I would recall it, but no, I am not certain."

"Thank you," says Stern. He looks back to Marta, who actually winks. "Since you have told us that you received no information from anyone on the government witness list or from any government agency, may I ask if you recall as you sit here *where* you received the information that led you to call these doctors?"

Moses is up quickly, and Marta's pen hits the floor. The judge stares down darkly at Stern. She has turned quite peevish.

"Mr. Stern," Sonny says coldly, "please be very mindful of my ruling."

"I surely am, Your Honor," says Stern. "I am simply trying to confirm that Ms. Hartung's denials are based on a present memory, and not because she does not recall her source."

He is correct in his logic, as far as he is concerned, but Sonny's baleful look does not change.

"Move on, Mr. Stern."

"Just so," he answers. He turns back to the witness and, settling himself with a familiar gesture, touches the center button of his suit coat.

"Ms. Hartung, you have testified that you spoke to the personal physicians for five patients who were being treated with g-Livia and who passed away from a sudden death syndrome, traceable, perhaps, to an allergic reaction to the medication. Are you aware that federal law prohibits disclosure of patient information to someone like a reporter?"

"Yes."

"Does the *Wall Street Journal*, as a matter of practice, publish that kind of confidential information without the patient's consent?"

"In general, our policy is not to publish confidential medical information, unless our editors conclude there is a paramount public interest in doing that."

"Did those physicians have the consent of their patients to speak to you?"

Moses objects, saying, "Hearsay." Sonny sustains.

"Did you speak to any of the family members of the five patients?"

"No."

Stern stands still, calculating. "Did you *believe* these patients' rights of confidentiality had been waived when you spoke to those doctors?"

Moses objects again. But this time Sonny overrules him.

"Yes," says Hartung.

Stern looks back to Marta. She understands that her father is about to break that iron rule about never asking a question to which you don't know the answer, but she shrugs: nothing to lose.

"And what was the basis of that belief?"

Sullivan and his colleagues stir on the front bench and in response perhaps, Moses tries a half-hearted objection that Sonny promptly overrules. If confidentiality had been waived, the patient information became public, which might be critical under the insider-trading laws.

"I had signed waivers," Hartung answers.

Surprise, like some measurable voltage, passes through the courtroom. Stern can see Moses staring at Hartung. Obviously, he had no idea about this.

"Do you have those waivers with you?"

Sullivan rises again and says, "Your Honor, may we be heard?"

Sonny wheels toward Sullivan and actually bangs her gavel on the wooden block on the bench.

"Mr. Sullivan, you are in contempt. I said before that you are a stranger to these proceedings, and I have told you not to interrupt. Furthermore, Mr. Stern and Ms. Stern have articulated a clear theory of relevance, which I have allowed. How much money, sir, do you have in your pocket?"

No one moves for a second.

"Your Honor—"

"How much?"

Sullivan reaches into the pocket of his woolen suit, a subtle plaid, and pulls out a pile of bills neatly folded into a gold money clip.

"Four hundred sixty dollars," he answers.

"You can keep thirty for a cab to the airport and a hot dog when you get there. Give the rest to the clerk."

Luis, the clerk, stands and extends his hand. Sullivan looks forlornly toward the judge, then steps forward to surrender his money.

"Now, Mr. Sullivan, if any further matter arises where I think it would inform the court to hear from Ms. Hartung's representatives, I will call on you. Otherwise, refrain from interrupting again in any way. Ms. Hartung, the question was whether you have the written waivers you testified about with you. Do I take it that they are in Mr. Sullivan's possession?"

"Yes."

"Mr. Sullivan, please come up here to the sidebar and show the waivers to Mr. Stern, Mr. Appleton, and me."

Miller Sullivan, who has the look of a gong that has been struck, has not moved since he sat down again. Summary contempt, which is what Sonny just convicted him of, is a crime, and bar disciplinary proceedings will follow automatically. He now directs a whispered comment to the young lawyer beside him on the front pew, and she sorts through her briefcase before handing a manila file folder to Sullivan. He brings it to the sidebar, and all the lawyers follow him. He gives the folder to the judge, who pages through it briefly. Quick as a lizard, a tiny smile passes over her lips and disappears, then she hands the folder to Stern. Marta is over his left shoulder and Moses and Feld are on his right as he opens it. Marta actually reaches up to give her father's arm a quick squeeze. This is gold. The five waivers are all written on the stationery of the Neucrisses' law firm. The wording is identical, except for the signature and the name written below it of the family member who is identified as the executor of the estate of the patient who died.

"May I inquire about these?" Stern asks the judge.

"Yes, of course, Mr. Stern, but give Mr. Appleton time to make objections to any question."

The lawyers prepare to depart from the sidebar.

"Your Honor," says Miller Sullivan.

"No!" Sonny responds, loud enough for the jury to hear, as she points at him. New York lawyers travel elsewhere accompanied by various presumptions, that they are pompous and overaggressive, and those preconceptions have undoubtedly worked to Miller Sullivan's disadvantage. Sonny is angrier at Sullivan than she was at Stern earlier in the case.

Sullivan, met by his colleagues who have remained several feet behind, trudges back to his seat, while Moses and Feld whisper together before getting back to the prosecution table. For a prosecutor, nothing is worse than the unexpected.

Facing Hartung again, Stern has her acknowledge that the documents he is showing her are the waivers she received from the Neucrisses' office.

"Before receiving those waivers, did you have conversations with one of the Neucrisses?"

Stern actually holds up a hand to give Moses time to object, and he shakes his head no. He is done trying to protect the *Wall Street Journal.*

"Anthony Neucriss."

That's one of the sons. No mystery anymore who Hartung's source was for these stories. That leaves the eternal question of what underhanded deal the Neucrisses made to get the information in the first place, but Stern knows there will be no answers here. That is like asking where a dog got its bark. The best guess may still be the FDA, although the Neucrisses also might well have paid someone there for the information. The civil lawyers will get to fight that out with the Neucrisses through several layers of appeals over the next few years.

"Now these waivers, as you understood them, Ms. Hartung, are unqualified—are they not?"

"Yes."

"Meaning the patients' legal representatives had given up any right to keep the medical information related to these deaths confidential."

"That was how I understood it."

"So, if someone happened to have heard about these deaths and chose to sell stock in Pafko Therapeutics, they would not have been doing it on the basis of confidential information?"

Moses objects this time. "Calls for a legal conclusion from a nonlawyer. Speculative."

"I'll sustain the objection to the question as argumentative," says Sonny.

"But when you published the information about these deaths, you did not believe it was confidential."

"It wasn't," says Ms. Hartung. This is an unexpectedly good moment for the defense. Feld has already signaled how the government will respond: The information remained confidential in Kiril's hands, because he had a duty to act in his shareholders' best interests and not to unload his stock before they had an equal opportunity to do so. But that is a complicated legal question that Sonny will have to decide before turning some part of the issue over to the jury at the end of the case. At least, finally, the Sterns will have something significant to say in reply to the insider trading charges. The rest of what Stern and Marta have planned by way of defense is, at best, smoke and mirrors.

"Now, Ms. Hartung, when you spoke to Anthony Neucriss, you understood his business to be as a plaintiff's personal injury lawyer, did you not?"

"Yes."

"And you understood, as you were writing your story, that the Neucrisses intended to file lawsuits against Pafko Therapeutics on behalf of each of these families, seeking in each case many, many millions of dollars in damages?"

Moses stands up, just as a placeholder, while Feld and he confer at the prosecution table. Moses then shakes his head at the judge and sits down.

Hartung says yes.

"So you were aware when you published your article that it would be detrimental to PT and Dr. Pafko?"

Bias is always relevant. Hartung understands that she has to wait for Moses, but he again declines to object.

"That wasn't my intention, Mr. Stern, but yes, I understood that would happen."

"Did you ask yourself, Ms. Hartung, why personal injury lawyers would want this information published before they filed suit?"

"I thought about that."

"And what was your conclusion?"

"I knew nothing for sure."

"Did it occur to you that if the information was published, that would appear to be the source of information for the lawsuits they filed?"

"Yes, that occurred to me."

"Meaning, as a result, the Neucrisses could hide the fact that they were the actual source of your information?"

Moses, apparently feeling this has gone far enough, stands to object and Sonny shakes her gray curls severely.

"Veracity," she says, meaning that Stern is entitled to test the truth of what Hartung has said on the stand or in her stories, by showing that she understood that there was a deceptive element.

"You could put it that way. I also thought, frankly, that because they would have the first lawsuits on file, several other families might contact the Neucrisses to be their lawyers, after my story was published."

Stern nods approvingly. "Your story was part of their business development strategy?"

Moses has no interest in protecting the Neucrisses and remains seated when Gila Hartung again looks in that direction.

"You could say that."

"And did the Neucrisses ever indicate to you how or from whom they received this information about the problems with g-Livia?"

Stern feels considerable anticipation. The next answer could tear the government's case wide open. On the front pew, the male lawyer who came in with Sullivan, much shorter than the senior partner, stands. Sonny smacks the gavel even before he can speak.

"This is not a game of whack-a-mole. Sit down, sir. If I have to warn any of the three of you again, you will walk to the airport." Knowing the habits of big firm lawyers, Stern takes it for granted there is a limo waiting downstairs, but Sonny has made her point.

The judge asks the court reporter to read the question back, and Hartung shakes her head.

"They would not discuss that."

Stern nods. He looks to Marta, unsure of whether he is done, and she motions him to the table. She has Hartung's initial story in her hands and she's marked a couple of lines in yellow. Stern stares at his daughter, awaiting the somewhat telepathic process that has always gone on between them in the courtroom. After another instant, he takes her point.

He faces Hartung. Perhaps there is something militant in his posture, because out of the corner of his eye, he can see several of the jurors straightening up.

"Now, even though the patients had made an unqualified waiver of their rights to confidentiality, you did not publish the names of the physicians or the patients?"

"I did not."

"And your article says, 'Names are being withheld to protect the privacy of the patients and their families.' "

"That's what it says."

"And had the families actually made that request?"

"I hadn't received that request from the families."

"You received that request to withhold the names from their personal injury lawyer, Mr. Neucriss?"

"Yes."

"And was that request in fact made by Mr. Neucriss the first time you spoke to him?"

Hartung says yes.

"And he had contacted you, rather than you contacting him?"

"True."

"And he said in substance, I have some interesting information for you, but you have to agree not to print my clients' names."

Stern is aware of another flurry of motion to his right from the three lawyers from New York. He actually turns to see if any one of them dares to stand up again. At the *Journal*, allowing source conversations to be heard in open court is probably a firing offense for the lawyer who lets that occur. Half crouched, Sullivan approaches Moses, who waves him away. For the prosecutors, the damage is already done by the waivers, and they won't make it worse by trying to hide more from the jury.

"That is the substance."

"And do you understand the business of being a plaintiff's personal injury lawyer?"

"To some extent."

"Do you understand that plaintiffs' personal injury lawyers typically get paid on a contingency, a percentage of what the plaintiff ultimately receives, somewhere between a third and forty percent?"

"That's my understanding."

"Meaning that the Neucrisses had many millions of dollars at stake potentially."

"Potentially."

"And do you also understand that a plaintiff's lawyer typically receives nothing if a new lawyer convinces the client to sign a representation agreement, especially before any suit is filed?"

"I would say I know that."

"So by not publishing the patients' names you were preventing other lawyers from contacting the families in hopes of representing them?"

"Mr. Neucriss never explained why he didn't want the names published."

"My question is this, Ms. Hartung. You're an investigative reporter, with years of experience. Did it occur to you that Mr. Neucriss was protecting his business interests with that request?"

She takes a second for a deep breath.

"Yes, that occurred to me."

"And yet you still said in your article that the names were being held to protect the patients' privacy?"

Given the way journalists see their obligations, they, in Stern's experience, are customarily resentful and defensive when they are caught fudging. But Gila Hartung has faced truths about herself far more difficult than this.

"I should not have said that in my article," she answers.

"Thank you," says Stern and goes back to his seat.

23. A WOMAN UNKNOWN

Once the jury is gone, Marta gives her father a quick hug. "What a fucking triumph," she whispers.

Kiril, as always, is gracious with his compliments, but he heads immediately for the little adjacent cloakroom where his coat hangs, moving off so quickly that Stern hurries after him and takes hold of Pafko's sleeve to slow him down.

"A word, Kiril?"

Pafko immediately checks his watch. Stern assures him he needs just a moment across the corridor in the attorney-witness room, where he immediately steers his client. Kiril looks unusually good today. He has been worn down as the proceedings have gone on, but he appears to have had a good night's sleep, relieved perhaps that the courtroom confrontation with his son is over. His mood seems brighter, judging from a new yellow pocket square he sports in his blazer.

"Is Donatella well?" Stern asks. She was not in court today. Nor did she return to court yesterday afternoon, following Lep's testimony. These have been the first sessions she has missed since the trial began.

"Oh, yes," says Kiril. "In the pink. Just busy with her things. You know Donatella." Kiril offers the bland, humoring smile that so often helps him politely evade further questions.

"I hope she will be joining us tomorrow," Stern says.

"I would imagine," says Kiril.

Stern, in spite of himself, finds that he is shaking his head.

"Kiril, I am certain she has had to neglect many responsibilities to be here, but by now the jury is accustomed to her presence. I would not want them getting the wrong idea and thinking there was something in Lep's testimony that made her support for you waver."

"Yes, of course," says Pafko. He nods, but shoots another furtive glance at his watch.

"Also, as long as I have you, Kiril, I wanted to remind you that we are quite likely to see Innis on the stand tomorrow."

"Ah," says Kiril, but no more. The back of his manicured hand drifts through space, signaling again that Innis is of little account to him these days.

Stern explains that he has sent Pinky back to PT for a few more documents regarding Innis's severance package.

"Since the jury will be told that Innis left after a disagreement with you, it might do well to show that you treated Innis generously nonetheless, unless you are aware of some reason not to do that."

"No, no," Kiril says. But it is clear to Stern that he does not really have Pafko's attention, and after another moment Stern lets his client go.

Despite Kiril's nonchalance about seeing Innis across the courtroom, Stern takes an instant to assess his own mood. Over half a century, he's cross-examined several persons who were friends, at least until he stood up in court, but given his brief time as a single man, he doubts that list includes a woman in whom he had even the faintest interest. Perhaps tomorrow there will be some little game of I-dare-you between Stern and Innis, as each tries to steer away from confrontation. In the quiet room, he finds himself smiling.

More and more often with Innis, he discovers himself in a response pattern familiar from much earlier in his life. Reason is compiling long lists about why Innis is not a good idea for him, but instinct seems to have a mind of its own. Whether he likes it or not, there is something about Innis he finds deeply compelling, a point demonstrated to him when he got to the courthouse this morning and realized he had left his cell phone on the table at the University Club after their breakfast. Pinky and Vondra made immediate calls to the dining room manager, and by now the phone is safely in hand at Lost and Found, where Stern asks Ardent to take him once he gets into the Cadillac outside the courthouse.

On its upper floors, the University Club operates a hotel, so the members' out-of-town visitors can be accommodated. The rooms are simple but clean—chenille bedspreads, old TVs, and decades-old bathrooms, but perfect for those traveling on business who want to be economical. The Sterns often make arrangements here for lawyers coming to Kindle County to consult with them. Lost and Found is at the hotel reception desk off the lobby, and as Stern approaches, he is stunned to see Kiril in line in front of him. In his confusion, Stern's first thought is that for unfathomable reasons, Kiril has come here to pick up Sandy's phone, a notion he quickly lets go of as making no sense at all. Instead when Stern comes abreast of Kiril in line, he notices that Pafko is holding a key card.

"Why, Kiril," says Stern. He pats his friend's arm.

Pafko's face jerks with a rictus of surprise, then relaxes into that well-practiced, uncommunicative smile.

"Sandy," he says. Kiril stares another instant at his lawyer, then pats Stern's arm in return and departs with nothing more said.

Stern steps to the counter and informs the young receptionist about his phone—then ceases midsentence. The interlude with

Kiril was too strange. He reminds himself: The client has a right to his secrets. But that doesn't quiet a nonspecific sense of alarm. He apologizes abruptly to the clerk and follows around the corner where Kiril disappeared.

Stern arrives just in time to see Kiril stride into the elevator, arm in arm with a woman in a stylish coat. Stern has a very senior moment. In his shock, it takes him a fragment of a second to place her, or, perhaps, to believe what he is seeing.

Olga. No question. It is Olga.

Court Wednesday morning sees a parade of recordkeepers trudge to the witness stand to introduce various documents essential to the government's case: phone records from Kiril's office, as well as trading records from Kiril's broker. Ordinarily, the Sterns would have stipulated to all of these documents, that is to say, agreed that they could be received in evidence without the boring testimony the law requires about how each paper was created and kept. Yet because of the government's tactical decisions, they need a live witness to testify about the trading records, and Feld also ultimately declined the stipulation about the phone records so he can use the live testimony to reemphasize certain calls from Kiril's office extension. The first was to Wendy Hoh in Taiwan on the evening of September 15, 2016. The second set of calls occurred twenty-three months later, on August 7, 2018, when Kiril returned Gila Hartung's call and then reached Innis instants later. Seconds after he was off the line with Innis, he called his young stockbroker, Anahit Turchynov.

As often happens, however, these things are more complicated to prove than Feld anticipated. Because the call to Wendy Hoh was international, two different witnesses are required to explain VoIP. This morning, Feld tried to reverse field and accept the Sterns' stipulation, but Marta refused, knowing that the jury would blame Feld for the ensuing boredom.

After that, the government moves on to the records of the sales of Kiril's grandchildren's stock. The sponsoring witness is a functionary from Kiril's brokerage house, Morris Dungee, a very thin man whose shirt collar over his tie gaps on him noticeably. He is fully bald and Stern wonders, with kindred feeling, if Dungee might have recently been through chemotherapy. Feld again examines Mr. Dungee, and does smoother work of it than he managed with the telephone records.

When Stern first heard about Ms. Turchynov, he suspected that she would prove to be another attractive young woman who'd flirted her way into Kiril's life. Instead, it turned out that Anahit is the daughter of Donatella's manicurist, a Ukrainian immigrant. Donatella urged Kiril to use the young woman as their personal broker to help Anahit get started. Generally speaking, vast experience is not required to preside over the tame mix of index funds and bonds in which most of the Pafkos' assets are invested. By company edict, the brokerage arm of the investment bank that brought PT stock to market handles transactions in PT stock for all PT officers and employees, because they have a clearance arrangement with Mort Minsky and his firm. On his own, Pafko placed the accounts for the grandkids' trusts with Ms. Turchynov, even though they held PT shares, because he knew he could not profit personally, and because no one entertained any thoughts of selling that stock for many years.

Feld has the brokerage house records up on the sixty-inch monitor that he's pushed in front of the jury box while he questions Dungee.

"And there in the upper right," Feld says, using a laser pointer, "do you see the notation 'unsolicited order'? What does that mean, in the pattern or practice of your company?"

"It means that the broker didn't solicit the order. The broker didn't ask for the sale."

"It was the client who initiated the sale?"

"Yes," answers Dungee obediently. He would sit up and bark if that is what Feld wants.

Marta rises halfway, as if to object, and then plops down, passing a hand before her nose, as if the question is too ludicrous even to be worth the effort.

The jury almost certainly would prefer to hear about Kiril's conversations with his stockbroker directly from her, but Turchynov presents a problem for the prosecutors. She had clearly taken Pafko's call as a sign that PT's shares were about to tank and used that knowledge as the occasion for insider trading of her own. After receiving Kiril's order, Ms. Turchynov eventually sold not only the grandchildren's shares, but also all the PT in her own account, as well as that of a few favored customers.

Moses has chosen not to force Ms. Turchynov onto the stand by granting her immunity, since juries in general do not like to see witnesses get away with the same crime for which they are being asked to convict the defendant. Moses tried to negotiate a plea deal with Turchynov and her lawyer, but facing the reality that a conviction will end her career in the financial industry, Turchynov decided to tough it out. Her young attorney seems to hope that once Moses convicts Kiril, Appleton will lose interest in Anahit. Yet after many encounters with the SEC's Enforcement Division, Stern regards that as a bad bet, especially because Turchynov engaged in a practice called 'front-running.' Realizing that a $20 million sale was going to weaken the price of PT stock, Turchynov sent her own order to the trading floor a few minutes before Kiril's, increasing her profit by at least $20,000.

The people who engage in insider trading almost always have the money to hire clever lawyers like the Sterns. Furthermore, these cases most often arise in New York City, where the financial industry is a major influence in the economy and where the judges of these cases are bound to know lots of people in the world of finance. All these factors have caused insider trading law to evolve with many arcane distinctions that serve as constant obstacles to the prosecution of these charges (in notable distinction to cases involving the theft of physical property, most often brought against the poor). Given all of that, Ms. Turchynov might have had a good chance of walking away, if she'd stuck to selling out her own positions, even those of a few customers. Yet by front-running Kiril's sale, a more straightforward offense to prove, Anahit probably doomed herself to the penitentiary, especially by not making a deal when the government needed her testimony.

Ms. Turchynov's fate, however, is of no consequence to Marta when she rises to cross-examine.

"Now, Mr. Dungee, you've given Mr. Feld several answers about the usual practice in your business."

"Yes."

"But you, Mr. Dungee, have no idea what was said on these phone calls between Ms. Turchynov and Dr. Pafko, do you?"

"Just what the records say."

"But you weren't on the line?"

"No, no, miss. I wouldn't do that."

"In fact, you can't even say for certain it was Dr. Pafko, rather than his assistant, who called Ms. Turchynov, right?"

"I don't think she could take an order from his girl," says Mr. Dungee, meaning no offense with his choice of words. "But no, I don't know for sure who was on the line."

"But we do know from the other records that Mr. Feld offered in evidence that there was an exchange of phone calls between Ms. Turchynov and Dr. Pafko first thing in the morning on August 7, 2018. And that was followed by a sale of an Asian index fund in Dr. Pafko's personal account, right?"

This is a coincidence that has nothing to do with the case, which does not mean that the Sterns won't take advantage of it.

"And as to the calls that took place later between Dr. Pafko's office and Ms. Turchynov's, you don't know for sure if they were discussing that index fund sale or PT, do you?"

"Right. Er, no. It's just how the records lay out."

"And you haven't asked Ms. Turchynov about any of these conversations?"

"No, no."

"By the way," says Marta, "was Ms. Turchynov at work when you came over here this morning to testify?"

Feld pops up with a furious objection. The government's decisions about who to call as witnesses, just like their decisions about who to prosecute and immunize, are completely at their discretion and not for the jury to evaluate. Sonny sustains the objection. Nevertheless, she can't conceal a smile at the art of Marta's question. For his own sake, Stern notes how much more leeway Marta gets, as opposed to her senile father.

Undeterred, Marta strides back to the monitor where Feld displayed the brokerage house records, asking for it to be illuminated again. She is moving with confidence. Over the weekend, Marta had her hair cut. His daughter is a little like the younger Hillary Clinton, with her revolving hairdos. Marta has never found a style to stick with—or a color either, for that matter. As she has grayed, Marta has asserted the primeval right of women of a certain age to dye. For the last decade, her hair has always been some shade of red, everything from strawberry blond to magenta, a color range Stern assumes she has chosen, consciously or not, as an homage to her redheaded mother.

"Mr. Feld called to your attention this box that says 'unsolicited order.'"

"Yes."

"And you told us that meant that the broker didn't originate the sale."

"Yes, ma'am."

"Doesn't an unsolicited order carry a lower commission? A broker charges less, because the client isn't getting the benefit of the broker's advice?"

"Yes."

"So don't brokers often mark orders as unsolicited so their clients get a better price from the brokerage house?"

"I believe that happens."

"Well, let's look at some other orders. In fact, you and the brokerage house have handed over the records of several other trades in PT that Ms. Turchynov placed the same day, did you not?"

Feld objects that these transactions are irrelevant, but since all are marked as 'unsolicited orders,' Sonny overrules him, and Marta has soon introduced the records of all the other PT trades Turchynov made that morning. Stern and she have agreed that she will do this without fanfare, leaving it to Stern in his closing argument to make what he can of these transactions to boost Kiril's defense. He has something in mind he would prefer not to tip to the prosecutors now.

Innis will testify after lunch. Stern confines himself to the attorney-witness room, where he is nibbling at a sandwich and studying his notes when Pinky knocks.

"Can I get a minute, Pops?" He is wary of the look on his granddaughter's face, but reluctantly beckons her in. "So I, like, asked Vondra to look at your calendar for March 24 this year."

"March 24?"

"Shit, Pops. The day you got nailed on the highway."

This is how Pinky has gotten herself into trouble all her life, by refusing to take instructions. Or at least trying to avoid them. He reminds her that he has explained at least twice why further questions about the white Malibu are off-limits.

"Okay, but I can't look at, like, *your* records? Not from PT. Just yours?"

"The answer clearly is no," he answers. They stare at one another. "All right, tell me quickly what it is you found."

"So you met with Olga Fernandez on March 24. She's the little hottie who was bumping Kiril, right?"

"Good grief, Pinky. How would you even know something like that?" That's the kind of damaging information about a client both Marta and he are always at pains to keep cabined.

"Jesus Christ, Pops," she answers, "you made me sit through two seasons of *Downton Abbey* with you." That is hardly the way Stern remembers it; he has little to no idea how to retrieve recent episodes of a TV show. Apparently, it offends Pinky's self-image to think she was enthusiastic about a British costume drama.

"What, dear Pinky, does *Downton Abbey* have to do with Olga Fernandez?"

"Christ, Pops, weren't you watching? The servants always know who's messing with who."

"Are you saying that the employees at PT have been gossiping with you about Kiril's personal life?"

"Like duh," she answers. "Super duh."

"'Super duh,'" he repeats. "At any rate, Pinky, you think Olga had some hand in running me off the road?"

"When Oscar—the parking lot dude?—when he was telling me last week how the fleet works, he said Olga took the Malibus way more than anyone else. Apparently, she, like, never brought them back. So maybe that day you were asking her questions she was desperate not to answer."

Stern decides he will explain the Investigative Fallacy to Pinky later, which is what happens frequently with the police: They develop a theory about a crime and then jackhammer the evidence until a couple of pieces fit. There is no earthly reason he knows of that Olga Fernandez would want to harm him. On the other hand, there is no question Olga has been evasive whenever Stern has spoken to her. She would not even acknowledge her relationship with Kiril. 'Ask him,' she told Stern once. Whatever else, Pinky's mention of Olga is far more provocative after the unwelcome sight of her with Kiril yesterday at the University Club. Given Pinky's frequent mistakes, some of which verge on catastrophic, it is natural to dismiss her wilder speculations, but it is clear to Stern today that there is much about Olga he doesn't know.

He tells Pinky to ask Vondra to find his notes of his conversation with Olga. He will look at them when he returns to the office.

"And no more on this subject without my specific approval," he says. "Do you understand?"

"Great," she answers, clearly a nonresponse, as she closes the door.

24. DR. McVIE TAKES THE STAND

Dr. Innis McVie," Moses announces to start the afternoon session on Wednesday. One of the FBI agents rushes to the swinging doors at the rear of the courtroom, which have button-stitch padding that always gives Stern fleeting thoughts of a torture chamber, and Innis strides in with her head high and her eyes forward. Before taking the witness stand, she stops and faces the bench and, at the judge's instruction, raises her right palm in the air. Sonny also takes to her feet, her own right hand lifted.

In Stern's early years in practice, when he was seldom in the federal courthouse, he once came here to observe the obscenity trial of a famous comedian. In the same pose as Innis strikes now, with an open hand aloft, and before the judge had a chance to utter a word, the comic said, "How," imitating the blank tone of Tonto, the Lone Ranger's sidekick. In the days before identity politics, the joke was merely impertinent, rather than racist, not that that would have mattered to the comedian who had become famous by violating all borders. The judge, predictably, was not amused, but the defendant's timing was perfect. Hilarity rolled like a tsunami through the courtroom, including the jury box. Acquittal became preordained. Laughter, it turns out, is the soul of liberty.

With Sonny and Innis, the ritual goes typically. "Do you swear or affirm that you will tell the truth and nothing but the truth?"

"I do." Innis is in a black suit with a pleated skirt, discreet makeup, hair styled. She straightens her skirt before sitting down, and at that point glances briefly at the defense table, issuing a taut smile of acknowledgment to Stern and to Kiril. It is exactly as Stern sensed yesterday. Innis has spent her whole life in the competitive spotlight. The courtroom holds no fear.

From Marta, Stern hears a faint groan, and a second later she slides Stern a note. "Your girlfriend is about to stick it to Kiril."

Everything about this comment is alarming. His first impulse is to defend himself in response to 'girlfriend,' but then the larger import of Marta's prediction settles. He shakes his head once to disagree, faintly amused that even in his advanced age, Marta remains a bit possessive.

Innis's direct starts as Stern would expect. Moses goes through the letter agreement she reached with the US Attorney's Office, which promises she won't be prosecuted if she is fully truthful in her testimony and in all her conversations with the government. Then he elicits details of her impressive educational background, eventually arriving at her professional relationship with Kiril for more than thirty years.

"And did you become friends as well?" Moses asks.

"We did."

"How close?"

"Very close," she says casually, as if there was nothing more to it.

Moses always prepares his witnesses, so his direct is almost staccato. Question. Answer. Nothing longer than one line on either side, if the witness cooperates. In that rhythm, Innis explains her duties as chief operating officer at PT. Finally, with the preliminaries out of the way, the United States Attorney gets down to the bad part for Kiril.

"And calling your attention to September 2016, did you have a conversation about the clinical trial of g-Livia with Dr. Pafko?"

"A brief one."

"When?"

"It was a week or two after Labor Day. We all knew the trial was going to be completed soon."

"Where were you, and if you recall, who was present?"

"I was alone with him in his office for a second."

"And what did he say and what did you say?"

"He looked troubled and I asked what was wrong. He said, 'There's a problem with the dataset.'"

"Did you ask what the problem was?"

"I don't think so. It was a very quick comment."

"And did you ever talk about the trial again?"

"We had another quick conversation about it a few days later."

"Where were you?"

"Not positive. His office, I believe."

"Who was present?"

"Just the two of us."

"And what did the two of you say?"

"I just asked him, more or less to be polite, how the problem with the dataset had turned out, and he said, 'Fine. I did some things to take care of it.'"

Stern realizes he has unconsciously gripped his chair arm. 'I did some things to take care of it' is far more incriminating than the version Innis repeated to Stern—and the FBI for that matter. On those occasions, she related that Kiril had said 'the problem was solved,' words that could be dismissed as reflecting Wendy Hoh's reassurance that the reported fatalities were a mere coding error. Even Moses appears to miss a beat following Innis's answer. In his unhappiness, it takes Stern a second to register that his daughter has planted an elbow in his ribs.

"Did you ask Dr. Pafko what he meant by that remark?"

"No. We weren't speaking much by then."

That answer becomes the prelude to Innis's account of her retirement from the company, as soon as g-Livia came to market in January 2017. Then Moses turns to the phone call on August 7, 2018, the centerpiece of her testimony. The government has provided every juror with a set of noise-canceling headphones, so the sound is sharp. The recording is played in its entirety, then Moses re-cues certain snippets to ask about Innis's end of the conversation, starting with her comment that she had asked Pafko to stop calling.

"Yes. He'd gotten obnoxious about asking me to come back to the company. The calls came late at night and it seemed to me that he'd had something to drink. I told him this was turning into harassment, that my lawyer had told me to record the calls so we could get a protective order."

"Not true," Pafko writes on the yellow pad between Stern and him. Kiril's version is that he called Innis infrequently with business questions, for answers only she would know, and that once or twice he diverted to the personal. But she never said anything about a protective order or a lawyer or recording him, until the phone call he made after he heard from Hartung.

"And can you explain what you meant when you said, 'Sell your stock'?"

Stern objects from his seat. "The recording speaks for itself."

Before Sonny can rule, Moses rephrases: "Immediately after saying 'Sell your stock,' what is the sound on the recording?"

"I am laughing."

"Why did you laugh?"

"I was speaking in jest. Both Kiril and I knew that was the last thing he could do."

"Objection to what Kiril knew."

"Sustained."

"Can you explain the compliance training you received from

the lawyers for PT?" Innis lays it on thick, the many sessions the jury has already heard about from Mort Minsky, where all officers were warned against selling shares of Pafko Therapeutics without the prior approval of the outside lawyers, except for the 10b5-1 plan.

"By the way, we've heard several times that Dr. Pafko didn't sell any of the shares held in his own name. Did you ever talk to Dr. Pafko about why he wasn't going to sell any of his stock after the approval of g-Livia?"

"Not after. I'd left the company then."

"I'm sorry. Before that, did you have a conversation about his plans concerning selling his own stock?"

"It was a few weeks before g-Livia was approved. Sometime in December 2016."

"Tell us where please, and who was present for the conversation?"

"We were working nonstop to get ready for the roll-out of g-Livia, and sometimes everyone would have Chinese for dinner in the kitchen. There were already articles speculating that Tolliver and another big pharma concern were going to get into a bidding war for PT, and the stock was soaring. A tender offer would terminate the 10b5-1 plan and the restrictions on our options, and most of us couldn't wait to sell while the market was going nuts. It would be a huge windfall for each of us, but after one of those conversations, Kiril looked at me and said, 'I won't sell my stock then.' "

"Did he say anything to explain that remark?"

"He wanted to remain the controlling shareholder of PT, so that even after a tender offer, he was in a position to negotiate an employment agreement for himself with the acquiring company. He wanted to have leverage so he could continue to be CEO of PT."

In Stern's chest, it feels almost as if his heart has jammed in surprise. In Florida, he told Innis that Kiril was indifferent to selling his stock or cashing in on a buyout offer and she never responded with anything resembling what she has just said. She has laid waste to a central plank of the defense, and worse, suggested that in the conversation with Yan Weill, the investment banker—the one that culminated in Kiril's remark about marrying rich—Pafko was actually just playing dumb.

Kiril leans over to Stern and whispers, "She is lying about everything."

On Stern's other side, Marta is giving him a look that is easy to read: I told you so.

"Your witness," says Moses.

Stern comes to his feet slowly. He is so surprised that he is literally somewhat off-balance. He looks down at his notes, hoping to reassemble himself.

"Now, you told us that you and Dr. Pafko were close friends for decades."

"Yes."

"In fact, for much of that time, there was no one in the company he was closer to, except perhaps Lep. Would you agree with that?"

"Not in the fall of 2016," she answers with a cold look. A splinter of fear lodges in his heart, as he recognizes that he has given her an opportunity to mention Olga, but her own pride holds Innis back. She adds, "Before then, I'd say that was correct."

"Yet Dr. Pafko never told you that he did anything to falsify the trial dataset, did he?" This is a safe question, because Innis has told the government repeatedly that she never heard anything about sudden deaths or altering data. There is no evidence to suggest otherwise, but it remains notable that Innis's claims of ignorance, just like Lep's, have protected her from being sued in any of the civil cases.

"No. But as I was just saying, we weren't speaking all that much at that time. I wouldn't expect him to."

"And this second conversation about the trial—"

"Where he said, 'I did some things to solve the problem'?" Some little wrinkle of triumph passes through Innis's lips as she says the words again.

"You said it occurred in Dr. Pafko's office?"

"That's my best memory."

"Were you often in his office?"

"Not so much in that period, but generally many, many times, thousands of times over the years. He had the biggest office. You know how corporate hierarchies go. I came to him. We all did."

"Your office was beside his, was it not?"

"Exactly. Lep on one side, me on the other."

"And you had thousands of conversations over the years?"

"As I said."

"And yet you still recall this conversation clearly?"

"If we're talking about 'I did some things to solve the problem,' yes."

"And in general, Dr. McVie, does your recollection of events get better as time passes or worse?"

"My memory is probably like everyone else's. I usually remember more clearly closer to the time something happened."

"In fact, when you asked Kiril Pafko about the problem with the dataset, he told you merely that the problem was solved, did he not?"

"Yes, he said 'I did some things to solve the problem.'"

"You testified before the grand jury on December 5, 2018?"

"I did."

"You raised your right hand and took an oath to tell the truth, just as you have now?"

"Of course."

"And you did not tell the grand jurors that Kiril said 'I did some things to solve the problem,' did you? You testified instead that Kiril said merely 'the problem was solved.'"

She shrugs. "I was reporting the effect of what he said, that the problem was solved. But if you want his exact words, they were, 'I did some things to solve the problem.'"

"Well, here is the grand jury transcript, Dr. McVie." He marks the page as an exhibit and asks the judge for permission to approach the witness. "Do you see that 'the problem was solved' appears in quotation marks?"

"I do. But I never said 'quote unquote' or anything like that. Whoever wrote this down, the stenographer, that was his mistake."

"When was the first time, Dr. McVie, that you told the prosecutors that Dr. Pafko said 'I did some things to solve the problem'?" This, too, is a secure avenue for attack, because Moses is too upright to let her lie without correcting her, whatever other prosecutors might do.

"I don't know." She looks over to Moses, who is studiously writing notes. "I don't know if I ever did. Does it make a big difference?" Innis is acting as if Stern is being a petty stickler, and she may actually be winning the point with the jury. Certainly, he knows that by re-emphasizing her version of Kiril's statement, he is making the same mistake Dan Feld has at moments and simply deepening the damage. He, too, might as well be holding up a sign that says, THIS REALLY HURTS THE DEFENSE, but he is too far down the road, and too confused at heart by Innis, to do anything but follow through. He reviews with her the three times she met with the criminal investigators and the fact that their memoranda show that on each occasion she said 'the problem was solved.' Innis continues to act as if she can't tell the difference between the statements. As a liar, she reminds Stern of some police officers who appear so matter-of-fact in uttering untruths that no person who believes anything about body language could ever doubt them.

Furthermore, he is beginning to realize how cleverly Innis has outflanked him. It was she who was getting critical information in their meetings, not the other way around. She knows she can alter what she previously said to make it more incriminating, because Sandy has told her that the Sterns are committed to a strategy of concealing her long-term affair with Kiril. Without being able to paint Innis as the woman scorned, they have little concrete way to explain why she would suddenly make things up to injure Kiril.

As with almost anything else that happens during a trial, Stern has been here before, taken by surprise by a witness. But the personal element here feels unique. Overall, just as happened after his blurtings early in the case, he feels truly old, unable to make sense of things. He has been standing for several seconds at the defense table, with his back to the witness, as he looks over the notes for his cross sketched out on his yellow pad. The next bullet point calls for Stern to get Innis to agree that Kiril sounded surprised by what Hartung had told him on the phone. But he can think clearly enough to know that she will say that was not how he sounded at all. Overall, Stern is starting to think he should just take his drubbing and sit down, rather than make things worse with something he hasn't thought through.

Seeing that her father is at sea, Marta pushes a note toward him: 'Kiril's statements about not selling stock.'

Stern nods.

"Now, you say you spoke to Dr. Pafko about his intentions not to sell any of his own stock in the company?"

"Right."

"And would you agree that this statement, too, is one that you never mentioned in your three different FBI interviews, or in your grand jury testimony?"

"I never even thought about it," she says, "until you mentioned the subject a few weeks ago."

Stern stops. She might as well have slapped him. Their meetings are supposed to be off the record. He gets it, though. With Innis, there are not going to be any rules besides damaging Kiril as much as possible, at least without hurting herself.

"Now, you had this conversation about Dr. Pafko not selling his own stock in late 2016, as g-Livia was about to go on the market?"

"Correct."

"In the kitchen, you said? With other people around who were working late?"

"I don't think other people were there. They'd eaten and gone. We were alone for a second."

"And you had decided to leave the company by then, in light of the disagreements between Dr. Pafko and yourself?"

"I had."

"And unlike the other officers, under the last 10b5-1 plan, you were going to sell all your own stock as soon as you could after the FDA approval?"

"Yes. That was definitely my intention. I wanted to be completely done with PT."

"How much did you make, by the way?"

"Objection," says Moses.

"Sustained."

"As you talked to Dr. Pafko about his intentions not to sell stock, how much money did you think you would be making by selling yours?"

"Same objection," Appleton says, but this time Sonny shakes her head.

"Overruled. That goes to her recollection of the conversation."

"No one knew what the stock price was going to be when g-Livia went on the market. But it had shot way up already, because the FDA advisory panel had recommended approval of g-Livia, and the press was already speculating about a buyout by a bigger company. I knew I was going to make many millions, Mr. Stern."

"Now going back to this 'I took care of it' statement, you told us that you didn't ask for details because you and Dr. Pafko were speaking very little."

"That's correct."

"Fair to say in that time period you spoke to Dr. Pafko only when you had to?"

"True."

"And yet you claim that during that same period when you and Dr. Pafko were speaking rarely, that he nevertheless took you into his confidence and explained his strategy to remain CEO of the company by not selling any of his personal stock?"

Innis has just been aced. It's the first time Stern has scored at all, and she sits back just a little in the witness box. She smiles a bit.

"Everyone knew that," she says. "It wasn't a confidence."

"Really? Did he speak of his plans not to sell any stock in the presence of anyone else you recall?" Innis knows the Sterns would be able to bring that other person to the stand, where they would likely deny hearing Kiril say anything of the sort. That would be risky for Innis. Violating your oath to God is near the top of Moses's list of sins, even if the false swearing is helpful to the government. Therefore, a provable lie might jeopardize Innis's nonprosecution agreement, even conceivably lead to her being indicted for perjury. But Innis clearly senses that she's at the edge of the cliff and steps back.

"Not that I can recall specifically."

"Even though you recall your conversation with Dr. Pafko specifically?"

"Yes. That's what I remember. In fact," she says. "In fact, you're right."

"I am?" Stern says and feels stupid as soon as the words escape him.

"I remember that's why I talked to Kiril about this. I wanted to be sure there wouldn't be any new restrictions on selling all my stock in the event of a tender offer. I asked him as CEO, since he would know, and he said, 'I won't sell any of my stock until I have an employment agreement in place to remain CEO. I need—'"

Innis, who seems to be enjoying making it up as she goes, stops midsentence and stares behind Stern. He turns to follow her eyes and sees at once what's disturbed her. Olga Fernandez, clacking along in her heels, is about halfway down the aisle between the spectators' benches.

25. BRILLIANT PINKY

Olga has clearly spent a minute primping before arriving in the courtroom. She is wearing the same belted trench coat Stern saw her in yesterday evening, the lapels turned back to reveal the plaid lining, with a matching silk scarf flowing symmetrically around her throat. Her big blond do has also been carefully arranged as she strides forward. At her side, she holds a small briefcase of glossy red leather that matches her shoes. Overall, she is moving with an air of tremendous importance, which seizes the attention of the entire courtroom.

She pushes through the swinging gate in the turned walnut rail dividing the gallery from the well of the court and heads straight for the defense table. Instinctively, Stern wants to call out to stop her. She is going to embrace Kiril, he fears, right in front of the jury. But he is wrong. Instead she reaches Pinky, opens her briefcase, and hands his granddaughter a file.

Moses is on his feet at the prosecution table. "Your Honor, this is Ms. Fernandez, who is on both sides' witness lists." Anticipated witnesses, except for the FBI agents and the defendant, are barred from hearing other testimony. Moses is also savvy enough to realize that Olga's presence will unsettle Innis, who up until this instant has looked as cool as a gangster machine-gunning enemies. Olga, in the meantime, looks up at the mention of her name.

"May we take a very quick recess to deal with this?" Moses asks.

"All right," Sonny says. "Let's take a little break. Mr. Stern, you'll explain to Ms. Fernandez?"

"Just so, Your Honor."

Kiril, Stern, Marta, and Pinky cross the corridor and direct Olga to the attorney-witness room. Stern keeps his eye on his client, who nods to Olga circumspectly, just as Marta is shutting the door.

"Pinky asked for these records," says Olga. "I knew Innis was testifying, so when I saw them, I thought, '*Chica*, you better get downtown.' I texted them, too, but I didn't think any of you guys would look at your phones during court." It has required several trips to her aunt's pillory to get Pinky to understand her device must stay in her purse while court is in session.

Again Stern feels very old and confused. "Pinky asked?"

"You wanted everything related to Innis's severance," Pinky says. "So I asked for the detail. I thought, What the hell. Could be something."

It is more than something. There are several pages there, printouts, and Olga lays a bright red nail on one line.

"I did a reverse directory."

Stern's pulse is quick; he might even be having another instant of tachycardia. From some crag in his memory, he identifies the number. There were periods in the past when he called for one reason or another.

To regain control, he does what experience has taught him. He lifts his hands and tells everyone to stop. He needs to get things in order. He asks both Olga and Kiril for some background about the documents, then thanks Olga profusely but tells her she must go now. She departs agreeably, and after asking if he's needed, Kiril follows quickly. With Marta beside him, Stern looks through the records, until he is sure they have seen everything of consequence, then he sends Pinky back to the courtroom to make copies on the small portable printer they have with them as part of their trial gear. Before Pinky departs, Marta stands up to hug her niece.

"This was brilliant," Marta is telling her. "Really brilliant. Right, Dad?"

"Inspired," says Stern.

Beaming exuberantly, an apple-cheeked smile he virtually never sees, his granddaughter looks like she may actually topple from pride.

Once the door closes, however, Marta's expression subsides to pique as she looks at her father.

"Honest to God, Dad. Men are idiots. I could see the minute that woman walked into the courtroom that she was going to fuck Kiril over any way she could."

Even now, Marta loves the moments when she is playing ahead of her father. He considers whether this remark is a comment on his perspicacity or his vulnerability. Probably both. He is also waylaid just a second with the thought that if he made a similar remark about women, his own daughter might threaten him with a lawsuit. On the other hand, as the law teaches in defamation cases, truth is an absolute defense. He finally nods.

"Well perhaps, then," he says, preparing to use a word that seldom crosses his lips, "we can now fuck her over in return."

"Now, Dr. McVie," says Stern, even before the courtroom is fully settled after the break. It has been years since he has felt this kind of eagerness about a cross. Whatever the irony, Innis has indeed made him feel young again. "This call between Dr. Pafko and you on August 7, 2018, which you recorded. The number Dr. Pafko called"—Stern recites it—"was that a company cell phone?"

"No, that was my personal cell phone."

"Did PT have business cell phones?"

"When?"

"When you left the company?"

"Yes."

"Did every employee have a company cell phone?"

"Every 'key' employee who had a reason to make outside business calls had a company cell phone."

"And were the cell phones part of your responsibility as COO?"

"Yes." She actually laughs. "I thought I had more important things to do, but I ended up spending a lot of time on cell phone policy."

"Feel free to explain, if you don't mind."

Innis is suddenly lighthearted. Watching her, Stern recognizes a sad truth: Innis loved every minute at PT, every tiny involvement.

"We went through several plans," she says. "At one point, we just reimbursed each employee for their cell phone use. But the IRS came in and told us we had to add the personal portion of each phone to the employee's W-2. So then I had eighty employees using work time to go through their phone bills line by line, and two people in accounting adding it all up and submitting it to the CPAs. After a year of that, I realized we'd save a lot of money if I just gave everybody their own business cell phone and told them in writing only to use it for business purposes. To satisfy the IRS, we made everybody list their personal cell phone number and carrier. Even paying for eighty phones, we had a huge cost savings."

"Did you get billing detail for each company cell phone?"

"No. It wasn't like your personal cell phone. In order to save money, we only got a bulk bill each month. If we wanted to know about individual phones, we could go online and look at the statement for the period."

"And did anyone at PT look at that online statement?"

"As I said, the point was to reduce accounting costs. When the main bill came in, somebody down in accounting was supposed to look at the detail online, just to be sure no one was calling a BFF in Zanzibar four times a week, but I know I said that if the bean counters spent more than half an hour on this, I would kill them. I was sick of wasting money and time on cell phone accounting."

"And how long does the provider keep that detail for each individual phone, the backup for the bulk bill for the company cell phones?"

"I have no idea. As I said, in accounting they barely looked at the current month. I'm pretty sure the provider doesn't keep that material online very long."

Moses stands. "Your Honor, I understand why Mr. Stern wants to distract us from the central points in Dr. McVie's testimony, but may I ask if there is any other reason for this line of cross-examination?"

"Mr. Stern?" the judge asks.

"If the court will indulge me for a few more minutes? I promise it will be clear."

He tries, as best he can, to look like his old self as he appeals to Sonny. Since no one, including the judge, can understand the point of his questions, he is afraid she will suspect him of engaging in more addled behavior. If she forces him to explain, it is likely to ruin what he has in store. The judge makes a face but says, "A few more questions."

To be safe, he moves on to a subject with clear relevance.

"Now, this nonprosecution agreement you reached with the government included a provision that you would provide the government with personal data. You would turn over your computer, your tablet, your phone, your bills, correct?"

"And I did that," says Innis.

"And before that, you had entered a severance agreement with PT when you left the company in January of 2017, did you not?"

"I did."

"And one of the benefits was that you were allowed to keep your company cell phone for two years, and PT paid for it?"

"Right. But as I've explained, that's for company business. Which I stopped doing."

"But my point is that you did not provide the government with the records from that cell phone."

"I couldn't. The company has access to the billing, not me." She offers a tight, arrogant smile. Stern can see that Innis has been playing things ahead, trying to understand this line of questioning. She is sure that this is going to be Stern's point and that she's beaten him again. "And as we've discussed, I'm sure the bills aren't online anymore. And the other thing, to be honest, is I don't even know where that phone is."

"Did you destroy it?" asks Stern.

Innis takes a second.

"Why would I destroy it?"

Stern stares her down.

"Would it surprise you, Dr. McVie, to learn that because of the IRS regulations you mentioned, despite the bulk billing, the cell provider maintains the online billing detail for each individual business cell phone for four years?"

Innis says nothing. You can see the weight of what he has just said accumulating on her. She thought she was several strides ahead of him, as she has been throughout, and she suddenly knows she miscalculated. She is probably terrified, but her face is stone. The score has changed suddenly. Her opponent, who was prostrate on the court, has gotten to his feet and is now serving at 200 miles per hour. Match point is coming. But she has years of training and won't even blink.

"May the record reflect, Your Honor," says Stern, "that Dr. McVie appears surprised."

Sonny smiles tartly at Stern's showmanship and says, "Can you answer, Dr. McVie?"

"Yes, I'm surprised."

Keeping his eye on Innis, Stern extends his hand to Pinky, who gives him the file Olga brought.

"Now, I believe you said a second ago that you never used that cell phone after you left the company?"

Innis lifts her hands, showing the pink on her nails.

"That's what I remember."

"Well, do you remember, Dr. McVie, that you used your company cell phone on August 7, 2018, the day you spoke to Dr. Pafko about his call from Gila Hartung?"

"Did I?"

Moses tries to save her.

"Your Honor, does Mr. Stern have documents in his hand that the government has not seen?"

Stern limps over to the prosecution table and places a copy of the phone detail in Moses's hands.

"We just received these, Your Honor, from Ms. Fernandez when she came into the courtroom."

Moses and Feld flip through the pages. Innis looks over to them for some useful sign, but the prosecutors don't understand yet. In the meantime, Stern marks another copy as an exhibit and hands it to Innis.

"Now, calling your attention to August 7, 2018, on this bill that you knew no one looked at. What is 322-446-8080?"

"I don't recall."

"In fact, if you page through Defense Exhibit McVie Telephone-1, PT's cell phone billing details that you knew no one would look at, you will see, Dr. McVie, that you called that number sixteen times between April and August of 2018. Do you see that?"

"I don't know."

"Are you denying, Dr. McVie, that that's what is shown on the document?"

Innis looks down at the paper and quietly says no.

"Do you know lawyers named Pete and Anthony and Christopher Neucriss?"

Innis now straightens again. Unbowed, one might say.

"I know them."

"Are you aware, Dr. McVie, that shortly after Gila Hartung's article appeared in the *Wall Street Journal*, the Neucriss law firm filed wrongful death lawsuits on behalf of the estates of five patients who'd been on g-Livia and whose physicians spoke to Ms. Hartung? Do you know that?"

"I know that now."

"You knew they were going to do that on August 7, 2018, did you not?"

Stern regards Innis harshly. Wrath is an emotion that eighty-five years have taught him to take little pleasure in, one that is downright dangerous in the courtroom, where reason must prevail. But he is enjoying the moment richly, in spite of himself. It has all fallen in place now. The identity of the lawyer from Kindle County who asked Innis to marry him more than a quarter of a century ago, the man Stern might even know, is now obvious.

"Am I correct in thinking that you have known Pete Neucriss well for many years?"

There is a laser shot of anger in Innis's look. It's unfair, she is thinking—that part of their conversation was private. But it is far too dangerous for her to deny it.

"That's correct."

"And the sons who practice law with him, Anthony and Christopher, you've known both since they were little boys?"

"Yes."

"And when you spoke to the Neucrisses on the morning of August 7, 2018—which one was it?"

"I'm not sure."

"Pete, was it?"

"It might have been."

"Whichever Neucriss, did he tell you that Gila Hartung was about to call Kiril Pafko?"

She wiggles her head a little bit while she calculates. If Innis knows anything about Pete Neucriss—and she knows quite a lot—she will realize that he will not die on anyone's cross but his own. In the face of the phone records, Pete will not lie to save Innis. Among other things, Shyla, the third Mrs. Neucriss, who came on the scene after Innis turned Pete down, will probably have a fit when she finds out that her husband was having regular conversations with Innis, who has been treated far more gently by the hand of time than Shyla.

"I don't remember."

"And by the way. This recording you made of Dr. Pafko after calling the Neucriss firm. How many times had you recorded Dr. Pafko before that day?"

"Never."

"But you had the software on your phone and at the ready?"

"I explained. I'd warned Kiril that if he called again, I'd do that."

"Even in your version, Dr. McVie, that warning to Dr. Pafko had come many months before, correct?"

"Objection to 'your version,'" says Moses.

"Sustained. Rephrase, Mr. Stern."

He eliminates 'your version' from the question and Innis says yes.

"But the recording software was cued up and at the ready, was it not, when Dr. Pafko called?"

"I don't remember if it was cued up. I just opened the app when I saw Kiril's number."

"Allow me to ask again in the hope that your recollection is a little sharper. Did Pete or Anthony Neucriss tell you that Gila Hartung was likely to call Kiril Pafko that day?"

Moses objects that the question has already been answered, but Sonny overrules him, since Stern is also asking if her memory is now clearer.

"It's possible, that's all I can say."

"And knowing that, did you realize that Kiril Pafko might well call you next?"

“Objection to ‘knowing that,’ ” says Moses.

“That much is stricken,” says Sonny. She looks down at Innis. “Did you know Dr. Pafko might call you, Dr. McVie?”

With the question coming from the judge, toward whom Innis has turned, she betrays less of the iron confidence she’s tried to exhibit with Stern.

“I don’t remember exactly. I might have thought that.”

“And the fourteen other phone calls to the Neucrisses, Dr. McVie, are you going to tell us that between April and August 7, 2018, you did not advise the Neucrisses about potential problems with g-Livia that would lend themselves to personal injury lawsuits?”

“I’m not sure. I don’t remember.”

Stern again peers at Innis across the courtroom until she finally weakens and looks away. He ponders a second, then goes to Pinky, to whom he whispers.

“Give me the file, dear Pinky, under your elbow.”

She looks up at her grandfather with her dark-ringed eyes.

“That’s mine, Pops,” she answers under her breath.

“I promise to give it back, Pinky. Look at it first, then hand it to me.”

Pinky gets it quickly and is perfect in her moment at center stage. She even sports a tiny, confident smile as she hands over the file.

“Now, Dr. McVie, looking at these bills, in addition to the phone calls, I see billing five times from April to July of 2018 for text messages. Do you see that?”

“Yes.”

“And all to the same number?”

Slowly, she agrees. In front of the jury, Stern actually pulls out his phone from the vest pocket in his suitcoat and thumbs through it carefully, until he has opened his contacts.

“322-204-8080. Is that Pete Neucriss’s cell phone?”

“I think so.”

"Asking again, in the hope your recollection is refreshed, did you advise Mr. Neucriss of the possibility that in the second year of use, g-Livia could cause fatal allergic shocks or some other sudden death syndrome?"

"Did I?" she asks Stern, afraid he can answer the question with what's in the file in his hands. Thus prompted, Stern opens the folder and looks down at the document, which is a flyer for a rock concert next month by a group apparently known as Fire-Breathing Cattle.

Moses stands. "May we see the document Mr. Stern is holding?"

Stern nods. "Before I display the document to Dr. McVie, Your Honor, I will certainly show it to Mr. Appleton. But first, I would like a clear declaration for the record. Do you deny, Dr. McVie, that in April and May of 2018, you advised Peter Neucriss that g-Livia had a history of causing sudden deaths?"

"In April?"

"Yes or no, Dr. McVie. Do you deny that in the spring of 2018, you discussed with the Neucrisses that g-Livia could cause sudden fatalities to patients?"

Innis casts a look at the prosecutors, then at her lap, and says, "No, I don't deny that."

With that, Stern glances furtively at the jury box. Gray-haired Mrs. Murtaugh is nodding knowingly, and Ponytail Guy is looking over his shoulder at his pal and smiling. The reporters are shifting around and Stern hears one of them rushing to the door. Without looking back, he guesses it is Carla Mora, from the Kindle County *Law Bulletin*, who has gotten good copy out of the Neucrisses for decades.

"Now, calling your attention, Dr. McVie, to December 5, 2018, when you testified before the grand jury here in Kindle County, do you recall telling those grand jurors, 'I knew nothing about g-Livia causing sudden deaths until after I spoke to Dr. Pafko on August 7, 2018.' Did you say that?"

Innis has finally wilted. Her eyes are skittery and her mouth is moving like a landed fish's, desperate for breath. Her bright eyes again drop to her lap, and then Innis revolves abruptly toward Sonny.

"Do I have to answer any more questions?" she asks.

Sonny flinches, plainly caught off guard. She stares at Innis for a second and then turns away, threshing the fingers of one hand through her thick hair. The gesture is striking because Stern has seen Sonny do this a hundred times in private, but not once on the bench. After a second, the judge gestures to Moses.

"Mr. Appleton, may I ask: Is Dr. McVie here under subpoena?"

He stands. "Yes, Judge."

"All right," says Sonny. "I'm going to excuse the jury for a second."

While the jury is filing out, Marta arrives at her father's shoulder and quietly takes the file and opens it. "Cute," she murmurs with a still face.

As soon as the jury room door has closed, Sonny addresses Innis. She has sat on the stand, with a vacant look and what she would probably regard as poor posture She is thinking, Stern hopes, using the word of the hour, 'I am fucked.'

"Do you have counsel, Dr. McVie?" the judge asks. "A lawyer to advise you about your testimony?"

"Not at the moment," says Innis.

The judge asks Moses to see Innis's letter agreement with the government. Although the courtroom remains packed, it is silent enough to hear Moses's shoes scuffing on the floor as he approaches the bench. Sonny studies the letter for a moment, then addresses Innis. Thinking back to Sonny's prior question, Stern understands what's on her mind. Because Innis is under subpoena, she is being compelled to answer questions.

"Dr. McVie—without deciding that it's actually possible but assuming it is—are you asking me if you can invoke your Fifth

Amendment privilege against being compelled to be a witness against yourself in order to avoid answering further questions?"

Innis looks up at the judge for a moment.

"I guess," she says. Then she nods with her entire upper body. "Yes."

"All right," says Sonny. "All right. I'm going to discuss this with the lawyers back in my chambers. If you would, Dr. McVie, go across the corridor to the attorney-witness room. The deputy marshal will show you where it is. But please do not talk to anyone about your testimony. Do you understand?"

As a group, they sweep into Sonny's chambers. Her clerk helps the judge remove her robe and she motions the lawyers to the chairs around her conference table.

"Well, you live long enough," she says. "Let's just talk this through a little. No one is committing to anything. I just want to take your temperatures. Moses, am I correct, that Dr. McVie has never had a court-ordered grant of immunity?"

"Yes, Your Honor." Under the law, while the US Attorney's promises can protect witnesses from prosecution, only a formal statutory grant of use immunity is sufficient to overcome an invocation of the Fifth Amendment and force a witness to testify.

"And do you want to give her a grant now in order to complete her testimony?"

Moses's face is still as he deliberates.

"Well, first I'd like to see those text messages Sandy has."

Understanding his position with the judge, Stern says immediately, "I have no text messages. Nor did I ever state that was the case."

A sound of exasperation blows through Moses's lips. Sonny studies Stern, probably replaying in her mind the sequence of events in the courtroom.

"Head fake?" she asks.

Stern nods.

"Good for you," she says. "Well, Moses, I guess you'll need a subpoena to get the body of those texts."

"If the company still has those records," says Feld, who is indignant.

Sonny shrugs. "But either way, are you going to grant Dr. McVie formal immunity?"

Moses slowly shakes his head. "I doubt it." Granting Innis immunity now would greatly complicate a prospective prosecution against her for perjury and make it next to impossible to bring charges for any other offenses she might have committed along the way. No prosecutor would be eager to do that for a witness who broke her deal to tell the truth.

Feld detains them for a few minutes with a suggestion that the testimony Innis has given thus far waives her right to invoke the Fifth Amendment. Minnie, the court reporter, comes in and reads aloud portions of what Innis said on the stand, and Elijah, one of Sonny's clerks, brings in several cases. Neither side disagrees when Sonny concludes that Innis maintains the right to assert the Fifth Amendment in this proceeding, at least with regard to questions about what she knew concerning fatal reactions to g-Livia.

"Okay," the judge says after the legal discussion is concluded. "Then what do we do?"

"I think her testimony should be stricken completely," Stern says.

"No!" Marta has raised both hands. She whispers to her father. Marta has already thought this through far more completely than Stern has. The recording Innis made of Kiril will come into evidence anyway. The forensic guys have already verified its date and time, and someone else—Lep, for instance—can identify the voices. And if Innis's testimony is stricken, the defense will be prohibited from making any reference to her lies in closing argument. On the other hand, if what Innis has said on the stand remains of record, Moses, being his upright self, will never endorse her truthfulness, while the Sterns will be free to ridicule her.

"I withdraw my suggestion," Stern says.

"So you'd stand pat?" Sonny asks.

"We want her to invoke in front of the jury," Marta says. She means assert the Fifth Amendment before the jurors.

Feld opposes that. The jury will take a meaning from that, he argues, that the law doesn't support. While the Supreme Court has said repeatedly that the Fifth Amendment may be properly utilized by anyone who reasonably fears prosecution, whether they are in fact innocent or guilty, jurors are likely to ascribe only one meaning to it if Innis pleads the Fifth before them: She broke the law. Marta argues that the judge can correct that inference with instructions and that Kiril's right to confront the witnesses against him means the jury must see Innis's testimony to the end, however it concludes. Like many of the legal disputes between the prosecution and defense, the issue is quite complicated and Sonny actually dispatches both her clerks to do computer research. After almost an hour has passed, the judge returns to the bench. Innis is summoned to the courtroom and stands in the well of the court, immediately below the judge.

"Dr. McVie, is it still your desire to assert the Fifth Amendment in response to further questions?"

Innis says she'd like to talk to a lawyer, but Sonny refuses to delay the trial for that.

"I'm sorry, Dr. McVie, but you had plenty of time to seek counsel before today."

Innis says, "I'll plead the Fifth then." She's regained her composure and looks stalwart as she answers.

"All right, you will be excused as a witness."

When the jury returns, Sonny says, "Dr. McVie has decided to assert her constitutional right not to answer further questions from either side. So her testimony is concluded and we are done for the day."

In addressing the jurors, Sonny has made it sound as if this happens all the time, but when the fourteen have exited once more, she looks at the lawyers and says again, "Live long enough and you'll see everything."

26. STERN'S NOTES

Kiril is in a rage when court ends.

"I cannot believe it," he repeats. "I cannot believe it." Everything that has befallen him in the last fifteen months traces back to Innis and her tip to the Neucrisses: the *Journal*, the lawsuits, the FDA voiding its approval of g-Livia, and worst of all, Kiril's prosecution. As Stern was frog-marching Innis through the phone bills, he was thinking only a question or two ahead and did not fully tease out the implications Kiril has recognized. The question, which Stern must ponder when he has more time, is whether Innis intended all that or if she found the damage cascading after her spiteful decision to leak the information about the problems with g-Livia to her old friend Pete.

Stern tells Kiril they can talk all this over back at the office, but Kiril doesn't want to return. Stern immediately understands: After having traveled down to the Center City with the phone records, Olga is now warming a bed at the University Club.

"I am sorry, Kiril," Stern says, "but I must see you at the office. You and I have an important discussion to take up in private."

Kiril is clearly taken aback by his lawyer's tone. The two are invariably courtly with one another, but Kiril agrees and says he will drive over. In the meantime, Marta and Pinky join Stern in the Cadillac with Ardent.

As soon as the door closes, Marta hugs her niece with both arms.

"I mean, amazing. Right, Dad? So smart."

"Genius," says Stern. "Truly, Pinky, you completely changed the course of this trial."

Marta asks Pinky how she even thought about the business cell phone.

"So, like, I knew that this morning the prosecutors were going to be putting in the records of Kiril's phone calls from his office, and I said to Janelle when I was out there last night, 'God, think how much better off he'd be if he'd called the broker from his business cell phone.' You know, I'm like everybody else, thinking those records evaporate after a few months. But Janelle knew the detail has to stay online for four years. So it dawned on me, Well, okay, as long as we're getting all these papers for Innis, let's get those records, too. It was just a guess," says Pinky, but she still has her wide smile of uncontained pride.

"I think," says Stern, "that come what may, Kiril will be paying for your tickets to see the Fire-Breathing Cattle."

The car rocks with laughter, even from Ardent in the front seat, who does not know exactly what the joke is.

Back at Stern & Stern, the three of them head off separately. Waiting for Kiril, Stern finds Vondra has left a file on his desk, which proves to be the notes of his interview with Olga last March, which indeed was the same day he was run off the road. He studies the single sheet of yellow foolscap, eventually recalling more of his meeting than the neurologist would have told him was possible.

He goes through some conjectures about what Olga took from his questions, then moves to the window, in the mood for reverie. From here on the thirty-eighth floor of Morgan Towers, the river is slate and, as the sun declines, is decorated like a cake with a raspberry gleam. Over time he's come to comprehend the nuances of the Kindle's many tones. Stern can tell from the density of color if the barometer is dropping, if the cloud cover is likely to lift. That is the value of experience, he supposes, to be able to read the meaning of signs, to know the large impact signaled by small things.

Although he gave the matter no thought until now, his cross-examination of Innis is, in all likelihood, the last he will ever undertake. In order to let Sandy concentrate on his closing argument and, God save them, Kiril's testimony, Marta will handle the one or two government witnesses remaining. Cross is the high art of defense lawyering, the essence of what the Constitution means by granting criminal defendants the right to confront the witnesses against them. Stern's last time at bat will go into the record book as a grand slam; what surer sign of success than forcing a witness to assert her Fifth Amendment right to silence in the midst of her testimony, a first even for him? But what will actually stay with Stern, he knows, is the complete disorientation he felt at first, the ineptitude. He wasn't even swinging and missing; the bat was staying on his shoulder while he tried to figure out what game they were playing. It is a good time—past time—for him to leave the courtroom. Thank God for Pinky, he thinks. That, too, may be a first.

Vondra phones him: Kiril is on his way back. Stern takes a seat behind his desk, like the school principal. This will not be pleasant. He does not come to his feet when Kiril is shown in. Pafko looks jaunty again today, with a more energetic posture. Across the office, Stern can smell that Kiril used the ride over to douse himself from the bottle of aftershave Stern has seen on occasion in his glove compartment. Until now, Stern did not make much from the fact that Pafko was so often intent on freshening up.

"I know you are in a rush, Kiril, so I will get to the point quickly. We must have a word about Olga."

"Olga?" Pafko throws his trench coat—a match for Olga's—over the chair arm and crosses his legs. He is doing his best to appear baffled.

"How is it, Kiril, that Olga knew we were looking for the records related to Innis's severance agreement? Document production is not in her area at the company, is it?"

"Dear me, Sandy. Are you complaining that she took initiative? I thought you'd be thrilled with her."

"Kiril, you are not answering my question. How did she know?"

"Sandy, back at the headquarters, there is constant discussion of what is happening in court. The *Tribune* has an hourly news feed. It is open on most computer screens."

"But the *Tribune* does not report about the documents we are looking at. I have told Janelle several times not to discuss that with anyone but the company's outside counsel. We do not want to give the government grounds to accuse us of influencing witnesses. So how was it that Olga knew what we were looking for?"

Pafko pouches up his mouth but does not answer.

"Kiril, you lied to me about your relationship with Olga."

Pafko's last efforts at a cheerful affect fade. "Ah," he says.

"Ah," repeats Stern. "You sat where you're sitting now only a few days ago and lied to my face."

"Actually, Sandy," he says. Stern interrupts.

"No more artifice, please, Kiril. We have known each other far too long."

"You saw us last evening at the U Club?" Pafko asks.

"Just so," says Stern.

"May I explain?"

"I would rather you think carefully before telling me anything further that proves to be untrue. You know, the denouement of Innis's testimony was a great triumph for your defense, but Moses will rally after a bit and ask the logical question. Granted, Innis knew about the sudden deaths, and probably long before she left the company. But how? Medical research was not her area. Who told her? Who else, Kiril, but you?"

"Really, Sandy—"

"No." Stern is holding up a hand. "I prefer you listen. You may lie to me about Innis. And about Olga. But not when doing so exposes me. Which leads me to my last subject. As we have seen, Pinky's instincts as an investigator are far better than one might think. And right now, she has a theory that you will not share the records from the PT motor pool because you know they will suggest that it was Olga who ran me off the road last March."

"Olga?" Kiril's nutshell face cycles through a variety of expressions, but none of them strike Stern as particularly sincere. "And do you share this thought?"

"I think it may be a bit fancy," says Stern. "But it is a question worth asking. As it happens, I had spent the afternoon back in March, right before leaving PT, with Olga. We found my notes, Kiril. Here they are." He holds up the manila folder. "What secrets does Olga have that she does not want me to know?"

"Well, I have no idea, Sandy."

Stern shakes his head. He is gut-sure that is untrue, even though there is nothing he can put his finger on in the notes of his interview with Olga. At the time, Stern had just learned about Kiril's e-mail to Olga attaching the screenshot of the unaltered dataset, and Stern had gone at her hard, especially when she claimed she didn't even know how to read the attachment. As a notetaker, Stern has never been much in the way of a stenographer, feeling he should concentrate on interaction with the person he's speaking with. By habit, the questions and answers he's recorded are summaries of longer conversational exchanges. His goal is simply to preserve an outline of what was discussed.

'Why Kiril send db you can not read????' the notes say. 'A: can't explain what other people do.

'How in drug industry 20+ years, cannot interpret dataset? A: Not my job.

'Who at PT to confirm you not read db? A: Not sure.

'Who helps read similar data coming a-x your desk? A: Someone in research.

'Who? Lep? He's 3 doors down? A: Wouldn't bother Lep. Barely talk to him.

'Kiril? A: Don't ask CEO to help do my job.

'Who? A: Don't know really. Never even looked at attachment, so can't say.'

It had been a fairly testy exchange. Before leaving Olga's office, Stern had tried to smooth things over, explaining he was merely role-playing with her, to see how she might fare on cross if she was called to the witness stand. But the unpleasant air between them remained. Olga was probably ruffled, thinking that Stern should not have practiced dentistry on the gift horse and instead been grateful she was backing Kiril's story. But looking at the notes before Kiril arrived, trying to determine why the encounter might have alarmed Olga, Stern wondered if she was scared that he was trying to figure out what lesser light Kiril could implicate for the government, in the event Stern persuaded him to plead guilty. Given the federal sentencing guidelines, it is always beneficial to a defendant to hand the government another case, even against someone less culpable. Because Kiril had sent Olga the database, Olga was the leading candidate for Pafko to turn on. It's hard to believe, but perhaps she was panicked enough about that prospect to go after Stern.

"Sandy," says Kiril, "I still don't understand why you've become convinced that what happened to you was not an accident."

"To be frank, Kiril, I am not convinced of that at all. The fact that PT owns six white Malibus may be only a coincidence, and I may have been the random victim of some dangerous maniac. But the fact that you have been lying to me about Olga makes me wonder what else you are hiding in order to protect her or yourself. I am asking you very emphatically to let us see all the records at PT that have anything to do with the fleet of Malibus, including the sign-out records for the last week of March of this year. It is essential to the confidence between the two of us that you allow us to do what is necessary to put our questions to rest."

In Kiril's eyes, the color deepens, the first actual sign of worry.

"If you insist, Sandy."

"I insist."

Kiril nods several times, then stands with his coat.

"Well, this is very confusing," Kiril answers.

"That much we can agree on," says Stern.

His client looks baffled and elderly, but once he arrives at the door Kiril seems invigorated. It is a second before Stern realizes that what has possessed Kiril are thoughts of the University Club.

V. CLOSING

27. THE PROSECUTION RESTS

For the first time since the trial started, Kiril is late to court Thursday. Stern immediately fears that his client's tardiness has something to do with how harshly he spoke to Pafko last night. When Stern woke up this morning, he was full of regret. Yes, as happens too often with criminal clients, he has seen a lot in Kiril he does not admire, but his job is to represent the man, not judge him. And besides, there was a moment in an examining room at Easton med school a few years back that no decent person should ever forget, when Kiril truly resuscitated Stern's spirit.

Pafko arrives just as the judge comes on the bench. Among many thoughts, Stern has harbored the hope Kiril is late because he is bringing Donatella, who has still not returned to the courtroom, but Kiril is by himself. Reflecting, Stern realizes he should be unsurprised.

Before the judge summons the jury, Feld asks to be heard. For the prosecutors it must have been a long, difficult night. Their case did not completely collapse yesterday afternoon. Innis, in essence, was merely a corroborative witness, backing up Lep and Hartung; Kiril's remarks remain on the recording she made. But her lies, previously undetected by the government, are hugely damaging, and the prosecutors probably spent many hours trying to conjure ways to recover. Feld's first request is that the government be allowed to replay portions of the audio recording between Innis and Kiril on August 7, 2018. At the podium, Marta's first response is, "That's ridiculous," and Feld does a better job of defending the idea than Stern expects. His logic is that because Innis is unavailable for redirect, the government ought to be allowed to rehabilitate her by other means.

"Not by repeating evidence the jury has already heard," Sonny answers. "I have no doubt that Mr. Stern would be happy to answer that by rereading the latter portions of Dr. McVie's cross-examination. I won't allow that either. What's next?"

The government also wants to recall their securities law expert to talk about the legal issues when a 10b5-1 plan is terminated due to a tender offer. The prosecutors clearly want to emphasize that their insider trading charges are unharmed by yesterday's events, and thus end their case on the highest note possible. The judge rebuffs that effort, too.

"You were within your rights offering expert testimony about how the securities markets work and the purpose of insider trading laws. Nothing I heard yesterday, however, justifies a repeat performance. That motion, too, is denied."

The one solace the prosecutors get is that over the Sterns' objections, the judge allows Special Agent Khan to testify as a summary witness to review the chronology of events from 2014 through 2018. Khan looks good on the stand—fit and slender, wearing a blue suit and a red tie, the part in his glossy black hair so perfect that it might have been done with surveying instruments. Feld has a number of charts to accompany Khan's testimony, but even so, it lasts no more than twenty minutes. After conferring with her father, Marta stands up, shakes her head, and says, "Nothing," meaning they will not bother with cross. Several of the jurors respond by smiling.

Once Khan is gone, Feld reoffers more than a hundred exhibits, just to be doubly sure they have been received in evidence. Then Moses rises beside Feld, looks first to the judge and then the jury, and says, with great portent, "The United States rests."

"All right, Ladies and Gentlemen," Sonny tells the jury. "You remember, I told you when we started that a trial has several different phases. You have heard the openings from both sides, and now part 2a, as it were, is concluded. The prosecution has completed offering evidence. Next, the defense may offer evidence, although, as I told you when we started, that is entirely up to Dr. Pafko and his attorneys. The Constitution of the United States requires only the prosecution to offer evidence at a criminal trial, and you may make nothing of the fact, if the defense chooses not to do so. Before that, I have some matters to address with the lawyers, so I'll send you home for the weekend and see you on Monday."

The jurors file out. Mrs. Murtaugh, with her crisp gray hairdo, who's been staring at Kiril frequently, is the last in line and again offers the defense table a backward glance before departing. Trying to read the meaning of these gestures is no better than the first guess in a game of charades. Is she stunned to be in the presence of such a genuinely evil person, or does she feel that a great scientist is being persecuted for some trifling mistakes? The Sterns will know only with the verdict—assuming that some of her colleagues don't change her mind before then. She seems far too agreeable to be a holdout.

"All right," says Sonny. "I am prepared to hear any motions."

The defense renews all of its objections to exhibits and testimony, then Marta launches herself into the defense's motions for a directed verdict, asking Sonny to declare that the government has not presented enough evidence to support any count of the indictment. Overall, this is the part of a trial that Stern basically hates, and he is glad Marta has agreed to handle it, even for their last time. This stage is little more than a bear trap for defense lawyers, who must venture every conceivable argument out of fear that if they don't, the appellate court will say the point was waived by not first presenting it to the trial judge.

Furthermore, the legal standards and institutional practice essentially prevent the defendants from winning now, even when they deserve to. The judge, under the law, may not substitute her judgment of the evidence for the jury's. Instead, Sonny is required to consider the proof "in the light most favorable to the prosecution." That means that even discredited testimony, like Innis's, must be treated as entirely true. Nor does it matter that the evidence about Kiril's stock sale would be more convincing if Ms. Turchynov, the broker, had testified; at this stage, the brokerage house records are sufficient to prove the transactions. The legal verbiage describing the standard is naturally quite dressed up, but what it truly says, reduced to the basics, is that at this point the judge must let the jury decide the case, unless only crazy people could find the defendant guilty.

Like all trial lawyers, Stern has mixed feelings about juries. On one hand, Stern venerates their role as fundamental to liberty. Yet back in the jury room, they will sometimes construct a reality that bears little resemblance to what they've heard. As a lawyer you are trying a case according to century-old rules, and they retire and decide they are playing SimCity or another game his grandchildren liked, where the universe constructed bears only occasional resemblance to our own.

Because of that, it is important, in Stern's view, that the trial judge think hard about whether the various factual questions presented are ones a jury really, under the law, ought to decide. To Stern, the murder charges are ludicrous. Having tried dozens of murder cases in the last half century, he knows in his bones that the state legislature never passed that law with any intention to see it applied to the CEO of a drug manufacturer who sent a basically good product to market. But at this stage, every trial judge wants to 'leave it to the jury.' The chance that Sonny will toss out that part of the indictment is virtually nil. In a case that has received so much public attention she would be even more reluctant to intervene. Then there is the fact that her dear friend is across the courtroom at the prosecution table; it would be a huge embarrassment to Moses if she told the world that he didn't even make out a case on his headline charges.

But those kinds of extraneous calculations pave the road to injustice. Once the jurors render their verdict, respect for their service—they will, by the end, have given up nearly a month of their lives as conscripts in a land of enigmas and arcane practice—means the judges of the appellate court will be equally reluctant to disturb it. Thus, if convicted, Kiril Pafko will die in prison for a crime that, under the law, he never should have been charged with in the first place.

And so it goes. The justice done in courtrooms is, in Stern's view, only rough and approximate. Sitting through the evidence, even as Marta and he have dismantled it piece by piece, Stern's visceral reluctance to accept Kiril's guilt has been greatly reduced. Yes, his old friend in all likelihood did something seriously wrong. But not so bad as to warrant a lonely death in a federal cell.

Inspired by a similar perception, Marta does a spirited job of attacking the indictment, particularly the murder charges. Sonny listens to her with a look of deep attention. Once Feld has answered somewhat bloodlessly with a perfunctory recitation of the law, Sonny says, "I want to reflect on my ruling overnight. I'm going to have the clerk make some changes to my Friday motion call. Come back at noon tomorrow, and then we can decide how we'll go forward."

The last remark all but says she will not be dismissing the whole case, but even Stern knows that would not be called for.

After court recesses, Kiril asks for a moment across the hall in the attorney-witness room, and Stern realizes how bereft Kiril must feel at the moment. His son has accused him. Donatella is absent. And Sandy, his friend and advocate, called him out badly after court yesterday. Stern feels as he did this morning. Whatever Pafko is—liar, philanderer, fake, a long unflattering list—Stern must remain on his side, first as his lawyer, but also as the grateful beneficiary of Kiril's talents. As soon as the door closes, Stern grabs Pafko by both arms, his hands on his biceps.

"I apologize for my tone when we met at the office yesterday, Kiril. Weariness is taking a toll." He means that. When he gets home each night, it seems that he is even more exhausted than the evening before, so tired that it sometimes feels like his bones may give way. In those moments, he has adopted a mantra: Just get to the end. Those unhelpful little spurts he feels from his heart now and then are increasingly frequent, although he knows they will calm down when he gets time to rest.

Kiril, much taller, nods several times. His face seems to have been loosened by uncertainty.

"What you said about Olga and the car—it was bewildering." Kiril, too, now appears very old; the thought required to find words is protracted and his speech somewhat labored. His eyes, with their yellowish whites, are unmoving while he finds his way. "But you were correct."

"About what?" asks Stern.

"There is something peculiar. With the Malibus. I stopped at PT this morning, on my way to court. I asked Janelle to find the records you have been talking about—the sign-outs from the fleet for the last week in March this year. I thought I would bring them to you, since they seemed to matter so much."

"Thank you."

Kiril nods several times, as if acknowledging Stern's gratitude, but there is still a lapse before he speaks.

"They are gone," Kiril says.

"Gone?"

"I had Janelle bring me the books. They're three-ring binders, Sandy. I don't know how it operates precisely, because before they suspended me, Janelle would get a car for me when I wanted one, if the Maserati was going to the shop or we needed another car for some reason at home. Apparently, Oscar, the security manager in the parking lot, keeps the binder out there. But the forms are gone for that period. Janelle and I looked at it together."

"Removed?"

"I assume. I thought I'd best tell you before doing anything further."

"Yes. Let us take it from here."

Stern now recognizes what is new in Kiril's aspect. It is a look Stern has seen often from many other clients at this point: He is finally and appropriately frightened. All the emotions Kiril has been denying have flooded into his eyes. He is near tears, beaten and uncertain and overwhelmed by the utter misery of being prosecuted.

"I cannot lose you at this stage, Sandy," Pafko says, sounding frankly plaintive. Stern understands. Kiril is afraid that the information he just shared will drive Stern even further from him. And it has already occurred to Stern that he must question Janelle closely, to see if Kiril was alone with those books before the discovery that the sign-out forms have gone missing. Even now, Stern is unwilling to dismiss the possibility that Kiril is covering for Olga, which might also be a reason for him to appear so distraught.

Yet it does not matter. Like a knight or a soldier, he swore allegiance to an ideal: the client, no matter what.

"You shall not lose me, Kiril. That I can promise." He grips Kiril's arm again. "I promise," he repeats.

Back at the office, Marta and Sandy resume the discussion they've had too many times before: What kind of evidence can they offer in defense?

"You know that's why Sonny wants us in court tomorrow. She

wants to know what to expect from the defense, so she can adjust her schedule."

Father and daughter again go through their options. They have hired two experts, both revered professors, one to address the FDA regulations, the other the insider trading laws. It's hard to imagine any expert being more effective than Marta has been in making hash of the clinical-trial regulations. On insider trading, they are better off offering their best defense in closing argument, rather than giving Feld a chance to reduce it to a threadbare fabric as he would by picking it apart during his cross-examination of an expert.

"Does Kiril still want to testify?" Marta asks.

Stern makes one of his expressions of futility—hands, brows, shoulders. Marta, like her father, knows that the defendants in fraud cases, generally speaking, are the hardest clients to convince to stay off the stand. A little like compulsive gamblers who can't resist another bet, no matter what the odds, fraud defendants always want to try to sell their story to someone else.

Stern, unlike most defense lawyers, prefers to see his clients testify, even if they will get bruised on cross. If the person seems likable and has an explanation for the crime that approaches the realm of reason, it's often worth doing. About 70 percent of acquittals come when the defendant testifies. On the other hand, when the accused 'gets up,' the saying is that there is no other witness in the case. It all comes down to whether he can be believed. Juries see the issue as binary. If they deem the defendant credible enough to raise a doubt, he will go free. If they don't, they will convict him, no matter what they thought about the prosecution case before he got on the stand.

Marta repeats what they both already know. "Under the guidelines, any chance he has of getting a kiss at sentencing—revered Nobel Prize winner, all that crap—Sonny will have to disregard. If he gets convicted after testifying, he'll have very little chance of leaving prison alive."

"If they convict him of murder, Marta, the result will be the same."

If there were some reason to think that Kiril wouldn't look like a hopeless liar on the stand, it might be worth the chance, with the goal of neutralizing the murder charges. But Stern is skeptical that Kiril's old-world schmaltz will play well with the group in the box. It will be lie after lie exposed on cross-examination—not knowing about the database on his computer, never calling Wendy Hoh, not remembering the conversations Lep testified to. And as a topper, the prosecution might well be allowed to bring out decades of falsehoods to Donatella about his affairs, which Sonny might deem fair game now that Kiril has put his credibility directly in issue. For that reason, Kateb, or other witnesses with similar things to say, could also be called by the prosecutors.

Like a man with a toothache who regards the extraction as the only thing worse than his current pain, Stern vows they will decide all this tomorrow after the judge's ruling. He goes down with Ardent to the Cadillac. As soon as they are out of the garage, he reaches into his pocket for his cell phone. Donatella recognizes his voice.

"Sandy, to what do I owe the pleasure?"

"I am calling, Donatella, to be sure, first of all, that you and I remain friends."

"Yes, of course, Sandy." She lowers her voice, even in the privacy of her own house. "What Kiril has done to this family is no fault of yours."

"So you are not staying away from court because you are put out with me?" His question is an effort at diplomacy. With Kiril marching around in public with Olga again, Stern has a clearer understanding why Donatella has stopped attending the trial. Whatever arrangements govern the Pafkos' marriage, Kiril has stepped over the boundaries and she feels no further need to support him.

"Certainly not."

"Then, Donatella, I must beseech you, please, to return." He explains to her, just as he has to Kiril, that the jurors might infer from her absence that she was taken aback by something she heard in the evidence. Donatella says nothing, although he can hear her husky breath in the phone.

"Truly, Donatella, I ask if not for Kiril's sake, then mine. This is my last case. I know you have seen the effort I have made. Please do not undermine that. We need you in court."

Even the entreaty in his own behalf is received again in silence. Yet that is not the principal business of this call. Stern pauses to ponder before going on to his next subject. He still has not really had time to fully process Kiril's news that the sign-out records have gone missing for the Malibus. Tonight, when Pinky comes home from the office, he will discuss next steps with her. But his granddaughter is clearly on quite a run and deserves, yet again, to be congratulated. It remains possible, of course, that the documents are simply misfiled somewhere, but even Kiril did not appear to believe that. After eight months of caution and denial, Stern's internal scales have shifted decidedly toward the unsettling conclusion that he was purposely run off the road. In six decades, he has learned a great deal about crime, the whys of it and the means of detection. But in every case, his calculations have been cold-blooded and detached. He is not surprised to discover that the anger—and fear—that go along with being the victim make rational deliberation a much more labored enterprise. Nonetheless, there is an alternative hypothesis for what happened he feels obliged to pursue.

"Donatella, this is too complicated to explain briefly, but may I ask: In the last year was it ever the case that you had to come out to PT to drive the Cadillac home after Kiril recovered the Maserati from the shop?"

On the other end, there is a different silence, more complete, as Donatella absorbs a question that must seem entirely random.

"That's happened, Sandy."

"Any way to recall when?"

"I doubt it. I can look at my personal calendar. I may have made a note."

"Check March 24, if you would, please."

She promises to look later and to get back in touch.

After Stern hangs up, he watches the dark city passing by the car window as they approach US 843. It is the way Olga strode into the courtroom yesterday that fortifies his suspicions. Olga understood, probably before anyone else, what the implications were of Innis's phone records. And she delivered them personally, and preened in advance, because she wanted Innis to see not only that Olga had a role in her downfall but the pure pleasure Olga took in seeing her rival completely vanquished. The sheer merciless power of Olga's ambition is part of what had seized the attention of the hundreds of people.

Stern will not say he fully believes even a little bit of what he is turning over. So far, they don't even know for certain that Olga had checked out one of the Malibus the day he was struck. Nor will they ever—that was the purpose of destroying the records. But if in fact Olga went tearing out of the PT lot late on the afternoon of March 24, Stern maintains a visceral unwillingness to believe she was actually after him, since he still cannot make out any obvious motive for that. On the other hand, the Cadillac Kiril and Donatella drive occasionally is close enough in appearance to Stern's old car to allow for a mistake, especially from someone in a state of high anxiety as they embarked on mayhem. Driving at ninety, there would not be much time to check details. But the Olga who powered into the courtroom would have had a more logical target than Sandy. She was finally going to remove the last obstacle between Kiril and her.

28. OSCAR

At a little after eight a.m. on Friday, Ardent drives Pinky and Stern into the parking lot at PT. Oscar is at the little flat-topped steel hut between the incoming and outgoing lanes, which is his principal workspace, and lifts the striped bar to admit them.

Oscar is a beefy guy, somewhere in his fifties with a full head of jet hair. He is wearing a puffy blue winter jacket that has a fake fur collar and the PT logo over the heart. As soon as Stern sees Oscar, he recollects him. Before the accident in March, when Stern was still driving himself out here, Oscar picked up Stern in his golf cart on a couple of occasions, as Stern was limping toward the front door from the handicapped spots. He is a vet, a good-natured guy who joked with Stern about also being a 'gimp.' From Oscar's gait, Stern's guess is that Oscar has a prosthetic leg.

It is a gray brisk day in the Tri-Cities area, too cold to keep the door to the hut open, but it is a tight fit for three people. Despite that, Oscar is an accommodating host and serves coffee from a pot breathing fog on the rear window. Oscar's desk is actually a shelf on the front wall. He offers Stern his seat, a bar stool with a back, which Sandy declines at first until Pinky insists her grandfather sit down. A little space heater with a fan chugs on and off intermittently behind them.

"So this about the logbooks?" asks Oscar.

"More or less," Stern answers.

Oscar nods. The main need for security at PT is not because of street crime but rather fear of industrial espionage. Oscar and his junior colleague are under orders to be wary of strangers and regularly drive through the lot in their golf carts, which now, as winter approaches, are fully enclosed with a plastic window and a canvas top.

Stern asks for a rundown of what happened with the book yesterday, which is not a long story. Janelle came out at 8:00 a.m. yesterday and asked for the binder for March. She opened it in front of Oscar and found that the sign-outs for the last week of the month weren't there, so they looked at April, thinking the papers were misfiled. Ultimately, they paged through every month of the year looking for the missing forms.

"Do you believe the forms were deliberately removed?" asks Stern.

"Gotta be," says Oscar. "I mean, you don't need to be Bernie Madoff to figure out how to grab them. The binders are just sitting out here and Bill and I, we're driving around the parking lot half the time. Wouldn't take thirty seconds to find what you're looking for and throw them in your pocket. I'm not asking why somebody would do that neither. Around here," says Oscar, rotating his head emphatically, "there's always stuff I'd rather not know."

With Stern's prompting, Oscar reminds them how the fleet program started, which was basically as a recruiting tool. Young scientists in particular are very sensitive about climate change, and at Lep's suggestion, Kiril and Innis wanted to create jobs for which a car wouldn't be needed. The PT facility is right across the street from a light rail stop, and the company buys a monthly pass for every employee who wants one. The fleet was meant to meet the occasional need to drive somewhere. But all of this started before ride sharing. Lep has already told Oscar that when the Malibus age out, the company will just pay for Uber or Lyft.

The system for checking out cars is straightforward. Oscar has a list of authorized users, who must first provide him with copies of their driver's licenses and insurance cards. Anyone who anticipates needing a car calls down twenty-four hours in advance and Oscar assigns a car by filling out a form. Last-minute requests are met, if there are still fleet cars available. Either way, the user signs for the vehicle right here. It's a simple form, a two-ply document that creates a yellow duplicate on the underleaf. The yellow copy is retained in a manila file on Oscar's desk until the car is returned. After that, the forms for the month are kept in a white three-ring binder on the desk, in case of any issues.

"And after the month?" asks Stern. "Do you file them?"

"Right," says Oscar. "In my very fancy file cabinet." He kicks a cardboard box on the floor. "End of the year, Innis said trash the lot of them. If you'd showed up to ask in January, there wouldn't have been nothing."

"Could it be that no one signed out a car in the last week of March? That would explain why there are no forms."

"First of all, it doesn't happen that a week goes by and nobody takes a car. Second, that week? That week was spring vacation." For the sake of athletic schedules, the Tri-Cities and suburban schools are on the same calendar. "Certain times—Christmas vacation, spring vacation, Easter, the summer, weekends—every vehicle is gone. Folks here, some of them, they think we got this fleet, so they don't need to rent a second car. Relatives in town, kid home from college, teenagers with no school—they sign out a car and forget to return it for a week or two."

"Who did that?" asked Stern.

Oscar rolls his eyes and shakes his head minutely. Rather not say.

"All of them at one point or another," he says. "Everybody in the C-suite, everybody who's a senior VP."

"Did Olga Fernandez ever do that?"

Oscar shoots an index finger at Stern. "You asked, okay? I didn't bring up her name. But Olga—you know, Olga?"

"I do," says Stern.

"Well, okay, so you know Olga, then you know she's kind of an operator. I mean, she's got sales calls, big meetings, running back and forth to the airport. I'm not saying she don't need a car. But you know, Jesus, once she's got it, good luck getting it back. Especially after her middle daughter got her license. Finally, I told her, I said, 'Listen, miss, don't let's have your kid taking driver's ed in my vehicle. She needs to scrape up a fender cause she's learning, let it be your Beemer.'"

"How did she respond to that?"

"Olga? She laughed. She thinks it's funny when you're onto her bullshit. But I mean, what am I gonna do? I'm not gonna go complain to Kiril about her." Oscar's eyes slant up for a second, to see if Stern gets his meaning. "Or Lep for that matter. His head's in the clouds."

"And did she ever bring a car back with serious damage?"

"Neh, neh. Couple scratches. Nothing major. Don't get me wrong. Olga, she wasn't the only one. The worst, for sure. But everybody who uses those cars regular holds on to them now and then. When Innis was here, she ran a tight ship. But once she was gone, a lot of people started in asking, What's the point of having six cars sit here all weekend? Fair enough. But you know, instead of rotating or something, the top folks just grab them."

"Kiril?"

"Whenever he had that car in the shop. Until they suspended him. Then the lawyers said no fringes for him."

"So Kiril never took a car after he was indicted?"

"Never."

"Who else were the big users?"

"Two groups, really. Mostly it was marketing people, the ones who work for Olga. Tammy Olivo and Bruce Wiskiewicz, who sell the Midwest. Each of them got a car a week at a time. I had a car reserved for Lep a lot, because half the time he works so late the train isn't running. Tanakawa, the associate medical director, he ran into town for meetings at the U or Easton med school. There were a couple of others."

"And all of those people held on to cars now and then?"

"Definitely. But in the last year and a half, since g-Livia is off the market, forty percent of the staff got RIF'd. I'm not gonna get worked up about this, because there hasn't been five times someone called for a car and I didn't have one."

Stern places his hand on Oscar's sleeve, so the man faces him.

"And Oscar, my friend," says Stern, "truly you have no idea who removed those forms?"

"Hand to God," answers Oscar, and lifts his arm.

In the car, heading back to Center City in the heavy morning traffic, Stern briefly takes his granddaughter's hand.

"Credit where credit is due, Pinky," he says. "Your instincts as an investigator are first-rate."

She beams again. An entire family, he thinks, and not one of them ever figured out that the best way to deal with Pinky is to compliment her. Of course, she's always done her best not to deserve it—the familiar perversity of humans.

"Should I call Detective Swanson?" she asks.

"Not until the trial is over. I do not want to trouble the waters further or ask Kiril to consent until then. But I expect the police will quickly reach a dead end. The sign-out records could have been destroyed by virtually anyone who works at PT."

"What if the cops find the body shop where Olga took the car?"

"Anyone trying to conceal a crime would be clever enough to pay with cash, and probably to use an assumed name—and not to bring the Malibu to a body shop anywhere near where the collision occurred. If this was a front-page crime or I'd actually died, the police might subpoena local parts suppliers to see which of them sold the paint or a Malibu fender that week, but that is a huge undertaking for a county police force and one with a very uncertain return."

"So Olga gets away with this?"

"I grant you, Pinky, that Olga deserves to be the prime suspect, but let's continue to hold an open mind. The pieces still do not fit together completely. Yes, she might have mistaken my car for the Pafkos' and tried to visit her rage on one of them." Olga's potential targets might even have included Kiril, with whom she remained deeply aggrieved over not leaving his wife. More likely, given that Kiril and she seem to have never really ended their relationship, Olga was after Donatella—even perhaps with Kiril's consent. The last thought is the kind of damaging speculation about a client that Stern, even now, prefers to keep to himself.

"But why would Olga suddenly have been moved to act on March 24?" Stern asks his granddaughter. "As you have pointed out, the only new element was that I interviewed Olga that day. That would suggest I was the intended victim, but I find nothing in my interview notes that convinces me she would have been eager to get me out of the way."

"You're not telling me again that you think it was just a coincidence that a white Malibu ran you off the road, are you, Pops?"

"No, Pinky, I have moved to your side on this. Oscar, who knows best, seems convinced that the sign-out records were destroyed intentionally, and that clearly indicates a bad actor with something to hide. But even assuming I was not struck by accident, we have not convincingly identified the culprit. Kiril has become such a complete mystery to me," Stern admits, relaxing his own rules, "that I still have moments when I have the reluctant thought he had a hand in this, although I can make absolutely no sense of that. And we cannot forget the possibility that the driver was someone else entirely whose motives we know nothing about as yet."

"Like who?"

"That is the point. We do not know, dear Pinky, and probably never will."

She sulks. The inability of humans to deal with ambiguity and uncertainty is always striking to Stern. We have an intuitive reluctance to accept the unknown. That is why there were sun worshippers and creation myths, to find some explanation for the otherwise inexplicable. But after another moment, these ruminations lead him suddenly to lift a hand in Pinky's direction.

"Pinky, you have just given me a critical thought for my closing argument." His closing is lurking in his mind right now at all moments. It has always been this way. As a trial nears its end, everything that happens in life is tested to see if it might add an element to his argument.

Pinky, for her part, is beaming again.

29. THE JUDGE RULES

When Stern and Marta enter the chief judge's double-size courtroom on Friday at noon, there is a lull. The morning session of Sonny's Friday call is over, and most of the journalists who have covered the trial won't bother attending a session when they know from experience that the outcome is preordained. To make time for her ruling, Sonny moved back a few matters, and two of the attorneys on a case, who did not get word about the delay, are haggling with the chief judge's docket clerk, Luis, so they can come in another day, rather than wait.

Looking around the grand courtroom for one of his last times as a lawyer, Stern is struck to realize that he now considers the solemn federal courthouse his home as an attorney. Admittedly, it is a more ideal place to practice law than the state courts where Stern started out. The judges have more time to consider briefs and write rulings. Here, unlike the state courts fifty years ago, it has always been a rarity for lawyers to engage in fistfights in the halls. The clerks and marshals are genial and, in proud contradistinction to their colleagues in the county courthouse of old, incorruptible. But Stern has never completely left behind the feeling that he is an intruder. He won his place of prominence across town in the Kindle County Superior Court, watching his back, avoiding the questionable dealings in the corridors whenever possible, proving over time that skill and smarts could prevail, even in that brass-knuckles arena. That remains the site when he dreams of being in court.

As Sonny comes on the bench, something about her strikes Stern as different. For one thing, he realizes after a second that she had her hair cut last night; the gray curtain now stops above her shoulders. More to the point, she enters every day with a stack of papers, usually orders she has to review cursorily and sign as chief judge. But today she is carrying a single law book, something that, in the day of computer research, is almost as much of an anachronism as a crank telephone. Even in Stern's office, the beautiful little law library where he drafted and redrafted hundreds of briefs over the decades is gone. The gold-spined volumes holding the reports of various decisions by courts around the country were all sold to an interior decorator, and the space was sublet to Gilbert Diaz, a former assistant US Attorney and a good young lawyer, who shunned the big law firms to open a shop of his own. The sight of the law book makes Stern feel like a guilty schoolboy, frightened with no real reason that Sonny, still affronted, will hold him in contempt for mentioning his own cancer to the jury.

Given her lengthy schedule of other matters, Sonny wastes no time. She calls the Pafko case herself, causing Minnie, the court reporter, to scurry back to her steno machine and computer at the foot of the bench. The judge also greets by name each of the lawyers who have come forward to the podium, so they do not go through the standard formality of identifying themselves for the record. Sonny notes the presence of Kiril, seated in his blazer at the defense table. Pafko knows what to expect and his mood is somewhat glum, although that may be because Donatella, unexpectedly, has arrived separately. Again, she has placed herself on the prosecution's side of the room. Stern is grateful that she has responded to his pleas, and he faults himself at once for not reminding her last night that the jury will not be present today.

"I want to turn to the motion to dismiss at the close of the government's case which Ms. and Mr. Stern have brought," Sonny says. As she starts to speak, she wears an air of grim resolve. The judge perfunctorily recites the lenient legal standard she is required to use at this stage of the proceedings to decide the adequacy of the government's evidence.

"Applying that standard, I have had no difficulty concluding that all counts of the indictment may go to the jury for their decision."

Stern feels his heart pinch, while Feld smiles and glances back to the agents and paralegals behind him at the prosecution table. Losing, even when you know it's coming, is always painful. As Mel Tooley, a somewhat oily defense lawyer now in the waning days of his career, once said to Stern, 'Let's face it, Sandy. You're never really ready to get kicked in the balls.'

Sonny works backward through the charges, starting with the insider trading and then the fraud counts, taking up murder last. She tosses aside the Sterns' arguments as she goes with an alacrity Stern finds dismaying.

While she speaks, Sonny's dark eyes are flicking up and down to papers on the bench that must have been folded in her law book. She has taken the trouble to write out her ruling and is reading it, which means she wants to be precise with her words, preparing for the matter to reach the Circuit Court of Appeals. Since the prosecution has no right to appeal after a jury has been seated, because of double jeopardy, that means the Sterns are going to lose on murder, too. That will be a real wrong, in Stern's view, but as is sometimes said, perfect justice is delivered only at the gates of heaven. He hears himself sigh.

"As we all know, the murder statute states, in relevant part, 'A person who kills an individual without lawful justification commits first degree murder if, in performing the acts which cause the death, he knows that such acts create a strong probability of death or great bodily harm to the individual or another.' I would note for the record that I began my career on the bench in the Kindle County Superior Court, where I presided over a number of murder trials, and I have found my familiarity with this statute helpful as I have considered the arguments of the parties." This observation is really intended for the appellate court. She is reminding those judges that, unlike many on the federal bench—including most of the appeals judges—who are inexperienced with state criminal statutes, for Sonny Klonsky it is not opening night.

"We all also know that the prosecution of the CEO of a pharmaceutical manufacturer under this law is unprecedented, but that means nothing in itself. But because the facts are unique, prior decisions are not directly on point, as I shall explain in a moment. Nevertheless, there can be no quarreling with the plain fact that seven people named in the indictment took g-Livia and, viewing the evidence in the light most favorable to the government, died as a result. Those deaths are terrible and tragic, and there is no legal weight to be offered to the occasional suggestions in cross-examination that those persons had a grave illness which would have killed them eventually anyway.

"But were they murdered? The government sees this as a simple case. Kiril Pafko acted to make g-Livia available for public use. Those acts were without lawful justification, because, they maintain, the FDA marketing approval had been secured by fraud when Dr. Pafko concealed a dozen sudden deaths that had occurred during the clinical trial. Knowing of those deaths, Dr. Pafko recognized a strong probability that some fraction of those who received g-Livia would also die as a reaction to the medication.

"According to Dr. Pafko and his lawyers, the acts alleged do not amount to murder as a matter of law, for several reasons. The most significant argument to the Court is the defense claim that by the statutory definition, murder is a crime about intending to kill or harm 'an individual.'" Her fingers draw the quotation marks in the air, as they have at other moments when she has used the precise words of the law. "Rather, the defense says that the evidence is unequivocal that Dr. Pafko never recognized a 'strong probability' that he would hurt any given person.

"While we could have done very well without the personal testimonial from Mr. Stern"—she smiles bitterly and raises her dark eyes to Stern to let him know he hasn't been fully forgiven—"the overwhelming evidence—indeed the undisputed evidence—is that for most persons with stage two non–small-cell lung cancer, g-Livia is a superior medication. From Dr. Pafko's perspective, therefore, according to the defense, the strong probability in any individual case was that g-Livia would aid that patient, not hurt them.

"The prosecution attempts to meet this by pointing out that the great bodily harm intended under the murder statute can focus on that individual 'or another.'" Again she marks the air. "Dr. Pafko, they reason, knew that even if any particular patient was far more likely to be helped than harmed, over thousands of cases, he knew well that *another* patient would die.

"The government is correct that the state's murder statute reaches to situations when another person is killed, rather than the intended victim. In *State v. Castro* and countless similar cases, a defendant was convicted of murder because he shot a gun at a rival gang member and instead killed a five-year-old girl in a passing vehicle. But Castro clearly intended to do great bodily harm to some person. Similarly, in *State v. Grainger*, the case the prosecution regards as controlling here, the defendant left a bowl of candy outside her house on Halloween, knowing that a few pieces had been laced with cyanide. Grainger did not know precisely who she would harm. But she knew there was a strong probability of great bodily harm to any child unlucky enough to get the poison.

"Accordingly, the government, under the words of the statute and the cases explaining it, can only prevail if they offered sufficient evidence that Dr. Pafko had a harmful intent regarding some individual. Dr. Pafko, if the government's evidence were believed, as it must be at this stage, knew that he was subjecting some patients to a risk of a deadly response. But the 'strong probabilities' "—again, she marks in the air—"in any individual case were that the patient was going to be better off with g-Livia than they would have been with any other available therapy. No rational juror could conclude that when he acted, he did so understanding and intending great bodily harm or death to any particular individual."

Shielded by the podium, Stern, with his eye still on the judge, nudges his hand from his side to grab Marta's fingers. It sounds like they have won. Yet caution tells him a 'but' must be coming, given the care Sonny has shown in explaining her ruling for the appellate court.

Then suddenly he understands. She is talking to the public, to the *Wall Street Journal* readers who have gotten daily summaries of this case, to the many laypeople out there who will feel that another rich guy has, literally, gotten away with murder. She has written her decision down, because she is going to publish this opinion, as judges should when they are dealing with an unprecedented case, for the benefit of lawyers and judges who must cope with comparable situations in future.

"So that will be the ruling of the court. Specifications 1 through 7 of the racketeering count, the murder charges, are hereby dismissed with prejudice from Count 1, which otherwise may stand. We must now turn our attention to what happens next."

The courtroom is utterly still. Even the lawyers here on other matters realize this is a moment of great consequence in an important case. Beside Stern, Moses and Feld are statue-still. They are not even bothering to confer. Across his shoulder Stern looks back to the prosecution table, where everyone is staring at the judge, as if they are awaiting another word that will erase what she has just said. Stern turns further and very quickly offers Kiril a wink.

Finally, Feld lifts a hand. "With great respect, Your Honor, isn't the issue you just articulated—what Dr. Pafko intended in any individual case—isn't that question for the jury, not the court, to decide?"

"Mr. Feld, I thought a good deal about that point. If there were any evidence that Dr. Pafko intended to hurt any one person who took g-Livia, I might agree. But there is none. I am not absolving Dr. Pafko. He sits here correctly charged with serious felonies that expose him to the risk of serious punishment. But on murder, there is a complete failure of proof."

Feld tries other arguments. The defense should have brought this motion before trial, before the jury was seated, when the government still had a right of appeal, but Sonny tosses her head in disagreement even while he is speaking.

"The government, too, could have brought a motion in limine before trial, Mr. Feld. More important, neither your motion nor the defense's would have been timely. This question could only be decided after hearing the evidence."

Moses still has not moved, at least not that Stern has seen. The US Attorney's recognition of the consequences must be slowly gathering. The next question is whether the prejudice to Kiril from the unwarranted murder charges is so great that the case cannot go on. That is where Sonny wants to direct the discussion now. She asks Marta and Stern if they have additional motions.

Stern, who has been clutching the podium for support, eases forward.

"Your Honor knows that we have maintained from the start that the prosecution has dramatically overcharged this case. The jury has been told that Kiril Pafko is a murderer, and we know now there was no evidentiary basis to do so. My impression, at first blush, is not only that a mistrial is warranted, but that the indictment in a circumstance like this, where the prosecution has unlawfully injected such enormous prejudice into the proceedings, my belief is that the entire indictment must be dismissed. But in candor, Your Honor, before proceeding with that motion, I would like to have cases to present to the court."

"I would love to see those cases, Mr. Stern. So why don't you send me a brief written motion, describing any decisions you think I should consider, by the end of the day on Saturday. The prosecutors can answer by six p.m. on Sunday—nine p.m. on Sunday." Sonny corrects herself, clearly remembering that Moses will spend most of the day in church. "And we can all gather Monday morning to discuss where we will go next. I will have the marshal tell the jurors that they need not be here Monday morning. The case will stand adjourned."

The Sterns return to Kiril at the prosecution table, whose face swims with uncertainty. Pafko asks, "I am not a murderer?"

"Not now. Not ever," Stern says. He is reaching up to grab Kiril's shoulder in triumph and reassurance, but somehow, as Stern speaks, his mind turns to all that remains unknown about the car that struck him on the highway, and his hand stops midair.

30. MISTRIAL

A victory of such consequence in a largely empty courtroom feels incongruous to Stern. The few reporters who were here have shot to the door to tweet the news. Stern tells Kiril—and Donatella, who has approached them—that they must meet immediately in the office to determine their next moves.

As soon as Marta and Stern are together in the back seat of the Cadillac, she turns a puckish grin on her father.

"I can't wait to read all those cases you're going to cite where indictments have been dismissed in situations just like this."

She is making fun of her father's hyperbole with the judge. Cases have been dismissed, but only when there is outright misbehavior by prosecutors. Moses and Feld may have been too aggressive, but Stern has never seen Moses act in bad faith and can't say he did so toward Kiril.

"But we *do* get a mistrial, right?" says Marta. "Sonny was basically saying that."

Stern read the judge's signals the same way. Moses made murder the centerpiece of his case and now has lost his bet. It's hard to imagine how this jury can arrive at a fair decision, after hearing Kiril called a murderer and seeing all those weeping loved ones on the stand. Sonny will grant a mistrial, which means this trial will be scrubbed. A new trial will start from scratch at some point in the future.

This is what the Sterns explain to Kiril and Donatella as they sit together at the end of the table in Stern & Stern's conference room. The associates who have treated this space as their office are back at their firm today, drafting proposed jury instructions. Vondra brings in lunch—salads and sandwiches—as Marta and Stern detail the law and the strategic considerations.

"This case ends without a verdict," Stern says about the prospective mistrial. "The jurors will be dismissed. And the prosecutors must then decide whether they will try you again."

"They will," says Kiril. He has always understood how Moses feels about him. And Stern agrees, as does Marta.

"So, what is the advantage?" Kiril asks. A white glob of mayonnaise hangs at the corner of his mouth. Donatella, with an audible sigh, signals to him with her napkin.

"Well, to start," Stern answers, "no one will be suggesting you are a murderer. In fact, I expect the judge will preclude any evidence that patients actually died as a result of g-Livia. Understand: The prosecutors likely may show there were such reports from Global and in the newspapers. But in the next trial, the government probably will not be allowed to go beyond that. And in the end the judge will tell the jurors not to consider whether it is true or not that there were patient fatalities." This was the original dilemma that impelled Moses to bring the murder charges.

"Besides that," Stern says, "we will gain several practical advantages. We will have a transcript of each witness's prior testimony. They will change their answers now and then, because frankly, Kiril, that is what human beings do. They rarely remember events exactly the same way. But some will end up sounding like liars as a result. For the government it will be a weaker case, for that reason and because the charges do not hold the same emotional impact.

Now it will be about failing to heed the rules of government bureaucrats, not primitive evil. And the jury will know there was a prior trial, at which you were not convicted for some reason.

"Finally, there is also a psychological burden to the US Attorney in again trying a case he did not win. Trial lawyers are a little like racehorses who never run as fast once they aren't first across the finish line."

Marta adds, "We'll lose some things. Without the murder charges, we won't get as much latitude in proving how effective g-Livia is. But Sandy is right, I think. It will be a weaker case for the prosecutors. Much as it will give Moses angina, he'll probably opt to grant Anahit immunity to lock down the proof of the stock sale, but that means the jury will know she got away with the same crime he wants them to punish you for. And, of course"—Marta smiles a trifle—"we won't see Innis. She'll probably be negotiating a plea agreement of her own."

"She will go to prison?" Dontalla clearly has heard about what she missed and undoubtedly rues that, given the way her eyes dance at the thought of Innis behind bars.

"Possibly," Marta says.

"While we are on the subject," says Stern, "I suspect, Kiril, that we could negotiate a very favorable plea agreement for you."

"How favorable? No prison?"

"Very little. Perhaps only home confinement. Certainly no more than six months in the federal jail down the block. Probably less."

Stern looks to Marta for confirmation. She nods.

"No," says Kiril. "I did nothing for which I should plead guilty."

The Sterns and Donatella are struck silent in the face of a statement that the weeks of trial have proved to be so dubious. Kiril adds, "Pleading guilty is even worse than being convicted by a jury. That I can call unwarranted."

Pride. Honor. Appearances. Stern has heard it before. But it never makes sense.

"And may I also ask, Sandy," says Donatella, "this new trial, when does it take place?"

"Six months? Inside a year."

With the answer, her eyes spark again, almost in the same way as when she thought of Innis imprisoned.

"And will Marta and you be beside me?" asks Kiril.

Stern was waiting for Kiril to get to that. He takes a breath before answering.

"No, Kiril. If I am honest with myself, I know this case has been far beyond my physical resources. I am like an old mule that just wants to make it back to the barn. I have promised Marta and myself that this will be my last trial. And so it shall be. I have been enormously honored to represent you, but there are wonderful lawyers here and around the country. We will make certain you have outstanding counsel. The change, by the way, may well delay the retrial even longer, if that is what you prefer."

Although Stern has not thought of it until this moment, ending his career by beating the murder charges and wrestling the government to a draw on the rest—that is a decent achievement on which to conclude. Any time a defense lawyer keeps their client out of prison, they have every right to take a victory lap.

Kiril is watching and thinking. He is more focused than he has been in weeks.

"Sandy, my dear friend, it is not at all clear to me that we will be better off next time. If we go on with this case, how does the judge explain the sudden disappearance of the murder charges?"

"She will say those charges no longer should concern the jury, and that they may not consider any evidence offered to support them. But who, Kiril, could banish from their minds all those weeping relatives?"

"So she will be telling them in effect that the prosecutors are liars?"

"One never knows for certain what a jury makes of this kind of situation. Most likely, they will assume something went wrong for the government."

"Isn't it better then to have this case decided by a jury that knows the prosecutors failed in all their pious denunciations of me as a killer?"

In the end this is a question of art. Some defense lawyers, who have a strong gut sense of the calculations within the jury box, might conclude that Kiril will never be dealt a better hand, that this jury will be more favorable than the next one. But Stern's abiding view is that criminal defense is practiced with short time horizons. What can I do today to keep my client free? No one has a crystal ball. A year from now, Kiril may not even be here.

"As we see it, Kiril, that is too much of a risk. It might work out as you hope. Or they may regard the fact that the other charges remain as the judge essentially recommending conviction on those counts. You can never predict how a group of laypeople will think about these things."

Kiril nods, thinks again, then says, "I think it is better to go on."

Donatella cannot contain her exasperation.

"Oh, Kiril!" she cries, and turns to the Sterns. "For nearly forty years he has acted as if the Nobel Prize citation said, 'From now on, you may believe whatever suits you.'" She makes a little exasperated click and closes her eyes. Her husband clearly has heard this observation before.

"Do you have a point?" he asks.

"Very much so. You are actually going to choose your view over that of your lawyers?"

"Why not? I am the client. That is my right." He turns for support to Marta and Stern, but Donatella will not be silenced.

"Your right? Sandy, is there not a saying about someone who tries to be his own lawyer?"

Stern chooses not to answer.

"I am a fool?" Kiril asks her. They are clearly touching the nerve of the persistent pain within their marriage. This is not the first time Donatella has insulted her husband nor that he has reacted with indignation.

Donatella, predictably, answers with considerable spite.

"Yes, you are a fool. And of a unique kind. Because at any moment, Kiril, you can convince yourself that you are living in the world you want, a place that is more convenient for you, or more fun." Innis, too, spoke of Kiril's tendency to dwell within his fantasies. Here, then, is the answer to how a man proudly accepts the Nobel Prize for research he stole, or sends a drug to market without admonishing its users of potentially deadly side effects. "You sold the *nietos*' stock because in that moment you were stupidly convinced that it was not a crime, if the sale did not benefit you personally. Even though you had been told a hundred times not to sell any shares without speaking to the lawyers. That is how much you know about the law."

"I was acting in haste. I had very little time," he tells his wife.

In Kiril's consultations with Stern, he has repeatedly told Stern that he does not remember calling the broker. It is never shocking when it turns out that a client has lied. It is a way of life. But as this little piece of the truth leaks into the room, Stern assays the consequences. This now is the ten thousandth reason that Kiril should not testify.

Stern says, "If you are really determined to proceed, Kiril, then we must decide what kind of case we will offer. Marta can correct me, but I suspect she will agree that we should simply rest."

"Rest?"

"Offer no evidence. Tell the jury that the prosecutors have not proved their case. Period. If you really want to take advantage of the court's ruling, this gives you the best chance. We cannot refer directly to the dismissed charges, but we can ask the jury if the government fulfilled the promises they made in their opening statement and imply they are not to be taken at their word."

"But I want to testify, Sandy. I want to tell my side. I did not do what the government charges. I had nothing to do with altering the dataset."

"Kiril, you do not have anything to offer the jury to explain all the evidence they have heard. Wendy Hoh said she spoke to a man. Shall we say it was Lep?"

"Not Lep," says Donatella.

Stern raises a cautioning finger.

"I am merely making a point. As I have explained before, blaming Lep is ludicrous. Starting with the fact that he was on a plane."

"Yes, of course that makes no sense." Kiril shoots a sideward glance at Donatella, then sits studying the table, as his frustration rises. "But Sandy, am I obliged to account for how something happened I know nothing about?"

"Kiril, if you know nothing about the crime, then you have nothing to tell the jury. If you are on the stand, they will expect you to explain."

Kiril sits, his face dark as he steeps in doubt and disappointment. Stern continues.

"And frankly, my friend, we have had very little to say all along in response to the insider trading charges. But there is less today after listening to Donatella and you. Shall we tell the jury you misunderstood the law, when it had been explained to you in detail a dozen times? And you a Nobel Prize winner to boot? How do you think it will sound to this jury of ordinary people when you tell them you believed it was honest and moral to put your grandchildren's millions ahead of the fortunes of your other shareholders, some of whom had trusted you with their retirement savings or college funds? You have a scant chance on these counts as it is, Kiril. Testify to that and your prospects sink to absolute zero."

Kiril appears for a second to literally chew on the bitter taste of everything Stern is saying. He slaps the table in frustration, looking near to tears.

"I want to proceed. I cannot live with this hanging over me any longer. I cannot."

"I understand, Kiril, that you are in purgatory. I know from a lifetime of this work how horrible it is when a person who has led a good life finds himself accused of a crime. But allow us to tell you: Anxiety or ostracism, whatever you are suffering now, is not worse than sitting in a prison cell for years."

Even while he offers this assessment, Stern wonders how much Olga is contributing to Kiril's urgency about getting the trial behind him. The state of war between the Pafkos, even though it may be long-standing, is now in the open, and Kiril's evenings at the University Club are almost certainly the reason. Even assuming that Kiril never really gave up Olga, he had decided to say so, perhaps to have some peace at home while dealing with the investigation and trial. Yet for whatever reason, he has now thrown caution aside. Perhaps Olga is pressuring him again to leave Donatella?

Marta takes a turn. "Accept the mistrial, Kiril. Leave the courtroom in victory, even if it is only temporary."

Pafko shakes his head no but does not speak. Instead, Stern tells him to take twenty-four hours to think it over, since they do not owe the judge an answer until tomorrow night. Perhaps someone—Donatella, or even Olga—will talk sense to him in the interval.

"I do not expect to change my mind, Sandy." Kiril stands and, still struggling to maintain his composure, leaves the conference room. "I am going," he says with no further parting word to his wife, who remains at the table with both Sterns. In his wake, they are all silent, sharing an instant of mutual bemusement with Kiril.

Marta, who needs to call the associates to get them started on the legal research about their potential motions, kisses Donatella and leaves.

"I was pleased to see you in court this morning, Donatella,"

Stern says to her, "although I am sorry I did not warn you it was not a day for the jury. But as it turned out, you chose a propitious time. I hope Kiril reconsiders your advice."

"No chance of that," she answers, her eyes downcast. "And I was not in court principally for Kiril's sake. I wanted to speak to you."

"Speak to me?"

Donatella wears a heavy necklace of obsidian today, and it frames her face much like the white collars of the guild members Rembrandt painted. Stern can see that the trial has cast a weight of weariness on Donatella as well. Despite her thick makeup, what he formerly saw as wrinkles are now more like deep grooves in each cheek.

"You asked a question yesterday about March 24."

"Of course." In the drama of today's events, all of that had slipped his mind.

"May I know the reason?" asks Donatella. That is why she wanted to see him in person, to put him on the spot. Since Stern's question concerns her directly, she is understandably wary.

"We are tying up loose ends, Donatella, just trying to rule out the very fanciful possibility that the wreck I had on the highway might have had some connection to this case."

"And how could that be?" For a person as smart as Donatella, failing to understand is a rare event. "If Kiril's car were in the shop, what is the implication?"

It would be ridiculous to share his suspicions about Olga, not only defamatory in legal terms but also unfair in human ones when Stern himself has no better than a hunch that she mistook Donatella's car for his. Under the circumstances, with Kiril cavorting with the young woman, Donatella would be likely to run straight to the police.

"I am sorry to be mysterious, Donatella, but I should say no more."

"Well." She opens her purse and withdraws a leather-bound

book. Stern realizes it is her calendar. "Neither Kiril nor I were anywhere near PT that day—or that week, for that matter. That was school vacation. Usually, we fly somewhere with all the grandchildren. Disney World when they were younger. These days, to the islands. But, of course, Kiril was on bail, so we could not leave the state. We had a vacation in-town, all of us. We took several rooms at a hotel and did something different with them every day and each evening. Cirque du Soleil. Museums. We had just come out of a matinee at the symphony when Kiril got a message that you were in intensive care. We were both devastated. I mean it."

"Ah," he says.

She offers him the calendar for his inspection, but he touches her hand and guides it back into her large purse.

She prepares to call a ride service to get home, and Stern instead summons Ardent to take her. Sandy helps Donatella with her coat and sees her to the elevator.

She considers him a moment longer. Donatella, he can see, is suffering.

"There really is no dignity in being elderly, Sandy, is there?" she asks. That, he suspects, is much more a comment on her life at the moment than his. Donatella sways her head with an air of deep sadness, then kisses Stern on each cheek and steps into the waiting elevator with Ardent.

31. FINAL MOTIONS

On Saturday, largely to stall, the Sterns file a motion to dismiss the indictment, which the government answers within hours. On Monday morning, when the lawyers are again assembled before the judge, Sonny talks respectfully about the decisions the Sterns cited, but says the situations are not the same and refuses to dismiss the indictment.

"Mr. Stern, do you have any other motions at this stage?"

Clearly, Sonny now expects Sandy to request a mistrial. Kiril has given them permission to make the motion, but only in the most minimal way. If they do not offer even a bare-bones request, then under the law Kiril will have waived many legal points, essentially giving up any reasonable chance on appeal, if he doesn't win his long-shot bet with this jury.

"Defendant Pafko requests a mistrial," Stern says.

Sonny nods. "Please proceed with your argument."

Stern answers, "Defendant will stand on his motion."

There have been moments during this trial when he has seen on Sonny's face an expression that has not been directed at him in almost thirty years. They started out as fierce rivals in a case in which Stern's brother-in-law, Silvia's first husband, was the target of a commodities fraud investigation. Sonny was at the end of her tether for many reasons, pregnant by a man she no longer wanted to be married to, working for a demanding and somewhat underhanded boss in the US Attorney's Office. She flared often in the course of her dealings with Stern, especially at the start, and on sight regarded him with a narrow-eyed look, awaiting his next trick. And that is what he sees now. She knows instantly that Sandy is trying to have it both ways—to proceed to verdict with this jury and then, if that goes wrong, to argue on appeal that Kiril was unfairly prejudiced when she denied his mistrial motion. Judges never like being middled in that manner.

"Any response, Mr. Appleton?"

Feld answers. "A mistrial is not warranted, Your Honor. Even without the murder charges, the prosecution was entitled to prove that g-Livia caused actual deaths."

"No, it wasn't," the judge answers tartly. "In proving fraud, you cannot go beyond what the defendant knew. Dr. Pafko was never confronted with direct evidence of any death. As to him, it was all hearsay. The reports of deaths required investigation, and as such they support your charges. But the weeping victims, the involved testimony about survival rates, let alone allegations of the most serious crime known to our law—none of that was in order in this case. The jury never should have heard it."

She is arguing the defendant's motion for them. Stern's heart rises in hope that she will declare a mistrial anyway.

After her expression of pique, Sonny plunges her mouth onto her palm and drums the fingers of the other hand on the desk blotter on the bench, while she tries to think.

"And if I deny your motion, Mr. Stern, what will the defense offer?"

"We shall rest, Your Honor."

His candor does a bit to calm her.

"The defendant will waive his right under the Fifth Amendment to testify?"

"He shall."

She has the full picture now.

"And your client is fully advised, including about the fact that you are making no argument in support of your mistrial motion?"

"He is."

"All right," she says. "All right. Given the fact that the defense refuses to offer any argument in support of its mistrial motion, I will deny it, since it is clear the defense has made a strategic choice to go to verdict with this jury, as is its right." Understandably, she is sticking it back to Stern as hard as she can.

She then calls Kiril to the podium and goes through the elaborate procedure required these days in federal court to waive his right to give testimony on his own behalf. Once that is done, she asks both sides to get her their proposed instructions to the jury and sets a hearing on them for 3:00 p.m. this afternoon, which Marta will attend. The defense will formally rest in front of the jury in the morning, and closing arguments in the case will follow.

"I will tell the jury that I expect to give them the case for deliberation after lunch tomorrow."

Following Descartes, who supposedly did his deepest thinking in bed, Stern has long composed most of his closing arguments here, a tray with food and several yellow pads beside him. He writes down little. Instead, he reasons through arguments, then phrases, uttering the same words again and again in his mind, and occasionally mumbling a few aloud to test the tone. Even at this age, he is confident he will retain it all in memory.

Perhaps because he is lying down during the day, or more likely because he breaks his own rules and occasionally feeds the little dog a scrap or two, Gomer leaps up on the bed and keeps him company throughout. It helps Stern to feel the heat of the dog's body beneath his hand, the dense fur, Gomer's breath and heartbeat.

Yet bed is a good idea in this case for more reasons than habit.

He meant what he told Kiril. This case has exhausted him, taken him far beyond his capacities. For the last couple of days, the racing of his tachycardia, like a small bird trapped in his chest, has been more frequent. He vows, not fully believing himself, that he will call Al, his internist, as soon as the jury is instructed.

What he has to say about the case comes easily. A good closing has always been in preparation every minute of a trial, and because he feels secure about that, he gives his body what it most needs and dozes. He wakes after night has fallen, to find it is not so much Kiril's past but rather his own that preoccupies him. His short-term memory remains good, but after living so long, there are moments when he wonders if his recollection is a work of fiction. He is no longer positive that Peter was a sleepwalker, that the scene in his mind of the boy in his pajamas, fully immersed in the bathtub except for his eyes and nose, did not come from a movie. And was Clara truly as stony and elusive as he sometimes remembers? He had never thought of himself as unhappily married, but now, in his waning days, he does not recall a waterfall of happy times. Yes, the birth of the children: absolute exultation. And the power and purity of his love for her at the start of their relationship was real. But her openness with him in the early days was what made him feel they had achieved something special. As time went on and her unhappiness became more deeply engraved and more complex, as adult life repeated rather than repaired everything that troubled her, she had become more closed off, more difficult. And in her subtle but unrelenting way, she let him know he was much of the problem.

Although he had never thought about it before Kiril first walked into his office, he now suspects that what drew Clara and Donatella together in friendship was not simply appreciation of symphonic music but the bond of women with impossible husbands—impossible in different ways, but neither genuinely committed to his spouse's happiness. They did not say much on that score, he suspected. Both women were too dignified. But even imagining the nods, the glances, the snorts of disapproval, is lacerating. Was he really the same kind of selfish buffoon as Kiril? And without a Nobel Prize in compensation.

He has never told himself he was without grave deficiencies as Clara's partner. He was in his office with his cigars, his books, his phone, his clients, from seven in the morning until nine or ten at night. When he returned, the children had been fed and bathed and put to bed. Clara waited with a book on her lap in the living room, something classical on the hi-fi at low volume, the aroma of his warming dinner in the air: an image of order, resourcefulness, self-sufficiency. She was like some Swedish minister, a character from a Bergman film, enduring existential torment in silence and low light.

Now, when his life stands in relief, as observed by the backward-looking eye, the trauma of Clara's suicide looms like a skyscraper. He has been trying to crawl out from the shadow of mystification and guilt for decades. They did their best, he supposes. She could not subdue her depression and he, given the turmoil and uncertainties of his youth, could only be a slave to his anxiety. But a part of him rebels. He did his best; but isn't that what everyone always claims? Was it really true, or only an excuse for having lived as he had wanted to? And her as well. Clara had killed herself at the beginning of the Prozac era but had refused all advice to take the medication. She did not want to be parted from her elemental self.

And would the Sandy Stern of today—the husband Helen had—have been attentive and empathetic enough to make Clara less desperate? Was it the darkest, the ugliest, the most unsettling truth that he simply did not care to make the effort, that at some level he understood he could live a happier life without her? And Clara's death had freed him. His children suffered. But with Helen he had found contentment. No, Moses could not bring murder charges against Stern. Yet he had sensed for years that Clara was standing on the cliff's edge. He did not push her, or even shout 'Boo!' But he had let her face the storm alone.

These were the kinds of truths that approached the unbearable, like performing torturous physical therapy on his heart. Here, at least, he bested Kiril, who could never for a minute bear the anguish of these kinds of questions. But he did not really know which of them was better off as a result.

Everything ends, of course. Life ends and thus all beforehand. Stern stands looking at his naked self in the mirror after his morning shower, confronting in the most meaningful way yet the approaching reality: By the end of the day, he will be a former trial lawyer. So much of his life's energy has been spent in actual courtrooms or the courtroom of the mind, where he would play out the next day's possible developments as an intricate mental experiment, that he cannot even gauge the precise effect of leaving this work behind. Although he would risk sounding like a lout, the fact, he knows, is that there will be moments when losing this career will be harder even than losing Helen. He loved Helen, and each day was far fuller with her. But her death reminded him of the existence of his fundamental being. Indeed, it is that something—soul, fragment, spirit—that remains most enigmatic, the subjective, ineradicable piece of him that seems to have always been here, unaltered since he was five or fifteen, the invisible space where he is who he has always been. He can imagine his grandchildren and great-grandchildren frolicking through life without his presence: graduating, marrying, suffering their own disappointments and even deaths; he can see the ice caps melting and Miami awash. But confronting the thought that this basic piece of his universe will be gone—that is somehow unimaginable. Not to say he can't accept it. For there is always this truth: He must.

Stern is in the office early, readying himself, sorting out the exhibits he will display to the jury and that Pinky will project as slides.

With that done, he takes up his familiar pose at the window to appreciate the rising colors of morning and thinks suddenly about his career. Was it really worth it? But he has no doubt. Some speak of the nobility of the law. Stern has not always found that to be true. Too much of the grubby bone shop, the odor of the abattoir, emanates from every criminal courtroom. It is at heart a very nasty business to accuse, to judge, to punish. But the law, at least, seeks to govern misfortune, to ensure that a society's wrath is not visited at random. In human affairs, reason will never fully triumph; but there is no better cause to champion.

At 8:30, he heads to the reception area to meet Marta.

"So, Mrs. Aquaro," Stern says, addressing her as she has been known in her private life, at places like her children's school, and as she will now be called far more often. "You are done now. How do you feel?"

"I know it's killing you, Dad, to stop, but I have to tell you, I'm not going to miss this. The idea that somebody's freedom depends on how I perform? I never had the same zest for it as you. Or the same gifts."

"Untrue," he says. "You are—were—a very fine lawyer."

"I agree with that. But I was never Sandy Stern."

"Lucky for you," he says. "But we had an outstanding partnership."

"I agree with that, too."

She hugs her father. They hold on to one another for a moment.

Knowing it is the finale, the entire office staff is lined up to see them off. He passes between these loyal friends, feeling like Marta and he are passing under the raised swords of fellow officers. He thanks every person for their help, the hours they have given him and Marta and their clients. At the door, he turns, touches his heart, bows. Then he offers Marta his arm.

"Let us go forth one more time," he says, "to slay the zombies."

32. CLOSING

Ladies and Gentlemen of the jury," says Mr. Alejandro Stern. With both hands on the knob of his walking stick, he has come to his feet, a little like a boater poling out of the mud. He is in the same outfit he wore for his opening—blue suit, white shirt, a red-and-blue rep tie, which was a gift from Clara when he argued his first case after leaving her father's law office. Whatever the fashions, he has worn it for every argument he has given since then.

"I am an old, old man. Alas, you may have noticed." They smile, all of them. A good sign. "I have spent much of my life in courtrooms or thinking about being there. Not all of those places have the architectural grandeur of this one"—he raises his arthritic hand toward the ceiling coffers and the glorious chandeliers—"but they are all beautiful places in spirit, because they are where we as a community come together to try to do justice—all of us, lawyers and laypeople, the judge, the court staff, you as jurors, all of us united in the same all-important enterprise. 'All important,' I say, because truly, there can be no society, no civilization, without a reliable and accurate system of telling wrong from right, a system that punishes those who are a danger and frees those who have been unfairly accused.

"Please forgive me if I seem to lecture you. You are my last jury.

It is inevitable that it will be your faces I see in whatever time I have left, when I think about my career in court. So I hope you excuse me if, in talking about the case against Kiril Pafko, I share a few lessons learned over a lifetime."

He gives them a long look, stirred himself by the way the river of time has carried him forward to this moment.

"I admit that not every client I have stood beside is Kiril Pafko, with a lifelong record of aiding humanity. You can understand, I suspect, why I tell you how proud and honored I am to be here speaking for him, why I am so pleased to be able to tell you that the charges against Dr. Pafko are unwarranted and entirely unproven, and to be doing that in the culminating act of my career.

"But even when I have represented clients whose record in life is not as glorious as Kiril's, I have been glad to do this work. In my own mind, what I have done for more than half a century is defend liberty. She, the figure of Liberty, has truly been my other client in every case. In *every* case, I have defended the right of each American to remain free unless and until the state has met the mighty burden of proving them guilty beyond a reasonable doubt. We do not live in a country, unlike many others, where people get locked up on mere suspicion. Or simply because they have displeased the powers that be. We live in a country that cherishes every single person's freedom and takes as a central belief that, as we have all heard said, it is better that a hundred guilty people go free than one innocent person be convicted. That is why the burden of proof on the state is so, so heavy.

"It is a horrible thing to be convicted of a crime. For a person like Kiril Pafko, it is the end, in every sense. An end to a long life as an honored individual. To his medical career, of course. The end. You know that. You do not need me to go through the details of what might follow. But please accept my thanks, Kiril's thanks, for approaching your duty here with a sense of the utter gravity of your deliberations and your conclusions.

"This system in which you today play a central part, our jury system, goes back more than eight centuries. In the Magna Carta, the Great Charter, the British king made a promise that our government still follows today, a vow that in a matter so serious—a matter where liberty, where a person's very existence will be changed forever—in such cases, the decision whether a defendant deserves to face the court's punishment—that decision belongs in the hands not of other government officials, or even a group of lawyers, or even an extraordinarily able judge, like Judge Klonsky"—he faces her and delivers his characteristic little cutaway bow, which she answers with a minute nod—"not any of them. No, the decision belongs in the hands of Kiril Pafko's peers, the people who live and work and worship beside him, in the same neighborhoods and streets. What an amazing concept that is. Think about it, please. Yes, we elect our leaders. But no decision our government makes, not how to spend the national budget, not how to deal with foreign countries, not how to levy our taxes or pay out social security, none of those decisions are entrusted to the people, even though a little common sense would probably help in all of those arenas." He smiles, they smile.

"This decision alone, guilty or not guilty, to punish or not, is laid before so-called ordinary folks—because, in the end, you are not ordinary at all. You, as good citizens, as good people, know *every* bit as much about right and wrong as prosecutors or defense lawyers or judges. And therefore you alone, the jury—not the judge, not the prosecutor, not the defense lawyers—you alone, as the voice and conscience of our community, will render the verdict in this case. There will be no critics to review or contradict your decision. The verdict you will return is right and just, for one simple reason: because you all say it is.

"This life I have lived has taught me immense respect for juries. Kiril Pafko has won the Nobel Prize in Medicine—The. Nobel. Prize. He is a genius, frankly. But he knows, I know, that the twelve of you who will deliberate, you together are even smarter than he is. Yes, there are remarkably complex government regulations at the heart of this case, mysteries of science like what causes and cures cancer, and of course complicated issues of law. But you together will figure out whatever can be known and said about this matter.

"Yet you must approach that task with a willingness to speak what I, as an old man, can tell you are the hardest words in life to utter: 'I do not know.'" He touches Pinky's shoulder as he passes her. "When we say that—'I do not know'—we are apt to feel like it means we are unintelligent. Or uneducated. Those words—'I do not know'—might even mean that we are confessing for a moment that life does not make sense. But you must go into that jury room gripped with the courage to speak those words if you determine they are appropriate.

"For that is what a not guilty verdict means. It means, in plain terms, We do not know, not for sure. 'Not guilty' does not mean innocent, not necessarily. It means something a bit different. If you say 'not guilty,' you are saying, as a group, We have thought hard about these charges and this evidence, and we do not know for sure. That is the wrong answer if you were back in school taking an exam. But not in the jury room. Do not feel you have failed because you come to that conclusion. In fact, it is your solemn obligation to say those words if they are true. You must convict *only* if you are convinced beyond a reasonable doubt. But if doubt remains—and frankly it must in this case—if you find reason to doubt, then it is your duty to come back here, stand before us all, and say, in substance, We do not know for sure. You have together sworn an oath to God or to whatever else you hold sacred to render a true verdict, and if, in the end, that is your conclusion—We do not know for sure—then the oath you have taken means you must say the words 'Not guilty.'

"Now in this case, there are *some* certainties. Data was altered.

That has been proven. Stocks were sold. Proven. But we do not know for sure how those events occurred." He stops for a second to brace himself on the defense table. With all the adrenaline, it feels like there is a hamster on a wheel inside his chest. He can see the look of concern on Marta's face, and after a second, he winks at her. He will make it.

"In the summation he gave before I started speaking, young Mr. Feld went through the elements of each crime the government has charged, the particular facts that the prosecutors must prove beyond a reasonable doubt, and how, in his view, the evidence fits the law. I am sure that over the course of this trial, you have been impressed by his intelligence, but as you would expect by now, he has not emphasized the points that are more troublesome for the prosecution. And that is fine, because that is my job, not his.

"I will start with the obvious. The government in several counts alleges that Kiril Pafko committed fraud. The different counts name different victims—the Food and Drug Administration, the Medicare system, the patients treated with g-Livia who, supposedly, received a mislabeled medication—but it is the same fundamental charge: fraud—and I will address it as such, as one crime that the government has given several different names. And I tell you to start that the evidence has not shown that the FDA or anyone else was fooled or tricked at all.

"The officials from the FDA who testified before you—they are not bad people. They are good people who are trying to protect us all. Kiril and I know that. But they are bureaucrats. They make rules. And like a parent or a prosecutor, a bureaucrat wants the rules to be obeyed. They are angry when the rules aren't followed. And they act in anger.

"g-Livia is a remarkable medication. From witness after witness you heard the evidence about the lives g-Livia saves." He dares, very subtly, to touch his chest. "At times, I have wondered if the only great wrong proven in this case is that the FDA's actions have driven g-Livia from the marketplace, with thousands of lives shortened as a result."

For the first time, Feld objects. "Your Honor, there is no evidence of that."

Sonny looks at Feld, longer than Stern might expect.

"Well," she says, "I'll sustain the objection, but only on grounds of relevance. The FDA and its decisions are not on trial here, whatever the evidence might be."

Her phrasing is clearly a subtle nod to the defense. Stern continues.

"Now, you will forgive me for being frank, but Mr. Feld glossed over a very very important point. He said—" Stern moves slowly back to the defense table for his yellow pad and turns a page. "Mr. Feld said, 'Of course, if the FDA had seen the true data from this clinical trial, approval of g-Livia would never have gone forward as it did.' To which I answer, Really?

"'Of course' is not evidence. Mr. Feld's view of what government officials could or would or should have done—that is not evidence. Evidence is *only* what has been presented to you in this courtroom. And what evidence did you hear? Think, please, about Marta's very skillful cross-examination of Dr. Robb. Forgive, if you will, a father's pride, but remember what Dr. Robb admitted to Marta: Given everything we know today, she, Dr. Robb, would hesitate to express her original opinion that g-Livia has not been shown to be safe—"

"Objection," says Feld. "That is not what Dr. Robb said at all."

"Overrruled," says Sonny. "The jury heard the testimony and can recall it for themselves. Mr. Stern is entitled to argue what he regards as the reasonable inferences and Mr. Appleton will get an opportunity to respond, and it will be up to the jury to sort things out. Proceed, Mr. Stern."

"Thank you, Judge Klonsky," says Stern, and then lifts a finger straight before himself, as if to set the record straight. "I repeat:

What Dr. Robb said indicates that knowing what we know today, even including the allergic deaths—even knowing that, given the longer survival of g-Livia patients, the medication would have been approved for the marketplace. Certainly, the government has not proven the reverse beyond a reasonable doubt, as they must.

"Now, as Judge Klonsky has just mentioned again, while the defense speaks only once at the end of the case, the prosecution speaks twice. Mr. Feld delivered his summation, now I am responding with the closing argument for the defense, and when I finish, Mr. Appleton will be allowed to answer by delivering a so-called rebuttal to my points. I understand that that may not seem fair to you—that the government gets two chances to address you, while we get only one. To be honest, it has never seemed fair to me either." He smiles at himself, knowing he has been a bit of a wise guy, and a number of the jurors join him. If nothing else, they have come to appreciate his sense of humor. "But the law at least has a reason. The government in a criminal trial carries that heavy burden of proving a defendant guilty beyond a reasonable doubt. The defense by contrast must prove nothing. So the law says, in light of the great burden the government must meet, we will let them have the last word.

"I suspect it has been clear to you that Moses and I have been in these positions before, prosecutor and defense lawyer, and thus I am able to predict a bit of what Mr. Appleton will say. As I speak to you now, I will do my very best to answer. But of course, the US Attorney has not given me any previews. So if it happens that he says something you think I did not address, please, when you get back to the jury room, ask yourself, What would Sandy say to that? As I have told you, I have faith in your intelligence. It is greater than mine, and together you will think of the right response.

"To be guilty of the various frauds charged—mail fraud and wire fraud, lying to the FDA or the Medicare system or mislabeling—in all cases the supposed misrepresentations made must be 'material.'

Judge Klonsky will tell you that. Now that is a strange word, 'material.' It is not the kind of word normal people use every day, unless they are talking about making new drapes."

There is a ripple of laughter in the courtroom, coming also from three of the women in the jury box, including, to Stern's surprise, the female CPA.

"But that word has a specific meaning in the law, and that, as Judge Klonsky will tell you, is that the alleged lie had a natural tendency or a capacity to influence the FDA. And the decision as to whether an alleged statement is a material lie—that is your decision, not the government's, and it is a decision you must make beyond a reasonable doubt. So you will be faced with this question: Is it really material beyond a reasonable doubt, does it truly matter that some data was scrambled, when the FDA's official in charge says, Well, looking at it today, knowing everything, assuming normal precautions are taken, I would hesitate to say g-Livia cannot be on the market. Is it a crime beyond a reasonable doubt to make a statement that the test of time shows doesn't matter anyway? That is your decision, of course. But this is the first point when I say to you, Are you really sure? Are you really sure that is a crime?"

He delivers a long, somber look. They hear him, they are listening, thinking. These are the Sterns' 'I don't have a dog' arguments: Kiril tried to fool the FDA, but it didn't matter in the long run. Kiril didn't report the deaths, but the regs requiring those reports are ultimately beside the point, as Robb acknowledged. The fourteen people in the box appear to be giving serious reflection to these questions.

"Now, of course, the government's main evidence on these counts about the altered dataset, about Kiril's supposed false statements, that comes from Dr. Wendy Hoh. Dr. Hoh says she spoke to someone on the phone who said he was 'Kiril Pafko.' She never wrote the name down, but that is what she says now.

"So, for a second, let us assume it actually was Kiril. I am sure after all the difficulty that this changed dataset has made for Kiril Pafko, you might anticipate an attack on Dr. Hoh. You might expect me to emphasize that Dr. Hoh admitted that she lied about what happened in that phone call. She lied when she was first questioned by her employers after the news stories about g-Livia, including questions about the clinical trial, began appearing in the fall of 2018. She told her bosses at Global that she had no idea how the dataset was changed. She lied. She lied, and now she comes here under oath, asking you to believe her. There is an old saying in the law: False in one thing, false in all. With liars, you just do not know what to believe. Dr. Hoh's lies, the lies she admits, mean you have every right to disregard everything that Dr. Hoh said.

"But let's assume you look past that point, that you say, as a group, We saw Wendy Hoh, we understand that she told a lie to save her job, but we won't reject all of her testimony for that reason.

"So allow me to tell you what may have actually happened."

Stern has always taken some pride in the inventions he can perform on the admitted evidence, constructing, as the law calls them, 'hypotheses of innocence.' It can become a beguiling fantasyland of what-ifs. The problem for the defense lawyer, especially when the defendant has not testified, is that the jurors may not tolerate an endless parade of 'it might have beens.' Sooner or later they start thinking, 'Very amusing. Very imaginative. But your client knows what actually happened. And so do you. So stop telling us bedtime stories.' Stern will be telling them a number and will be watching for the moment when their body language tells him they've heard enough.

"You saw who Wendy Hoh was when she testified before you: Eager to please. So excited to be speaking to this Nobel Prize winner—no matter who was actually on the phone. Thrilled to be involved with this remarkably important, lifesaving medication. And delighted also, no doubt, to be involved in a matter likely to make her company millions of dollars in revenue, *if* further testing went on. So we know that for many reasons Wendy Hoh wanted Kiril Pafko to be happy. And despite her lies to her employer, perhaps her story to you is true, that is, in her eagerness to please this person calling himself Kiril Pafko, she did what she thought he asked.

"But what actually was said? Remember how this whole clinical testing procedure works, how long and involved it is, and how prone to error the normal rigmarole makes it." He lifts a hand to Pinky, who illuminates Stern's next slide. "The clinical trial subject, the patient, talks to their doctor and nurses about how they are doing, and the site staff performs tests—blood work, scans. The doctor, the nurses, the staff relay this information to someone else they work with, who keys that information into the database maintained by the CRO. If there is a problem, someone at the CRO, like Wendy Hoh, informs the research supervisors at PT. The research supervisors report to Dr. Lep. And Lep then speaks to his father about whether to inform the outside safety monitors."

With each line of this summary, another line slowly appears on the 'Clinical Trial' chart with an arrow beside it.

→ Patient
→ Doctor/Nurse/Staff
→ Keypunch operator
→ CRO
→ Testing supervisor
→ PT Research Supervisor
→ PT Medical Director
→ PT CEO
→ Monitors???

"It is like the children's game of Telephone, in which a message is passed along a line of boys and girls. Each child repeats to the little boy or girl on the left what she or he has heard from the person on the right." Stern acts this out, turning first one direction with his hand to his ear, then revolving the other way and pretending to speak. "What started as 'The sky is blue' comes out at the other end sounding a little like the government's case: 'I don't know why or who.'"

The quip gets quite a laugh from the jury. Even Sonny, who has always had a wicked sense of humor, fails to stifle an audible chuckle. Moses, God bless him, is shaking his head but laughing, too.

"My point is that the people in this system have good reason to doubt whether what has been reported is what actually occurred. That is why the data that has been recorded must be scrubbed and analyzed before it can be presented to the FDA, because there may be things on paper that are simply strange statistical oddities.

"Judge Klonsky will tell you that good faith is an absolute defense to a charge of fraud, that someone acting sincerely, without an intent to deceive, is not guilty, even if they were stupid or stupidly hopeful. Now remember, please, what many witnesses said: Allergic reactions appearing only in the second year of use of a drug or biologic are virtually unprecedented. It does not happen. Remember what Dr. Kapech said, what Dr. Hoh said, what Dr. Robb said. This kind of sudden problem with a medication that has performed so well for a year is utterly baffling. It does not make any sense. And so any experienced researcher, certainly someone like Kiril—or Lep—their first impression would be that what was recorded by Global was not right. What is that term they like to use? 'Noise in the data.' It was noise, numbers that appear as supposed results but which have no real statistical significance.

"So could someone like Kiril Pafko have thought, looking at the unblinded database, 'This is nonsense, this is noise.' That would be a logical, reasonable, good-faith thought to have as he got on the phone with Wendy Hoh.

"So you have Kiril on one end—*perhaps* Kiril, but let us assume as much right now—Kiril, with well-founded skepticism about these reports of sudden deaths, and on the other end, Wendy Hoh, so, so eager to please this Nobel Prize winner.

"Now, you heard Dr. Hoh speak English. You have heard me speak English, for that matter. You know, from listening to me, that I was not born here. Now and then, I am sure, the way I pronounce words has left you baffled for a second. I do my best.

"Imagine, please, what happens when *two* persons who were not born speaking English are conversing. You know that Kiril Pafko passed his youth in Argentina. You know from listening to her that Dr. Hoh has difficulty with spoken English. Dr. Hoh, of course, speaks English far, far better than I could speak any dialect of Chinese, of which I do not know a word. But she told you that her difficulties with spoken English are one reason she prefers e-mail.

"With respect, could what happened on the phone have been a miscommunication? Could the person on one end, with natural doubts about what gets repeated down the line, unwilling to believe that a biologic would produce sudden deaths only in the second year of treatment, could that person have said something like, 'Are you sure about this data, have you checked with the investigators, could this be a programming error, any chance that patients who withdrew were reported as fatalities?' And could Wendy Hoh have thought her caller was saying that was what happened? A scratchy international connection. Two people conversing in a language neither of them was born speaking, and in which one of them struggles to this day. They are not face-to-face. They get none of the clues we see from one another's expressions.

"Can you say for sure that is *not* what happened? Was that why Wendy Hoh lied at first to her employers? Because she suddenly realized she had corrected something she had not even been asked to correct? Did she tell you what she wants to believe now, with her job at stake? People do that, remember what they wish happened rather than what occurred. But can you be certain that she did not simply misunderstand what Kiril was saying, the questions he was asking? We do not know. We do not know for sure.

"One thing that is beyond doubt, however, is that the way the government viewed all this, what they told you to start—that is not true. Something was very wrong with the way the government conceived of the evidence at the beginning of this case. You know they did not prove what they told you they were going to prove. You know now that their opening statement was dramatically incorrect."

"Objection." It is Moses this time who stands. "Your Honor has asked the lawyers to make no reference to the dismissed evidence."

Stern answers at once.

"Thank you for that reminder, Mr. Appleton. I am well aware that the judge has told the jury to pay no mind to much of the evidence you introduced. But I am speaking about your star witness, Dr. Innis McVie."

Stern looks up at the judge, who is stifling the smallest smile at the way Stern mousetrapped Moses into talking about what she said could not be mentioned.

"Proceed," she says.

"There is clear evidence in this case that one person—and only one person—knew that g-Livia carried a risk of sudden death in its second year of use. One person. Innis McVie."

Feld, clearly agitated, gets up again.

"That's not what she said, Your Honor. A failure to deny is not a confirmation."

Sonny narrows her eyes at Feld.

"Enough, Mr. Feld. You had your turn to talk about the evidence. Mr. Stern is entitled to his without interruptions concerning his interpretation of the testimony."

The judge's look at her former clerk is even sharper than her tone. When Feld sits, Moses places his hand on his arm and whispers to him forcefully. Stern's guess is that from now on, the US

Attorney will make the objections. Stern takes his time watching them, in the hope jurors will notice, too.

"Innis McVie told her friends, the Neucrisses, that there were problems, unexplained deaths in the second year on g-Livia, and the Neucrisses went out and called doctors and lined up patients to sue PT. And then to hide Innis McVie's role, they planted a story in the *Wall Street Journal*, so the world would think it was Gila Hartung's scoop, not Innis McVie leaking information, that led them to their clients.

"Yet you heard directly from Innis McVie—you saw her caught in her deceptions by phone records she thought no longer existed. We do not know the entire story, because Dr. McVie stopped answering questions. But she knew that g-Livia carried the risk of sudden death in the second year of use—because that is exactly what the Neucrisses told Gila Hartung after speaking to Dr. McVie. And Dr. McVie pointedly did not deny that, as she sat before you on that witness stand, even though she had previously raised her hand to God and told the grand jurors"—Stern reads from a transcript page—"'I knew nothing about g-Livia causing sudden deaths until after I spoke to Dr. Pafko on August 7, 2018.' But when she was confronted with her calls and texts to the Neucriss law office, you heard something very different.

"She came here to lie, to convict Kiril Pafko. You saw that. She was willing, even on the witness stand, to alter the statements she had attributed to Kiril, which were fictitious from the start, to make them even more incriminating. Dozens of times before this trial, she had spoken about a conversation that supposedly had taken place in Kiril's office in September 2016, during which she claimed Kiril told her 'the problem was solved.' But that was not good enough. During this trial, it became Kiril saying, 'I did some things to solve the problem.'

"When Mr. Appleton gets up here to speak his final words, listen carefully. See if he tells you that Innis McVie was a truthful witness.

He is an honorable person. I predict now that he will not do that. He will tell you to listen to the recording she made. As if Innis McVie were nothing but a robot with a microphone attached, as if all the lies that are behind that recording, as if all the scheming with the Neucrisses, do not matter. But we know now that she was laying traps for Kiril with every word, so the prosecutors could pounce on any ambiguity.

"The truth that the government wishes desperately not to admit is that they have no case on fraud without her. Due to Innis McVie's lies, they cannot tell you what actually happened at PT in September 2016. Innis and her lies stand for nothing, except—*except*—that the events at Pafko Therapeutics in late 2016 are a black hole in the prosecutor's case. How did Innis know what she did? The prosecutors have not told us. What did Innis, who desperately wanted to leave the company, do when she found out there was a problem with the medication? What course did she set to preserve her path to the exits? How many other lies has she told about Kiril, and when did they start? We can speculate, but the prosecutors, and the evidence they have offered, do not tell us.

"Yet we surely have a fair basis to ask whether Innis's determination to leave Pafko Therapeutics and sell all her stock had something to do with what she—and she alone—had discovered about g-Livia. You have heard during this case about 10b5-1 plans, which are these schedules corporate officers and other insiders, like members of the board of directors, agree to in advance to sell their stock in a company. They must stick to this prearranged schedule for share sales to minimize any questions about insider trading. As you heard from Yan Weill, a new 10b5-1 plan was adopted at PT late in 2016, after the FDA made various public announcements that indicated g-Livia would soon be approved for sale in the US. You will have that written plan back in the jury room with you—here it is on the screen, Defense Exhibit MedInvest-3—and I urge you to pay very close attention to the intentions of two of those insiders. As Yan Weill explained, most of the officers and directors, like Lep, or Yan Weill, or Dr. Tanakawa—a number of officers and directors adopted an orderly schedule to sell some but not all their shares at regular intervals in 2017 and 2018. A prudent course and unremarkable.

"But two people stand out in contrast." The document is on the monitor, and Stern uses a laser pointer Pinky has handed him. "The first is Kiril Pafko. Notice again, please, that Kiril was the only insider who made no plans to sell any of the shares he owned personally during this time frame. Now I hope Mr. Appleton can explain something to you, because it makes no sense to Marta and me. If Kiril Pafko knew he had defrauded the FDA into approving g-Livia, if Kiril realized there was a problem with the medication that was going to appear in its second year of use, why in the world did he not make plans to sell as much of his stock as fast as he could under the law? If you know you are aboard the *Titanic*, you find the life jackets. Yet he made no such provisions.

"Who did? One person. Only one officer. Innis McVie. Wholly unlike Kiril, Innis was determined to sell every share of PT she owned as soon as she could, even though—as Gila Hartung put it in the *Wall Street Journal* article you will have back in the jury room—even though PT was becoming the hottest biotech stock on the market, rising in value like a rocket. Only Innis was determined to sell every share without waiting to see what offers to buy Pafko Therapeutics emerged. Why do that? She said on the stand she just wanted to cut ties with the company as quickly as possible. Was that the reason? Or was it because Innis McVie knew there was a problem with g-Livia that might be discovered at any moment and drag the share values down close to zero? Innis sold out completely—and then tipped off the Neucrisses as soon as she had gotten her money and had nothing left to lose. It is Innis McVie who should be sitting in this chair"—Stern has found his way behind Kiril and has put a hand on his client's shoulder—"charged with fraud and, of course, perjury.

"So much for the many fraud counts."

Stern lets his eyes drift over the jury box, assessing. Two jurors, both men, seem to be shifting in their seats, which he reads as discomfort with what he is contending. They are probably thinking, But how did Innis know about the problems with g-Livia in the first place? Who told her, if not Kiril? Stern cannot answer those questions, for the jurors or even for himself. Yet it is not his job or theirs to solve every riddle, and with luck, they will understand that.

"'All right,' you say, 'Sandy, Mr. Stern, we agree. We do not know for sure what happened on the phone with Wendy Hoh. We cannot see how the FDA was actually defrauded under the law. And surely, we cannot count on anything said by the demonstrated perjurer Innis McVie. You are correct, Sandy,' the group of you say. 'About the fraud charges, we must declare we do not know for sure.

"'But what about the insider trading?' you say. 'That seems a little clearer.'

"No, I tell you. It is not.

"What proof did Mr. Feld offer you that Kiril Pafko actually gave the order to sell these shares? 'Circumstances,' he said. 'The chain of events': Gila Hartung's call to Kiril. The ensuing conversation with Innis McVie, where she told him to sell his stock. A ten-second call that followed to Dr. Pafko's broker, with the unusual name of Anahit Turchynov. And her return call a few minutes later. That is their evidence: two or three lines of the phone records, along with documents showing that the grandchildren's shares were sold an hour or so later that day. That is the beginning and end of the government's proof on these counts. Calling the trade 'an unsolicited order,' as you learned, is meaningless and tells you nothing about who originated the sale. And in fact, we know that an unrelated security, an index fund, was also sold in the Pafkos' personal account the same day, which could just as well have been the subject of those phone calls between Anahit and Kiril's office.

"You do not know more. And you do not know because of the way the government decided to go about proving these charges. Ms. Turchynov, the stockbroker, was not called. For that you cannot blame the defense. Judge Klonsky will instruct you that the defense is under no obligation to produce any evidence—let alone witnesses—and from that you can draw no inferences against the defendant.

"But what about the government? You know, from what you have seen, that the government, with their power to grant immunity from prosecution, the government can force any person to come to the stand and answer questions. Anyone. They can even force a son to testify against his father.

"But they chose not to utilize that immense power to allow you to hear from Anahit Turchynov. Why? That is Mr. Appleton's business, frankly. And goes beyond the evidence you have heard. But having made that choice, the government must live with the consequences. And in this case, the consequence is that you simply do not know for sure what happened.

"What the evidence shows you, from these order tickets that the government introduced"—Pinky now brings them up on the screen—"is that Anahit Turchynov was selling PT shares—her own, those of other customers—she was selling them *before* she entered Kiril Pafko's orders. Look at these time stamps." Stern again directs the pointer.

"If Anahit's first indication that there was a problem with PT stock came from Kiril Pafko's call, then why were Kiril's shares not sold first? Or did she have another way of knowing, another source of information?

"Remember that for some reason Gila Hartung, the reporter, could not say for sure that she did not speak to Anahit as Hartung was investigating her story. And there is one more set of mystery people in this case: not just Anahit Turchynov, but, yet again, these lawyers by the last name of Neucriss. You have heard that name since this trial began. They are the plaintiffs' lawyers who, months before August 2018, received information about the problems with g-Livia from their friend, the spiteful Innis McVie.

"I am sorry to tell you, Ladies and Gentlemen, but the sad fact is that the government did not do a proper job of investigating this case. They were so eager to get Gila Hartung on the witness stand that they allowed the lawyers for the *Wall Street Journal* to obstruct them. You saw that Gila Hartung, like all journalists, was very reluctant to reveal her sources. And you saw the lawyers who protected her in that goal. They were here in front of you, from New York, from Wall Street, three lawyers to listen to the testimony of one witness. Tireless attorneys, yes, but also completely disobedient. A law unto themselves, unwilling to listen even to Judge Klonsky. Total obstructionists. And rather than take a hard position with them, Moses Appleton and Mr. Feld—who, I must say in fairness, have many other things to do—decided they would settle simply to get Gila on the witness stand to testify about her supposedly incriminating conversation with Kiril Pafko.

"And so they did not know, until we exposed the truth right before your eyes, a truth the prosecutors with all their vast power had not bothered to discover, that the Neucrisses were Gila Hartung's source. And not knowing that, they never forced any of the Neucrisses to answer questions, the first and most obvious of which is, Who told you about g-Livia? And so the prosecutors accepted Innis McVie's perjury at face value.

"Again, I will imagine my dialogue with the group of you: 'You are correct, Sandy, the prosecutors were thwarted by the Wall Street lawyers, they never got to the bottom of this, as they should have before the trial started, but what does that have to do with insider trading?'

"My answer is, Everything. The Neucrisses live here in Kindle County." He motions to Pinky, who brings up on-screen the written waivers of medical confidentiality that were signed by representatives of the estates that became the Neucrisses' clients. "You can see their address on the patient waiver letters that are in evidence. They were talking about the problems with g-Livia with Innis McVie. Did their knowledge of this—or Gila Hartung's—find its way to Anahit Turchynov? That kind of information—what the *Wall Street Journal* was about to publish, that PT shares were going to crash in value—that moves like mercury, through any little crack. And it easily could have made its way to Anahit Turchynov. Remember a very very important point. Remember what these letters written on the Neucrisses' letterhead demonstrate: The information about what had happened to the patients who had suddenly died was *not confidential.* And to be guilty of insider trading, as Mr. Feld acknowledged, you must be buying and selling stock on the basis of information you have a duty to keep *confidential.*

"I certainly understand that the law in this area probably sounds to you like an incomprehensible mess. You saw when PT's outside counsel, who was in charge of explaining the law to people at PT like Kiril—you saw on cross-examination that even attorneys experienced in this area have a hard time explaining its many nuances. Gobbledygook, no matter how many times you hear about it, remains gobbledygook.

"But remember, the medical history of the Neucriss clients who had taken g-Livia and died, that was no longer confidential. Confidentiality was waived so the doctors could speak to Gila Hartung. And therefore, stock trades based on that information—on knowing there was a medical problem for some patients—such trades were not a crime. Any person who realized that the stock was destined to plummet, because they knew what the doctors were saying, any person who traded on that expectation would not have violated the law.

"And thus, the Neucrisses could have told Anahit about those problems, and even that they were going to file suit shortly and publicly expose the issues with g-Livia—they could have shared that information with Anahit without breaking any law. And having been told that, Anahit could have sold the shares of all her clients, even Kiril Pafko, completely lawfully, because she was acting on nonconfidential information.

"Is that in fact what happened? You do not know. Is one of the young Neucriss lawyers dating Anahit Turchynov, or do they live in the same condo building, or go to the same health club? You do not know for sure, because Mr. Appleton chose not to call Anahit Turchynov or grant her immunity, and he did not force one of the Neucrisses to the stand, even after their names emerged through the defense."

Moses, who has appeared increasingly agitated by Stern's accusations of investigative blunders, has come to his feet.

"Objection. We are not obliged to call or immunize witnesses."

Stern again spins with that grace that has eluded him elsewhere for decades.

"Yes," he answers, "but you are obliged, Mr. Appleton, to prove your charges beyond a reasonable doubt. Surely you do not object to that." Across the well of the courtroom, he faces Moses directly for a second, like gentlemen at a duel. Moses, knowing it is not his turn to speak, beyond making objections, blinks several times, trying to calculate a response.

Sonny, briefly silent in the face of the byplay, now says, "Given how Mr. Stern puts it, the objection is overruled."

Stern nods, then returns his attention to the jury.

"Now what will Mr. Appleton say in rebuttal? 'Oh, Sandy is having flights of fancy. He is making things up. It is obvious that Kiril called Anahit and initiated this sale.' Fine, let's consider the prosecutor's point. You may assume that Kiril Pafko, a physician for more than fifty years, understands the rules of patient confidentiality. When Gila Hartung says, 'I have talked to these doctors,' he knows that what she is telling him cannot be confidential information, and therefore that he, like anyone else, can freely trade PT stock on that basis. And how can Mr. Appleton possibly answer that? Well, I imagine, as my dear, dead wife liked to say, he will 'try to slice the bologna a little thin.'" Again, some smiles. "He will say, 'Yes, the patient information was not confidential any longer, but the information about the *Wall Street Journal* story, *that* was confidential until it was published, and thus Kiril could not trade any PT shares.'

"Is Mr. Appleton right under this incomprehensible mess of laws? I leave that to you. Because it does not matter. Because to commit this crime, Judge Klonsky will tell you that Dr. Pafko first must have *known* he was violating a duty of confidentiality, he must have *known* he was doing wrong. Even Mr. Feld admitted that much when he described the elements of the offense. So let us go back in time to August 7, 2018: In that moment, when Kiril Pafko got off the phone, shocked and concerned about the fate of his lifesaving achievements, about a possible flaw in PT's very careful research, about the future of his company, and about his grandchildren, could he have made a very understandable mistake about what this hodgepodge of laws required? Mr. Feld called your attention to the repeated warnings Kiril received from PT's outside counsel, the lectures they had delivered about when he could and could not sell shares of the company. But what does that tell you? Think about this, please. That elaborate education about the law means, of course, that Kiril Pafko would not have proceeded *unless* he believed he was *not* violating the law, *not* engaging in insider trading, because the patient information Gila Hartung related was no longer confidential."

Stern again is behind Kiril. Pafko, who has generally followed his lawyer's admonition about not reacting to the evidence or arguments, is nodding in agreement, which immediately earns a black look from the judge. A defendant who has not subjected himself to the prosecutors' cross-examination is cheating at the margins when he tries to signal the jury this way. While speaking, Stern places his hand on the back of Kiril's neck and applies a firm squeeze, which freezes Pafko at once.

"Now, Mr. Appleton, I predict, when he gets his chance to speak last, will come to this podium and ridicule me. He will not be doing that because he likes to make fun of old people."

The remark, to Stern's surprise, provokes a gale of laughter around the courtroom. It is comic relief mostly, but the hilarity is widespread. They are chuckling in the jury box, Sonny is holding up a hand to mask her mouth, even Moses, seldom inclined to levity, is smiling again. Only Feld seems to find no humor in Stern's remark.

"But he will say, 'Oh well, really, my friend Sandy has given you some far-fetched hypothetical explanations of how this could have happened. Wendy Hoh misunderstood on the telephone. The Neucrisses told Anahit about g-Livia. And Kiril Pafko, a Nobel Prize winner, was confused because he knew the medical information was not confidential. What a coincidence,' Mr. Appleton will say. 'All these things going wrong for this unlucky fellow Kiril Pafko. And here he sits, poor man, accused of federal felonies, after the value of his stock rose to close to 600 million dollars. How unlucky. What a coincidence.'

"But truly. Does it make more sense to believe that a winner of the Nobel Prize in Medicine would throw the work of a lifetime, a worldwide reputation, a long and noble life and career straight out the window at the age of seventy-five? How believable is that to any of us?

"Peculiar chance occurrences, coincidences, accidents—whatever we want to call them—happen in our lives all the time. If I had the opportunity to have a conversation with each of you and say, 'Tell me about the strangest coincidence you heard about this month,' you would each have plenty to share: Your sister's mother-in-law and father-in-law died of separate causes the same day, he in surgery, she in a car accident as she was racing to the hospital. Your best friend dated a woman for six weeks before realizing she was his long-lost first cousin. Your doctor and your priest, no relation, are both named Joe Flynn. Those things are unlikely. But they happen.

"Moses has a job. I have a job. You stand between us. And I stand beside Kiril Pafko, whose achievements are legend and who has been accused of a crime for what he did in developing a medication that is destined to save thousands of lives. Yes, Dr. Robb says there should be a black box warning, whatever that is, and so we can assume there will be one in the future. But g-Livia will return to the market, and cancer patients will live far longer. And in hospital rooms and houses, at grandchildren's softball games, as parents put a child to bed at night, or live to attend a wedding or graduation, they will all say, 'God bless Kiril Pafko. He was once accused of something bad. How,' they will ask, 'how could that possibly have happened?'

"They will not understand. Do not compound the errors that have occurred already, the mistake of being taken in by Innis McVie, of being thwarted by Wall Street lawyers, of not calling the right witnesses, of relying on a sloppy mess of laws and regulations even the regulators do not understand, of trying to brand a man revered around the world as a felon. Let the parade of mistakes stop here.

"In this life, we know many things beyond a reasonable doubt: That we love our children. That it is raining when the drops fall from the sky. That stars are out. That you love pizza. That Innis McVie is a liar.

"But that Kiril Pafko is a felon, that he committed these crimes? Do you know that? Do you know for certain? Do you know for sure?"

He looks to them, his last jury, shaking his head, shaking it again and again until he takes his seat.

VI. JUDGMENT

33. THE VERDICT

It is Marta's voice that retrieves him from a region of unsettled dreams. As he rises toward the world, he undertakes the inventory that has become routine. Alive? Apparently. Pains? Not much worse. At home? He doubts that but opens his eyes, only to find his vision somewhat blurred. After another second, he knows: the hospital. He comprehends as much from the feel of the sheets and the infernal bleating of the monitors. But he closes his eyes again to orient himself. He recalls finishing his argument, plunging into his chair with one thought: I did it. Meaning not that he won the case—that remained unlikely—or even that he'd delivered a stirring argument, although Marta had whispered an adoring compliment, with her jaw clenched like a ventriloquist's so the jurors could not read her lips. He was relieved because he had made it to the end.

As Stern was completing his remarks, while he was mutely shaking his head time and again, his heart once more felt like it was trying to run away and escape his chest. When Moses stood to deliver the government's rebuttal, an immense weariness overcame Stern, and with it a brutal headache, as if a huge pliers were clenched against his skull. His temples drummed. Breathing was futile. To Marta he whispered, 'You make the objections.' One more thing comes back to him: a piercing scream. Pinky?

He begins to follow the conversation taking place beside him.

"Marty," says Al Clemente, Stern's internist, addressing Marta by the nickname from her teendom, "the job of a physician is not simply to sweep up the pieces of a human being after they're broken."

"Al, what do you think the chances are I could have talked him out of it?"

Somewhere, like a cold drip from the roof of a cave, the thought arrives that Clara had once shared their daughter's confidence that Al was Marta's first sexual partner. But they were pals more than lovers, even in high school. Years ago, when Stern had accepted the advice—probably from Kiril—to find an internist younger than he is, Al had been Stern's first thought. Now Al is close to turning himself out to pasture, another doctor eager to leave behind a noble profession whose pleasures are largely lost in the course of an unceasing war with insurance companies and hospital administrators.

Al is dryly wrathful with his old friend.

"Does that mean I wasn't entitled to express my opinion to him? When I read the papers and realized he was in the middle of a month-long trial, I nearly ran down to the courthouse to kidnap him. Some calamity was inevitable. You know, he doesn't have a normal physiology, even for an eighty-five-year-old. Remission or not, he has metastatic disease, and God only knows how this kind of strain affects that."

"I know," says Marta sullenly.

"He's had a wonderful quality of life because he's still so sharp."

"Most of the time," says Marta.

"Okay, most of the time. But he could live a really good life for another decade—if you don't say 'Okay' when he decides to climb Mount Everest. This verged on suicidal. Is he still depressed about Helen?"

"I guess. Normal. Recently he's seemed a little interested in someone, so maybe he's moving on."

"You should encourage him."

Stern decides it's time to clear his throat. Al stops midsentence and on reflex reaches for Stern's wrist to take his pulse. Both Marta and the doctor are sheepish at first.

"Did you hear us?" Al asks.

He nods and Al lowers his round face to Stern's. He is not very good at accepting the advice he dispenses about dietary habits.

"Sandy, never again."

"I have promised that," he says.

"Well, promise me."

"I promise you, Al. And myself. I know this was beyond me. I am not pleased about it. But I accept the fact."

His doctor is finally pacified.

"May I ask what happened to me?" says Stern.

"Well, the bad news, to be medically precise, is that you were dead. The good news is it didn't last long. You went into cardiac arrest, Sandy."

"Cardiac arrest? Because?"

"Ventricular tachycardia, apparently. Later today you'll meet a very fine cardiac surgeon named Sarita Panggabean, who's going to implant a device in your chest to prevent any reoccurrence. You'll be out of here tomorrow morning."

"Is today still Tuesday?" Stern asks.

"Wednesday," Al says. Stern had been sedated overnight, after being brought in by ambulance.

Marta describes the chaotic scene that unfolded in the courtroom after Stern had slithered out of his chair and face-planted on the carpet. Ultimately, Feld and Moses and Harry, the court security officer, lifted Stern onto the defense table, and Marta says that Sonny and she took turns administering mouth-to-mouth.

"Pinky was the hero, though," Marta adds.

"A wonderful new trend," says Stern.

"She remembered there was a defibrillator in the corridor. She had to smash in the glass with her bare hand, but she came rushing back with it, so Kiril could apply the paddles."

Stern takes no pleasure in his vivid reimagining of the scene—his shirt torn open, his sunken, scarred chest exposed to view, his flesh a bloodless white.

Al says, "You had outstanding judgment, Sandy, collapsing beside a Nobel Prize winner in Medicine."

"I have had a charmed life for years now, Al." Stern looks to his daughter. "A verdict?"

"Not yet. They only got the case a couple of hours ago."

"How did our friend Moses do in rebuttal?"

"Going down for the count was not a good tactical decision on your part. Sonny sent them home yesterday and let Moses start again this morning, after telling the jury you were doing well."

Fairness to the prosecutors would have required the judge to say that, even if Stern's body was in cold storage at a funeral home.

"And the argument?"

"Strong. Very good. Not as great as you were. But he definitely benefited by getting overnight to sort things out. He started out with the 'Aw shucks,' stuff. 'I can never be as eloquent as Mr. Stern.' "

"Then ripped me to shreds," says Stern.

"He tried. Moses didn't spend a lot of time on the fraud counts."

Stern is surprised by that.

Marta explains, "I think they felt their case on fraud sort of collapsed. Just too many things went south on them. He told me afterwards that he thought the jury was going to buy your argument about Wendy Hoh enough to raise a doubt. He went all-in on the insider trading. 'No matter who the government called, Mr. Stern would be able to name another witness we should have brought before you. You have all of Ms. Turchynov's phone records. There are no calls to either of the Neucrisses' numbers. And don't you remember Mr. Stern's cross-examination of Gila Hartung? Ms. Hartung agreed that the Neucrisses were determined to keep the problems with g-Livia a secret in order to prevent other plaintiffs' lawyers from trying to jump into these cases. There is no chance they would allow word to leak to Anahit Turchynov. It's a pipe dream that Ms. Turchynov sold PT for any other reason than what she learned from Kiril Pafko. But that's the wonderful part of being a defense lawyer. You don't have to prove anything, so you can say one thing one day and something else the next.'"

"It sounds effective," Stern says.

"The jurors were listening. You know the rest of it. 'No one is above the law, no matter what their achievements.' 'Twenty million dollars is not a minor offense.'"

"And our client?"

"The usual. Cloud nine. Concerned about you but certain he is destined for freedom."

Stern thinks about Kiril for a moment, then shakes his head as he reconsiders the impact of Moses's argument.

"He was an idiot not to take the mistrial."

The following morning, Thanksgiving Day, Stern is shocked to see his younger daughter, Kate, come through the hospital-room door early in the morning. She embraces him. The tallest person in her immediate family, Kate is too thin, but still the same beautiful, quintessentially sweet human being. Her second husband, Miguel, a Spaniard, is quite a bit older than she and nothing like John, Pinky's father, who maintains the distinction of being the only person any of Stern's children paired with whom Stern ever disliked—but, as Stern often says, he disliked John enough for ten. Miguel is far more worldly and has broadened Kate's life in a way she clearly longed for. But once she was happier, she was unwilling to allow Pinky to disrupt that, and it is no accident that she supported Miguel's desire to move to Scottsdale, where they live most of the year, closer to Kate's other two kids in Seattle. The older Kate has gotten, the more she reminds him of his sister, Silvia—another bright, kind, beautiful woman, basically withdrawn to a protected realm of wealth.

Kate had flown in last night as a holiday surprise for her father, and so it now falls to her to tell Stern he will have to stay here one more day. The hospital is short staffed; it would take hours to get Stern discharged. On top of that, Al thinks Stern will benefit from one more day of enforced rest. Court, Stern knows, is closed for the holiday, but Sonny has asked the jury to return and resume deliberations tomorrow morning. If there is no verdict by late Friday, they will probably send out notes about being hung.

"Thanksgiving in this hellhole?" Stern asks.

But it turns out rather well. Marta brings the entire dinner down to U Hospital and they eat in the family lounge, eighteen people, including all three of Marta's kids and Henry's girlfriend. Stern is delighted to see Pinky and her mother seated side by side, conversing amiably all night. With Kate earlier, he lavished praise on Pinky's work throughout the trial, not to mention her heroics when he collapsed.

'Marty says the same thing,' Kate allowed. Like everyone, she was also deeply impressed by Pinky's quick thinking and bravery in smashing her way to the defibrillator.

'I think she has a solid future as a private investigator,' Stern said. 'She has many strengths suited for that role.'

Kate was clearly pleased to hear all this, but she has been disappointed by Pinky much too often not to remain guarded.

Peter, with whom Stern has been trading voice messages since yesterday, rings his father's phone with a video call while they are all around the table.

"I hear you nearly got your fondest wish," he says as soon as Stern is on-screen.

"What is that?"

"To be buried in a courtroom." Peter laughs. As usual with his jokes at his father's expense, only Peter sees the humor. "How are you feeling, Dad?"

"Some pain at the incision. Otherwise, surprisingly energetic. When I am awake. Al has me on sleeping pills."

"Good idea. I talked to Al. Exhaustion was a big part of your problem. But you're going to be fine. Your ejection fraction is over fifty percent. We should have done this a couple of years ago. But most of the time you seemed to be getting by well."

Stern asks to see his granddaughter.

Rosa is adorable and determined to hold her father's cell phone.

"Ho'd," she screams. "Ho'd."

When she calms down, Stern clucks at her and plays peekaboo.

"Rosa," Stern says, "tell your father, as soon as I can fly again, I am coming to spend a few days with you. Retirement has its benefits." In the face of Peter's silence, Stern says, "I have read the script, Peter, and your line is, 'We'd love to see you.'" Peter actually laughs, and Stern passes the phone to other family members to offer Thanksgiving greetings to his son.

The chemically aided sleep Stern has gotten the past few nights has been delicious, like floating carefree in a warm sea. It is nearly nine thirty when Stern awakens on Friday morning, and Kate is reading from a tablet in the chair next to his bed. She smiles with heart-lifting sweetness when she notices he is awake.

"Clarice and Marty ran down to court."

"A verdict or a jury question?"

"Marta said she would come straight here after to tell you all about it."

That sounds like a verdict. After a day of thought over the holiday, the holdouts have come over to the other side. Stern knows he could tune to the local news channel on the radio and find out, especially if there is a decision. But he is pleased to ride on the ether of ignorance for a few more minutes, just as would be the case if he were actually in the courtroom. Those moments, awaiting the announcement of a verdict, are dizzying. Something huge has happened—to your client, to the community—but it is a secret only twelve people know.

In another half an hour his cell on the table beside the hospital bed is buzzing—undoubtedly reporters seeking comment. He's sure now: There is a verdict.

His older daughter and his oldest granddaughter arrive in twenty minutes. He is pleased to see Pinky and her mother greet one another this morning in a sincere embrace.

"*Dígame*," he says to Marta, who has not even taken off her coat.

"Not guilty all counts except 23," says Marta.

"Guilty on 23?"

She toughens up her mouth and nods.

Insider trading. It feels like he's been shot. He groans.

"I should have told them not to compromise." It's a standard argument, based on a line from the judge's instructions about their deliberations. 'Do not surrender your honest beliefs about the case.' The subtext is, Don't make a deal just to get out of the jury room. This happens all the time, jurors thinking they are doing a defendant a favor, or expressing an opinion about the merits of the charges, by convicting only on a count or two. One count or one hundred, Kiril Pafko is now a felon and faces punishment accordingly.

Stern is astonished by the depth of his disappointment. He knows, for one thing, that Kiril committed the crime. And it sounds like Moses, in rebuttal, solidified this part of his case. But still. Hope, that blind songbird. It flies through the bleakest skies. He is so sad. For himself, in all honesty. It would have been such a glorious way to depart, notching what the media painted as an impossible win. And his heart is broken also for his stupid, stupid client. He finds that Pinky has stolen to the chair beside him and, with nothing else said, has taken his hand. A bandage of gauze and tape is still wrapped around her knuckles.

"It's a great result, Dad," Marta says. "The guy was charged with murder and ended up with a moving violation."

"You do not go to the penitentiary for speeding."

"Neither will Kiril. Not for long anyway. The guideline will be high," she says, referring to the time in prison prescribed by the federal sentencing guidelines, "but with the NG counts, Pafko's cancer research, the lives he's saved, and his age—all of it will give Sonny solid reasons to depart," Marta says, meaning that the judge will be free to ignore the guidelines in this case. "The last thing Moses said was, 'Call me.' They know Kiril has a whopping good chance in the appellate court, with the murder evidence and Innis taking five. If Kiril waives appeal, we might get an agreed sentence, or a cap. Six months in, six months home confinement? He'll work in the infirmary. It'll be like going on a medical mission."

"How did Kiril take it?"

Describing that part drives Marta down into a leatherette chair on the other side of the hospital bed.

"Terribly. He cried. You know, he rose for the verdict. He stared when it was read, then he looked over at me and asked, 'I am convicted?' When I nodded, he just crumbled. He put his head down on the table, sobbing like a baby. Then two of the jurors started crying."

"But they held to their verdict when they were polled?" asks Stern. After the decision is announced in open court, the defense may request that the judge ask each juror individually, Was this and is this your verdict? In the federal system, all twelve jurors must agree to a conviction, and if even one person changes their mind and sticks to it, the case ends up a mistrial—as this one should have been.

"I really thought one of them was going to buckle," Marta says.

"Mrs. Murtaugh?"

"I bet you can date her, Dad."

"Totally," says Pinky. "She's just totally in love."

"I am retired, Marta. From the courtroom and matters of the heart." Given how little he had staked on pursuing things with Innis, he is shocked by how hurt he is—or perhaps just humiliated.

"One is a good idea," says Marta, "the other maybe not."

"Bail?"

"Yes, Sonny left Kiril on bond. Until sentencing. The usual."

"As soon as I am able, I would like to go see him. You will come, Marta?"

"Of course."

"Al says I can leave the house on Monday. Please call the Pafkos to see if we can stop over then."

34. DONATELLA'S NEWS

Kiril and Donatella have lived for two decades in an English manor house in Greenwood County with steep slate mansards. Within, it is appointed in the tone of a British barony, with lustrous antiques of chestnut and cherry, long velvet drapes in scarlet, and sterling pieces heavy enough to double as murder weapons. Despite Donatella's Italian bloodlines, her Anglophilic decoration is in the style of the Argentine upper class, which gravitated toward English mannerisms in the nineteenth century as a way to repudiate the influence of Spain.

Stern has been here several times before for the huge holiday parties that the Pafkos hosted. It was just the kind of scene that pleased Kiril, a confluence of many of Kindle County's most influential citizens—although 'interesting' would be the word Kiril would prefer—pols, musicians, many figures from Easton and the U, artists, business leaders. Still at heart the frightened young stranger who arrived here, Stern was always a little thrilled to be included.

It is an odd visit from the start. A few minutes late, Stern and Marta find themselves standing outside on the front step for an eternity, even after ringing the bell several times. Marta has her cell phone in hand, about to call the house line, when Donatella sweeps the front door open. She blusters apologies, clearly harried, a rare mode for her, and shows them into the living room, where Stern is surprised to find Lep standing there to greet them, tall and slender in his corduroy sport coat.

Donatella offers refreshments. They chat about Thanksgiving and the latest musical achievements of Lep's daughters. Finally, after several minutes, Stern says, "Where, may I ask, is our friend Kiril?"

Donatella and Lep exchange looks. The son finally says, "We don't know."

"Excuse me?"

Donatella says, "I have not seen him for three days."

Stern tries to think of some way around the question, then finally asks, "Is that common?"

"Common? No. He was not here for several nights before the arguments began, but then he returned all last week."

"When did you see him last?"

"He drove off early Friday afternoon."

"Did he say anything as he left?"

Donatella purses her mouth. "He said, 'Please forgive me, *cara*, for all of this.' "

That does not sound good.

"What was his mood?"

"He seemed to be recovering a little, Sandy. The verdict had come only a few hours before." She looks to Lep, who nods to support that assessment. Donatella continues. "He knew about this appointment. Marta, you spoke to him yourself. He was eager to thank both of you. He thought the defense you mounted was brilliant. Both Lep and I have been expecting him to come through the door any minute."

"Has he been to PT to look at his mail this morning or on Friday?" Stern asks Lep. The answer is no. He has not shown up at the lab at Easton either. Nor has Kiril responded to e-mails or calls.

"Lep, have you asked anyone else who might have seen him?"

"He missed his poker game Friday night."

"Anybody else?" Stern means Olga but does not want to speak her name in Donatella's presence. From the way Lep's mouth knots, he takes it that Lep, understandably, has not found a way to question her.

"Are you concerned he might have harmed himself?"

Donatella's sudden snide laugh is surprising given the somber mood.

"Kiril? He cannot imagine the world without him."

Stern looks to Marta.

"Where does he keep his passport?" she asks.

"He gave it to the probation department long ago," Donatella answers. "Surrendering it was a condition of his bond. You both know that."

But something in Donatella's response strikes a false note. As a straightforward person, she is not an accomplished liar. An immigrant is always an immigrant in some part of their soul, a guest who never takes citizenship or belonging entirely for granted. Stern realizes there is a question he should have asked long ago.

"Does he have an Argentine passport as well?"

Donatella looks down to her doughy hands in her lap.

"Both of us. When we visit family, we have renewed them over the years."

"And where is that kept?" Stern asks.

"We have a little safe upstairs."

"May I ask you to look?"

She is back in a few minutes.

"It's gone," says Donatella, somewhat breathless.

Marta groans. This is big trouble.

Stern says, "We are obliged to report Kiril's disappearance to the court, Donatella. The attorney-client privilege cannot provide a refuge for a crime. Jumping bond is a serious offense, the more so after conviction."

The woman who was derisive a few minutes ago now seems gripped by a new sadness. The disappearance of Kiril's Argentine documents has clearly taken her by surprise. She now realizes that there is a chance she may never see Kiril again.

The Sterns and Lep depart together. It snowed last night, less than an inch but enough to make things slick, and Marta brings the car up so her father does not have to walk on the gravel drive where the footing is unsteady.

"Lep," Sandy says, as they are about to part, "at some point, I would love to ask you a few frank questions, just between two gentlemen."

Lep, with his fair eyes, stares back at Stern.

"You know what my lawyers have told me, Sandy. I can't go into this, even with you."

"The trial is over."

"Does that matter? There will be an appeal, if Kiril turns up. And all these lawsuits? I need to keep things to myself."

He is right, of course. As Marta's SUV rolls up, Stern says, "Once it is all settled, perhaps."

Lep smiles and offers his hand. "I don't expect that, Sandy." He means it without rancor. He's walked through a minefield and has no intention of retracing his steps.

From the Pafkos', Stern and Marta head to the Center City. Stern makes a call to announce their visit as they are driving in, and together they wait in the chief judge's anteroom until Sonny is off the bench. She has started another trial, a civil case, and openings should be wrapping up momentarily.

The judge has a separate entrance to her private chambers directly through the courtroom, and one of her clerks opens the front door to admit them about twenty minutes later. Sonny, without her robe, rises from behind her desk and advances to hug them both. She holds on to Stern for quite some time.

"You scared the hell out of us."

"It is a mystical experience," Stern says of the few moments when his death had started. He had no memory of it at first, but now he is beginning to recall more: the white light that so many people speak of. It has made the prospect of the time soon, when he will not be called back, much less frightening. It had felt shockingly natural.

"We have come on two missions," says Stern. "The most urgent is to report to the court that our client seems to have decamped."

"For sure?"

"By all appearances."

"Shit," says Sonny. A fugitive is always a black mark for the judge who admitted him to bail. It means she made a poor assessment of his character. With chagrin, Stern explains about the second passport.

"I should have asked," says Stern.

"Me too," Sonny answers. "Any idea where he's gone?"

"There is no evidence thus far. But the marshals will be able to check the flight manifests, assuming he went by air." Stern has already put some thought into the judge's question and could make a good wager at this point, but his obligation is to report the facts they know, not share his hunches. Even so, their responsibility to assist in their client's arrest comes with an unavoidable consequence.

"Since we are witnesses against Kiril now," says Marta, "we will be filing a motion to withdraw."

"Granted," says Sonny. She tosses a hand and calls out to her docket clerk. Luis's face emerges through another doorway. Across the room, the judge says, "*US v. Pafko.* Granted: Oral motion of Stern & Stern to withdraw as counsel for Defendant Pafko." She does not want any formality to slow the Sterns in sharing information with the Marshals Service, which will begin the hunt at once. Next, the judge calls in her deputy marshal, Ginny Taylor, to inform her.

The entire situation leaves Sonny shaking her gray head. Stern will forever see Sonny Klonsky as the peasant beauty with whom he was once for a minute in time so deeply smitten. Yet now, in another part of his mind, he will always be calling her 'the judge.' Unexpectedly, his thoughts light upon that detail Marta shared, that when he collapsed, Sonny took a turn or two administering mouth-to-mouth. After all these decades, their lips had met, as neither ever envisioned, his mouth soft as puddled wax. What comedy! We live, we change. It is part of the adventure.

"What terrible judgment your client seems to have," Sonny says then. "May I safely assume it was his idea to go to verdict with that jury?"

"We cannot comment," says Stern, "except to note yet again the court's great perspicacity."

Sonny is amused by Stern's delicacy. He sits forward in his chair, both hands on the ivory knob of his walking stick.

"My other reason for coming is to apologize to you."

She laughs and waves a hand.

"Advocates are advocates, Sandy. And you have always been the best. Frankly, I thought you'd pulled the rabbit out of the hat with this one."

"Marta says I was not a wise tactician to collapse and give Moses extra time to prepare his rebuttal."

"He did a very fine job."

"Moses and I spoke on Saturday," Stern says. "I congratulated him and he was very gracious. We shall have lunch." That has always been the Sterns' custom with Moses after a case against one another. The loser pays, which has worked out to Moses's advantage over the years, as it should. "Nonetheless, I know I put the court in a difficult position at some moments."

"Apology accepted. But you know you will never lose me as a friend. And frankly, the court put the court in a difficult position. I was upset because I realized I should have stepped aside. I'll need to talk to Moses about how to handle these situations in the future. Whenever the case is over." She brightens then and laughs in her good-natured way. "And for you two, it is."

Stern has told himself at every step, the end is coming. His final cross-exam. His last closing. But when Sonny waved to Luis a moment ago to grant their motion to withdraw, that tiny back-of-the-hand gesture rang down the curtain on his career. Now, in every sense, he is a former lawyer. As is Marta.

The judge walks them to the chambers door and hugs them both again.

It is over.

35. ANOTHER INTERVIEW WITH MS. FERNANDEZ

By Friday, a week after the verdict, Stern is restless. Pinky and Marta are in the office, having undertaken the laborious business of returning files to the former clients who want them. Many have not responded yet to the Sterns' letter. His assignment, when he goes to the office next week, will be to call the clients they haven't heard from. He is looking forward to checking in with several of those folks. Together they endured tense times, although it is the nature of a criminal practice that even some who walked away unscathed would prefer to forget Stern's name, as part of a period of undeserved misery. Some others, who were convicted, won't pick up the phone because by now they have decided all their troubles were Sandy's fault.

With nothing much to do besides be outraged by what he sees on cable news, Stern dwells on Kiril's case. He is unsatisfied with the conclusion, not just the conviction and Kiril's departure, but the amount he still does not really know. After more than a year of arduous work, Stern has little insight into what actually occurred on September 15 and 16, 2016, when the clinical trial database was changed. He has concluded dozens and dozens of cases in which his client's lack of candor, combined with the blame-shifting and dissembling of government witnesses, has basically left him in the dark. And in this instance, Stern could tell himself to accept his own advice about how hard it is to say, 'I do not know.' But Kiril is—or was—his friend, so the dishonesty has a personal edge, especially given Marta's prediction from the start that Kiril chose Stern as his lawyer in order to lie to him. And then there is the lingering question concerning who deliberately ran Stern off the road.

On impulse, Stern calls PT and asks for Olga Fernandez. When he gets through, he tells her he would like to pay a visit. For an instant, it seems like the line has gone dead.

"*Que pasa?*" she asks then.

"Some loose ends," says Stern.

"Suit yourself. How long will this take?" She gives him fifteen minutes at 1:00. Stern calls Ardent, who will soon become Sandy's personal employee.

Not unexpectedly, Olga does not get up to greet him. Instead she motions Stern to one of the two contemporary office chairs in front of her desk. Since March, when he saw her here, she has moved out of Innis's office beside Kiril's, where Kiril had placed her. This glass-walled enclosure is considerably smaller. Olga explains that with Lep becoming CEO, without the prefix 'Acting,' he has promoted Tanakawa to chief operating officer.

"And I'm headed for the exit," she adds. "Lep doesn't want me around." Olga's success marketing g-Livia has earned frequent mention in the business press, but now that Lep is free to run the company himself, he apparently is unwilling to repeat his experience with Innis. He won't tolerate dealing with his father's lover on a daily basis.

When Stern saw Olga in court the other day, he registered something different about her, which, given his excitement over Innis's phone records, he did not try to identify. Now that he is less stressed, he sees that she is wearing the contemporary equivalent of braces, that plastic casing over her teeth. As someone often embarrassed by the mess in his mouth, Stern sympathizes. In his children's and grandchildren's generations—and those are Olga's cohorts—there is no surer marker of social class than what someone sees when you laugh or smile. As always, he gives Olga credit for her ambition and her matching efforts at self-improvement.

"You look good for a dead man, Sandy."

"A temporary departure, apparently. I am not certain, however, Olga, that you would have missed me."

"*Chacho!*" She draws back with a narrow look. With Stern, a fellow Latino, Olga reverts often to Spanish, but that is only to maintain the upper hand. For decades, his desperation to be a true American meant he did everything he could to obliterate Spanish from his mind. Spending time around Marta's home, where English and Spanish are spoken interchangeably, often in the space of a single sentence, has restored some of his comprehension, but he is still very slow to converse. In any event, Olga speaks the standard Spanish of the *boricuas* in which half the consonants are swallowed, which generally goes past him anyway. "Are we enemies, Sandy? I've never thought so. You came to ask me where he is?"

"That is one subject."

"I'll tell you what I told Marshal What's-her-name." Olga sits forward. With the arrival of December, the Tri-Cities are getting cold, seldom above freezing—twenty-nine today—but Olga has maintained her habits, and her blouse, beneath the large gold cross she wears, is open to reveal a healthy stretch of freckled décolletage.

"The marshal was here?"

"Wednesday. 'The US Marshal,'" says Olga. "All the time, I thought that was just in Westerns."

"They are the federal judges' right hands. The marshals pursue bail jumpers and other fugitives."

"Interesting."

"And why was it that they came to speak to you?"

"Apparently he'd bought an airplane ticket for me."

"Ah," says Stern. "So Kiril expected you to go with him?"

Olga just makes a face. "He called when he was on the way to the airport and told me what a great life we'd have down there. I wouldn't even discuss it with him."

"Was he crushed?"

"He was surprised, I guess," she says. "But what was he thinking? I have three kids." She points to the photos on her bookshelves. "The fourteen-year-old just started high school. Okay, I need to leave PT now, but emigrating? Come on."

"But you were hoping to marry him, I thought?"

"Did Kiril tell you that?"

"As you know, I cannot reveal what Kiril told me. But I am certain you and Kiril were seeing each other again. And that leaving Donatella had long been your condition for the relationship."

"Well, then you don't need to know anything from me."

Stern is still trying to make sense of this. After another second of staring at one another, Olga relents a bit.

"Sandy, maybe three weeks ago, he calls me and says, '*Mi amor*, I can't stand it any longer. I must see you. As soon as the trial is over, I will marry you. I swear.'"

He wonders if he should believe this, that the renewal of her relationship with Kiril is recent. It's hard at this stage to discern any reason for Olga to lie.

"And the wife he has?"

"Their marriage isn't legal. Not according to Kiril. He's always said that when he married Donatella, she wasn't actually divorced. It was years before the decree went through in Argentina. After that, she and Kiril never had a second ceremony. He says he spoke to a lawyer." Olga shrugs. It's not much to her now. "He didn't care about giving her all the money she wants."

"Did he tell Donatella he was leaving her?"

"That was my condition, Sandy. I wouldn't see him again until he did it. He promised he had. He spent a few nights at the U Club, so I was pretty sure."

Stern nods. That accounts for why Donatella stopped coming to court.

"Donatella said he was at home just before the verdict."

"He told me he slept in his study, but he needed to look after some things there. I guess he wanted to pack and get out fast, if the jury made the wrong decision. The marshal said he bought open plane tickets for both of us three weeks ago."

Stern takes a moment to absorb this information. Even before the verdict, Kiril had decided at the age of seventy-eight to restart his life in Argentina, with Olga as his wife. Did that mean he actually expected to be convicted? After all his happy talk?

"But, *mira*," she says. "He never said I'd have to marry him in another country." She gives her head a hard shake, as if trying to make sense of Kiril's plan.

Now that they are discussing her prospective marriage to Kiril, Stern shares what he has surmised in his recent mullings.

"I take it you expected him to be convicted?"

"Isn't that what you thought? For me, either way was fine. You get him off? *Está nítido*." It's cool. "I'm set. Including here." She tapped her desk, meaning the company. "But okay, yeah, I thought he was going down. Everybody said he was slabbed on insider trading."

Stern can't keep himself from smiling. Here is yet another meaning to the saying that every marriage is unique. Olga's idea of wedded bliss is to have a husband in the federal penitentiary and an inheritance of hundreds of millions when he dies.

"Don't judge, Sandy. He's a charming old guy. I enjoy him. And if they got him, it would still be what? Three months, four months before he was sentenced and went to jail? And I promise you, he'd have a very good time. Better than sitting at home with Donatella telling him over and over again what a fool he is. Compared to that, the joint would be a relief."

In the last few decades, given the circles Stern travels in, he has seen dozens of these May-December relationships, trophy wives coming—and often going. In such relationships, Stern thinks, no matter how much the heart—or gonads—sing songs of love, there has to be a cold-blooded understanding on both sides that the future has been bargained against the past. He—and it is generally a male—wants to return to youth, while she (though sometimes he as well) seeks a secure old age. On both sides, they are out to cheat time. After failing at three marriages before, perhaps Olga was right to wed for more practical reasons. Centuries ago, kings and queens, indeed most of the rich, married for power and money, and no one seemed to think the worse of them.

"And what was the destination of this plane ticket he'd bought you?"

"Don't you know?"

"My guess would be Buenos Aires. There is quite a bit of family money there he probably could never expatriate."

"So again, you don't need me to tell you anything."

"Have you heard from him since he arrived?"

"One call. A few seconds. I told him not to phone again, since he would just get me in trouble."

"He was in BA?"

"I didn't ask. A smart person wouldn't stay there, no? Won't they try to get him back?"

"Extradition is a very complicated legal procedure, Olga. First, insider trading must be a crime within the scope of the extradition treaty. Then our insider trading laws and the Argentine ones must more or less match. With a seventy-eight-year-old defendant, I am not sure our government will bother with a long battle."

"So, he did the right thing."

"Hardly," says Stern. "It sounds like he has damned himself to die alone."

"He'll find someone else. He's very smooth. Don't misunderstand, Sandy. I care about Kiril. Really. Okay, when I started with him, he was a means to an end. I admit it. But you know, over time?" Her lower lip turns down: not so bad. "His passion? *De verdad*. You want to love him back because it's so real. But some men, you know, they *need* to be in love." She shrugs in the face of the blunt realities.

Stern tells her that he really did not come to discuss her romantic life.

"*Que entonces?*" What then?

He prepares himself and inclines toward her, supported by the knob of his cane.

"I came to look you in the eye, Olga, and ask if it was you who ran me off the road last March."

Overall, Stern would have guessed that Kiril would have alerted Olga to Pinky's and his suspicions. But she draws back, doing a convincing version of surprise, and utters a remark under her breath. He understands only '*loco*.'

Stern adds, "You know I was hit by another car on the highway not far from here?"

"*Por supuesto*, but I thought that was an accident."

He explains some of Pinky's research concerning the white 2017 Malibus. "We have largely established that you had one of those vehicles that week."

"*Aiyaiyai*. And because of that you suspect me? Everyone up front here kept those cars from time to time."

"But I had just spoken with you that afternoon. Not a comfortable meeting. You may recall it. I did not leave feeling that you had fond feelings about me."

"Recall? How could I forget? I was afraid you were going to give me a whack with that cane of yours. You didn't seem to believe a word I was saying. It was that e-mail Kiril sent me with the screenshot you were asking about."

"And did you tell me the truth, Olga? I have always felt you knew much more than you have said."

"I told no lies."

"But there was more to say, was there not?"

"In this life, Sandy, there is always more to say, no?"

"Olga, you are a very capable person, but I do not think of you as a philosopher."

Olga laughs. Whatever else, she has a sense of humor. He stares until he has worn her down again.

"Okay, Sandy, so what I didn't tell wasn't really important. But I was with Kiril a couple hours before that e-mail was sent."

"Where?"

"Where do you think?" She gives him a slightly exasperated toss of her small eyes. "We had happy hour, you know? Back then, I'd meet him before five at the PT condo in Center City. Around six, I'd leave to make dinner for my kids. Usually, he was asleep. A couple hours later I got that e-mail. He hadn't said he was going back to work, but sometimes when he came in to meet me, he took the light rail in because of traffic and went back to PT later for his car. Next morning, when I asked him about it, he was playing dumb. *Se lució el chayote!*" Stern is not sure he gets that one. She seems to be saying that Kiril was acting like a squash—a dumbbell. "But what I really thought?"

Stern tumbles his hand toward her, beckoning her to continue.

"I always had this idea, I'm not even sure exactly why, but I figured he'd really meant to send that e-mail to Innis. You know, sometimes you call your girlfriend by your wife's name? That's why he made this big deal that he had no idea what I was talking about."

Stern ponders again. It would explain why Innis knew about the deaths, if Kiril had turned to her for help at that moment. No matter how angry Innis was, it was in her interest to solve the problem so she could get out of PT with the value of her stock options undiminished. He weighs that, then he runs Olga's words back and realizes that apparently she takes it for granted that Kiril's protests of innocence were phony.

"I wish you'd been frank with me, Olga. The whole case might have gone very differently if you'd shared your thought that Innis had some role in helping Kiril change the data."

"Nuh-uh," says Olga. "Papi—the guy I called Papi, anyway—he always said, 'Don't never tell nobody's secrets.' And what do I know anyway? Maybe I'm crazy, you know? But one thing straight, *hombre*. I'm the only person out here who never lied to you. *Verdad*." She draws her plump chin to her chest and gives him a fiercely direct look from her black eyes. "So, yeah, I remember talking to you that day. You were pissed when I said I couldn't read that dataset. 'Well, then who reads numbers for you?' But where you really jumped on me was when I said I never talked to Lep."

As unlikely as it seems, Stern believes he can recall that moment. Stern has been told that Lep, though normally ill at ease socially, loves to play teacher, to guide others through the realms where he is master. Because of that, everyone went to Lep for assistance on research issues or numbers. Granted, Lep would not have liked Olga's sporting with Kiril, but that was over by then (or so all had been told), and Innis said more than once that Lep was professional at work, no matter how little use he had for his father's girlfriends. All in all, Olga's statement that she would never talk to Lep struck Stern as odd.

"But I didn't run you off the road, Sandy. I had a meeting with an oncology group at the Hotel Gresham. That's how I finally got you out of my office, cause I had to boogie." That detail is a complete blank to him. She asks for the date in March and then pecks at her keyboard and swivels her huge computer monitor around to show Stern her expense report for that day. Stern finds his glasses and leans across her desk to examine the scanned documents: A parking ticket at the Center City hotel, with the entry time within minutes of when he had been hit, and a bill for cocktails there. She even has a date-stamped photo on her phone of herself at the podium, talking to the doctors. "I got there with, like, ten seconds to spare before my speech, by the time I was done talking to you, then Lep."

Does she flinch faintly when she hears herself?

"I thought you do not speak to Lep?" says Stern.

She waves a hand around.

"I don't run down the hall and ask him to help with my homework. But he's in charge of the company, Sandy. When we need to talk, we talk. In and out. No small stuff, not even weather. Just business."

"But you say you nearly missed your speech? It must have been an important subject."

"Whatever. *Quién sabe?*" Who knows? "I don't remember. Had to be he asked to see me."

He studies her, and Olga shakes her head without looking away. As always, he knows there is more that she will not say.

The office phone rings, and she picks up. Her next meeting is about to start. Stern reaches for his overcoat, which is on the other chair.

"And when do you expect to leave PT, Olga?"

"A month?"

It is hard to feel concerned for Olga. She will exit, undoubtedly, with a handsome package, augmented somewhat in the #MeToo era after her affair with the CEO. More important, given her record here, she is bound to be in great demand at other pharma companies. Stern says as much to her.

She shrugs. "I'll land soft. I just hate to pull my girls out of school. You know. They're at that age. And I would love to be here for the relaunch, when Livia comes back on the market. But Lep, you know. I can't leave fast enough."

She gives a little nonchalant wave but, shockingly, appears to flush. Like Innis, she has apparently developed a deep connection to the company. Stern finds himself trying to be avuncular.

"Olga, you have a brilliant future in this industry. And a brilliant record here. To be candid, I would not be surprised at all if Lep encounters some pushback from the board when he announces you are going."

"He won't change his mind, Sandy. By now he wishes he never knew me." She looks askance and then focuses on the wall. For a second she seems incapable of speaking. Then, suddenly, her flush deepens, and Olga Fernandez of all people is crying. Both eyes fill up and the tears, gray from her makeup, trail down each cheek.

"Oh, for fuck's sake," she says, and squeezes the back of her fist against her nose.

Stern struggles to make sense of what he is seeing. Olga weeping over a job? But then he reconsiders what she said, and the internal Geiger counter he has always depended on to register the truth begins to click and sizzle. Now he knows why she doesn't talk to Lep.

"There was something between Lep and you at one point?"

She resolves to stare out her window toward a garden area, colorless and bare now as winter approaches, with a small pond in the center that will soon freeze over. But she is not focused on the view.

"Something," she answers. The tears continue to spill. She has made no effort yet to wipe her face. "You know, they tell you—Papi told me—Don't shit where you eat. But you know, Sandy. He's *really* nice. *Coño!*" she says suddenly. *Damn!* "He ran over my heart with a semi, and I'm still sitting here telling you he's a nice guy." She laughs bitterly, followed quickly by an involuntary heave. With that she reaches into her drawer for a paper napkin, the remnant of some fast food meal, and scrapes it across her face.

"It was my fault. I admit that. That's always been my type, you know? The quiet pretty boys. Smarter the better. He kept saying

'No, no, no.' But you know, he needed it. I knew he needed it. He was living in a coffin. Between Kiril and Greta? And Donatella. His life was about everybody else. And he is such a sweet guy. And he was so grateful when it happened. It was really something. *A fuego.*" On fire. "I fell hard, too, man. Really hard."

"This was some time ago?"

"2014 we started. Finally I told him, New Year's 2016, 'Dude, you gotta leave Greta. We can't stay on the sneak forever.' You know, he never said he would—leave? It wasn't like he led me on. But we were in love. Really in love. And I didn't want to end up like Innis. But he just couldn't do it. You know, he wanted to. I knew deep down he wanted to. So I just thought, Well, if I make it hard enough on him, he'll come around." She wipes her eyes again.

Stern thinks about that for a second, before he understands.

"So that was the genesis of your relationship with Kiril? As a way to force Lep's hand with Greta?"

She nods.

"And did Kiril ever know about Lep?"

She glances back at Stern directly for the first time, a sharp look, as if he is an idiot. Then her eyes return to the window.

"You know, Sandy. People like me? You grow up knowing you're never gonna get what you want anyway. *La piña está agria. Siempre.*" The pineapple is always sour. "So you know, if you can't have the loaf, have a slice. And being with Kiril, that at least meant Lep couldn't fire me. I'd be damned if I'd leave before the med was on the market and all my options vested. But mostly, I thought I'd get him back. I figured he'd never be able to stand watching me with Kiril." This time she places the palms of both hands against her eyes and drags them down her face to stop her weeping. Then she again looks at Stern, seemingly for help.

"I'll be better off getting out of here, right? He's never changing his mind."

Stern does not answer. He is still trying to absorb the emotional impact of all this information.

"So the day I was in your office grilling you, Olga, on your way out you stopped to tell Lep that I had asked a lot of pointed questions about your relationship?"

She gives a weighty nod.

"Us? That's his deep dark secret. Cause Greta, man, there'd be no 'Sorry.' It would be *adios*. And I always promised we'd be on the D and the L. Even though I knew it would be the best thing for me if Greta found out. Whatever I did, it didn't make sense, even to me, but I was just always thinking, If I prove I'm really all-in for him, we'll end up together." She gives her head another solid shake. "I mean, Sandy, love is just so fucking strange. Right?"

He nods slowly as he holds her eye. It is a bit shocking how sorry he feels for her.

She picks up her cell from her desk and points it toward herself. He knows only from watching Pinky do the same thing that she is using it as a mirror.

"*Wepa*," she says at the sight of herself. Congratulations. Pure irony. "I got people coming in, Sandy."

He picks up his overcoat. He wants to offer a word or two of comfort, but he still has said nothing when he goes out her door.

36. DON JUAN IN HELL

That evening at home, Stern tells Pinky a bit about his visit with Olga and the fact that she was in Center City when he was struck on the highway.

"So who hit you?"

"Olga seems to think on balance that it was an accident."

"Bullshit," answers Pinky. Stern laments again that Pinky messed up with the police force, because she has a cop's instincts through and through, seeing the world as the site of wrongdoing until proven otherwise. Of course, in this case, she is almost certainly correct. But Stern has no idea yet how he prefers to proceed. For that reason, he will not be sharing his conclusions with Pinky, who is likely to go off half-cocked.

On Monday morning, twelve days past the insertion of the small defibrillator, Stern calls Al and asks how his doctor would feel if Stern went to Florida to visit Silvia, his sister.

"Get out of this mess and relax?" Al asks. "I'm all for it. There's supposed to be a blizzard on Friday. But remember the rules. Nothing heavy. Limited arm movements. No carrying your luggage. No swimming."

Given Al's reaction, Marta can interpose limited objections and on Thursday, Ardent drops Stern at the airport. He carries nothing but the newspaper and his tablet, since he always keeps a few items of clothing at his sister's. His itinerary is precisely the same as when he went down during the trial. His plane lands at Fort Myers, and the same young man, Cesar, is there to greet Stern in his gleaming black SUV, the shape of a toad. They lunch together at the same crab shack, before speeding down the highway to Naples. Looking at the lines of malls, Stern wonders if the play he was thinking of last time is called *Don Juan in Hell.*

Cesar parks in Innis's drive, right in front of the steps where she displayed herself so fetchingly against the lights. Stern rings. Inside there is stirring, and eventually he hears knocking on the long window beside the beautiful tooled door. Plump and dark in her gray maid's uniform, Maria, the housekeeper, shakes her head, repeating several times, "No home."

Stern answers at volume, "*Muchas gracias. Esperaré.*" He has told her he will wait. Knowing the way, he opens the gate and circles to the rear. He removes his suit coat and loosens his tie, then nudges a chair out of the sun on Innis's bluestone patio. In a second, there is a rustling at the curtain and he sees Maria peering out, scowling. He smiles and lifts a hand cheerfully, and the woman disappears. With luck, she will call her boss and not the police.

It is a tranquil day on the water and the sound of the waves is even. Here on the shore, the breeze makes the air a bit cool and Stern once more dons his jacket. He has brought his tablet, and he works his way through texts and e-mails that have come from several ex-clients. Most are pure business, but several sound like letters from camp, including two from men nearing the end of their time in confinement in the same federal prison camp. One characterizes it as 'punishment by boredom.'

He stops after a while to throw his face back in the sun. There is health and excitement in the bright breeze. Thus, he is badly embarrassed when he wakes up with Innis standing over him. He must have looked like a very old man, his head cast over the back of the wicker chair, exposing his bridgework and his fillings, looking very much like another one of those Floridians who is no longer quite in touch with the present and who has come south to wait in the anteroom to death. Taking in the expression of surprise and then alarm on Innis's face, he has the immediate impression that she had hoped it was a different man who was adamantly insisting he would not depart.

"Well, isn't this special," she says. "What the hell are you doing here, Sandy?"

Innis is in her tennis attire, a short pleated skirt and a white placket shirt. Her racket case is slung over her shoulder, and the forelocks of her hair are still glued to her forehead by sweat. She obviously ran over directly after the end of her match.

He straightens slowly. His back is getting worse and worse.

"I was hoping to have a frank conversation with you."

"Oh, I doubt that's about to happen, Sandy. I have no more to say to you. Do you realize I may end up in the penitentiary?"

"I am sorry about that, Innis, but generally speaking when you commit a federal felony, that is one of the risks."

Her mouth pinches in bitterly.

"Screw you, Sandy. Are you leaving or am I calling the police?"

He nods, although his body does not feel disposed yet toward motion.

"And who is your lawyer now?" he asks.

"I don't have one yet. Rex says it shouldn't be him." She is referring to Rex Halsey, who negotiated the nonprosecution agreement with the US Attorney's Office that Innis wantonly violated. Rex's thought, clearly, is that Moses and Feld will never believe he has any control over his client. "Feld gave me until the end of the year to find another attorney. Happy holidays!" says Innis. "All I want for Christmas is a plea bargain. I'm going to

New York next week to interview a few lawyers whose names I've gotten."

Stern finds himself instinctively shaking his head.

"A poor idea," he says, "if you don't mind me saying so."

She flicks her fingers forward, urging him to speak.

"Since Moses and Feld neither like you nor believe you at this stage, you would be much better served by one of their former colleagues in the US Attorney's Office, whose integrity they trust. I could give you a few names, if you like."

She considers that. "Come inside for a second so I can write this down."

She knocks and Maria opens the back door, allowing them to enter the lanai. Innis beckons Stern toward the living room, where she slams through the drawers in an antique breakfront looking for paper and a pen. In the interval, Stern admires the precise furnishings, each piece exquisite as jewelry. The walls are clad in dark metallic wallpaper, and the intense beam of tiny spotlights shows off gorgeous little trinkets on the sideboards and console tables. Two tall Chinese vases stand like guards beside the sofa.

"I suppose your friends the Neucrisses may have some ideas about lawyers for you, too," Stern says.

Her look in response is purely vengeful. As was Stern's sarcasm.

"They don't seem to be answering their phones," Innis says.

"So surprising," says Stern in a tone far from kindly. "You do realize, don't you, Innis, that they will be telling the prosecutors and the FBI that they had absolutely no idea about the content of your prospective testimony?"

"Oh sure," she says. "I've already seen the view from under the bus. Do you realize that in the last two weeks I've been named as an additional defendant in two of the class actions where I actually gave those assholes the information that helped their buddies file suit in the first place?"

"Now you are beginning to understand why the Neucrisses have always been such favorites among their colleagues in Kindle County." At the annual bar association Christmas show, there are reliably at least half a dozen Neucriss jokes sprinkled among the skits, none of them remotely flattering. Stern keeps to himself a thought about Innis's taste in male companions. If he knew Neucriss was Innis's old beau, Sandy might have realized that he isn't a big enough jerk—or at least the right kind of jerk—to be of interest to her.

"You are aware, Innis, that our mutual friend Kiril has run for the hills?"

"I read the papers."

"We were required to withdraw as counsel. So it dawns on me that you do not have a lawyer and I do not have a client. Perhaps we could have a conversation for the purpose of legal advice. It would be privileged."

"Would that hold up in court?"

He thinks about it. "Almost certainly, yes." His license to practice is good for a few more weeks.

"Except you hate my guts," she says.

"That's a bit of an overstatement. I certainly understand why you were so eager to get even with Kiril."

"Oh, you don't know the half of it."

"All right," says Stern. "This will be the bargain: You will tell me the truth, and I will give you my best advice on how you should proceed, once you have found your new lawyer."

Innis lifts her face to think, then gives a little hiccup of a laugh.

"About six people have said to me, 'It's too bad you can't go to Sandy Stern.'"

Innis motions him to the sofa and calls to Maria for something to drink. She asks for white wine, while Stern requests club soda. The couch where Stern takes a seat is red brocade, and the glass-topped coffee table is again Chinese, black lacquer with a dragon breathing flame. For Florida, the room is surprisingly dark, probably to preserve the expensive artwork on the walls.

"How did you know I was even in town, by the way?" Innis asks. "Am I being followed?"

"Nothing quite so intrepid. The pairings for the Southwest Florida Tennis Association's year-end singles tournament are posted online. You seem to be advancing just as you expected in the seventy-pluses."

"I'm kicking ass," she says. "The trophy will be a nice touch in my cell, don't you think?"

Stern smiles. In extremis, we all come more clearly into view, and this afternoon he is getting a much better idea of who Innis is, with her anger and self-pity and, as of yet, no sign of shame. Much quicker, he thinks suddenly, than finding all that out after years of dating. That notion brings him close to a snicker.

"'Hate' puts it much too strongly. I admit that I do feel a bit humiliated by how easily you manipulated me. Especially your flirting. You did everything but bat your eyes."

She smiles at the description. Innis knows the lesson that seems to be on the news a few times every week: A man is never too old to be led astray by his penis. Consider Kiril with Olga. Stern can't recall the name at the moment, but he had an acquaintance, a lawyer who was older than he is now, who died after falling out of bed in a physical-rehab facility while trying to pinch a nurse's behind.

"But what was the point, Innis? You surely do not require an elderly cancer patient with a cane to convince you that you are still attractive."

"You don't really need me to explain that, do you? I wanted to turn the tables on Kiril. I wanted to disappoint him, which would be a small repayment for the way he disappointed me. I wanted him to believe I would show him some mercy—and then give him none. I know him, Sandy. He would be eager to believe that I still loved him. And I don't."

Stern could challenge her assertion, but there's no gain in that.

"So I was collateral damage?" he asks.

"If I was going to take him by surprise, Sandy, I had to take you by surprise. Neucriss always said those are the hardest cross-examinations, when the witness goes off in a direction you're entirely unprepared for."

He understands her logic. But she also must have taken some pleasure by seeing how easily he was led along.

"So what really occurred, Innis? In September of 2016? Did you and Kiril plot together to alter the dataset?"

She gives Stern a triumphant smile. "I knew he was too proud to tell you the truth."

Stern considers this idea, a variation on Marta's original theme. He was the wrong lawyer for Kiril, not because Pafko wanted to lie to him, but because Kiril would be reluctant to damage Stern's high opinion of him.

"Believe me, Sandy, he deserved everything that happened to him. Everything."

"Perhaps I should start by telling you what I have surmised, Innis?"

He'd been willing to waste a day of what life he had left on the bet that Innis would talk in the end. And she now looks eager to hear what he has pieced together.

"I believe, Innis, you were part of whatever happened in September 2016."

"How do you get to that?" she asks.

"It's a rather clear deduction. We learned in court that you knew about the problems with the medication. How soon? Certainly before you left, because you alone were hellbent to sell all your stock as soon as you could, rather than riding the market. And it is doubtful that whoever altered the dataset would have shared such a dangerous secret casually with anyone. Logic says that if you knew, you were part of it from the start."

"Go on," she answers.

"But you could not have altered the dataset on your own," Stern says. "Not that you lack the technical acumen. But the initial information about fatalities came up through the research staff. So you required the aid of someone who had the authority to reassure Dr. Tanakawa. Lep. Or Kiril. Or both."

"Okay." She drinks half her glass of wine in a gulp. "And this is all privileged, right? Whatever I say. Wild horses can't drag it out of you."

"It is privileged," Stern answers. "Barring a court order, it goes with me to the grave."

From her seat on the sofa, she considers Stern. There is a lot going on inside her, clearly—anxiety now, and a lot of the anger that drove her in the first place.

"Have you had one of these tête-à-têtes with Lep?"

"Regrettably, not. His lawyers still do not want him speaking to me."

"And Olga?"

Stern is surprised to hear Olga's name in this part of the conversation.

"I have. Are you saying she had a role in altering the dataset?"

"I told you last month, Sandy. Everything begins and ends with Olga. If she had an ounce of shame—or could keep her knees crossed—none of this would have happened. You know, everyone liked to laugh at Kiril behind his back for falling for her stuff, but nobody ever seemed to see the obvious. Including you."

"And what is that?"

"If the girl is going to sleep her way to the top, do you think she would have started with Kiril? Is he the most attractive alternative? Lep is handsome. Kind. A genius. And about to become very rich. I give Olga credit. As a schemer. She can play a long game. Do you think Lep ever really aimed to become CEO? He wants to do research. He'd be only too happy to have someone he trusted run the company, once Kiril finally let go."

"So that was Olga's long-term objective? Becoming CEO?"

"It was always apparent to me. I just didn't realize how low she would go, once Lep turned his back on her."

"Is it Lep who told you about his relationship with Olga?"

"Lep told me nothing. I was Olga's boss. I began to notice Lep and she were always on business trips at the same time. You know, in a small company, no matter how discreet people are, folks pick up on things. I remember years ago in the lab at Easton, one of my colleagues told me she knew I was seeing Kiril, because I'd stopped talking to him at work." She smiles. To Innis, it's still a bittersweet memory. "You have to feel sorry for Lep. I'm sure he never had a chance with Olga. You know, Sandy, it amazes me how easily taken in by all of that men are. A woman who other women see as a tramp, wearing her clothes a size too tight? And you idiots stand there panting. She is not a subtle person, Olga. I'm sure her come-on wasn't subtle either. But she could see how much Lep needed something at that moment to boost his self-esteem."

"And why was that? I'm still not following."

"I've told you this much before: g-Livia is Lep's work. An egotist like Kiril, he could explain to you how consequential his contributions were, but I was there, Sandy. Lep Pafko is the principal creator of g-Livia. The breakthrough in understanding RAS's positioning and how to reverse it? That was all computer modeling. Once Lep publishes more about how he did this, it will change the way pharmaceuticals are discovered."

"And Lep did not resent that Kiril took credit?"

"That's what I'm trying to tell you. He was incensed. Naturally. But he suffered in silence." For an instant, Stern takes note of Innis, bent emphatically across the cocktail table, carried away by the volcano of emotion still boiling up in her. "There is probably nothing in life that Lep Pafko prizes more than his father's adulation.

And he never gets it. I'm sure that as all the attention on g-Livia mounted, Lep was hoping his father would allow him to hear some of the applause. But that's not Kiril. So there sits Lep in September 2016. His father has claimed his discovery—and then his girlfriend."

"Lep made no protest about that either?"

"I have no idea. I never spoke to Lep about Olga. That's in the vault with him. But *I* told Kiril, when he started catting around with her, 'Ask your girlfriend about her relationship with your son.' He gave it the back of his hand. 'Then she has found a better man.' Can you imagine? Some father."

When Stern had decided to travel down here, he was gambling that this is what would move Innis to speak: She would want Stern to know what a complete shit his friend Kiril Pafko is. No matter how tortured the logic, or how deep her anger and embarrassment, she had a need to demonstrate to Stern that she wasn't the only one who'd failed to realize how base Kiril is.

"So that night, when all of this went down—" Innis says.

"September 15?"

"Right. I saw Lep sitting in his father's office."

"What time was this?"

"Seven?"

"I thought he was on his way to the airport."

"He had his stuff with him. It's fifteen minutes to the airport on the light rail."

The prosecutors had never wondered why Lep would go home, half an hour in the wrong direction. But then again, neither had Stern nor Marta.

"He was a wreck," Innis says. "I mean, that guy never looks happy—maybe Olga made him smile, which he deserves, frankly—but I mean, it was like his dog died. Three dogs. And I asked, and he said, 'We're screwed on Livia.' "

"And why was he in Kiril's office?"

"Apparently, he'd come in there with the unblinding codes to tell Kiril what Global was reporting about the trial. He wanted to give his father the courtesy of examining the dataset with him. And instead he found out that Kiril had skulked off without telling anybody where he was going and wasn't answering his phone. Meaning he was humping Olga somewhere. Nice moment for Lep, right?"

What was the old line? You don't get to pick your parents.

"He'd already unblinded the dataset when I saw him there," Innis says.

"Lep had?"

"It was right on the screen. He showed me. That's completely legitimate, by the way, with people dying. That's why the sponsor gets the codes. But you're supposed to report it. Anyway, it was a bad moment looking at those numbers."

"You realized that your road to the exit had just been barricaded?"

"That was the first thing I thought: I'm fucked. I'd given my life to PT, and that med was my whole future. Either I stayed and watched Kiril cavort with Olga, or I walked away to live like an old lady who can't afford to eat anything but cat food. And so I actually said it out loud, 'Let's fuck Kiril.' I had no idea how Lep would react, even then, but talk about a guy who'd finally had enough. We war-gamed it. It was his idea to call Wendy Hoh and say he was Kiril."

Stern frowns. "I have thought of that," says Stern, "but I know that Lep could have come up with far cleverer ways of altering the database that would have fooled the safety monitors and satisfied Wendy Hoh."

Innis laughs lightly. "Naturally. But we had to do something that would look like *Kiril*. Given a problem, Kiril's first instinct is always to try to bullshit someone. We both thought it was a long shot Wendy would change the data, but once she believed she was talking to the world-famous Dr. Pafko, she would have danced the boogaloo to make him happy. If Lep told her to change her own name, she would have."

"So instead of another trip to Stockholm, Kiril goes to Marion?"

"At that moment, both of us would have enjoyed that outcome. But the truth, Sandy, is neither of us gave any serious thought to the idea that these were anaphylactic deaths. Normally, if a medication produces an allergic response, you'd expect to see that in some part of the patient population long before a year. We were ninety percent sure we had a simple, solvable issue here—a drug interaction with some medication all these patients took, or a manufacturing problem. Lep thought the protein was denaturing and becoming toxic, which could be prevented by constant refrigeration until g-Livia was administered. Whatever the problem was, we assumed we could figure it out and solve it quickly."

Stern says nothing, but he makes no effort to hide his skepticism, and Innis leans closer to be more persuasive. She looks far different today, compared with his visit last month, when her casual appearance was more managed than he realized. Today he has truly caught her unaware, and he can see what light makeup hid—an unevenness in her complexion and a lack of color. Her posture is no longer what was taught in the day in finishing schools, and she slumps a bit. But it is bitterness that's most decidedly changed her appearance: a curl at the lips, the weight of anger throughout her face. The day he was here last month she had controlled every detail for maximum appeal. He reminds himself that the same is probably true of the story she is telling now.

"I don't want to pretend that we weren't grown-ups and professionals," Innis says. "We knew the right thing to do was stop and investigate. But as experienced researchers, neither of us saw much merit in the idea that after a year of use, some new lethality had emerged that was inherent in the medication itself.

"And the other thing you need to understand, Sandy, is that we did it all quickly. There wasn't a lot of time for second thoughts—or much thought at all. Lep had about forty minutes before he had to go. Everything was done in half an hour."

"And what about the patients who might die, Innis? You still realized there was a chance of that? No thought of them?"

"Compared to the ones whose lives were prolonged? This is a great, great medication. I don't have to explain that to you of all people. As a general matter, I think the FDA is in a no-win position, because people blame them no matter what they do. But as a society, we build highways and drive cars because it's convenient, even though 40,000 people die every year as a result. And don't even get me started with handguns. We balance benefits against harms all the time. There is no question in my mind that more people have died because the agency forced us to yank g-Livia from the market than expired due to allergic reactions."

"So, given when Lep boarded his plane to Seattle, it had to be you, Innis, who e-mailed the screenshot of the unaltered dataset to Olga. Did Lep agree to that part, too, or was that your improvisation?"

"I did it after he left." Innis's teeth are perfect and white, but her smile is nasty and vulpine. "I reached Lep right before his plane took off. I wanted him to know, so he was prepared if Olga talked to Kiril about the dataset. Lep actually laughed at first. He isn't the president of Olga's fan club either. But after he had a second to think about it, he was pissed—he said it was an unnecessary risk. But we agreed that if Kiril asked about the e-mail, Lep would say it was a prank. Things were tense enough between Kiril and Olga and Lep that his father would believe that Lep could be a bit juvenile for a second and enjoy giving them both heart failure."

Lep's reaction on the plane was correct, though. E-mailing the incriminating version of the database was an unnecessary risk—although Stern is not long in realizing Innis's point.

"This way, Innis, if investigators ever caught wind of all of this and Kiril went to Marion, you might get the pleasure of seeing Olga in an adjoining cell."

"She's a scheming twat, Sandy."

Stern is not much for name-calling, but if he were, it's not Olga he would single out that way. Measuring the look on Stern's face, Innis adds, "She ruined my life, Sandy. Don't ask me to feel sorry for her."

"And why inform the Neucrisses, Innis? Just spite?"

Her brow narrows in offense.

"Hardly. Not at all. The FDA maintains a postmarketing database of adverse event reports for all drugs and biologics. It's public, but far from comprehensive, because most physicians don't bother filing when a patient has a bad experience. But when I started to follow g-Livia, about a year after I left, I got a sick feeling. I could see that Lep and I had been too quick to minimize the problem. There were a lot of sudden deaths noted, and I knew that was just a fraction of what was actually occurring given the way reporting goes. There were even a couple of pathologists who'd looked at the data and were speculating about an allergic response. But what was I going to do then? The only way to correct the situation without getting myself in hot water was to call Anthony. I told them how to examine the database and suggested they call any doc who'd reported more than one sudden death episode. Most of them hung up on Anthony, but there were a few who were glad to hear from him."

Stern takes a swallow of his club soda, so he has some time to think over her explanation. He suspects it's mostly after-the-fact justification. Notably, Innis became public-spirited only when she had sold all her stock and banked about $100 million. If a form of the electrocardiogram ever were invented that could assess the feelings in someone's heart, such a contraption hooked up to Innis when she first called Anthony Neucriss would probably have sketched out the shape of vengeance rather than concern for patient safety. She was tired of waiting for Kiril's world to blow up and decided to light a match.

"So the Neucrisses let you know a year ago August that Ms. Hartung would be making contact with Kiril, and you had your recording app ready. Why were you so sure Kiril would call you?"

"His great project in flames? Of course he'd call me. Is he going to ask Olga for advice in a life crisis? Or Donatella, who'd simply exult in another opportunity to tell him he was a fool? Lep's a genius, but not in managing a situation like this."

"What would you have done if Kiril said that he knew nothing about any sudden deaths while you were recording him? Or asked if you did?"

"That's what I expected."

After thinking that through, Stern smiles reluctantly.

"You recorded the call so you had your denial on tape when the prosecutors came to your door?"

Innis elevates her hands: Voilà. She'd made the recording not to ensnare Kiril so much as to clear herself. The FBI would never accept Kiril's denials, because of the evidence on his computer. Yet when she said she had no idea about the sudden fatalities, Kiril, who truly knew nothing, would be unable to contradict her. The recording would prove definitively that she had no role in the fraud.

She must have savored every step as the plan unfolded, taking a special private glee in the secret ways she had mocked Olga and Kiril, by sending Olga the e-mail or using the phone Kiril and PT were still paying for to call the Neucrisses. Both gambits were dangerous, but they undoubtedly deepened the joy in vengeance. Revenge had clearly been on Innis's mind long before she saw Lep sitting in his father's office. Even now, given the largely shameless way she has told the story, she seems to regard her actions as justifiable. What had she said to Stern down here last time? With Kiril, she had settled for less than most people want—and then he took away even that. She remains, in her own view of the entire saga, the biggest and least deserving victim.

"Well thought out," says Stern. It is not the first time he's complimented a criminal.

"Thank you," says Innis. "The only complication was when the criminal investigation began. Lep seemed to be losing his nerve because he was afraid Kiril would slowly realize what had happened. Even after all of that, Lep was still unwilling to have a confrontation with his father. We actually met in Oklahoma City. I spent a day trying to calm him down. But then I had an inspiration."

"Which was?"

"I told Lep to talk to Donatella."

Stern feels the deepest jolt of full-on surprise yet. His glass of club soda is halfway to his lips, and he finds he has held it there in the air, as he stares at Innis over the brim.

"And what role did Donatella play?"

"I don't know the details. You'll have to ask Lep. But I was certain Donatella would never side with Kiril against her son. She adores Lep." And loves to hate Kiril, Stern thought.

"So now," says Innis, "you're going to tell me what to do. Am I going to get out of this?"

Stern thinks a while. "You have a very good chance," he says, although he cannot completely erase a note of disappointment in his voice.

He has several ideas. He writes down a list of lawyers. Young Diaz, who has been officing in Stern's former law library, is his first choice. He had been the chief of the Major Crimes Division in the US Attorney's Office, and Moses thinks the world of him.

In terms of strategy, Innis's best course is to wait. Feld may never call while Kiril remains on the loose, since it's hard to benchmark anybody else's punishment until Pafko has been sentenced. After that, she should keep her peace. What Innis said at trial is not quite definitive enough to convict her for perjury—she took the Fifth at the right time. And there's no direct proof of her role in the fraud. If Moses wants to hear the whole story, she should talk only under oath with a statutory grant of use immunity. That will sorely compromise Moses's chance to prosecute her for anything, which makes it highly unlikely he'll ever go that route.

"What about those texts between Neucriss and me?" Innis asks.

"Hmmm," Stern answers. "Last I heard, Moses was having some problems authenticating them. I don't know the details." The messages are almost certainly gone. The FBI will press the Neucrisses, but whatever story they tell will protect their freedom and their law licenses. They will all be emphatic that they had no idea Innis intended to lie under oath. The serpent Eve met in the garden took lessons from the Neucrisses.

"And what about the civil cases? Am I going to lose my house?"

"I doubt it. The kind of class-action lawyers who pal around with the Neucrisses are vultures. They want money, not justice. With the testimony Dr. Robb gave at trial, and the pressure from patients and oncologists, g-Livia will be back on the market soon. PT will be making billions, and the company will pay for a global settlement on behalf of the company and all its officers. Lep will be happy to buy you out of trouble, because he'll be doing the same thing for himself."

Stern's assessment, entirely sincere, makes Innis brighten for the first time in the hour-plus Stern has been here. The hangdog look didn't suit her well, and with a little more confidence, much of her robustness is restored.

Stern finishes his drink. Innis offers another trip to the balcony to watch the sunset. Stern is tempted but instead says, "I'll leave you to that," and prepares to depart.

Unlike his meeting with Olga, he would not say that hearing Innis's side has improved his opinion of her. He's most struck by her mean streak, which is deep and wide. But after three decades, Kiril had to know that about her. And he trampled her anyway.

Innis sees him to the door, and surprises Stern by coming close again—for a fragment of a second, he gets a sense once more of her sensual presence when she kisses him on the cheek.

"I really do prefer older men," she tells him with a comical eye, and Stern heads out to Cesar in the limo, laughing in spite of it all.

37. A DINNER

Stern's flight from West Palm Beach lands in Kindle County late morning on Monday, after another soothing weekend with Silvia. Stern and his sister can sit for hours in the sun, looking out at the Atlantic in almost complete silence, yet both will come away feeling deeply sustained.

He takes a taxi to Center City. At Stern & Stern, the business of closing the doors is proceeding full speed. The staff is boxing up files to go back to clients or to storage, and many of the pictures have been removed from the walls with a rectangle of whiter space where they were. In the reception area, some of the freestanding furniture has been picked up by its new owners. Several dustballs are left where the pieces stood, which Stern briefly mistakes for mice. The Sterns' landlord has already re-leased the space. The firm will vacate on December 31, and Marta has proposed an open house late that afternoon, a final bash for their many loyal employees and friends in the bar and elsewhere. Stern and his daughter both like the idea of celebrating the end. After thinking at length about Kiril and Lep, he has a deeper appreciation for his partnership with his daughter. And the truth is that much of his joy in the practice of law has been palling around with other attorneys, despite the vexations he's felt with difficult opponents. The public scorns lawyers—except their own—but Stern has relished their company, the particular kind of smarts so many share. For better or worse, they are his people.

One thing he concluded over the weekend is that he cannot keep from Marta his conversation with Innis, which remains privileged within the firm. As soon as his daughter hears that he was in Naples, she is irate.

"You are worse than a teenager," she says. "Do I have to take away your credit cards? You aren't three weeks out of surgery."

"And my heart is stronger than it's been in years. Really," he says, merely to provoke a reaction, "I am wondering if I should rethink my decision to retire."

Marta starts to scream until she sees him smiling. She shoos him from her office but is back at his door in a few minutes and takes the chair in front of his desk to find out what Innis said.

Marta thinks it all over slowly.

"When are you going to say that you were right about Kiril and I was wrong?"

"I would never say that," answers Stern. They are both smiling.

"And why didn't Kiril point the finger at Innis and Lep? He must have figured out some of this."

"I have been contemplating that, Marta, with no real answers. He couldn't accuse Innis without including Lep. I have asked myself if it is possible that he decided to be a good father and not to sacrifice his son for the sake of his freedom."

Marta scowls. Overall, her dislike of Kiril seems to have been fortified over the last several months. Not that she is alone.

"A guy who wouldn't give up his little *chiquita* for his son isn't going to the pokey for that kid either."

There is, of course, another unanswered question. Once Marta leaves, Stern makes a call to Chicago. His phone rings again in half an hour.

"Pierce Shively, Sandy. I've relayed your request to talk to my client and he politely declines. Lep wants to put his father's trial behind him."

"Did you tell him that I've spoken to Innis?"

"He has no idea why that should make any difference to him."

"Very well," Stern says. Lep is going to hold the line.

He begins taking down his diplomas, his licenses from the State Supreme Court, the federal district court, and the US Supreme Court, where he argued once. He lost 9–0, but it was a thrill to be there. Everything he touches unspools memories, most good, but even the unhappy ones feel far more innocuous, given that he managed to survive.

This reverie is interrupted when Vondra puts a call through late in the afternoon. Donatella Pafko.

"Short notice, Sandy, but I was hoping to offer you dinner at my table tonight."

"A soiree?"

"No, just the two of us. It is the least I can do to express my gratitude."

Stern arrives at six thirty. He has brought his hostess a small bouquet, which Donatella receives as if he had presented the Hope Diamond. They enjoy a glass of champagne in the Anglophile living room and then go in to dinner. The dining room table is set elegantly. Donatella occupies the head, formerly Kiril's place, and Stern sits immediately to her left. Neither of them hears well enough any longer to engage in the formality of sitting at opposite ends.

He allows Donatella to mention Kiril first.

"You have been interviewed by the marshals?" Stern asks.

"They are here every week. I tell them everything."

"And what is that?"

"Whatever Kiril says when he calls."

"And how often is that, Donatella?"

She worries her head a little, to indicate the number does not really matter to her. She has dressed for dinner, with a high lace bodice and a heavy necklace in which Stern suspects the many jewels of imposing size are real.

"Once or twice a week. He keeps asking me to join him there. He has a lawyer who has convinced him that the government of Argentina will never consent to extradition. Do you think that is true?"

Quite deliberately, Stern has not studied the matter. His guess, however, is that Argentina has the same kind of rich-people's exceptions to the insider trading laws as the US and that something—the fact that only the grandchildren benefited, or that the medical information about the g-Livia patients was no longer confidential—will provide ample fodder for an argument that what Kiril has been found guilty of is either not a crime under Argentine laws or is not one covered by the extradition treaty between the two countries.

"Are you considering joining him?" Stern asks.

"Not really," Donatella answers. "As you know, we always visit Argentina once or twice a year and I will continue to do that. I have reached the point in my life when a few days with Kiril now and then will be quite enough." It is none of Stern's business why, only now, Donatella has reached this decision. He would have thought she had reached her limit a few years ago when Kiril first announced he was abandoning her for Olga. She had asked only to be treated with dignity and respect for appearances while he wandered, and in the end he was unwilling to grant her even that. Although Stern has not worked out the particular geometry of this, he suspects that Donatella's decision to stand by Kiril during the trial might have been more about protecting Lep than her husband.

Still, it makes a gloomy end to what had been a grand romance, at least as Kiril told the story. Stern had heard it from him years ago during one of their annual lunches at the Morgan Towers Club during the holiday season when the courts and Kiril's lab were all but closed. Kiril brought wine from the family vineyard in Mendoza, which they drank slowly as the winter light weakened in the room and the staff turned the other tables for breakfast.

'I was shameless,' Pafko said, meaning that he had refused to accept Donatella's insistence that he stop flirting, wooing. He had met her after coming to Buenos Aires as a medical student, determined to ingratiate himself with BA's prominent families. She was tall and beautiful, six years married and still childless. Her husband, in the Italian way, was two decades older, and perhaps Donatella already sensed that her destiny as a mother was going to be thwarted due to a failure not her own. Certainly, Ricardo, the husband, never fathered any children after the end of his marriage to Donatella. Kiril, with the predatory instincts of a panther when it came to romance, sensed a vulnerability.

But in his telling, he was stirred by more than just the appetite for a difficult conquest. He felt instantly that Donatella and he operated on their own frequency, a channel only she and he could hear, and one that they each had long assumed had no other listeners. He invented excuses to see her, showing up at events he knew she would attend. Catching her as she went to the cloakroom, he would get as close as possible and whisper that she must agree to meet him. Or in a crowded hall, when others broke off and left them together an instant, he would murmur, 'I am in a fever.' She rolled her eyes; she told him to stop. But she never involved any outside authority whom it would be dangerous to ignore, like her husband or her priest. Kiril sent flowers that would arrive midday when Ricardo was at work. He found a drifter on the street, who followed her to a shop and placed a small gift in her hands: a thin chain, a bottle of scent, something too tiny for her husband to notice.

'I wore her down. It took months.' The day she accepted from him an antique tiger's-eye ring was the day he knew she would soon be in his arms.

Kiril says he understood that by then a person of her intellect and capacity would yearn to escape the narrow boundaries of a marriage her parents had regarded as wise to another of BA's regal families, with large tombs at the Recoleta Cemetery. Kiril promised America. And a life at the forefront of science. They ran off together. He married her in front of a judge in Kindle County, years before her husband actually agreed to a divorce.

What we hope for in the love of others, Stern has decided, is often illusory. Happy marriages—and Stern has had at least one—begin with an understanding of the limits on what can be asked. For Donatella, it was the deal made by women in the eons when they knew they had little chance to be great themselves. But Kiril had delivered. She was the wife of a Nobel Prize winner and never had to surrender that distinction. He was great because she had helped him be great.

"Kiril asks me in every call if I have spoken to you," Donatella says now. "I have a number if you want to talk to him yourself. He knows he put Marta and you in an embarrassing position by departing."

Stern shrugs. "He is not the first client to misuse his lawyer. Marta has said from the start, Donatella, that Kiril chose us as his counsel because he knew that I would not challenge his lies."

"Well, Sandy, you are an old friend. And still a magnificent lawyer. You were my suggestion, if you must know, and I remain convinced that I gave Kiril excellent advice."

"Because I would not demand the truth?"

"And what truth is that, Sandy?"

"About Lep, certainly."

Donatella, so graceful, tries not to falter, but her eyes dart off quickly at the mention of her son. She fingers the heavy sterling spoon over her Limoges dinner plate, which has been reserved there for dessert.

"I have a request, Sandy. A personal request."

Now, Stern thinks, we get to the point of dinner. He nods, meaning only that he will listen.

"Please leave dear Lep in peace," says his mother. "He is a wonderful son, a wonderful scientist, a wonderful father. This has been a horrible time for him. For years now."

If the roof caves in on Innis and the prosecutors extract the truth from her, Lep's horrible time might get considerably worse. But Lep has excellent lawyers and they will know, if they ever hear Innis's story about Lep's role, that it is uncorroborated and the word of someone easily attacked as a perjurer. Moses is far too responsible to bring charges on that basis, as long as Lep is wise enough to keep his peace and not contradict himself. Given that, Stern understands why Lep's legal team has advised him to stay clear of Sandy.

Donatella watches Stern avidly, as he works these things through.

"I must address one matter with Lep," Stern says then. "For my own sake. I do not need to discuss any of the evidence against Kiril—datasets, none of that. But I need to be face-to-face with him. And with respect, I demand that. I would hate to send the Greenwood County Sheriff's Police to his door. He will understand what I mean by that." Her dark eyes are stilled by caution, even alarm. He sees the words coming to her and adds, "Please do not ask."

"And can you promise, Sandy, that no harm will come to Lep?"

A challenging question. "I am sorry, Donatella, but I can promise only the reverse. If he will not see me, then his troubles are going to multiply manyfold. Certainly, if we speak, I will remember he is the son of a very dear and valued friend." He takes Donatella's old hand as he says this, with a touch firm enough to be reassuring. "But if Lep is evasive with me or shades the truth, I will do as he fears."

She nods a bit, then looks at the candles aflame at the center of the table in the heavy sterling silver candlesticks.

"Now, I have a question for you, Donatella. I understand that you recommended me to Kiril, expecting that I would be reluctant to advise Kiril to turn on his son, whom I have known since he was a boy. But that does not explain Kiril's compliance, undergoing a trial on murder charges of which he knew he was innocent. What is puzzling is that up to that point, he exhibited little ability to restrain himself for Lep's sake."

"Oh that, Sandy. That is simple." Stern waits. Donatella again eyes the spoon, turning it over in her knotted fingers, while a smile forms, a rare moment in which she exhibits deep appreciation of herself. The heat in the house comes on, adding a whisper behind them that further conceals Donatella's lowered voice. Stern edges forward to hear her better. "I told him if he accused Lep of having any part in this that I would take Lep's side, even if that meant giving testimony against Kiril. The law? I know nothing about that really. But Lep's revenge on his father—that, frankly Sandy, was well deserved." It was of course a revenge for his mother's sake, too, whom Kiril was planning to leave in her dotage. Stern has not recognized that part of Lep's motivation before, but Donatella would have grasped it instantaneously. "Whatever Lep said to escape responsibility, I would raise my hand to God and say that Kiril had admitted to me doing exactly that. Perhaps a brilliant lawyer could poke holes in the government's case and contrive a way to secure Kiril's freedom. But the path out of this maze could never come at Lep's expense."

As she says, it is simple—even if it reveals more of the brutal truths of her marriage to Kiril.

At the door, Stern hugs her. At this age, it is common for him to wonder when he parts with old friends if he will ever be with them again, and in this case, he knows he has seen far too much of the pain in Donatella's life for her to seek out his company in the future. After the door opens, he lifts her hand to kiss it and then says, resolutely, "Goodbye, dear Donatella."

38. THE OTHER DR. PAFKO

The following evening, Stern and Pinky have just returned from the office and are about to settle down to soup when the front doorbell rings. Pinky goes off to answer, but Stern recognizes Lep Pafko's voice and rises as Pinky admits Lep through the storm door. The fur-trimmed hood of Lep's parka is around his face. Pinky says nothing to him but instead strikes one index finger against the other, as if making fire. The gesture seems comical, but Lep stops cold when he takes in the fierce look Pinky is giving him. Stern eases her out of the doorway, and Pinky stalks off without further word.

He points Lep to the living room. This is the only space in the whole house that feels slightly haunted to Stern. He has never experienced any discomfort about continuing to inhabit the place he shared with Helen or sleeping in their bed. He feels her presence and enjoys it. The living room is another matter. It had a kind of mausoleum quality even when Helen was alive. It was reserved for guests and always pristine. Despite owning two housefuls of furniture between them, Helen insisted on newly redecorating this room and, once that was done, barely used it. Formality was never a comfort to Helen. There was not a breath of it in her. Stern always adored Helen's unwillingness to be guided by other people's social expectations, an attitude she had helped him assume to a degree.

As for the living room, it is a nice enough space with a beautiful malachite hearth on the fireplace, but when he is in here Stern feels like a visitor. Nonetheless, with Pinky about to throttle Lep, it is a safer choice than the family room behind the kitchen, where Lep would feel the weight of Pinky's black stare.

He offers a drink to Lep, who asks only for a glass of water without ice, and Stern returns to the kitchen.

"Give me a minute alone with him," Pinky says, as she's studying her phone, "and I'll beat down his scientific ass." Pinky would be giving away at least eight inches and seventy pounds, but if Stern had to wager on the outcome of those fisticuffs, his money would be on his granddaughter.

"Very gallant, Pinky. I shall let you know if I need any help."

Returning, Stern puts the water on the coffee table in front of Lep. With his forlorn expression, he has the look of a prisoner who knows that his interrogation may devolve at any second to brutality. He has declined to remove his coat, simply pulling back the hood and opening the zipper, and is perching on the edge of the sofa. He clearly wants nothing to detain him if he decides to race for the door.

"Donatella said you needed to talk to me," he says.

"I assume you understand why."

Despite his natural good looks, the blondish froth of hair and sharp features, Lep did not weather the trial especially well, and no wonder. His eye sockets are now rings of gray, and his nostrils seem permanently edged in red. Has he been crying? Possibly. Possibly for years now.

"Maybe it's better, Sandy, if you just tell me what's on your mind."

Lep is not about to volunteer any confessions, which is not a promising start.

"What is on my mind, Lep, is that you tried to kill me on the highway."

Assuming Donatella passed along Stern's remark about the Greenwood County Sheriff's Police, Lep has arrived knowing the subject of their conversation, but even so his eyes go still, and his jaw moves unconsciously.

"Do you deny that?" Stern asks.

Lep shakes his head but still doesn't speak.

Stern continues to stare hard at Lep and says finally, "Explain yourself, please."

"'Explain' myself?" He manages a sound that approaches a sardonic laugh. "Sandy, you hear people say they're losing their grip? I lost my grip about five years ago. In my whole life, I was never an impulsive person. I mean, even as a teenager, I'd look at what other kids did and think it was crazy. Climbing the water tower to write your name? Or jumping off the Heights into the Kindle? What was the point? But then I got involved with her." He is reluctant even to pronounce Olga's name. "Before that, I sort of thought I understood the way things go. You look at a woman, but you're married. Your father makes your blood boil, but everybody's got a father. But once I, I don't know, gave in, whatever you call it—now it's like there's a leak in me somewhere. Something happens and there are moments when I can't seem to pull back."

Many of the persons Stern represented throughout his career could have given Stern the same speech, but most were not even self-aware enough to recognize their condition. After Clara died, Stern had found himself shockingly out of control for a brief period. And overall, it had informed the rest of his life—and for the better. He restrained himself out of wisdom, not fear. But Lep, thus far, does not seem to have learned many lessons.

"Were you in love with Olga, Lep?"

Lep looks up abruptly. Stern might have pinched him. Sandy wonders if he's the first person to ask Lep that question out loud. It is actually none of Stern's business, although it explains why Lep's persistent anger with Kiril boiled over. But the younger Dr. Pafko turns his head ruefully several times.

"I really don't know. It was exciting. It was really, really exciting, and new that way. She said she was in love with me. But I love my family. I always knew I loved my family."

Stern decides he is not entitled to any follow-up. Affairs, by their nature, rarely follow an established etiquette. He returns to the subject that brought Lep here.

"And what was it I did to turn you toward homicide?"

"I was terrified, Sandy. Completely terrified. Back in March, that afternoon, Olga came to my office as soon as you left her. We don't speak much. Never, really, now. So it was very strange to see her there, but she said, 'I want to warn you. Your father's lawyer was asking me a lot of questions about our relationship. Me and you.' She seemed to think you might have figured that out."

Stern asks, "And if I had?"

"Then you'd figure out everything else eventually."

Was that true? Possibly, yes. He certainly would have been well on the track once he recognized the dimension of the rage Lep had to feel for Kiril and the perversity of their situation.

"Lep, I could not offer a defense your father did not approve of."

"I wasn't thinking like that. And besides, Kiril will always do what's best for him in the end. It just seemed to me that if you knew, sooner or later it would all come out in court. I'd lose my family. And maybe end up in the defendant's chair, too." Lep flaps his arms like a flightless bird. Even describing his fears does not seem to do justice to their magnitude. "I mean, I'd waited every day for two and a half years for the whole thing to unravel. And then I was terrified it had. I was barely holding it together with Kiril under indictment, and then, thinking you'd pieced it all together, I really felt like I should just swallow a bottle of pills." He actually reaches forward and sips sparingly from his water.

"You've probably never had a real panic attack, Sandy, but it doesn't necessarily get better with time to think about things. Sometimes, when you get in your head, your fantasies, it all just multiplies. I was sitting there with my heart flying apart for about an hour after Olga left, and then I saw you limping out to the parking lot."

"So you signed out a car?"

"I already had the keys. Once I became CEO, I mean Acting, there were weeks at a time when I was in the office later than the train ran. Oscar would just sign out a car to me and bring the keys by my office. When my schedule lightened up, I'd return it. Nobody really asks you questions, Sandy, when you're the boss."

"But looking out the window, you decided to kill me?"

"I decided to follow you. I wasn't sure what I was going to do. I don't know, maybe I thought I'd signal you to pull over and explain the whole thing to you and beg you to keep quiet. I don't know. The thinking part doesn't have a lot of room next to the panic. I was literally driving ninety down the highway, and then I saw your car. And swerved into you. But at the last second, I pulled away from the driver's door, I really did. And I can't tell you how I felt when I hit you. It was like, No, no, now it's all worse. Now I had something even more terrible to be panicked about. I was so happy you recovered. Really. I know how stupid it is to say that, but I was, like, ecstatic when I heard you were going to be okay."

"Especially when it turned out that after brain surgery, I was none the wiser about Olga and you. I assume you took the Malibu directly to a body shop?"

"I drove back to Nearing. I mean, every second I was waiting for the cops to pull me over and put me in cuffs. But I got to a body shop on the other side of town and told the guy it was all super embarrassing. I was the big boss and had cracked up a company car because I wasn't paying attention and hit a concrete barrier on the highway."

"So if you had the car repaired, Lep, and Oscar thought little of you keeping it for a week, why bother stealing the signout forms?"

"By the time I brought the car back, I knew from Kiril that you were saying that the car that hit you had a PT decal in the rear window. I just wanted to be sure there was no record that I had one of the Malibus the day of the collision. I didn't think Oscar would be sure one way or the other if there wasn't a paper trail.

"Half the time when I return one of the Malibus normally, Oscar is out in his golf cart. So I just drop the keys on his desk and find the form and sign the car back in. The day I brought the car back from the shop, I drove by a couple of times until I could see Oscar out checking the parking lot. Then I just stood in his little hut and made like I was signing in, while I actually crumpled up every form for the week it happened."

Lep, whose eyes have not risen from the floor for several minutes, reaches out and sips again. He stares at the glass at length before he resumes speaking.

"Sandy, my life has been chaos for five years now. I mean with Olga, I slipped, or fell, or gave in, whatever stupid word people put to that, but I cannot even remember what it was like to be me in 2013. Truly I cannot. I'm not sure I'll ever do another piece of scientific work worth discussing. That kind of concentration is a thing of the past for me. I can barely add two plus two. There are days when I just go from one thing to another in my head and realize I've spent the whole day sitting in a chair and looking out the window. You know, Kiril—he can forget about anything, or pretend it's not happening."

"So I have noticed. Have you spoken to your father?"

Lep tosses his head minutely, his eyes closed, to indicate no.

"My father and I haven't really had a conversation in more than three years."

Stern does the math first, then asks, "Do I take it you had a disagreement about Olga?"

"I mean, she knew it was killing me. That was the point, right? She'd go flouncing by my door into Kiril's office ten times a day. But finally, I figured I'd tell him the truth and ask him for a little mercy. Not even to stop seeing her. But get her out of the office. Give her some monster severance and get the whole thing out of my face."

"He did not agree?"

Lep winces at the memory.

"He already knew about you and Olga, I take it?" Stern asks.

"I was surprised, but I guess she'd told him. He just shrugged that part off. But he looked at me and said, 'If you've created a situation that you cannot tolerate, Lep, then perhaps you are the one who should think about leaving.' And I knew what that was about really. When g-Livia went on the market in a few months, there was going to be a huge fanfare. All kinds of attention. And he would be just as happy to have me gone, so he could tell all the reporters how he'd basically done all this himself."

"Even though you were the one who deserved the lion's share of the credit."

"Science is always collaboration, Sandy. It's not like writing a poem. Kiril made real contributions."

"But nowhere as large as yours, Lep."

"You know, at least he could have said we did it together. But when Kiril tells the story, it's like he's the architect and I was the carpenter."

There is, of course, considerable justice to what Lep did to his father. If Kiril wanted all the credit for g-Livia, then he also deserved all the blame for its problems.

"So that was the last time you and Kiril spoke, when you asked him to fire Olga?"

"I mean, the conversation went south, which was my fault in a way."

"How so?"

"I don't have his skill with people. I don't. I know that."

"And what does that mean?"

"I said to him, finally, 'Don't you understand she's just trying to get even with me?' "

"Ah," says Stern. "I take your point."

"He just smirked at me and said, 'On the contrary, Lep, she seems quite happy.' "

Stern cannot stifle a small sound. An ugly scene.

"My whole life," says Lep, "I've never really understood my father. There's a different Kiril inside my head, I guess. And that Kiril never shows up. But that moment, when I asked him for just a little empathy—that was the end. I mean, guilty isn't even the word for how I've felt about what I was doing to him. Because lying, all that, it's not me. But I never doubted he deserved it. I hugged him in front of the jury because Feld told me it would be a great touch."

Lep drinks the rest of his water and heaves a great sigh.

"I want to ask you to forgive me, Sandy. Please forgive me." Lep manages for the first time to actually bring his fair eyes to Stern's, albeit not for long. He has the pink-eyed look of a rabbit.

Sonny, when she talks privately about sentencing, says she always gives convicted defendants credit when they say they're sorry. Not that she thinks they mean it, in most cases. But at least, she says, it shows they know how to behave.

Yet in Lep's case, Stern does not doubt his sincerity, or his self-analysis that his emotional life has descended to chaos. And if Innis is correct that it is Lep who made the most significant breakthroughs in the development of g-Livia—and a number of scientists at PT have hinted the same thing—then Stern feels obliged to give proper weight to that. Yes, Lep put Stern's life in peril. But, in Lep's better moments, he had a signal role keeping Stern here on earth.

"Are you talking to someone, Lep?"

Lep nods repeatedly, but it turns out that his apparent yes actually means no.

"I know I have to. I've gotten names. But I just don't even know where I'd start. I can't even imagine admitting all of this to someone else. I feel crazed just sitting here, realizing you know as much as you do. You've heard people say they feel like jumping out of their own skin?" He tries and fails again with another effort to meet Stern's eyes.

Before Lep arrived, Stern had given some thought to whether he would go to the police, if Lep was insincere or dishonest. It would be a cruel thing to do to Donatella in her current circumstances. But a distraught mother is often in the back of the courtroom weeping when someone who deserves it is convicted. Yet the man in Stern's living room seems to have been forthright—and responsible—and Stern made a commitment to his mother to consider her.

"Here are my terms," he says to Lep. "I will keep this to myself, if you are taking concrete steps to get yourself under control. You can go to a shrink or go to jail. And not one or two visits. A genuine course of treatment. You will authorize whatever psychiatrist you choose to inform me every six months or so whether you are still attending your sessions."

When they'd met, Helen had far more faith than Stern in the talking cure. But once they had decided to get married, he had spent quite a bit of time with someone, trying to get a perspective on Clara, her death, and his family, especially Peter. And it had helped. Not changed everything. But helped.

At any rate, the proposal he has made Lep is one that he has fervently wished a wise prosecutor had made to dozens of his clients over the years. Not all of them by any means—many were incorrigible and had repeated their behavior often enough that they deserved to spend time in the penitentiary, just to grant the rest of humanity a reprieve. But there were quite a few who felt enough shame to make genuine efforts to prevent a reoccurrence of their conduct. Punishment for its own sake, to make the victims feel better, had a purpose, too. But in this case, Stern does not require that. For almost sixty years now, he has stood before sentencing judges, preaching the need for second chances. He will give one to Lep.

39. RETURNING

As Stern might have guessed, traveling with Pinky is not easy. Although it was done outside Stern's presence, he knows that Marta—not in complete jest—informed her niece that Pinky will suffer the tortures of the Inquisition if anything happens to Stern on this trip. Marta, in fact, was initially fiercely opposed to this journey, even when Stern proposed taking Pinky as a companion. But Al approved, and Marta relented when her father said, 'You must understand, Marta, what it would mean to me at this point in my life to see BA again.' Pinky and he depart Christmas afternoon and will return December 30, back in time for the great New Year's Eve finale at Stern & Stern.

The only other living creature toward whom Pinky has assumed a caretaking role is poor moth-eaten Gomer, so there is no subtlety or practice when she hovers over her grandfather. Seeing this, the flight attendants seem to assume Stern is utterly incompetent and speak to him as if he is a kindergartener. It is all that Stern can do to remain polite, and he is relieved that Al's pills allow several hours of sleep during the night portion of the flight.

Meanwhile, Pinky remains herself. The trip takes roughly fifteen hours, including their layover in Dallas, and—beyond asking Stern every ten minutes if he's all right—Pinky and he have few conversations of longer than three or four sentences. Instead, she sleeps or watches her tablet. It is only near the end of the second flight that Stern realizes she has not been viewing the same movie over and over, but rather a string of them, in which, again and again, some person with superpowers saves the world amid much crashing and intense bursts of light.

It goes without saying that Pinky is in no way like him. For instance, he has given up on trying to interest her in reading. Both of Marta's boys, on the other hand, are often said to have completely channeled their grandfather, and he adores each of them as much as breath. And yet, enigmatically, if he were forced at gunpoint to answer the question—which he might not respond to even in those circumstances—he would say that he is closest with Pinky of all his grandchildren. This is not simply because of their recent living circumstances, but also because of the depth of their understanding of one another and the acceptance that goes with it. For the trillionth time in a long life, Stern wonders if he will ever fully comprehend love.

Looking out at BA as they speed in from the airport, he can feel the might of the place, almost as intensely as he experienced it as a child. On the outskirts, the architecture of the public housing is essentially Stalinist, big squares of concrete, but he is not surprised to find that within the city limits BA remains a place of great beauty and vibrancy, with its twelve-lane avenues, where the traffic moves at reckless speeds by free-for-all rules, and its grand old buildings whose graceful details like the huge arched windows and balconies over the streets are reminiscent of Paris or Madrid.

The travel agent booked them a place in Puerto Madero, the old harbor district that fell into disuse and recently has revived as an area of curving glass-and-steel skyscrapers beside the river. Their hotel, a reclaimed grain mill, is palatial. The furnishings in the lobby bar remind him of his office, and he snaps a photo that he texts to Marta—'My taste explained'—but it is his mother he is soon thinking of. She would have looked through the doors and clucked that she did not own clothing fine enough for her even to dare to step into the lobby. Poor Mama, he thinks. She never got the chance to learn everything money cannot buy.

As soon as Stern has washed his face in his room, he texts Pinky, who is next door. Marta made them swear an oath to rest when they arrived, but Stern's approach to jet lag is to get out in the daylight. When he offers to show Pinky where he grew up, she is enthusiastic.

Mysteriously, Stern's Argentine Spanish became more accessible the moment the aircraft touched down here—*that*, Stern realizes, is the language he cannot make out in his dreams, where his mother, often conflated with Clara, mumbles. He directs the taxi driver to the Balvanera neighborhood, where the Sterns had moved when Alejandro was five. They came here from Entre Rios, a town of European refugees whom Stern's father served as a physician. In his full beard and pince-nez, Papa had trod behind barefoot Indians to his clinic every morning, wearing his full-length white doctor's coat despite the dust, as if he might not remember who he was without the respectful gestures of the townspeople prompted by the outfit. Even as a child, Stern could feel the full measure of his father's anxieties. After the family was forced to flee from Germany in 1928, the man was like a piece of broken crystal glued back together. Seeking something more secure, Papa had relocated them here to BA, where his hopes were immediately disappointed. They were regarded as rubes, while his father's noticeable insecurities made it difficult to attract patients and build a medical practice. There was never any money.

In this part of the city where the Stern family settled, the Jewish community might have numbered as many as 300,000. Even the gentiles referred to the adjoining neighborhood—where the Sterns moved eventually—as 'Villa Kreplach' instead of Villa Crespo. In some ways, their life was not markedly different than that of Stern's American friends who had grown up in Brooklyn or the Lower East Side in Manhattan. There were three Yiddish dailies, kosher butcher shops and bakeries, tiny storefront synagogues. These were poor people—shopkeepers and factory workers, dockhands and meatpackers—who, as Mama put it, sold their labor to survive. But they accepted, as they had for centuries elsewhere, that in time there would be some grotesque outbreak of anti-Semitism, much as there had been a decade before when thugs, swinging tire irons and barrel staves, had roamed through the neighborhood breaking windows and skulls. During World War II, when Argentina was aligned with the Axis and there were giant Nazi rallies in Luna Park, his mother stored blankets and canned goods in a closet, preparing for the night they would be rounded up for the camps. Perón, whatever else could be said about him, was far more willing to accept the Jewish community. As a boy in the US, Stern had been the target of slurs, but never assumed, as he had during most of his upbringing in Argentina, that being a Jew left a question mark over his existence.

With Pinky, he walks two blocks, keeping up a brisk pace despite his cane and the heat. It is over 90 degrees American, as Stern would say, with close air and a sun intense enough to seem menacing. The little electrical device in his chest, whose spurts Stern believes he can feel occasionally despite the doctors' denials, has dramatically increased his stamina.

The grubby neighborhood is less changed than Stern might have predicted. Many of the residents are now Peruvian immigrants, but the streets are still full of hole-in-the-wall *tiendas* whose doorways are crowded with upright bolts of colorful fabrics. He asks Pinky to stop in front of the Templo de Paso, the main Ashkenazic synagogue. Predictably, the gray building now looks half the size and one-tenth as grand as he saw it as a child. It is, in fact, a bit of an architectural hodgepodge with a large golden Jewish star high up beneath the arches on its facade—not to mention prominent security cameras, presumably added after the Iranian bombing of a Jewish community center near here twenty-five years ago.

It was from the temple, one Saturday night in 1944, that his family of origin—his mother, his father, his brother, his sister, and Stern—took their final stroll home together. Pinky looks over in alarm at Stern's small gasp, as he is nearly knocked from his feet by the surge of love he feels for each of them, in memory.

"What, Pops?"

"I am remembering," he says. "Mostly my brother."

"*Brother?*" cries Pinky. "Get out of here. You and Aunt Silvia had a brother? Why didn't I know that?"

A moment of despair takes hold of Stern. Too pained to touch the subject, he has apparently said little about Jacobo. Despite his recent calm about the prospect of death, the way even titanic figures like Jacobo can vanish from the memory of future generations desolates him.

"He was extraordinary," says Stern, "destined for greatness. He wrote poems published in the newspapers. He won contests for oratory. Year after year, he received the highest marks in every subject. And he was also quite a rogue—that was an important aspect of his character—always in the midst of one scrape or another. Filching fruit from a stand." Stern stops briefly, struck for the first time in his life by the possibility that his attraction to the smart-asses and schemers he has represented for decades began with his love for his brother. "For a period when he was sixteen, he would sneak out at night to keep company with the mother of one of his friends."

Predictably, Pinky loves that detail and utters a lascivious laugh.

"He sounds like he was something else," she says.

"That he was," says Stern. "He was the child the world adored. Including my parents. Being the younger brother, I found his achievements a terrible burden—and the source of seething jealousy."

Would Stern have been able to ascend to the same prominence if Jacobo had lived? Intuitively, he knows the answer is no. But even so, he feels the mammoth vacuum left for him by his brother's loss.

"When did he die?" asks Pinky.

"1944. He was seventeen."

"Jesus," says his granddaughter, and asks how.

"He had fallen in with a crowd of rich Jewish kids. My mother was a terrible social climber and was thrilled at first, until she realized that under their influence he had become a passionate Zionist. He decided to go to Palestine to fight with the Haganah. My parents never had any control over him. Jacobo went up the gangway of the boat they were taking, tossing kisses. This was no more than a block from the hotel where we are staying, Pinky. We stood on the dock that Sunday, with my mother shrieking out loud that she would never see him again. And she did not. The US claimed that the ship was sunk by a Nazi U-boat, but the Germans blamed the Americans. I was sure my mother would die of her broken heart, but it was my father who was gone within six months."

The family was left penniless. Even as a child, Stern was aware of how much his mother loved the rare nights she and her father could attend the opera, when she displayed her opulent figure in a formal gown with a plunging neckline. It was probably melodrama to imagine that she had done any more than enjoy the admiring glances of other men, but with Stern's father gone, she had immediate suitors. Without the kindness of those men, the family might have starved. Her most passionate attachment, to a lawyer named Gruengehl who represented one of the few anti-Peronist unions, proved their undoing and required them to flee again in 1947, when Gruengehl was jailed. With displaced persons throughout Europe clamoring for entry to the United States, and Argentina's diplomatic ties to the US in question after the war, legal immigration was problematic. Instead, they traveled by train as far north as Monterrey, Mexico, from where they were driven across the border to Brownsville by a medical school friend of his father's. His mother's aunt met them in San Antonio and brought them home with her, by train again, to Kindle County.

Sandy Stern, Boy Illegal. In those days, the INS did not scour the cities for violators. He had many friends, Irish and Poles and Italians, who faced the same plight. The best advice was to mind your p's and q's and if you were ever arrested, bribe the cop, eminently possible in those days for any offense short of murder. Stern always kept fifty dollars cash inside his shoe. When he was drafted right after college, he felt none of the resentment of most of his fellow soldiers about conscription. The iron-headed manner of the military was laughable, but he woke every day knowing that he was now guaranteed to achieve a relentless ambition: He would become an American. He was sworn in as a citizen, along with Silvia, now his dependent after his mother's death, only two months after his honorable discharge.

God save him, but he loves the United States. He'd had his hard times as a young man, and the terror of poverty and homelessness still dwells in him like something in the composition of his bones. But America, as it had done from its beginnings, had taken him in, allowed a frightened foreign boy to find his talents and to prosper.

"Clarice," he says, calling Pinky by her proper name as he does perhaps once a year when he requires her attention. He receives it now, as she stares amid the raccoon blackness of liner and shadow. "We live in a great country. Never take it for granted." He thinks a second about poor Argentina and adds, "Democracy and the rule of law are much more fragile than most Americans realize."

She nods as if she understands.

Darkness now is creeping over BA, and Stern feels exhaustion taking hold, like some unseen masseuse loosening his limbs. In the taxi back, he fumbles with his phone until he finds Kiril's number.

"Does Pafko know we're coming?" Pinky asks, as he puts the phone to his ear.

"I asked Donatella to tell him."

Kiril responds enthusiastically when he hears Stern's voice.

"Ah, Sandy. You are here! Come tomorrow. Lunch."

"I am with Pinky."

"My savior! I want to bestow laurels on you both."

Kiril's predictable blather. Nevertheless, Stern finds himself looking forward to the meeting, as he did throughout the planning. He does not feel he has a score to settle with Kiril; however foolish, Pafko had the right to his choices. But something remains that Stern needs to know, even though he cannot say precisely what.

Given their frequent trips back to BA, the Pafkos have always kept an apartment in Recoleta, still—as it was in Stern's childhood—the home to BA's elite. The neighborhood has the air of the Upper West Side in Manhattan, with the tall trees and smart shops and cafés amid the six- and seven-story residential buildings whose many window air-conditioning units dribble moisture down onto the street. The Pafkos' glass-doored building is a block from the stately old Hotel Alvear. The amiable elderly doorman shows them to the tiny elevator, and at Kiril's door, a young woman about Pinky's age receives them. She is perhaps Peruvian or Asian and is dressed in khakis and a polo shirt. It is possible she is an employee, a maid or an assistant, or Olga's replacement, as she predicted. The way the young woman greets them gives no indication. From the door, she yells, "Pafko! *Sus visitantes.*" Your visitors.

Kiril insists on opening a bottle of Brazilian sparkling wine to celebrate now that they are all together, and tells Stern how well he is looking. It is Kiril, however, who appears noticeably better. He has tanned in the Argentine summer and even looks a bit trimmer in a pair of pleated bright blue slacks and a white-on-white shirt, short-sleeved and open at the collar.

"I understand, Kiril, that yet again, I am in your debt for your medical attention."

Kiril demurs but clearly enjoys Stern's gratitude. It leaves him in his favored role of grand importance. Pinky looks askance when Kiril makes no mention of her critical role in finding the defibrillator.

The living room here is the polar opposite of the house in Greenwood County, far more contemporary and more Italian than English, the other side of Donatella's heritage. The tall windows of the living room are uncovered. There is good light and sleek furniture.

"So Sandy, what have you come so far to say?"

"Kiril, I feel obliged to encourage you to return to the US."

"To go to prison? My lawyer here believes he can defeat extradition. And even if not, he says the Argentine courts move no more quickly than trees grow. Sooner or later, he says, the Americans will lose interest."

"Even now, Kiril, I think that whoever represents you at home—and it cannot be us—but whoever your lawyer is could strike an excellent bargain on your behalf. Moses wants to be done with the case. And knows he would face a difficult appeal."

"No, no, Sandy. I will not go back. I will have a good life here."

"Word of your conviction will follow you quickly, Kiril."

"For a financial crime? Selling stock for my grandchildren? This is a country where generals who disappeared thousands were received in polite society. The Argentines are not as idealistic as Americans. Have you forgotten? Besides, Sandy, they are very very proud of their few Nobelists. Here I will be treated as a returning hero. And I am certain to be more of a free man here than I could be in the US, even after I was released from prison."

"And how is that, Kiril?"

He spreads his hands wide and smiles. "No Donatella."

Stern stares. "She says you urged her to come down here."

"What else? Had I told her to stay away, she would have been on the next plane."

Stern's guess is that Kiril is also somewhat disappointed, especially now that Olga has refused to join him in exile. Kiril and Donatella could not have dwelled together for so long without ambivalence being a dominant motif. Yet say what you like about never knowing the truth of anybody else's marriage, the Pafkos' elegant manners have concealed more than usual, especially the degree to which they lived in a state of open warfare from which neither, for fear of being the ultimate loser, could ever withdraw. Although it has required a criminal conviction to separate them, it is possible both might find themselves somewhat happier in their final years.

In contemplating things on the way down, Stern realized there is little that beckons Pafko to return. The jury verdict requires him to be dismissed from PT, and Kiril will never have any relationship to speak of with his son, or even Lep's children, after the events of the last few years. Dara is her mother's daughter and probably has long accepted Donatella's view of things.

"I owe you thanks, Sandy. And you too, my dear." He lifts his champagne flute toward Pinky, who has just stood up to help herself to another glass. Stern suspects that Kiril has forgotten her name, but Pinky is doing her best to ignore him anyway.

"I would have much preferred a complete acquittal, Kiril."

"Yes, I too. I had my hopes up. But you had my side at every moment, Sandy. I could tell you never lost faith in my innocence."

Stern nods rather than say anything.

"I am not certain, Kiril, that you might not have been better served with another lawyer who did not know your family and to whom you therefore might have been more comfortable telling the truth."

"I was stymied, Sandy, no matter who represented me. Donatella saw to that. I said I wanted to testify because I knew the prospect terrified her, the chance I might implicate her precious son. But she had kept the upper hand. I realized that whenever I stopped to think. She'd have backed Lep from the stand. Yet please recognize that I never lied to you, Sandy."

"About being guilty of fraud, I grant you. But you were not straightforward about other matters. Olga?"

Pinky, who has been twirling her hair around her finger, is suddenly alert.

Kiril says, "Olga and I had nothing to do with one another for close to eighteen months. It was as much your questions about her as anything that made me reconsider the prospects for the two of us."

This is a new low. Clients have blamed Stern for a lot during his legal career—losing cases that should have been won or cozying up to the prosecutors—but never for their infidelities. Even Kiril seems to recognize the absurdity of what he has just said.

"Not to lay my decisions at your feet, Sandy. I mean only that things came together at that moment, the idea of starting fresh down here with her."

"You were planning on coming down here with Olga even if you were acquitted?"

"Exactly." Bringing Olga and marrying her would be Kiril's own revenge on Innis and Lep and Donatella, who had all punished him for his relationship with the woman. "But having set a course, Sandy, it was time to get on with it. A mistrial and another year of being roasted over fires of uncertainty—that was unacceptable. I had hopes of a complete not guilty—perhaps greater than you. And naturally, I would prefer the freedom to go back and forth between my two countries. But even were I acquitted, Sandy, it would be years—years I do not have—before people stopped looking at me with suspicion."

"That surprises me, Kiril. I thought staying in control of PT was important to you."

"When PT was seen only as the maker of a medication that is a remarkable advance in the fight against cancer, yes. But the company for most of the next decade will be enmeshed in litigation and struggles with the FDA. That is Lep's mess—let him deal with it. And g-Livia will be my legacy anyway." He takes his champagne down then in a single draft, then looks directly at Stern, as he adds, "It's all a lie, you know."

"About you altering the trial data? Yes, I understand."

"Not merely the dataset. The medication. g-Livia? Donatella has told me for years that I did nothing but ride Lep's coattails. And she would have said as much in court. But my son would have been entirely lost without my contributions. Believe me. The credit is properly mine."

When Stern understands, he needs to stifle a gasp. Because only now does he finally comprehend Kiril's motive for enduring the false accusations against him, and the nature of the bargain he tacitly made with his wife. If Kiril implicated Lep, Donatella would have testified that her husband was uncontrollably jealous of their son, knowing that sooner or later the scientific world would recognize that Lep made the principal discoveries underlying g-Livia. Mother and son would both say that Kiril was lying, not only to escape blame for a crime, but also to discredit Lep in order to cement Kiril's false claim about his scientific achievements. So in the end, Kiril had decided to accept indictment and trial rather than lose the accolades he, yet again, did not deserve. For more than three decades, Kiril Pafko's life had been built upon the lie that he is a genius, worthy of the Nobel, and thus capable of formulating g-Livia. He would risk prison rather than forsake that.

After a quick lunch, fish nicely prepared, Pafko hugs Sandy at the door. He is happy. That is what strikes Stern. At seventy-eight, Kiril—the poet, as Innis put it—sees his life as pregnant with welcome possibilities. Pinky lifts one hand lamely, says "Bye," and without a backward look at Kiril precedes her grandfather down the corridor, waiting for him at the elevator.

Outside it may be 100 degrees. They look for a taxi, but on the corner Stern spots a tobacconist. In Argentina, like Europe, one can buy Cuban cigars, still embargoed in the United States. Stern had quit smoking as a kind of penance after Clara's death, backslid eventually, and finally stopped cold after the cancer diagnosis. But now the appetite seizes him. Despite Pinky's protests, he buys a Bolivar, a Robusto, and then goes to the café tables set up on a small tile patio adjacent to the shop. Pinky and he can have coffee and a pastry while he smokes. In the shade of the café's black awning, the heat is tolerable.

Helen often commented that among the men she knew, Stern had few vices. He didn't gamble, didn't chase, didn't drink to excess, didn't spend for pleasure. But he loved tobacco. Even now, with his disease stalemated by g-Livia, he knows that in the final analysis, a pathologist is likely to conclude that it's the cigars that killed him. But he relishes the moment, here where he started, conceding to pleasure, and in the company of this grandchild whose prospects others find dim and whom he loves without reservation.

She points at the cigar like a culprit.

"If you go back to smoking after this trip, Aunt Marta will be mad enough to try to rip my tats right off my skin."

"Pinky, my love, I suspect that I will get no further than three puffs."

He warms the cigar in the light of his first match, then with another draws the flame to the tip. Even the first touch of the nicotine to the tender membranes of his mouth makes him dizzy. He holds the smoke there and exhales, then sets the cigar in an ashtray, savoring the richness of the flavor. Only old Bordeaux deliver the same depth of tastes throughout the mouth. He will have a puff or two more, assuming he's sure he'll be able to stand up afterward, and then never again. He has been saying that about so many things that have given him happiness. But he allows himself no sentiment, no sadness.

Pinky, however, appears morose, shaking her head as he lifts the cigar again. She touches his hand, which she has been doing far more often lately, and says, "I don't want you to die, Pops." Amazingly, she is close to tears.

Stern suddenly recalls Peter crying the same thing in panic at the age of five or six. The remark devastated Stern, because he wanted to soothe his child, but could not really do it without offering an evasion Peter would later resent.

Pinky, though, is not asking him to change the nature of existence. She is merely saying that she will miss him. He encloses her hand in his.

"That is a very kind thing to say, Pinky. But that is not a reality we seem to need to face today."

She studies her grandfather. She has such beautiful green eyes. The family lore is that she takes after Clara, but Stern realizes only now that he is sitting in BA that those eyes are his mother's, who had similar coloring to Stern's wife.

"Are you scared of that, Pops?"

"Of dying? I enjoy living, so I am reluctant to go, Pinky, but I am not certain that is the same thing as fear. Certainly, I feel a bit more comfort today, since I answered the question that drove me down here. It was very selfish, I realize."

"Meaning what?"

"I have concluded I would rather have lived my life than Kiril's. Nobel Prize and all."

"No shit," says Pinky, for whom it is easy to choose Stern as a better grandfather. Yet the question he had put to himself is not as simple as Pinky sees it. One night, while Marta was preparing for another long evening of research for one of her crosses, she remarked matter-of-factly, 'I really missed the boat with this career. With law.'

Hearing his daughter say that petrified Stern, fearing he'd misled her in some way that had kept her from discovering a better destiny for herself.

'How so?' he asked.

'I should have done science,' she said. When she entered college, Marta had been heading in the same direction as her older brother and was intent on medical school. She had the aptitude, perhaps more than Peter, but in her father's house she'd developed a fascination with sorting right from wrong, and ended up in Political Theory. 'Science is where the truth is in our world,' she said that night in the office. 'What once belonged to religion or philosophy is now the business of science. That's where we'll learn what's really unknown about being here on Earth.' Stern had realized she was correct the moment she'd said it.

"I do not dismiss the importance of Kiril's scientific contributions," Stern tells Pinky, "even if they have been greatly exaggerated. It may well be that the principles and discoveries he has had some hand in advancing turn out to be critical to the course of humanity for the next century or even longer. The same will never be said of my work.

"One of the tragedies of Kiril's life, Pinky, is that he has such large gifts as a treating physician. I tell you that from experience. That part of Kiril that people like Innis and Donatella talk about all the time, his great talent for convincing you of what he wants to believe, gives him a unique ability to engage the psychological element of healing. He could have been like some guru or shaman, the doctor people traveled thousands of miles to see. But they do not give Nobel Prizes for that, and so apparently those abilities were not adequate to match his grand vision of himself.

"And that is what stands out to me. Even if he really were entitled to all the laurels bestowed on him, Pinky, it is plain that Kiril has found his life disappointing at some base level. All these lovers? This insatiable hunger for recognition for its own sake? It is still true, Pinky, that even if our best efforts as humans are expended in aid of others, and even though we deeply need their love, we still live with no one more than ourselves. And recognizing that, I feel I have had better company than Kiril."

Though often puzzled by irony, Pinky understands this comment perfectly and laughs out loud, but in another moment she has subsided to a gloom that leaves her studying the marked surface of the round black café table. Pinky has been badly unsettled by their interview with Kiril. The minute they were out the door of Pafko's apartment, she had uttered several obscenities. Kiril is a lot to absorb, Stern knows, especially for someone like Pinky, who is far more sheltered than she realizes. She has starred in her own pornography, but she hasn't yet accepted that humans are neither innately good nor bad.

"There are just always so many people like him, Pops, who get away with so much crap. I mean, that case ended up as a total shit show. I've been listening to you the last couple weeks. Do you realize who the only person is who's going to serve time in jail?"

There is no one, so far as he knows.

"Anahit," says Pinky. "The stockbroker."

"Ah," says Stern. He is struck, both because of the purchase Pinky is developing on his world, and because she is, in all probability, correct. When Moses accepts that he can't extradite Kiril, that he doesn't quite have the goods on Innis or the Neucrisses, he'll be left with his unequivocal evidence against young Ms. Turchynov. Wrong is wrong for Moses.

"Is that right, Pops? I mean, are you okay if that's the result of your last case?"

He takes his final puff, and in that dizzy instant decides his answer is yes. He is at peace with the limitations of the law. It is not unjust that Anahit Turchynov be convicted, even if her greed was dwarfed by Innis's, for example, or her deceptions and destructiveness by Lep's. Justice is good in its own right and makes life among other people more dependable. Yet Stern accepted long ago that even perfect justice will not change who we are. The law is erected on many fictions and perhaps the falsest one of all is that humans, in the end, are rational. Without doubt, our life—so far as we can tell—is one of cause and effect. That is what science depends on. But our most intimate decisions are rarely based on the kinds of calculations of pluses and minuses Jeremy Bentham, or the free-market economists for that matter, have wanted to believe in. We are fundamentally emotional creatures. In the most consequential matters, we answer faithfully to the heart's cry, not the law's.

"I mean, it's just not fair, Pops. Life isn't fair."

"Well, dear Pinky," he says, again taking her hand, "it has been far fairer to me than many other people. And to you, too, I dare say, although it may not always seem like that. But in the end, Pinky, we must heed the response of a revered philosopher—I forget his name—who was famously asked by a student if he believed life was fair."

"What did he say?"

Stern stubs out the cigar, tightening his grip somewhat on Pinky's soft fingers.

"He answered, 'Compared to what?'"

ACKNOWLEDGMENTS

For many reasons, the regulatory framework that governs the clinical testing and approval of new medications is one of unrivalled complexity that makes even the Internal Revenue Code seem straightforward. The pharmaceutical regulatory scheme defies easy understanding—at least by me, despite practicing law for more than forty years—and inevitably by readers, who are seeking the pleasures of fiction rather than the drudgery of a text. My goal has been to avoid outright mistakes and misrepresentations about that process, but readers should be aware that the preceding pages have substantially simplified what happens in practice.

In understanding that system, I have had the help of several persons. Among them, I owe special thanks to Shawn Hoskins, who was generous with his time.

I had the benefit of incisive readings of earlier versions of this book with extended commentary from Rachel Turow and Julian Solotorovsky—as well as my first reader and untiring champion, Adriane Turow. Dan Pastern, Duane Quaini, Stacee Solotorovsky, and Eve Turow were also kind enough to read the manuscript and share their reactions. I am also indebted to Liz Turow, who provided valued opinions on related issues.

I am very grateful to my editor at Grand Central, Ben Sevier, for his patient guidance and sound suggestions, as he nudged me toward making this a better book across multiple drafts, and to his chief lieutenant, Elizabeth Kulhanek, for the careful attention she gave countless details, including her thoughtful line-editing of the manuscript. The copy editor, Rick Ball—and the senior production editor, Mari Okuda—saved me from several blunders. (Remaining errors—including in my questionable Spanish—are entirely my fault.) And as always, I have had the benefit of the wisdom of the World's Greatest Literary Agent, Gail Hochman.

I again want to thank my friends at Farrar, Straus and Giroux for allowing me to steal from myself and republish a few short passages, albeit a bit changed, that originated in my first novel in which Sandy was the central figure, *The Burden of Proof.*

I initially started writing about Sandy Stern in the mid-1980s, and he has appeared as a character, sometimes center stage, usually in the background, in every novel I have published. I feel like thanking him, too, for the pleasure of living again in his skin.

ABOUT THE AUTHOR

Scott Turow is the author of eleven bestselling works of fiction, including *Testimony*, *Identical*, *Innocent*, *Presumed Innocent*, and *The Burden of Proof*, and two nonfiction books, including *One L*, about his experience as a law student. His books have been translated into more than forty languages, sold more than thirty million copies worldwide, and have been adapted into movies and television projects. He has frequently contributed essays and op-ed pieces to publications such as the *New York Times*, *Washington Post*, *Vanity Fair*, *The New Yorker*, and *The Atlantic*.

For more information, you can visit:

www.ScottTurow.com
Twitter: @ScottTurow
Facebook.com/scottturowbooks